F A L
The Dragon Harper

by
Peter Patterson

Illustrated by Johannes Steuck

HAWTHORN PRESS

Published by Hawthorn Press
1 Lansdown Lane, Lansdown, Stroud, Gloucestershire, United Kingdom. GL5 1BJ

Cover illustration by Terry Thomas.
Cover design by Nick Allen, Old Convent, Stroud, Gloucestershire.
Typeset in Sabon by Patrick Roe, Glevum Graphics, 2 Honyatt Road, Gloucester.
Printed and bound in Great Britain by
Biddles Ltd, Guildford and King's Lynn

British Library Cataloguing in Publication Data
Patterson, Peter J.
Fal, the Dragon Harper
I. Title

A catalogue recording this book is available from the British Library

ISBN 1 869 890 43 4

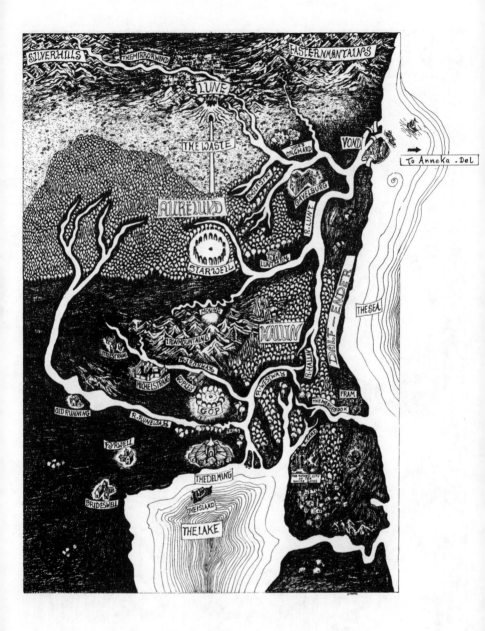

Dedicated to
The Middle Kingdom of
Craig Wen, Hafodydd Brithion
and Castle Mead.
Thanks.

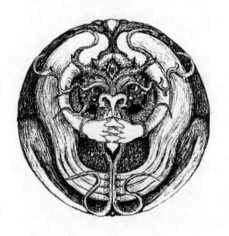

THE AUTHOR

Peter Patterson spent the first six years of his life behind King's Cross station in central London. During his childhood he became increasingly fascinated by the study of forests, mountains and other wild places and he now lives with his wife and two teenage children in New Zealand.

Peter is a musician, well-known for his many settings of J. R. R. Tolkien's poems, and a storyteller whose imaginative and traditional tales entrance audiences of all ages.

ONE

The mist clung to Sulthind's dark form, drawing in behind him as he pushed through the brambles at the top of the cliff. The rocky stairway glistened and he had to wipe the dew from his eyebrows before they froze.

He hesitated. No, he would not risk the ice on the stairway, he would be able to see from here.

His fingers tore at the wall of mist and made a window in it. Not too big. He was not sure how close the intruder was and he did not want to be seen. One form of attention might attract another. He moved the window from right to left, scanning the waters of the lake.

He smiled. Yes, of course. It was Fal, out there all by himself, drifting along in that odd little boat of his, floating so close to the mists of the island.

He watched for a long time. He knew all about the people from the mainland, he knew about their petty arts and crafts. But Fal, Fal was different. There was something unfathomable in his mind, tantalizingly elusive. Was it the music in him?

The watcher knew little of music, he did not understand it; certainly not that kind of music, the music of the boat. No-one understood it. And what was he doing so close to the island?

He disliked things he could not understand, and yet he longed to be with Fal in that boat. Fal was a doorway to many things, not least to the world beyond the island.

"It's high time we did something about this," he murmured. "High time".

But a new thought struck him and he stood again for a long time watching the boat drift, almost motionless now, out there in the sparkling sunshine.

"You and your boat," he whispered at last.

He sealed the window in the mist and walked briskly back to the house. It was time to start things moving.

———

Reflections in the water, cloud-images, clouds that sailed above the lake, castles, gods and goddesses, giants growing and changing. All day he had watched their solemn dance, and again and again a meaning had seemed about to appear. It was long enough.

Fal sat back and pressed his ear against the mast. He liked to hear the water talking through the hard wood. Even when the lake was still it would speak of its everlasting secrets. He knew people who listened to trees like that — or through them, rather. Rowan was said to be the best. But the boat was Fal's oracle. The boat and the harp.

He touched the twining patterns on the ivory, the patterns that were his. They were carved everywhere into the lightly built instrument. They were carved all around the boat. And they were carved into his mind, where they lived a life of their own.

He ran his finger-tips along the loops which pulsed rhythmically down the slender white pillar beyond the longest string. He played a deep note, and the water rippled as the boat quivered in response. The mirrored clouds were split and juggled wildly, then gathered and re-knit into heaving shapes.

He glanced at the sky. The real clouds, the giant kings and queens up there, had ignored his little trick. They wouldn't even have noticed. Or maybe they had — on such a day, when all the world is born again. Quite likely all is aware of each, and each of all, he thought, on such a day. He frowned, feeling suddenly watched, and glanced around the lake. But the waters were quite empty.

He tried to go back to looking at the reflections, but now he had become too aware of himself and of the way he was seeing. He could go no further on that path. He had felt the difference, yes, it was enough, he would go back soon.

It was his day of preparation, when all the rest of the town left their workshops, their kitchens and their hearths and went out together, looking and sharing.

They would have seen the signs. A bird's nest freshly made, gleaming with eggs, and crazy hares, boxing and leaping. It was always the same, yet always new. The new life.

Estera, the morning star, had been walking in the woods and in the meadows calling out the new life. "Awake!" she cried. "The dance begins!" Then darkness and loss are forgotton, and all can look, look as on the first day when the world began.

He stretched and yawned. Who had been the first to see the hares this year, he wondered? Last time it had been old Aren, the master weaver, who had leaped around and frolicked after them in such excitement that he had been taken ill afterwards and missed the Praise Song in the evening. Poor Aren. He'd been sent to bed like a child.

"The plaited pattern of your heart is going all the wrong shape, old friend," the master smith had said. "When it's re-woven you can rise. Till then, stay in your blankets!"

Yet it was not old Aren but the smith who had died, in that long, dark year with its chain of misfortunes. And now Ilmarin was the master smith, perhaps the youngest the city had ever known. And Fal was the new master harper, the weaver of sound in the forge of patterns.

A breeze was springing up, and he moved to unfurl the sail. He would tack across to the shore rather than use his harp. The strings must sound fresh and clear at the Praise Song that night, his first festival as master harper. It had been a perfect day, brimming with energy, and he'd been storing it within himself. He would not touch the handle of that inner door until the time came and the people were waiting.

He stood by the mast, his finger-tips fitting into its knotted patterns. The water was all a-ripple now, licking and sucking against the hull. A pair of black-headed gulls wheeled around, watching him hopefully.

"You can come to the Praise Song if you want feeding," he said, "and if you want a free ride, I'm heading that way!"

He wondered where they nested. Somewhere out on Sulthind's island, maybe. It lay to the south-east, nearer to him now than was the mainland. He should have been able to see the outlines of trees and buildings, but it was still shrouded in its cloak of winter mist. You'd think that today's clean, warm sun would have dispersed it. It was strange about Sulthind. They'd been close enough at one time, the three of them, — Fal, Ilmarin, and Sulthind. But that was often the way with growing up, Ilmarin had said. Friendships lost their colour and faded and were forgotton. There were other things and other people to think about. Still, the memory was painful to him. He had loved Sulthind's daring nature and infectious laughter. But the laughter seemed to turn to mockery as they grew older, and the mockery to a gift for cutting, bitter wit which had in the end soured their friendship. It was more than five years since they had tried to spend any time together. What was he like now? Part of Fal longed to know yet he feared to penetrate the mist which had been growing like a white mound all these months out over the waters of the great lake.

"Like a ferment round a lump of rotten cheese," he caught himself thinking—and checked himself, wondering at the resentment that he felt.

The slanting sun was beginning to shine through the white swathe and make it glow a golden orange as if lit from within. "It's quite beautiful really," he thought. "You see? Well, one day...!"

He shrugged. The boat bucked as he trimmed the sail and the wind caught it. He came about onto a new tack and found himself looking across to the little town which was his home. The Delming, the last of the forges of the east, where he was master harper, and where Salpin, his teacher, had also been among the winter's dead.

But the thought of Sulthind would not go from his mind. Sailing was good for the memory to come into its own. Voices, laughter, shouts from years and years ago were crowding around him. He wanted to think of other things, the Praise Song and the solemn music of the re-birth. But instead he thought of the time when Sulthind, his red hair flowing out in the wind, had tried to call a monster from the depths of the lake, waving his arms in such a grand gesture of exhortation that he had toppled in head first.

"Ah, monster," Ilmarin had said as their wet friend surfaced and clutched frantically at the sides of the boat, "what message dost thou bring us from the depths of the wondrous lake? Speak, I bid thee!"

Sulthind had spouted a mouthful of water at them, then began yelling that something had grabbed his heels and was trying to pull him under. The boat certainly did tilt pretty violently as they hauled him out, but they never discovered whether it was all true or whether Sulthind had just been trying to scare them.

They had seen a strange creature once, though — with two dark eyes watching them quietly from just above the surface. No-one had been calling it. Ilmarin said afterwards that he rather felt it had been calling them.

Eyes... Yes, there had been the time when Ilmarin had fallen from the tree which grew by the white wall round Sulthind's house, bringing a whole branch down with him. That tree must have been half rotten, eaten up by the fungus which oozed and bubbled its way out of the twisted old trunk. It was a wonder Ilmarin had not been seriously hurt. Sulthind's mother had come to the gate then and looked at them, and Sulthind had turned very pale. She hadn't said anything, just stared out of her cold blue eyes. Fal had preferred the water-monster.

It wasn't often that you met Sulthind's mother. It was all servants in the white house on the island. She'd been dead some time now, anyway. She must have died just about the time the boys' friendship had fallen apart, when Sulthind had become really unbearable. He can't have missed her very much, surely, he thought, she had seemed to scare him terribly, and he hardly ever spoke about her. Though Sulthind did once say that his mother had taught him more than they ever dreamt, or something of the sort. Anyway, now he ruled the roost on the island all by himself. Lord Sulthind it was, by all accounts.

Of his own parents Fal knew nothing, he was not even sure how old he was. He might have been seven or eight when he was found, unconscious and near to death, afloat on the open lake in his patterned boat. The masters of the Forge were never able to find out whether he'd come from the River Ironway, which flowed into the lake through several mouths east of the city, or whether the boat had drifted from further afield across the water. There had been little wind that long, hot summer, fourteen years before, so many claimed he must have come down the river from the north. But others called this a groundless argument, for it was a magic boat and had a will of its own unless it was guided, and all had looked in wonder on the strange patterns which covered mast, gunwale, and tiller. For weeks he had lain in a deep dream, murmuring jumbled words, and when he woke he was bewildered and even frightened when they asked him where he came from. All he'd brought was a simple leather bag containing his harp, made of white ivory and patterned like the boat. The thin, dark haired child had remembered only how to tune and play it, and even the guests of the Forge who had travelled far away had never heard melodies such as he played. He used that music to guide the boat and control its power.

He had no memory of his earlier life unless the strange wisps of dream from his long illness were in some way links with the past. But much that he thought might be true memory was coloured with such impossible details that it was useless to relate it to anything he now called reality. Sometimes he worried about it and about the fact that, though probably an orphan, it was quite possible that somewhere he was missed and mourned or news of him was sought. But mostly he accepted the mystery about himself as most of us accept the mysteries of the world — what binds the rocks to earth, what makes the grass grow straight, what lies behind the stars? And he loved the Delming, not only on account of its folk, who had welcomed and cherished him, but also for what it was: a college of age-old skills, skills forgotten in the rest of the world, with its busy craftsmen and teachers, and, in its centre, the ancient forge. There, in harmony and industry, worked a people of another race, akin to the elves it was said, together with men and dwarves. And the fruits of their labours were carried far into the world, over lake and land.

———

As he approached the quay with its assortment of tubby barges and shallops, slender skiffs, punts and rafts, he could see three stocky figures moving in a very curious fashion. At first, from a distance, he thought they were dancing. They seemed to be leaping and cavorting in such a way that whenever one was on the ground, the other two appeared airborne: one up, one down. It was like a humped caterpillar making efforts to run but not being able to leave the spot. Then he realized that they were trying desperately to attract his attention and communicate something. His heart sank. Not more bad news! Surely there had been enough that winter. It must be over now! But as the breeze swept him in, and his eye made out the odd movements, he saw that they were hopping and dancing in the peculiar fashion of dwarves when they are very excited and need to share something which has pleased them tremendously.

There were the brothers, Skelfir and Skirfir, hard to tell apart. And Theck, easy to distinguish by virtue of his wide-brimmed hat, woven of straw, without which he was never to be seen, summer or winter, indoors or out. Theck was particularly agitated and was quite out of breath by the time Fal was within hailing distance. He waved and shouted "Hurrah!" then sat down, dangling his legs over the jetty, staring happily at the boat of patterns as it glided towards him. Skelfir and Skirfir grinned broadly as Fal threw a rope to them.

"We are greatly happy, Master Falimbravel," explained Skirfir. "Theck's daughter, Amba, was the first to find eggs and the first to see hares at sport, so much honour has come to his family and indeed to all the dwarves, for mostly it is the tall folk who see the hares."

"Though dwarves have been known to find skylark's eggs in the grass," said Skelfir.

"Or moorhen's eggs by a pond," said Skirfir. "But these were bright blue throstle's eggs!"

Theck had come back to life and was helping Fal out of the boat.

"But throstle's eggs are high up, in a thick bush or tree," Fal protested skilfully.

"That's just it, master," said Theck, who had decided that the dues of modesty had been sufficiently observed and it was time to join the conversation. "Half a baby she is, by our reckoning, but she spotted them and climbed up and gave the call, all by herself. And everyone came running. Then she rode off in triumph on the shoulders of the Lord Dringskel," (this was the dwarves' name for Ilmarin) "and so it was that she spotted the hares first, too!"

"And it's the first time a dwarf has ever been the first to find them both," shouted Skelfir, and they all began their dance again, this time leaping over each other like three balls in a juggler's act. Then the two brothers hugged Theck from each side, and his hat was so wide-brimmed that it looked as if it were being worn by some extraordinary three-headed dwarf. Fal began laughing, both on account of the odd sight and also because he loved them and was infected by their joy, and the dwarves went on tumbling and somersaulting, the brothers slapping their thighs, and Theck gripping his hat with both hands.

A crowd of townsfolk had gathered round, smiling and applauding. But Fal felt a tug at his sleeve. It was Dan, an old man from the house of Ilmarin.

"Come, good master harper," he said. "The time of the Praise Song is not so far off. Behold, the sun is setting."

And so it was. Between the mists of Sulthind's island and the distant western shore the sun was a dusky crimson globe, already slipping behind the water of the lake.

————

Only a part of the heavy portal of the forge could be seen from the gates of the elves' court where the folk of the Delming thronged, awaiting the procession which would welcome the new year. The massive stones of its frame appeared to shift and vary in size as if they were made of living shadow, holes in the twilight, rather than hard grey stone. It was an entertainment the townsfolk never tired of watching, though there was not one among them who had not seen it from his earliest days. To them it was the readiest pledge and proof of the magic life that was their livelihood and that brought the ancient peoples together in harmony.

Often the red flicker of the furnaces would shine through the doorway and through the tall, narrow windows above it. But since the full moon the fires had been allowed to burn themselves out. They would be rekindled during the ceremony.

The last flush of gold from the dying sun turned to the grey stillness of evening and the openings into the forge became black holes of silence between the shift and flow of the magic wall. A stuttering glimmer, then a flare of light from within told the waiting crowd that the apprentices, bearing torches of resinous wood, had passed through the elves' house. They were dividing on either side of the forge stone and preparing to enter the court, to light the master craftsmen in. They would flank the edges of the white path, the Pointer, and make an avenue — for the masters and for the finders of this year's signs. There they would stand in silence until the first music sounded, facing the gigantic tree which grew against the south wall, the emblem of the Forge of the two hills, the town by the lake, the city of the tree.

They called it the Golden Tree, though at the feast of Estera its branches were still black and bare, and when the new spring came upon the land, they were clothed in fresh green, not gold. But whatever the season it could be seen from afar among the glittering spires of the Forge: black in winter, green in spring, golden yellow all the summer, and in the dying of the year blood-red.

Delicate runners of young ivy enhanced its grey bark, as if new life had erupted around the ancient trunk only moments before. No other green leaf was to be seen in the elves' court at that time of the year.

Once, not many months after Fal's mysterious arrival in the Delming — out of the lake, as some said — he had been noticed by two of the dwarf craftsmen examining the large smooth-edged leaves of the great tree. For almost an hour he stood alone under its heavy boughs handling the foliage carefully, studying first the golden, red-veined upper surfaces, then the paler, almost silvery undersides. Suddenly, feeling himself observed, he looked up. The whole community of dwarves had gathered around him and was watching him with large, thoughtful eyes.

"Will you read the patterns of the Tree, young master? There is no writing on the leaves." It was Thengir who had spoken then, and his dark eyes seemed very close to Fal, who was as yet scarcely taller than the dwarves.

"Writing?" he said, as if awakening from a long, rare dream. "I haven't yet learned to read."

Some of the dwarves smiled, the youngest giggled, but the eldest still stared solemnly. Then he had been overcome with a dreadful embarrassment and had run between them and hurried out of the court.

But now the apprentices, in pale grey tunics, glinting with silver embroidery around the neck and cuffs, had entered like a company of will o' the wisps, their flames a symbol of the life given to the earth. Between them, tall, youthful and golden haired, robed in white and bearing the silver hammer of the elves, came Ilmarin, the new master smith. Behind him should have come two finders, but this night there was only one small figure, the dwarf child Amba, dressed in palest blue her dark eyes large with wonder and crowned with a wreath of daffodils. Ilmarin stepped aside and ushered her to the very tip of the white Pointer. Next was Melauriën, mistress of the city, the mother of Ilmarin, upright and stern but still lovely, bearing in her hands the Forge's golden key. Then Fal, master of the harpers, Aren the weaver, in a richly embroidered robe, and Celbring, the master of the dwarvish crafts.

The moon had risen to greet the solemn company, as the first tones of Fal's harp rang out amid the lines of burning torches. The dwarves among the crowd had to grip each other's hands, some twisting back and forth with effort to suppress their need to shout out their joy. And when little Amba turned her head and smiled, first at the folk in the left gate, then at those in the right gate, and then at those who sat upon the walls, they all smiled back, and all the tall folk nodded while many nudged elbows with their neighbours and their eyes all shone like a host of stars.

Fal played, and as the clear notes sounded with all the freshness and goodness of that spring day and the court of the elves was filled with the light of the moon, the singing began. Apprentices, masters, and townsfolk blended their voices in stark but resonant harmonies:

O flow of wonder, glow of light,
    the wonder of the spring,
the radiance born from out the dark,
    the world enlivening!

And there, above the chorus of the Praise Song, rang out the two ancient bronze bells from the tall central spire of the Forge, vibrant and pure, merging with the singing as if the music had been created around them, as it perhaps once had, leading the strong rhythms from verse to verse:

The lovely queen who ends the night,
    who heals the winter's sting,
who rises from the ashen waste,
    a bird with shining wing!

O glory of the wonder-wood,
    fair leaf and blossom bright,
your dance brings back the meadows' green
    at ending of the night!

At last the song was ended and silence fell over all the folk of the Delming.

The mistress of the city raised her hands, and the wide sleeves of the golden gown fell back so that her slender arms shone in the white light of the waning moon, symbol of the dying year. Suddenly the Tree quivered, as if air stirred its boughs, though none there felt even the faintest breeze, so hushed and still was that perfect night. The sigh of the Tree's bare branches was echoed by a gasp of amazement from all the people, then an outburst of talking, like the buzzing of a hive of bees.

"Be silent, good people!" cried Melauriën. "Perhaps this is even as it should be, and we poor folk have grown forgetful!"

Then she turned quickly towards the West Court and led the procession out into the city. Wonder was still on every face as the crowd made way for the light of the rebirth to be carried through the maze of narrow streets that surrounded the Forge and away under the moon and the stars into the meadows and woods of the lake-town.

TWO

When all was over and the streets had emptied, Fal felt tired and happy but far away from sleep. Sensibly, he did not imagine that the Speaking of the Tree, as people were already calling it, had happened through any skill or virtue of his. Nevertheless he was too excited to think of going to bed and he longed for the stillness of the lake and the open sky.

The quayside was bright from the moon, now high and dominating in the southern sky, as he strode along towards his little boat-house, past the bobbing, creaking boats, the tangs of watery and woody smells, and the dark forms of fishermen wrapped in their blankets, some already snoring. Most of them would be out before dawn, hauling their nets in the rich fishing grounds around the river esturary. They were good men, hardy and dour, less rooted in the Delming than most of the townsfolk, often spending the winter months far away beyond the horizon along the south coast of the lake, catching and trading. Fal liked them. They brought back news and travellers' tales and sometimes even new songs. They enjoyed his company, too. Perhaps because they felt that he, also, was less a part of the Delming's walls, as they put it, than most. But tonight he walked quietly. He wanted to be alone again for a while, alone with the lake and with the boat of patterns.

A sudden movement in the shadows made him start.

"Master! Forgive me, master, but I thought you might be coming down to the boats." It was no fisherman but Theck, the dwarf, with his straw hat, looking more serious now as he stepped into the moonlight. "I guessed you might want to go out on the lake again. Hard to think of sleep after so much song and wonders." He spoke in a low, husky voice. "I've got your boat all ready for you, Master Fal," he grinned. "Sorry if I did wrong."

Fal thanked him and said he'd guessed his intentions very well. Theck looked sheepish, and something stirred under his cloak.

"'Tis not the icy northern blast which moves this cloak of stone, but the fiery heart of Earth that scorns the tempest's moan," Fal quoted. He loved the lore of the dwarves and knew more of it than any other harper of the Forge. And the dwarves never failed to appreciate an appropriate rhyme. But this time it was not only Theck who nodded. A head popped out from the cloak and smiled shyly. It was still wreathed in little wild daffodils.

"Said she'd love to go out on the lake for a bit as well. Too excited for bed I expect. It's a special day for her, master, but do say 'no' if it's too much to ask."

Amba had stepped out from her hiding place and stood waiting for her answer. Her heavy, knitted tunic, of grey or blue, glistened almost like chain-mail in the moonlight. She was only six inches shorter than Theck, but even so she hardly came up to Fal's waist. By the conventions of men or elves she was not beautiful, for her jaw was too large and her nose too thin and angular. But her eyes were dark, deep pools, full of the newness and wonder which is the world's gift to childhood, whatever the race or people.

Fal had been looking forward to being alone. But he could not possibly spoil the joy of these gentle folk.

"But of course, Theck; if you don't think it will be too much for her?"

"Not too much, master. Here's my cloak to wrap her in. Just let her roll up and drop off as soon as she starts looking sleepy. She won't be doing any talking."

Fal nodded and smiled as little Amba darted forward and clutched his hand firmly with her tiny fingers. He looked out over the lake. The air was very crisp and clear, the water a sheet of molten silver under the magic alchemy of the moon. Suddenly he caught his breath.

"Theck, look! There's Sulthind's island. The mist's all gone!"

All three of them stared out at the island, now clearly visible, several miles away across the water.

"Funny it never went before, though, if y'ask me," muttered Theck, twisting his beard round his fingers and glaring out over the lake. "Clear as clear can be, in more senses than one."

Fal suddenly felt Theck's bony hand gripping his arm, just below the elbow. "Don't go there tonight, master," said the dwarf. "Such lop lollies as that young Lothur are best left alone; and folk do say he's been turning his mind to sorcery lately, like his mother before him."

Fal hadn't intended going anywhere near the island and he looked at Theck with surprise.

"Oh, yes, master, a wonder if you haven't heard. The dwarves have been talking about it all winter." He leant forward and reached up, standing on tip toe, to whisper towards Fal's ear. "Some say he killed his own mother, once he learned all the tricks of the trade from her, as you might say."

Fal looked into the intent eyes before him, half in the shadow of the wide hat brim, and saw the dwarf's urgency and concern.

"I'd be glad if you wouldn't go out there tonight, master Fal."

"Alright then, Theck, I won't," Fal said with some amazement, for the moment unable to say anything else.

Theck let go of his arm. "Thank you, master, thank you," he said. "I know you'll look after the little one. She'll soon go to sleep, I expect."

He smiled again and helped Fal and the dwarf-child down into the waiting boat.

Now that the Praise Song was past, Fal had no mind to use the sail to tack against the now steady on-shore breeze. There was power left in him to spare, the power that the boat was made for, that found its visible expression in the patterns with which it was engraved. He would not be called on the next day for work in the Forge, and he wanted to enjoy himself. He plucked the strings of the harp swiftly and strongly, and the boat glided forward as if borne on the back of some mighty fish, silently and without effort.

Little Amba sat next to him in the bows upright and eager as they sailed straight out along moon's bright path across the shimmering expanse of the lake. A white glint to the right of the rippling causeway, obscure with distance, marked the cliffs or maybe even the buildings on Sulthind's island.

Was Lothur, as the dwarves called him, really turning his hand to sorcery? Fal remembered the earnestness of Theck's face. Dwarves were not gossips by nature. Even among themselves they spoke only to the point. Or was it natural but exaggerated fatherly concern? Again, the dwarves were not usually fearful. And could Sulthind really be so reckless? He would know the price a sorcerer paid, no matter how masterly his knowledge or how lofty his aims. Sorcerers reckoned to force others to pay the price for them — but it would spring back on them in the end. Sulthind's mother had already paid the price if Theck's account was true. He would have to ask them more about it in the morning, the story was too unpleasant and improbable to be believed lightly. He wanted to thrust it from his mind.

But Amba had been yawning and was beginning to rock from side to side. He folded Theck's cloak as an under-blanket and quietly wrapped his own cloak around her. She sighed contentedly and allowed him to make her comfortable at the bottom of the boat. She fell asleep at once.

He looked at the stars and saw that, in spite of the moon's brightness, the air was so clear they still shone out with fierce, liquid brilliance. Estera, star of evening and star of morning, had already set in the west, and in the eastern sky the wild hunters were chasing the royal hind across the heavens. "Until she turns and shows them the yellow jewel that shines between her eyes. Then shall they at last be satisfied and shall break their arrows across their knees; and of their bows shall harps be made, and the world will change." So prophesied the dwarves.

In the north, above the twin hills, glittered the Traitors, those who had failed in their trust and had not kept their word. And about them were the dragons which had issued from their mouths when the great falsehoods were spoken.

Above, alone and silent, stood the heroes, the gods and goddesses of the Deep, and the birds of heaven, Thendril and Cefwin, flying across the pathway of the gods, the Crystal Chasm of the dwarves, the Flower Trail of

the elves. For a moment something stirred deep in Fal's mind, like a
memory too lovely and too precious to be grasped, and he heard, and at
once again forgot, the Great Music. But he was at peace with the world,
and a contentment fell upon him such as he had not known all that long,
hard winter.

————

Whether he had slept or not he did not know, but he was suddenly aware
of feeling very cold. The moon had sunk low in the west, and in the east the
stars were giving way to the first flush of dawn. Somewhere close by a
skylark began to sing.

Where was he? With alarm he saw before him, not more than a furlong
or so over the open water, the pale cliffs of Sulthind's island. He spoke
quietly to the boat and stilled its motion. Involuntarily he looked up and
studied the cliff-tops. Dimly, in the pale light, he could make out the steps
cut in the rock-face, where, years before, he and his two friends had
clambered up and down. This was not far from Rushkel, once the main
settlement, but long since deserted. The trees from here obscured any view
of the crumbling roof-tops. The small harbour was further to the right.
The boat appeared to be drifting in that direction, towards the rocky
headland which formed one arm of the harbour bay. He thought he would
use the oars to pull out from the rocks; the dawn air was very chill and it
would get him warm.

But the light was increasing and he was held by familiar landmarks: the
clump of boulders where they used to pull up the boat over the crunchy
sand; the wooden door they had made from driftwood over the small cave
where they had made their den. He wondered whether the boxes and
cushions they had once used to furnish it were still there. He was tempted
to go and find out. The boat was still drifting to the right. The edge of the
wall had become visible around the side of the trees. One of the boulders
on the sand shifted and wavered. It uncurled and straightened up. It was
Sulthind.

"Good dawning, friend Fal!" he called. "Has your promotion to the
rank of master gone to your head that you come spying on me so soon?"

Fal sat tongue-tied for a moment, partly with surprise at Sulthind's
unexpected appearance on what he had taken to be a deserted shore, partly
at the silly accusation, but also because he was always at a disadvantage
with Sulthind's clever way of speaking. Not that it was unfamiliar to him.
It was a perfect balance between hen-bane and honey, carefully chosen
words and half-hidden mirth. It could be good humour or withering scorn,
you could never be quite sure with Sulthind. Certainly he could be very
funny when he wished, but the barbs, when they struck home, always went
deep.

"Come, come," Sulthind called persuasively, "not lost your voice after
the noisy old Praise Song, surely? Or a sore throat through leaving your

cloak at home? A foolish oversight at this time of the year, if I may say so."

Fal cleared his throat and said, "As a matter of fact, Sulthind, I was just thinking about old times and looking at the door of the cave. I didn't realize you had anything worth spying on." He decided to take a chance. "I didn't notice any green flames flickering round the keyhole or magic fumes drifting up the cliff-face."

As Sulthind threw back the hood of his grey cloak he revealed his remarkable aquiline features; yet in spite of the long, sharp nose and narrow cheek bones, the large grey-green eyes were full of life, and his face, set in a mass of tousled ginger hair, was decidedly handsome. Fal had not noticed how close to the shore the boat had drifted.

Sulthind laughed, drily and mirthlessly. "Not bad," he said, "actually not bad at all. Thinking about old times! When elves ruled the world and men roosted in the tree tops like pigeons, eh? But all you meant was cooking sausages on the beach and climbing around looking for gulls' eggs. Well, well; why not? Don't just sit there. Bring her in and come up for breakfast, have a good old chat."

He was obviously being friendly after all, and Fal felt mean to have misjudged him. People were sometimes sarcastic to mask embarrassment or shyness, he knew, and men brought up on islands did not have much chance of learning to mix. Anyway, the boat was already moving in, Sulthind seemed to be beckoning it or pulling it, something no-one had ever managed to do before.

Just then there was a movement in the front of the boat. Little Amba, disturbed by the voices, yawned and stretched, then climbed up and peered over the edge towards the beach. Her eyes were cloudy with sleep, but when she saw Sulthind standing on the shore, his arms outstretched towards her, she involuntarily threw up her hands in a vigorous gesture as if to ward him off. At once the boat stopped moving, and Sulthind coughed or maybe sneezed with the sound of a red-hot stone when water is poured on it. Then he drew a quick breath to speak but instead checked himself and smiled gently.

"Behold the harper's missing cloak! What an injustice I did you, old friend, accusing you of folly and oversight. I should rather extol your chivalry and courtesy towards this little... little...?"

"Dwarf maiden," said Fal. "This child was yesterday's double finder who stood before us all on the tip of the Pointer." He would have said more, for he missed Sulthind's friendship, but he was interrupted, and Sulthind's eyes had for one moment opened wide with surprise and unfeigned interest.

"A dwarf child with you on the Pointer, was it?" he said. "That... that might explain why you have brought her with you. Your new accomplice! or... maybe as a special treat for being such a clever little girl. How interesting, how novel! Then how about *both* of you coming up to breakfast in uncle Sulthind's white house! Come along! For old time's sake. Fresh buttered rolls with hot goat's milk and honey, to warm you up. Then back home on the wings of the rising sun. Eh? The perfect outing!"

He had been speaking directly to Amba, who all this time had been kneeling on the bench in the angle of the bows staring at him open-mouthed. Fal was half inclined to give way but was wondering how he could reconcile breakfast on the island with his promise to Theck.

Sulthind again stretched out both arms towards them, inviting and imploring, and he was smiling broadly, but little Amba spoke: "My daddy doesn't like you, Lord Lothur," she said.

Sulthind's arms dropped to his side with the suddenness and completeness of a marionette whose strings have been cut. He pouted, putting on an exaggerated show of hurt feelings. But Fal caught a glint of genuine annoyance in his eyes. He disliked being called Lothur.

"Your daddy doesn't *like* me, child? Does your daddy know me then, have I met him, has he been here? Who *is* your good daddy?"

Fal thought he had better interfere before insults began to fly and a feud of the dwarves of the Delming with Sulthind of the Island erupted around this child's family honour. He knew how touchy dwarves could be and how unendingly complicated such situations could become.

"Her daddy is probably standing on the quay," he said, "and wondering why we're staying out so long. I think we'd better go back for now. We can come another time when it's been properly arranged," he managed to add affably.

Sulthind stared at them in silence for a moment as if trying to read Fal's thoughts.

"Very well then," he said, "that might be the better way. Bring Ilmarin with you. And of course bring little... ah... what did you say her name was?"

"I didn't," said Fal, laughing. "You'll have to keep guessing till she tells you herself — next time! But for the moment, I'm afraid we really must be off!"

Deftly, Fal unfurled and fastened the sail which puffed out stiffly in the fresh dawn wind. "Good-bye, Sulthind."

The little boat pulled away and Sulthind bowed in mock courtesy. He did not speak again but stood watching after them for a long time as the sun rose, gold and clear. The light caught in his eyes and flamed in them as in cut rubies; but Fal was already too far away to see it.

Little Amba snuggled up to him for warmth and comfort and looked at him with large, solemn eyes.

"That was a very narrow escape, wasn't it, Master Imbravel?" she said. "And you'd better take your cloak. You look frozen."

THREE

Fal was finding it very difficult to prepare his mind for the patterning. Five days ago a brightly painted barge had come in from Angarth, a prosperous little town on the southern shore of the lake. The winter had been bad there, too. Now her mariners brought grain for the Delming — and work for the forge. Ceremonial bowls were asked for, inlaid with gold, "to banish blight and bane, dearth and drought, to quicken corn and hallow harvest." The undertaking was commonplace for the craftsmen of the Delming, but designs were never repeated, each item was unique and had to be matched to the place and people who were to use it.

His thoughts kept pulling him back to the dwarves' accusations against Sulthind. There was obviously some embarrassment among them that Theck had spoken of the matter, and further information was not forthcoming. They insisted that the affairs of the island interested them in no manner at all, and beyond that they would not be led. Fal knew there was nothing that incensed them more than mockery in a man's voice and he could see there was going to be no way of taking Amba to tea parties on the island. And to go without her would lead to more difficult questions from Sulthind. Better let the matter slide. Icicles will hang until the sun grows warmer, as they say.

Well, let them hang then. But it is hard to put suspicions aside once the mind has listened to them. They spread like thistles in a meadow till all else is suffocated, like the soft rot in timber that turns strong planks into crumbling fungus. He thought of the fog that had concealed the island all that winter, of the illnesses, the accidents, deaths. No, it was too absurd, too unlikely to bother thinking about... and yet he was longing for the patterning to begin, to help him thrust out the torment of these wretched thoughts.

He stood between four other harpers, two of them apprentices, two much older men, perfect in their knowledge of the Delming's music but ungifted in awakening the magic which lies in all things. Did they never find this ceremony of waiting round the forge-stone as tedious as he? Today it seemed endless. If only the patterning would begin! He sighed deeply, and caught sight of the master weaver smiling across at him. He was on the other side of the circle, to the left of Ilmarin, his eyes sparkling with amusement and understanding — like a wise old owl, Fal thought, or like an oak in a copse of saplings among all those apprentices of his. Aren had spent hundreds of hours waiting like this, of course, ready to watch the twisting lines of light, to bring knowledge to them, as he said. Fal managed to smile back.

The dwarves were coming in now, following Celbring, their master. They were dressed identically in grey with plain leather belts and, except for Celbring, carried neither lantern, hammer, nor any other object for, like the weavers, they too came only to add alertness of the mind and fineness of the eye. When they were all in their places Celbring returned to the north door and laid before its threshold the hammer of polished copper that he bore, emblem of the people of Chardec from whom they claimed descent. Some believed this was done to banish the forces of darkness which crept forever on the heels of the dwarves, while others said that the outer doors, at the further end of the northern entrance, were connected with this ritual. Ages ago they had been locked in token of the bitterness of the dwarves at the loss of their kingdoms, and none would so much as lay a finger on the Portal of Sorrow which had rusted into its frame, cracked and untended. Other doors now led from the passage into the house of the dwarves and thence into their courtyard.

Ilmarin stepped forward. At last it was beginning. He handed the silver hammer to one of his apprentices and Fal began to play. It was the music to open the stone, to let the life of the earth shine through the massive altar-like boulder as through a window — a window that looked down into the ocean of rock and crystal, vast reservoir of ancient power. And Ilmarin began to sing the invocation, the song of earth's hidden fire preserved ever since the mightiest of the elven kin had taken the light from the world and placed it in the sky — that earth could harden and come of age, that tree and bone could gain their strength.

Each syllable was drawn into many flowing notes, each word into a melody of its own, yet the meaning was not obscured but sounded clear to all who heard them:

> An tsilwe ah sulmirië
> eleonai emel i glor
> esthelia entirwië
> genna aréalnan
> ymurin ycsin derwinin!

— Thou memory of the wondrous sun that in earth's centre ever shineth as of old: we call thee to us, mother, sister, ancient friend.

The melody rippled as liquid as the blackbird's song, yet something was in it too of the robin's singing, silvery and ethereal. And all the while the hands of the singer moved over the stone as if protecting a delicate flame, newly lit, from the roughness of the world.

A flame it was indeed, gathering light, very faint at first and as intangible as the scent of wild roses, but ever growing until the smith held between his hands a ball of fire, fresh and radiant as the rising sun. And within that radiance lines began to weave, twisting and spiralling, and Ilmarin played with the light as a child plays with a toy, looping it in and out of his fingers, dipping, kneading, now weaving cat's cradles, now throwing out shimmering blossoms, while unceasingly he thought of the purpose the patterns were to serve — the blessing of the fields of Angarth.

For a long time it seemed but a plaything in his hands, tame and malleable. Then it burst into life, its brilliant lines plaiting and writhing in such a whirling glimmer that even the clever eyes of the dwarves, well used to beholding the Forge's wonders, were confused. Only Aren, master of all the patterns of weaving, could not be outwitted, and his eyes remained calm, his lips lightly pursed, as if critical of the wild dance and waiting for something more ordered and useful to emerge.

Several times the pace would slow, as if the energy were near its end, and Ilmarin would lean forward, working eagerly but carefully with both hand and mind, the complex patterns suggesting marvellous possibilities to him. Then they would flare up into yet another swirling dazzle and the work seemed to begin afresh.

But in the end, when noon was long past, the struggle was won and the patterns became completely still, shining steady and clear. Not for many days would they begin to fade but would stay poised and quiet above the stone, whence the craftsmen could copy them into wood, alabaster, copper and gold, and the weavers would learn from them, increasing their skills.

Now when the dwarves saw that the patterning was complete and the dance of light finished they stamped their feet and clapped their hands, according to their customs, and shouted aloud to show that the task was done. The silence of the Forge was broken and its daily work could begin once more; shuttles clicked and wove, the harpers practised their epics, ballads, and solemn incantations, the ringing of hammers was to be heard in the streets around the courts, and the folk of the Delming knew that all was well at the heart of their ageless city.

FOUR

"Only as a shadow or as a twist of the air before a boulder or a tree could they see him now, elusive still yet unable in defeat to escape their anger. And though he could not outpace them he showed no sign of tiring in his flight. The dawn of the third day of their pursuit was breaking, and still they could not overtake him."

The story-teller mustered her audience as if to reassure herself that everyone was still following the narrative that was unfolding before them. Would the harpers remember every detail correctly? Would the elves paint the figures aright for Aren to weave? The story was nearing its climax and its end.

"The enemy had led them far indeed, through a land wild and cold and unknown to them, for none of them had ever ventured so far as this into the north. Endless his flight might seem but it was not without purpose, for even in humiliation he was not bereft of reason, and one last hope drove him on.

"'In spring this is a land of blossoms, they say, and in summer of light beyond compare. But now autumn's upon us, and ice is in the air. We cannot go much further.'

"Gildor spoke, and his eyes were still dark with the silence of the tall pine forests which were their home.

"'Soon the sun will rise', said Orvin, 'the ice will yield to her warmth'.

"'Not for long!' cried Thelior. 'Look!'

"His right arm was extended towards the horizon, pointing out the way ahead.

"'The Wall of Ice!' gasped Orvin, 'for us this is the world's end. No horse of ours will climb those cliffs'.

"'Then we must ride like the wind or we shall lose him', cried Gildor, 'and our victory will be all in vain. That would be a sorry ending!'

"They swept forward, their hair flowing out as in a gale, and the sun shone on their armour so that each apeared within a flame of golden light.

"Ah, good folk!" — the story-teller smiled kindly at her listeners and raised her long-fingered hands amid the weaving of her tale — "no-one of you has seen a sight so fine, not even you, good elves. And there has been no feat like that riding in our age. But Gildor reckoned as their last hope with the pride of their enemy, that he would not in the end be able to slink silently away but would have to show himself and mock them when he reckoned safety to be within his grasp. Then they might yet approach him and assail him, for Orvin carried the Silver Bow and its one last arrow. Though even now they hoped not to slay him but rather to take him alive, that one day he might repent and light might enter his heart.

"Alas, slender hope! And what if they should lose him after all in the vast icy wastes of the northland? Years of vigilance would be their doom, watching for they knew not what, for already in his flight he had forsaken the form they knew and had become as a shadow, a bitter taint of hatred, leading them ever on.

"They had come almost to the foot of the cliffs, furrowed by deep cracks and gullies, sheer and very high. And they saw that a steep road had been cut out of the blue ice, rising in one straight sweep to the cliff top a thousand feet above the plain. And at the beginning of that road, clear against the shimmering ice, their enemy stood, waiting for them.

"Gross and clumsy he was now, or suddenly appeared to be, clad in dark leather and hoops of iron, coarse, gap-toothed and foul, and in his left hand he swung a heavy club, set with spikes, black and long. He spat on the ice and laughed loudly.

"'We shall meet again, pretty ones', he sneered, 'when the ice has fed my strength for a while. In the meantime it will be an evil journey you'll have seeking your homes. Now shoot your arrow if you will, Orvin rat-brain, it will have less power over me than a snowball!'

"He laughed again, but strangely, as if a sudden idea had struck him. Laying aside his club he knelt on the ice while the friends watched, uncertain what to do. Suddenly they realised: he was himself making a ball of snow! With a lurch he rose and hurled it at them, striking Gildor's steed full on the chest. The horse staggered and fell. Gildor jumped clear with an angry cry, and Orvin shot the arrow with a swift hand and a bright, cold eye. It pierced the club which their enemy again swung before him and stuck in it. Its wielder laughed and, pulling the shaft out, snapped off the head and dropped it into his pocket.

"'I'll keep this', he called, 'the ice feeds me already, and it will not be long before I shall return to you. There will be a few scores to settle then. And a few years of amusement to make amends'.

"They had dismounted and were crowding round the foot of the ice road as if to attack him, but he only spat at them over his shoulder as he walked up the white causeway. He knew they could not follow, for their strength would wane even as his grew.

"'This is a poor victory', Thelior whispered.

"'He is an ice-troll', said Orvin, 'surely this is his true form. Look at him with his club and great iron boots'.

"Gildor shook his head doubtfully.

"'Maybe', he said. 'Even so, do we try to follow or stay here staring like fools.'

"'We have our spears', said Thelior. 'We can't give up now'.

"'Our kindred do not belong to the ice', said Orvin, and Gildor hesitated, for he had never seen the great ice of the Ever Cold, and he was afraid.

"But then another voice cried out, strong and clear, from the cliff tops, ringing through the frosted air like a blade of steel. And yet the sound was clean and good.

"'Who takes what is ours, who drinks our wine, who drops his filth on the clean white snow?' And laughter came to the three friends down from the top of the ice.

"Their enemy had halted, not yet half way up the cliff road, and the companions looked beyond him in wonder. Over the brink of the ice, down the roadway, came four beasts, their foreheads high and domed, their red, shaggy hair sweeping the snow, their long trunks swinging between huge curved tusks. And on the neck of each, clad in furry skins, sat a rider. They carried spears, and already the foremost appeared to be taking aim at the dark figure that stood, murderous and grim, yet trapped and uncertain which way to turn.

"But the rider spoke again. 'Do not think to throw your snowballs at us, black dog, we have no fear of the snow, we who rule the northlands'.

"Then, to the amazement of the companions, their enemy began running up the snow path, swinging his club and crying out. But the beasts were too swift for his lumbering movements, and now too late did he regret the massive, troll-like form which he had drawn together for himself out of that world of ice, for a lithe trunk seized him round the wrist and flung him out beyond the precipice into the thin, clear air.

"Their foe cried out again, but in a strange tongue, as he wheeled through the air, cursing Gildor and his folk and all the ground they stood on. But when he struck the rocks he died, for in the air he found no strength to be rid of the new shape which he wore; and so at last, with help unlooked for, they were victorious indeed. But the land was withered all about their homes for many miles and nothing since has grown upon it."

The story was finished. Its teller looked slowly over her audience again and nodded. then she placed her hands on the heads of the animals which lay like sphinxes beside her — the alert, grey wolf and the drowsy, brown bear. She rose. The evening was at an end.

The plump she-bear was trundling ahead of them through a sea of bluebells, crushing scores of the lovely blossoms at every step.

"It's a language," Fal thought, "a language of opposites. We must learn to read it."

The wolf thrust its hard muzzle into his hand for attention, and he rubbed the cleft which ran backwards from its forehead to a point between its ears, then wriggled his fingers down into the heavy mane. The size of the beast's shoulders never failed to surprise him.

"Ay," Tholaiwin was saying, "there are still some big enough to carry a frail body for a few miles, though maybe they're a bit small compared with the creatures that trod the earth in the Golden Age. And fewer now are willing. Times aren't what they were. Times change."

She was the old woman of the beasts, wanderer in her own legends, the story-teller. Some said she hunted with a pack of wolves in the cold time of the year, riding Alfeng as if the wolf were a pony, wild and swift. Another, a merchant from over the lake, said Tholaiwin had been seen in the mists of the hills around the Starrill like a phantom astride the haunches of the white stag, hunting with a tufted owl upon her wrist. And others said she was the last mistress of Fram in exile. But to the masters of the Forge she was a good friend, teacher and tale-weaver, a traveller without possessions except the wise lore of many lands.

"Yes," said Fal, "if the stories of the past are anything to go by, times certainly do change. And that means that places change. Even the Delming is not what it was. When did the Golden Tree last blossom, I wonder?"

"The bluebells bossom, though, lad. Don't forget that. The woods are full of life. Don't want too much of the world. Think rather of what the world wants from you."

"That's all very well, but you can't deny that there was once a light and a life in the very air which has faded in the ageing of the world. The stories you've taught us are full of it."

Tholaiwin's eyes were pale grey yet they were themselves full of light as she glanced at Fal.

"Well, that's right," she said. "Yes, Gildor would have been the last of the elves to see the north before the coming of the great waste. That was a change, now. Yes, that really was a change."

She spoke half to a crow that had perched on the limb of an old beech above her and that appeared to be listening to the conversation with intelligence.

"That crow now — would have had a crest of silver with red tail and wings. A beak of pure gold, maybe; wings of glittering amethyst and claws of emerald."

She seemed to be quoting from something, Fal thought. But the little old woman was frowning at the bird and looking very thoughtful. It gave a squawk and flew off.

"No offence, no offence," laughed Tholaiwin. Fal watched the blackness of it flying away under the green canopy of the spring.

Another contrast, he thought: like the bear and the bluebells — or the wolf and the bear.

"If that bird should come your way again, ask it in for supper," Tholaiwin said. "It had a lean, starved look. Unnatural. Seemed to appreciate conversation, as well."

"Maybe it can tell a story or two itself when it's in the mood," said Fal.

"That wouldn't surprise me at all," said Tholaiwin, "but Bereldan's gone up into this little valley. Let's see what she's after."

They came to an outcrop of rocks around the entrance to a cave. The bear was desperately trying to get into the narrow opening. A badger would have found it a perfect fit, but Tholaiwin thought that it was more likely to be the lair of a wildcat. Alfeng sat on his haunches and watched while the bear snuffled and scraped.

"You'd be safer sticking to bluebells," said the old lady. "You'll be getting a scratched nose in a minute."

Bereldan loked briefly at her over her shoulder and sighed, then returned to her attack on the clay and rocks with increased energy.

"But I think you're right," said Tholaiwin. "There was certainly a power in the north which has gone to-day. Maybe the flickerings that you see in the northern sky on a clear winter's night are a last memory stirring of what once was."

"So the tales of shining elven cities and hidden dwarf kngdoms in the north might be true!"

"Oh, they are, without a doubt. Of course they're true! In the very middle of the Waste was Gelmindel, the city of fountains. It turned into Lune, the barren mountain, the hub of silence, the womb of death, and fifty other names which all tell the same story in different words. It's all very certain to be true."

"The dwarves have a saying," said Fal. "'Only a fool finds wealth easy to lose'. Where did it all go?"

But for once the old creature was not willing to be helpful. She shrugged and said, "I should ask the people of the Waste, if I were you, up at the fastness of Lune. They should know, if anyone does, living in the middle of it all. But it's getting chilly now that the sun's gone, isn't it!" She gave the young harper a quick, questioning look, but Fal missed it. "Let's get back and see if those dwarves have got a good fire going in the hall!"

She called the animals and began striding down the hill with such energy that Fal could hardly keep up with her.

FIVE

In the night that followed that walk in the bluebell woods, Fal had a dream. Even as it began it already seemed to have been rambling on forever without any hope of change or awakening. Endlessly and aimlessly he saw himself journeying through the world, doing this and that, everything and nothing, until at last he realized that he was very old and desperately tired, and wherever he looked, the world was dying. Great forests, once the home of many beasts and full of the song of birds, became lonely desolations of sand and rock where only a chill wind sang among the dry, cold stones. Meadows, tall with plumed grasses, mottled with flowers and heavy with the drone of bees, had withered into shifting deserts. He saw people, restless and wandering, sometimes alone, sometimes in hordes, their belongings packed on horses or even on their own weary shoulders. He saw others greedy for power and greedy for possessions, inventing, trading, building, all feverishly trying to ignore the growing emptiness around them and within them, an emptiness they could not understand.

And always the dying of the world went on — into the rivers, the lakes and oceans it spread, into the very cradles of life. And he saw the Delming a deserted ruin and the water of the lake filled with floating dead fish. Dark slime fouled the rocks and sands of the shores as the water shrank, and the horror and revulsion of it were more than he could bear and he cried out in his sleep. But he could not wake.

Then the scene changed, and he saw, at first far away, in the middle of a desolation of grey rocks, a castle. Mostly it consisted of one massive tower, silver roofed. And though there was a drawbridge and an iron gate, yet the castle had no windows or other openings but stood blind and featureless in that empty land, while Fal's horror at the dying of the world turned into comfortless misery, and in his sleep he wept.

And a hollow voice spoke like thunder out of the bowels of the earth. "I am the fastness, the heart and centre of the desolation, the guardian of the future," it said. "I am the one you seek, the one you have forgotten, bane and blessing, wisdom and waste, help and hunger. Long have you sought me, long, long."

Then at last the dream faded, yet still he did not wake but returned again to a deeper sleep, to a land full of shadows, always shifting, in which he could find neither rest nor comfort.

———

An old traveller and her animals, a wood of bluebells, a crow, an ugly dream — small things, and yet the unlodging of a tiny pebble can start an avalanche, a spark a forest fire. So it seemed to be with Fal, for his conversation with the story-teller touched off many thoughts about the nature of the world and his own place in it. Day by day the thoughts bred in his mind until a haunting mood engulfed him and all else faded, while at night in his dreams he saw grey landscapes, dismal without hope, and in the gloom the blind castle, silent now in the empty world over which it ruled. And in that dreadful land he walked, bent with age, tired and lost, seeking a remedy for the harm which had come to it.

On the morning after the walk in the woods he had gone straight to find Tholaiwin. He wanted to ask her more about Lune and about the people she said lived in the Waste; and he wanted to tell her his dream. But the guest house was empty. Tholaiwin had left before dawn to continue a journey of her own — to a destination nobody knew. "On the road to the west," Skelfir had said, a road which in the first thirty miles had as many paths leaving and joining it as there are lines on the palm of a man's hand. Fal had taken a pony with the hope of catching her at Fyrwell, but already only ten miles from the forge neither cottager nor wayfarer had seen the old woman and her beasts, and he knew he had lost them. Now it might be a year, even several years, before they would return, and day by day his restlessness led him further from the life which for so long he had accepted as his.

"I doubt whether Tholley could have told you all that much more about Lune," said Melauriën, trying to comfort him. "The fastness is a thing of the past and not of our age, by all reports."

"We were talking about the world and how different it used to be," said Fal. "About the story of Gildor and the coming of the Waste. I wanted to know more about it but Tholley said I should go and ask the people who live there myself, the people at Lune."

"Don't you think she was joking, Fal?" Melauriën smiled. "I've never heard of any people living in the Waste. Wolves — and flies — are all you'd be likely to find."

"She semed perfectly serious to me," said Fal wretchedly. "If only someone knew where she'd gone, I'd go and ask her."

"Perhaps she doesn't know any more than she told you," she said gently; but she was worried at his mood. She had never seen him like this, so restless and dissatisfied.

———

"I'm not worried whether Lune was an ancient fortress or not," he was saying to Ilmarin that evening. "It may be in ruins or have disappeared entirely by now, for all I care. That's not the point. But it's true what Tholley said, don't you see. The whole north has become a dead world, and perhaps we think it doesn't matter because it's far away. But it isn't just the north; that's only where it's worst. All the world has faded compared with what it used to be. Yes, all right, the bluebells still blossom. I know. But what about the Golden Tree? It's supposed to sing, according to the songs we teach the apprentices. Even the dwarves have stories of the Golden Tree. They say the wisdom of the stars speaks in its thousand voices. Whoever heard it speak with one voice, never mind a thousand! This year it trembled, and we thought it was a marvel. All it shows to me is that there must be some truth in the old stories, but that things have changed, changed beyond all recognition. And when will they stop changing, Ilmarin? Look at all the death and misery of this last winter. What will next winter be like?"

"The world grows old," said Ilmarin thoughtfully. "The hills are ancient. Maybe even the stars won't shine for ever."

"The moon still waxes and wanes, and after every winter comes the spring. But who knows for how much longer? The dying of the north is maybe entering our very hearts." Fal spoke passionately, longing to be contradicted, yet feeling more and more convinced that what he said was true and of terrible importance.

"I'm going to Lune, Ilmarin, I want to see if Tholley was joking. Will you come with me?"

Ilmarin shook his head sadly. "There's too much to do in the Forge. But I don't blame you for wanting to go. Maybe some of the dwarves will go with you. They all once came from the north, it's said."

"I'll go alone, I know there's a lot to do here. I'll leave soon and be back in the autumn, before the snows come to the Waste. If there's really no-one there I'll be able to return at once."

Even as he spoke he remembered some strange words in the Book of Laurin-men-Arkh, an old dwarf king. 'The roads of the heavy people will be bent, they will be full of corners. They will not turn to follow the shapes of the world but will be governed by laws of their own; hidden from us, yes, but hidden also from them. Yet there shall still be those who shall see, as from a mountain top, the patterns of the world, even the patterns in the paths of men.'

And a distant, silent part of him knew that it must be an inner mountain which was meant, an ascent of the mind, not the outer mountain he was seeking, but he said nothing. For he was angry and felt suddenly jealous of his knowledge of the ancient lore of the dwarves. And he did not think Ilmarin would understand the Book of Laurin.

———

As spring wore on towards midsummer and the festival of fire he spoke little of Tholaiwin's visit and of his own proposed journey, partly for the fear that his plans would meet with disapproval and partly because of his own indecision. Secretly, he asked the one and the other of the people of the Forge what they knew of the fastness of Lune, in the hope of learning

something that might sway him towards an irrevocable plan. In himself he
found only uncertainty and confusion.

The elves told him that there had once been another forge far in the
north, exceedingly great in importance and power, but they spoke with
caution, fearing to hurt his pride, looking upon themselves for the most
part as but visitors to the Delming. But when they saw that he was only
eager to hear as much as he could, they spoke more freely and said that the
northern forge was once the centre of the world, yet they were sure it had
been no fortress and in no way a place grim or forbidding but a wondrous-
ly fair city.

"It is what we call Gelmindel," they said, "and it was a very long time
ago when it ceased to be. There's no city or even village now beyond the
Forest of Aurëlund, Fal. The Delming is the only Forge. There are certainly
none of our people in the far, barren north — and we've never heard of
Lune."

When he asked the dwarves they only scowled. But he pressed them until
Skelfir said, "The Iron Mountains are wild and empty. Whatever lies
beyond — fortress, forest, or barren moor — can only be given to the same
emptiness. We do not speak of Lune."

"But have you ever heard of it?" Fal persisted.

"We do not speak of it," Skelfir repeated, and neither he nor the other
dwarves would say more.

. Only from Aren did he hear something to give him hope that his
yearnings might in some way be connected with a known reality. The old
master weaver remembered that there was indeed a mountain called Lune,
or Luin he thought it rather was, in the north beyond Aurëland Forest, but
he was interested in nothing beyond the spelling of the name.

"I feel sure it's Luin, you know, not Lune," he said. "Lune just doesn't
ring the right sort of bell. Luin, I'm sure."

———

A week before midsummer his restlessness again grew so strong that he
knew he would not sleep if he went to bed. He took his boat out on the lake
and tried to find peace in the gentle lapping of the water. The stars shone
only very faintly, for the sunset lingered long after the sun had gone and
clung to the sky behind the northern hills until, after a mere three or four
hours, the pale glow turned into a slow dawn. And in the south the moon
shone full. He knew about the shallow path of the midnight sun and was
not deceived into thinking that he maybe saw the light of which Tholaiwin
had spoken. Yet it awakened his longing even more to understand where
that ancient light had gone and how it might be regained.

The next day his mind was set.

"I'll stay for the nights of the festival of fire," he told Melaurïen, "then
I'll go a-journeying, for my heart leaves me no quiet; the call is too great."

To his surprise the Lady of the Forge said nothing to dissuade him. "I have seen your longing to be off, Fal," she said. "It's a good thing to get to know the world for yourself. Don't stay away too long, though; the winter in the north can be very fierce. And we need you here in the Forge!"

SIX

In the fields outside the city walls, on the eve of midsummer, six fires were lit, and all night long the people danced between them. The elves danced for the sun, the dwarves for the moon, the younger folk for the quicker planets, and the older ones for those which move more slowly, further from the sun but nearer to the stars. In and out they wove, circling and crossing, spiralling and looping, meeting and passing, while the fires were fed throughout the night till their heat and roar seemed a part of the earth and sky and the movement and the warmth were all that the dancers knew.

Fal led the harpers and their apprentices and the visiting musicians from the villages who had come in for the festival, and they played the ancient melodies a thousand times, while Aren conducted the dancing, calling, guiding the groups, reminding young and old of the duties and customs of the dancing stars.

And for a while Fal was one with the life and flow of the Delming again, as the people he loved stepped and chanted, the fires glowing hot on their cheeks.

But after the third night, when the day of rest came and the main part of the festival was over, he began gathering provisions to stock his boat for the journey up the River Ironway to the steading of Gopley. From there he would continue on foot.

Several times he had considered asking Ilmarin again to accompany him, perhaps at least part of the way; but he knew that the smith did not see the changing of the world as he saw it. He did not want to persuade him only for the sake of their friendship, quite apart from the difficulties Ilmarin's absence would cause for the work of the Forge, for the elven apprentices were not yet able to replace him whereas there were at least two harpers who could do the day-to-day part of Fal's work reliably.

The dwarves recaulked his boat, and Aren gave him a thick new blanket, backed with silk, for the cold autumn nights. It was dark red, and woven into it was a map of the Forge with its six courtyards, but all enwrapped in the branches of the Tree, which was clad in pale green and yellow.

That afternoon, as Fal was busy in his room re-sewing the buttons on his pack and cloak and thinking about his journey, there came a soft tapping on his door. It was Theck, in one of his sheepish moods; but that was not the strangest thing about him. He had removed his hat, which he now clutched nervously in both hands, revealing the glossy dome of his head, edged only by a little grey hair, so fine and fluffy that it was like the fur of a young rabbit.

"Master Fal," he began, blushing. "Forgive the intrusion, young master, but..."

"That's all right, Theck," said Fal, smiling, "I'm not doing anything special at the moment."

"Not writing a new ballad or anything?" said the dwarf, peering round Fal into the room.

"Just sewing my cloak where it looks worn. Come in, Theck."

"Oh no, master, thank you, I won't stay." He looked quickly up into Fal's face. "Only a quick word, Fal. We were wondering, some of us... That is, we hear you're going to be travelling northwards in the next few days, a long way northwards. Yes, master, people *are* talking about it. And we wondered whether you'd care to come to a modest meal tonight — in the Dwarves' House — a little farewell gathering, as you might say."

Fal gasped in amazement. It was not the custom for the dwarves to invite the big people into their house, and, though he had lived in the Delming since his childhood, he had never so much as caught a glimpse of the corridors that led off the dark tunnel between the north court and the inner forge.

Theck suddenly looked serious. "We've heard where your heart is driving you, master," he whispered, "and we're worried, very worried. If it lay within our nature and strength, we would come with you, yet that cannot be. But at least we'll make the farewell one of..." He hesitated, "...of importance, master; if you would do us the honour. Tonight, or tomorrow, if you will."

Fal smiled sadly. "I'll come tonight. But don't fear, Theck, I shall return. I'm no dwarf that holds a grudge against the north or the north against me. I go but on a journey as might any other man. Do not fear."

Theck glanced at him again and frowned. He seemed about to speak but, instead, bowed.

"The two brothers will fetch you tonight when all is ready. We are honoured, master."

He turned and was gone.

———

"You didn't expect to find an old dwarf-hall, carved out of living crystal and inlaid with precious metals," said Celbring with a welcoming gesture, "yet perhaps even so the plainness of our dwellings may surprise you. Remember, Master Falimbravel, that we dwarves of the Delming are a people in exile, or at least a part of that people. It would not be fitting to make imitations of our past glory. Rather shall that splendour live on in the old stories. Anything of less quality would tarnish the memory and would mislead the young into believing they knew what they do not by any means know."

He glanced at little Amba who was one of the dozen dwarves invited to the gathering in the simple, whitewashed hall. She smiled shyly and gazed at him with her astonishingly large brown eyes.

"The hall is simple," said Fal, "but pleasing and fitting for those skilled in the ancient arts."

There was certainly no great richness to be seen anywhere, yet much craft and care had been applied to humble materials. The rectangular table was of dark slate, almost black, but completely covered with the most delicate and intricate patterns, etched into the stone and filled in with the shining green of malachite. There was only one chair, of oak, which he knew would be for Celbring, as Master; but he guessed, too, that it would be offered to him and that he would be expected to accept. Otherwise the table was surrounded only by benches. There was enough space there to seat the Forge's whole dwarf community, but, as Skelfir and Skirfir had hinted, this was to be something of an intimate occasion. Fal thought the brothers had exchanged knowing, mysterious looks which made him wonder what was planned.

The only other furnishing was a large chest, of hornbeam maybe, vaulted and patterned with thousands of leaves. Celbring seemed to have a knack of reading Fal's thoughts.

"It wasn't made by the elves for all its patterning," he said. "They are not elvish patterns. A golden tree played a part in our lore, too, a long time ago; but it was only the leaves of that tree that were golden, not the blossoms. Wisdom was the flower it bore and knowledge its fruit." He smiled. "In the chest we keep copies of these and other texts and deem them our greatest possession."

He bowed and ushered Fal to the chair, which had a low, squat back but large arms, something after the fashion of a simple throne, though the seat was closer to the ground than Fal was accustomed to.

The meal began. Theck's wife served them: a dwarf so like Theck that, apart from the absence of a beard, Fal would have taken them for brothers rather than husband and wife. But he had met Aundvara before at festivals and knew her gentle, wifely nature. She smiled and nodded several times whenever she served him or passed his end of the table.

There was hare, braised in elderberry wine, with oat bannocks and fresh golden butter, followed by a rich fruit cake, full of delicious whole cherries, with strawberries and whipped cream to finish. A strong, rather bitter version of coltsfoot wine was brought round in tiny stone cups, though supplies were not limited, and he noticed that even Amba drank five. He himself stopped at three for he wanted to keep a clear head for whatever had been planned for the rest of the evening.

Celbring stood up. He cleared his throat. No-one else moved.

He's going to make a speech, Fal realized with some dismay. He began to feel uneasy, although the attitude of Celbring's people was always very modest and respectful towards him. Yet their faces were all unsmiling now.

Kindly still, but terribly serious. Little Amba's eyes, large for her size at the best of times, had opened to their fullest extent and were staring at him unblinking with the lofty gaze of a princess. Celbring, slimmer and with more angular features than Theck and the brothers, regarded him with dark, glittering eyes. Was he expected to speak or do something? But Celbring was beginning.

"Dear Fal," he said. "Good master Falimbravel! What we wish to speak about tonight falls hard upon us — yes, hard even so much as to mention. It has not been our custom to do so, not for a long time. But as you spoke of it to my people first and as, it is said, you purpose to journey to that place of which you spoke, then it falls to me to speak to you of it. For though we are, as many folk say, a people of few words, yet we cannot leave the touching of a wound without at least hearing why it was touched. In short, Master Fal, why are you wanting to go to Lune?"

He sat down at once, having put his question, and his face joined the silent array of staring eyes. Fal was ill at ease yet very much wanted to say whatever would soothe the feelings of these loyal people. Had Celbring meant that he had offended them? Or was this merely a dwarvish way of expressing their concern?

"The world has changed," he said at last, simply. "Much of its old glory has gone. I seek the cause and I seek also the cure."

Celbring nodded. "So we thought," he said, and sighed. He bent forward as if speaking to the table rather than directly to Fal. "And you think the evil came from a place that you can find, that you can walk to, as it were, on your legs?"

"The old tales make me think so," said Fal. He was wondering what this exchange was leading to.

"There are many tales," said Celbring, "many, and again many more. And the meanings of these tales are interpreted in many different ways."

"Then I'll go and find out the truth of them for myself," said Fal. "I'll go and see what is story and what is fact."

"By looking at a barren mountain?" Celbring interrupted. "You're a hopeful young man."

In spite of his love for the dwarves and the good will between them and him Fal was beginning to feel the first pricklings of irritation. He could not bear fatherly sermons.

"It is enough," said Celbring, picking up Fal's mood. "We do not wish to anger you. Nor am I your father to advise my son. And yet, Fal, for the love that is between us, we would like to share some things with you before you go, as we have shared our hall with you this evening, a hall that no man has entered in your lifetime, no, not since Forlëd came with the dwarves of Fram whom he saved in the war of the iron ships. You have done us this honour. Come, share one more thing with us."

He rose again, and this time all the company rose with him. They took

Fal to the vaulted chest and stood around it.

"As Master Celbring says, it contains our sacred books," Theck began in a voice which, Fal thought, betrayed rehearsal. "Some of them you know, for they were copied and studied, with our consent, by former harpers of the Forge. But others no man has ever seen."

"We show them to you as a token of our friendship," said Skelfir, "that should you come into dangers greater than you can foresee, we may feel united with you — and you in strength, with us."

Celbring took a large bronze key from his belt and handed it to Theck, at the same time telling some others of the company to fetch the chair for Fal.

"In the presence of our books it is our custom to stand," he said, "but you are our guest; you shall sit."

For a moment it appeared that the chest was full of cloths, neatly wrapped, and he recognized the weaving patterns of Aren or of those who came before him. One of the cloths on top was removed (it was pale blue with a design of silver and lilac leaves) and laid behind the open lid, so that the carved wood should not rest directly on the stone wall. Three identical, rectangular bundles were taken out, wrapped in soft, off-white linen with an edging of dark blue stars.

"This is the Triptychon," said Aundvara. "In it speaks a lady who once was very close to us. She belonged to the stars, but it is said she dwelt on Earth and ruled the dwarves as a mighty queen."

"It is not Estera, the Lady of the Delming," said Amba, "but one far greater."

Celbring frowned and gave the dwarf child a warning look. "This is not known with any certainty," he said, "neither who's greater nor even who is who; and though there may be some still in the world who have such knowledge, we of the Delming at least are cautious in our opinions, and in such subtle matters our books give us not guidance. But Aundvara wishes to read you some words of the Triptychon, some teaching which the Lady of the Stars once gave to her people."

The dwarves bowed their heads as Aundvara took off one of the wrappings to reveal an old leather binding. Indeed, the only difference from the books to which Fal was used was the way each page opened out double, with the writing inside the fold. Thus the book at first appeared to consist of nothing but thick, bare pages. They were of fibrous paper, as far as he could see — he was not invited to touch them — and inscribed with a tiny angular script, not unlike the writing the dwarves used for engraving their jewellery with mottos or names.

Aundvara had found the page she was looking for, and the dwarves bowed again. She began to read.

"Good people, I have instructed you, and you have learned. The Sun and the Moon, the fixed and the wandering stars, you have seen them from within the earth and you have found them where they shine in stone and in metal; and you became hushed and still with the seeing. And though I have praised you, both for your diligence and for your achievements, yet we must continue, for what you have done is only a beginning.

"What is the new teaching? Listen, for it is this: you have seen the stars as the people who walk above on the outside of the earth, and are dazzled, could never see them. You have seen the worlds, you have stood before the shining ones. Let your silence and your wonder grow and turn yourselves about. Look back and, beholding the earth from that far place without, look deep within; now whom do you see there?"

As she finished, the dwarves all suddenly looked up and stared at Fal. He felt very uncomfortable and uncertain as to what was required of him.

"It's very beautiful," he said. "I thank you for letting me hear these words."

Celbring grunted, a little disdainfully, Fal thought. He felt he had not said the right thing but he was quite at a loss to know how else he was meant to respond.

Just then a door clicked shut and there was a shuffling sound in the shadow of the deep portal. A person emerged whom Fal had certainly not seen before. He had once heard that there were some very old dwarves in the Forge who never left the dwarves' houses, but he had never so much as heard them named. Whatever he had imagined such an ancient person to look like, the reality exceeded any of his expectations.

The dwarf who slowly hobbled into the circle was apparently sleep-walking or at least so nearly asleep that Fal did not expect him to be aware of his surroundings. His eyes — or, Fal thought, more likely her eyes — were closed as the dwarf approached. She was short and squat, and her white hair fell straight down, almost touching the ground, and all but covering the grey gown which she wore beneath it. Below her long, gnarled chin was a clasp of emeralds in which the light of the high, narrow windows shifted strangely. But her face seemed to consist largely of wrinkles and warts which so disfigured her that it was hard even to be sure where her eyes were.

Fal could not imagine what she looked like with them open and began wondering whether she had any. Most likely she was blind, he thought. But as she joined the circle, the others respectfully giving way to make room for her, she opened her eyes and looked straight at him. He gasped audibly. They were the eyes of Amba, dark and young, and very penetrating. Suddenly he realized that he had never seen such a beautiful face.

"Read him the part about the star paths," she croaked and glared impatiently round the circle. There seemed to be some uncertainty as to which section she meant.

"Which part, grandmother?" asked Celbring.

In answer she took the book, almost snatching it from Aundvara, but Fal noticed that she was very careful in turning and unfolding the pages.

Her fingers were white and thin, smooth like alabaster near the tips, but terribly old. He thought he heard them creak.

At last she found what she was looking for. She began reading in a trembling voice.

"And now, dwarves, I have shown you clearly and to your very eyes which saw not before," — here she gave a quick glance in Fal's direction, to see if he was listening, he thought — "how that which quickens the trees is the cousin of the Sun and how you, in your substance, are even further from the Sun than are the rocks themselves and can so interpenetrate with the rocks, when you will, as the air and sunlight can mingle freely with one another. And beyond you, further still, is substance yet more removed which you do not see, just as beyond the Sun herself there are realms too different to be now described. And yet the road forms a circle and at both its ends there is starlight; and in that starlight, dwarves, is your true being."

She stared at him again for a moment then once more closed her eyes, this time, he thought, with displeasure at what she saw.

Again, he had no idea what to say. He felt unable to grasp the meanings of this book. Were the readers directing the words at him, he wondered, in some way that he did not understand? He felt very uncertain and said nothing.

Celbring gently removed the book from between the ancient fingers — she appeared not to notice — and wrapped it once more in its cloth.

"We will not read from our other treasures tonight," he said, "but you shall look upon them, for they're of fine craftsmanship and some are very old."

There were scrolls of parchment, tablets of marble engraved in gold, mostly with scripts Fal had never seen before and which he therefore could not read; a silver axe-head etched and completely covered with a minute, flowing script, engraved slates which had cracked and had been pinned together with gold, and bound books, full of such strange characters and repetitive patterns that he could hardly imagine that their shapes represented words.

He was amazed by the variety of all he saw and managed to say some suitable things, he thought, about the wonder of these ancient treasures; and he caught a glimpse of a strange pattern of spirals, a kind of symbolic map or chart maybe, engraved on the bottom of the chest.

Then the dwarves busied themselves re-wrapping their treasures and putting them carefully back into place. The lid was secured and Celbring took the key. Only now did Fal notice that the old grandmother had left them. Then they all nodded, smiled and bowed, and thanked him for honouring them.

The party had ended.

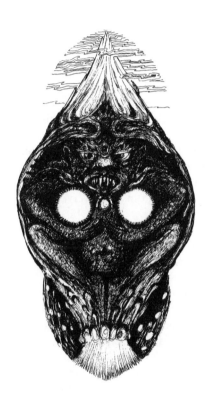

SEVEN

It was a day both of sadness and of festivity when he was at last ready to set out, and the quayside was thronged with people. All the folk of the Forge were there and most of the town-dwellers, too, and everyone seemed to be calling out advice and greetings at the same time.

Melauriën cast some freshly picked leaves from the Tree into the boat and spoke some words of blessing. The dwarves all wanted to shake hands. Little Amba had to be held up to give him a kiss; and he climbed into his boat.

"And if you happen to come across Sulthind on your travels, tell him we're still waiting for his tea-party," Ilmarin called out. "Don't forget!"

The two friends grinned at each other, the dwarves scowled, then laughed, and then looked glum, and everyone waved and shouted as Fal rowed out into the open lake.

"Good-bye!" he called.

"Good-bye, come back soon!" they shouted.

At last he was on his way.

———

There was a fresh north-westerly breeze, so he unfurled the sail to take him eastwards along the shore as far as the mouths of the Ironway. Then with his harp he turned the boat northwards against the sluggish movement of the river. He would need more power further up where the current ran faster but at first it was only necessary to play the flowing melodies after the two or three stops between one long sunset and the next to set himself moving again, for his will to go north was firm and deeply rooted, and even while he slept the boat went on.

There were several steadings where he could have broken his journey and found hospitality, for the masters of the Delming were welcomed in all the lands of the Ironway. But the weather was warm and clear, and he wanted to get as far as he could while it lasted. A few folk saw him and waved from the banks, but mostly it was only ducks, moorhens, coots; and, once, a family of swans that swam after the strange silent boat.

One evening, where the river was narrow and passed through thick forest and the reds and golds of sunset filled all that could be seen of the sky, he heard, as he first thought, a bird singing in the distance among the trees; and it seemed that the sound of that song was full of the growing of trees, of the opening of leaves, of the green of ferns, and the soft coolness of mosses. But then, as he stopped the boat for a while to listen, he thought it was perhaps not a bird but someone playing a pipe or flute. He longed to meet this wonderful musician and called out, but at once the woods fell silent and he knew it would be folly to blunder through the dense undergrowth of the pathless forest in search of the hidden player.

But the music stayed long in his mind, and from that evening on he was more at peace with the world than he had been for many months and his purpose lost some of its frantic urgency. And for the first time since he had left his friends at the Forge he smiled, and began to enjoy his journey.

———

At last the woods thinned out and gave way to grasslands, which stretched away to the left and right as far as the eye could see. Only to the west was there any distinct landmark: Gop Hill, a single mound against the distant skyline, and he knew that soon he would have completed the first leg of his journey. Then there were lazy herds of cattle, and once an old cow-herd came down to the water's edge and stared, disbelieving, as the boat, oarless and sailless, drifted upstream.

But when he came to Gopley Farm and the master of all that region was fetched to meet him, he was received heartily and as an old friend, for Gulmer had come down the river himself the year before with a load of cheeses and had lived for a while in the guest house among the craftsmen of the Forge.

That evening, for the first time in nearly a week, Fal sat at the table under a roof, and he was soon drowsy from the warmth of the fire and the crackle of burning wood. It was homely in the low room where Gulmer's family dined with their two chief farmhands, and where the meal appeared to be presided over by the watchful eye and penetrating gaze of an old black she-cat. No other animal was allowed in the house, Gulmer explained, but Nonney was to be treated in every way as a member of the family.

It was soon as much as Fal could manage to keep awake after the strong wine that came with the roasted meat, but he knew he must not disappoint his hosts by going to bed without some songs.

Then Gulmer asked him where he was bound for, and when he said he'd be passing through Little Strang, to the west of the Iron Mountains, and would be glad if he could leave his boat at Gopley in safe keeping, Gulmer looked pleased and said, "If you can wait here with us a day or two, Master Fal, I can help you and you me, so to speak. My young ones here, Tim and Feather, are taking a load of hides up as far as Little Strang, and I can send a spare pony with them for you. It's the first time they've been to the Strangs without company, and I don't doubt they'd be glad of yours."

He looked sideways at his son and daughter, who were perhaps two or three years younger than Fal and who appeared to be twins, for it was hard to decide which might otherwise be the elder. They smiled and nodded back in agreement, and he thought they would probably be easy and pleasant to get on with. They would also be a good introduction to the people of the upper Ironway who had a dour reputation and whose help and guidance he would need in order to find the ways into the Forest of Aurëlund.

The next day Tim and the two old cowmen helped him get his boat up into the barn. The lad was interested in the way he had managed to get so far up the river with so little effort and asked many things about his skills as a harper and his life at the Delming. Fal was surprised at the degree of understanding that the young farmer revealed and may have shown his surprise, for Tim said, "We haven't learned much of such matters from our father, yet even so you'd be wrong to think he'd grown cow's hoofs. But mother and granny were both a bit like you and we learnt a few things from them. Mother died when we were small, so it was granny mostly."

They locked the barn door and Tim showed him where the keys were hung, in case any of them were away or out on the plains when he returned.

"There's always someone around if you can wait an hour or two, though," said old Crombel, one of the two brothers who helped Gulmer run the farm. "Make yourself at home. Ay, that's what I said to Gulmer when he first brought his family to Gopley. Make yourself at home, I says."

And the hearty tone with which he spoke left Fal in no doubt that he meant it.

————

There were three additional ponies to make up their party, two laden with hides and a third to carry the travellers' packs, of which Fal's was by far the largest, together with the provisions they took. The journey to Little Strang was reckoned at three and a half days each way, four at the most.

At first they followed the river, riding up its west bank, with the grasslands still stretching all around them. Fal often rode between the twins, who turned out to be talkative people and who enjoyed telling him about their lives at Gopley. When there was a lull in the conversation, Feather — or Fethilian, as she said her name really was — would sometimes hum parts of the songs which he had sung on the past evenings. Even tunes he had only sung once she remembered without mistakes.

"There's more music in you than in some of our harper apprentices, Feather," he said. "You should come to the Forge and study in the harpers' school."

"You really think so?" She turned her dark eyes on him for a moment, fearing perhaps that he was mocking her. But seeing his face thoughtful and serious she smiled and said, "I'd like to get to know the Delming. It sounds a wonderful place from what father's told us about it. But don't you find it strange with elves and dwarves all working together in a city of men?"

"If you lived there you'd soon forget its strangeness," he answered, "and as for being a city, it's a tiny place as cities go and quite homely in its own way."

The day went quickly, yet by sundown they were already in sight of the woods which were eventually to lead them up to Michel Strang. This was the larger of the two towns which had been built in the old days when ore had been abundant in the west of the mountains and mining had made it rich.

Tim thought they should press on for an hour or so to reach the forest and then tether the ponies in a glade where the grass still grew thick, so that by noon the next day they could be passing through the town. In the end it was well into twilight when they unburdened the animals, lit a fire, and roasted some fresh Gopley steaks for supper.

The next day as they rode along together through the light birch woods that filled a wide loop of the river, Fal suddenly thought of asking Tim and Feather about Lune and wondered why he hadn't asked any of the menfolk at Gopley.

"Our granny used to tell a tale of Lune," said Feather. "She was a great story-teller, even though she did tend to tell the same tales year in and year out. But that's the way with old folk. You wouldn't learn much from granny's fireside stories if you want to know what Lune's like today!" She laughed and flicked her long black hair back over her shoulders. "Most people said they were only old wives' tales to while away the time."

"I'd still like to hear the story of Lune, old wives' tale or not," said Fal, "if you think there's time before we get to Michel Strang."

"Oh, it's not so very long, but there's enough foolishness in it to set every woodpecker in the forest laughing."

"Come on, sister," said Tim, "stop beating about the bush. It's a fair enough yarn; especially the part where the prince..."

"Now then, Tim," said Feather sternly — but Tim winked across at Fal — "even if it is an old wives' tale you're not going to spoil it by telling the end first. If it has to be told, I shall tell it in the proper order. Here it is then:

"There was once a marvellous city which stood at the foot of a very tall mountain. The king and queen who ruled there were as famous for their generosity as their city was renowned for its beauty and wealth. Both summer and winter the lofty summit of the mountain was crowned with ice, and at sunrise and sunset the light would catch on the ice-crown so that it was visible through many lands. Those who saw it were glad, for they said, 'The king and queen of the mountain are well and they greet their people far and wide'.

"But deep below that mountain, in a cavern, there lived a troll. Huge and terrible she was, with teeth like daggers and claws like billhooks. She said the mountain was all hers and she hated the city which was built at the foot of it. Her heart had become knotted with envy and cramped with malice towards the king and queen and all their people.

"As she failed to find ways of harming them she kept thinking of how she could perhaps at least match them in splendour. So she set about casting a spell to draw the power of the sun and of the moon down into her cavern and trap them there, so that the city would seem a mere nothing compared with the glory of her hall. For years and years she worked her spell, and so mighty did she grow in sorcery that at last the sky darkened and the mountain was filled with light. The people of the city were dismayed to see the sun and moon shining only as feeble silvery discs in the sky and amazed to see light gleaming out of the rocky chasms of the mountainside.

"Now, the son of that king and queen had been visiting far away countries where he'd won much honour, and he returned to find the city in twilight and the people greatly troubled. He wore a circlet of gold, which itself shone like the sun, and silver armour, which glistened like moonlight.

"The prince shouted into a deep fissure up on the mountainside and challenged the troll to fight. At first she only laughed at him and said she had already won her battle — why should she fight again? But when she looked out and saw his crown and armour, themselves shining with the light of sun and moon, the hate rose up within her and her mind was all befuddled, so that she rushed out with a roar to seize him.

"Then followed a dreadful conflict, for though the prince struck the troll again and again, her leathery skin was hardened by such wicked sorcery that his sword made no impression on it. Up and down the side of the mountain they fought, neither able to gain the upper hand, until, in wrath and desperation, the prince put all his strength into one last two-handed stroke.

"The troll leapt over the sword unharmed, but the terrible blow struck the mountain near the top, severing the ice-crown from it. It shot up and spun away to the north, where it struck the ground and spread, growing into the land of ice which is there to this day. But out of the mountain itself burst a tongue of flame, right up to the sun, which rekindled and shone even brighter than before. All day and all night flame and burning stone gushed thundering from the wounded mountain, and the city was utterly destroyed. Yet it was not only the city and its people that perished, for the old troll witch fell straight down the hole into the mountian of fire and was never seen again."

"What happened to the prince?" Fal asked.

"He went up with the flame to the sun where he's lived ever since."

"And the moon, what about that? You only said the sun was rekindled."

"The power of the moon stayed in the mountain. That's why the moon shines so much fainter than the sun, even to this day."

They rode along in silence for a while, for Fal liked the story and was still seeing the burning mountain in his mind's eye. Then he said: "I should like to have met your granny. Was she mostly like your mother or more like your father?"

"She was our mother's mother," put in Tim, "but she wasn't really much like either of our parents."

"She was thin and delicate, but strong and very upright for her age," said Feather.

"Father says she had some ancestry with the elves, and it was granny who gave us our names. People around Gopley don't usually have long names like Fethilian and Timbelor nowadays! That's why we're called Tim and Feather, you see."

"You'd have liked granny — and mother. We all miss them very much."

"Mother once taught me a song about Lune," said Tim, blushing. "Would you like to hear it?"

Fal looked at him in surprise, for Tim had shown some reluctance to join in their singing.

"Of course I would, Tim, I'd love to hear it," he said with emphasis, for he could see Tim was embarrassed.

"Mother said it was an old song of the elves, for they didn't speak of Lune but of Gelmindel, and the king and queen there were lords of the elf-kind, not of men."

"I didn't know mother ever taught you any songs!" Feather looked as surprised as Fal.

"Oh, it was a long time ago," said Tim shyly, "and I can only remember part of it."

Then, with a clear voice, softly at first, he began to sing till as he gained confidence the old elf-song rang out far into the woods.

> On terraces of carven stone
>   unstained as swan's white breast
> there shone a star through lands afar
>   to south and east and west.

> The streams that ran from fountains clear,
>   the waterfalls that fell,
> made rainbow veils of sparkling light
>   in ancient Gelmindel.

> There dragons walked about her streets
>   and danced by fountains fair
> to music played on silver pipes
>   by elves with shining hair.

> Now broken are the marble walls
>   and we have said farewell
> to fountains of the dancing light
>   that shone in Gelmindel.

The simple, ancient tune shone too, with a light of its own, and sketched vivid pictures of joy and wonder. Fal was silent for a while, for he was reminded of the hidden pipe player he had heard in the forest from his boat. An enchantment had fallen on the birch woods which he was reluctant to break, but at last he said, "Thank you, Tim. There seems to be more than one harper-apprentice here which the Forge is lacking!" and the twins both smiled happily.

But just then the trees thinned and beyond a half a mile or so of cultivated fields they saw the tumbled grey roofs of a walled town. They had come to Michel Strang.

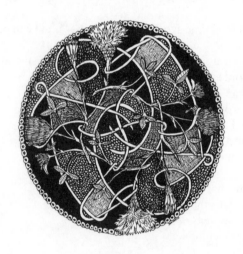

EIGHT

The twins wanted to make a mid-day break beyond the town rather than in it, but on Fal's request they led their ponies straight through the narrow cobbled streets and not on the easier road outside the walls; for this was the first time he had ever had the chance of seeing a town of a size even comparable to the Delming and he was curious to make comparisons.

It had apparently been market-day, and though most of the stalls were now empty or already dismantled, there were still more folk about than might be expected at noon-tide. Looks and whispered remarks make it clear that the sight of laden ponies entering the town at the end of the market rather than in the early morning was something of an oddity requiring explanation, but no-one was of a sufficiently friendly disposition to ask the travellers for one. That, Fal thought, would have been different among the cheerful lake-side people at home. But they were civil enough and there was no fuss about making room for the ponies and their wide packs as Tim had feared there might be.

Just as they were through the low vaults of the town's west gate, from which began the road up to Little Strang, Feather said, "Fal, you haven't actually told us the purpose of your journey, but do I not guess rightly that you plan to go on through Aurëlund to seek the mountains of Lune?"

"Yes," he said, "that is my plan."

"All tales agree that Gelmindel vanished long ago. What do you hope to find?"

Only a few days ago he would have been put out by such direct questioning, for he really had no idea what he hoped to find there and did not want to admit that his journey had no more cause to speak of than a chance remark of an old woman visiting the Forge. But he had quickly grown fond of the twins and felt very easy with them, so he said, "It may seem foolishness even more than old wives can muster in their tales, Feather, but as I can't live happily in a world I don't understand, I'm seeking the answers to some questions I have. And as I know of no-one in the south who's able to answer them, I want to find out if there's any in the north who can."

Tim had dropped back level with him and was listening to the conversation. Feather looked thoughtful but said nothing, and Fal went on, "It's hard to believe that a city can disappear without any trace, and even if there are no folk to talk to, maybe some memories linger there which a harper's art can revive. I'd like to catch a glimpse of the fountains of

Gelmindel, Tim, especially after your song."

Tim's eyes shone at the thought, but Feather said, "It's a dangerous journey to make alone, Fal. There are wild men in the Forest of Aurëlund, they say, and wolves in the north. I wish we could come with you. But we must go back to Gopley. It's coming into harvest time and we couldn't just ride off into the northlands and leave father without so much as a word."

Fal was about to say that if it was dangerous for him, it would be doubly so for them, who, apart from being younger, did not have the protection of a harper's skills. But as he glanced at Feather a light shone about her; and it seemed to him that her simple linen gown became covered with the flowers of the meadow, blue cornflowers and red clover, intertwined to form strange emblems, and she wore a crown of daisies. The leather bridle in her slender hands was all a-ripple with flowing inlaid patterns, glistening like quicksilver. Before he could recover the impression faded and Tim was speaking.

"You've left your boat at Gopley, Fal, that's one thing. So you'll have to come back our way to fetch it. Then you can tell us all about your adventures."

Tim smiled across at his sister to comfort her. He saw no radiance; to him there was a shadow about her, and he knew her heart was troubled.

"The world is built on mysteries," she said slowly. "You really think you can find some memories of a bygone age to explain them to you, Fal? Do you think people in the past really knew so much?"

Then, as they entered the wooded valley which led from the fields of Michel Strang up into the hills, he found himself telling the twins the story of the Praise Song, when the tree sighed; of Tholaiwin's visit, and of his dream. They listened quietly, and he was glad to be telling them for to his surprise he felt they understood him better than Melauriën and Ilmarin.

————

Little Strang had also been a prosperous mining town in the times when man and dwarf had worked together to win the metal which had made the neighbouring mountains famous. Now the rock was barren and if there were still dwarves there they never showed themselves. Most of the people of the town spun wool and they wove it well enough. Others worked leather. Yet the once flourishing town had shrunk to little more than a village, a few narrow streets and alleys around a dingy cobbled square. The houses were built of granite, the roofs of grey slate, and the drizzle of rain made Fal glad to be invited in to a cosy log fire.

The hides were unpacked by two young apprentices. Like most people at the Strangs they showed little inclination to speak and so stood in striking contrast to the master leather worker and his wife. They were jovial and red-faced and of homely proportions. It turned out, not surprisingly, that Gally Gaskins and Daisy had both come from Fram, in the east, to learn a trade when they were young. That had been a long time ago; meanwhile

Gally had developed the habit of wheezing a few times before he spoke, and as he spoke often, he always sounded out of breath.

He stood now behind the white, clean-scrubbed table supporting his bulk straight-armed on his knuckles. He grinned, wheezed and said, "Well, good masters, good mistress — fried eggs and hot oat-cakes fresh from the oven in a few moments if it please you be patient yet a while. Till then maybe a sip or two of cider won't be out of place."

He shuffled, panting, to a cupboard and came back with a tankard and mugs.

"We'll have those ponies loaded up with some very nice fleeces in the morning, if you insist on going back so soon," he panted. "It wouldn't amaze me at all if this rain didn't last a day or two. You'd be more than welcome to hang on a bit till it's cleared up."

He grinned at them showing a combination of gaps and brown, broken teeth.

"That's very kind of you, Mr Gaskins," said Tim, "but we did promise father to get straight back. The crops have been ripening early this year down at Gopley, and there's ever so much to do around the farm."

Gally gave a few understanding wheezes and said, "Your new cloaks of Little Strang wool will be very good at keeping the rain out, that's one thing." He poured out some more cider. "Anyway, here comes Daisy with the oatcakes."

That evening was spent sitting round the fire with Gally and Daisy, eating, drinking and chatting. Daisy was a plump, busy woman who believed in getting on with the talking while her husband wheezed and puffed. Whenever his wheezing grew louder as a prelude to speech, Daisy would get there first, apparently with the very words he had in mind, for he would nod and grunt, sigh, and sink back again into his enormous chair.

She asked a little about the folk she knew at Gopley, but as she knew none of the people at the Forge except perhaps by name, Fal was at first left out of the conversation. She talked about the various comings and goings at Little Strang, mostly involving people even the twins had never heard of, when Fal suddenly had an idea. He said, "Mrs Gaskins, do you ever get visitors from the north, from beyond the mountains, I mean?"

Gally began panting loudly, and Daisy said, "Not from *beyond* the mountains, now. There's nowhere beyond the mountains for anyone to come from, is there? Though we did have those people from that farm over to the east last year staying at the Dragon. What was the name of that farm now, Gally?"

He was wheezing with more vigour than usual, but Daisy said, "Ah yes now, that's right. Lunt. From Lunt Farm they were. And a more mournful looking couple you never did see, neither. Miserable looking lot, weren't they, Gally?"

Mr Gaskins had not yet subsided into his arm-chair but was still getting up steam when Daisy said, "A fair old load of cloth they bought though, so never mind their looks."

But this time she had not taken the words out of Gally's mouth for he appeared to have something else in mind. He was leaning forward and waving a hand, determined to get a word in.

"There's a man over at the Dragon right now," he gasped.

"Eh? Man over at the Dragon? What man?" Daisy was put out by what she suspected to be uncalled-for change of subject. "Not one of them Lunt folk again, surely. Sold 'em enough cloth to keep 'em going for a lifetime, I did, though they never took no leather. You'd think they'd have sheep of their own over there. Funny, do you know I never thought of that. Fancy coming from one end of the hills to the other just to buy cloth! Fair old way it must be. Oh stop waving your hand, Gally. What man over at the Dragon, then?"

Gally gave one gigantic sucking wheeze and said quickly, "Wiry little fellow, come all the way on foot with that great load o' deer hides on 'is back, was over here late this morning, asking to see you about woolly blankets. Hunter from the big forest up north, was over here just before noontide, thought you must've seen 'im." He collapsed in a fit of heaving gasps. The effort and excitement of avoiding interruption was too much for him and put him out of conversation for quite a long time. He had to make do with nodding.

"Oh him!" said Daisy. "How was I to know he was staying at the Dragon, then? You never said. Yes, of course I seen him. Quiet little fellow. Wasn't over-talkative, was he, Gally?"

Suddenly the obvious occured to her. Now she knew why Fal had asked about people from the north.

"You after some nice supple deerskins from Aurëlund, are you, young master?" she said. "Now hold on a minute, I'll just nip upstairs and bring down some really nice ones."

She bobbed onto her feet and was halfway to the door before Fal could stop her.

"Thankyou, thankyou, Mrs Gaskins," he said hurriedly. "I mean no thank you, I don't. It's news of the north I was after, not hides."

"Eh?" she said, stopping and looking startled. "News? What news? News about what? What's happened then?"

The twins came to the rescue and tried to explain Fal's interest in the Forest of Aurëlund.

"News about how to travel around there," said Tim.

"He's on a journey into the north," said Feather.

"To see what it's like," said Tim, each speaker overlapping the other, so eager where they to prevent any further complications.

"To see what it's like?!" Daisy exclaimed. "Anyone can tell you what it's like. There's miles and miles of forest then miles and miles of waste.

Hundreds of miles of nothing! Everyone knows what it's like."

"Ah yes," said Tim, "but Master Fal comes from down by the lake and *he* doesn't know what it's like."

"So he wants to visit it," said Feather.

"Visit it!" squeaked Daisy,now distinctly coming to the boil. She'd had little practice at listening to two people at once. "Visit what? Now just be quiet for a minute and tell me, visit what? There's not town, village, or hamlet even, north of here. Who or what's he going to visit?"

But Gally was wheezing again.

"Why don't you ask him?" he groaned.

There was a sudden silence and everyone stared at Fal. Tim's eyes were sparkling merrily, but Feather was looking bothered. She frowned, and Fal thought she shook her head slightly. She dreaded an argument with Daisy on the existence of Lune and the futility of seeking it.

Fal said, "It's important for harpers to travel around in the world a bit, Mrs Gaskins, before they settle down, as you might say. And the nightingales in the south sing different songs from the thrushes in the north, by all reports. So I was heading towards Aurëlund to hear them for myself."

"Ah, so that's it!" cried Daisy, delighted and rather fascinated by this novel line of thought. "Why didn't you say so before, then? I'll send one of the lads over to the Dragon and invite the hunter over to a flagon of cider. Banny!" she shouted, bouncing towards the kitchen door. "Run over to the Dragon, there's a good boy, and invite that hunter gentleman across for some cider and a bit of homely talk around the fire. The young master here from the Delming would like to meet him. Tell him he's interested in animals."

The hunter was indeed a man of few words, but looking at him in the firelight Fal was uncertain whether he was having difficulty containing his amusement or his irritation at the domestic comedy of Gally and Daisy at home. Daisy didn't look too sure either, for she made some excuse about seeing what her bread was doing in the oven, slipped out into the kitchen and stayed there. Fal feared his explanation involving nightingales and thrushes might pluck the wrong string, as the harpers say, for the hunter would of course be aware that the season for bird-song had already passed. So he sought a different approach.

"We harpers of the Delming are taught may old tales of the north," he began tentatively. "I was thinking of journeying around up there for a while. The emptiness of the Waste must be a wonderful thing to someone from the busy lands of the south."

He felt he was choosing his words very clumsily and stopped, feeling uncomfortable under the hunter's shrewd gaze. His thin, bony face was puckered with concentration as he listened to Fal, who had no idea what the man was thinking. So the response was in every way unexpected.

"My name is Frekk," he said suddenly with a lilting accent and a strong, rolled 'r'. "What is yours?"

"I'm Fal, a harper from the Forge." Neither Gally nor the twins knew he was the master harper, for news of the winter's changes had not yet travelled northwards, and Fal had no mind to appear more than people found him.

"I don't like it here," said Frekk. "I come on business. If you have no business why do you come?"

Apparently Fal's explanation had not made much sense. He plunged onto a different tack. "I have no home, as you perhaps have. I was found adrift on the lake as a child. My home is everywhere and nowhere."

The hunter's keen brown eyes widened a little then narrowed again, regarding Fal critically.

Feather seemed about to speak, but Gally was wheezing. "Take him with you," he said. "A bit of company for one another's a good thing, I reckon. Long way to walk an' all, ain't it? What do you do for food all the time — raw rabbits?"

He guffawed, gasped, then grinned at Frekk, displaying his gappy teeth, and the hunter's face creased into a smile in return.

"I do not need the company of strangers," he said. "But the harper can come to Aurëlund if he wishes."

"I should be glad of your company," said Fal. He hoped that the question of his further journey, the crossing of the Waste, could be left till later, when they perhaps knew one another a little, and Frekk did not press the point.

"With our host's help in selecting the blankets which I shall be carrying, I shall be ready by mid-day," he said. "The cobbler has my boots for re-sewing and has promised them by then. You're right, Master Gaskins," he smiled wryly again. "It's a long walk and hard on the footwear!"

NINE

It was raining heavily the next morning, but Frekk gave no indication that he took such things into account, and Fal had confidence in his own finely woven woollen cloak to keep the wet out. The hunter had gone to the cobbler's when the twins had finished loading their ponies for the return to Gopley.

"Good luck, Fal," said Tim. "I hope you're back to get your boat before the winter sets in."

Fal smiled, and Feather said, "In my thoughts I'll be watching over you. Sing to me sometimes on your journey." She stepped close to him and kissed him.

"Good-bye," he said and tried to smile again.

They mounted, and the cobbles in the square echoed noisily for a while from the ponies' hoofs. They waved and were gone.

He was still standing there staring at the empty gap between the grey houses when he felt a hand on his arm. It was Frekk, bowed under a huge pack of new blankets strapped to his shoulders. His dark hair was tied back behind a brimless leather cap and he was armed with a light bow and a quiver of arrows. He had no cloak, and in place of the linen tunic he had worn on the night before, there was a shirt and breeches of soft leather.

"For the raw rabbits!" he said, with his funny half-smile, and patted his bow. "Ready?"

Gally and Daisy had come to the door to say good-bye, and there was a lot of wheezing and "mind how you go" before they were stepping out through the dismal houses and into the hills. Clouds of varying shades of grey clung low around the distant peaks to their right, and it all looked very damp.

"I don't like it in that town," said Frekk after they had left it well behind them. "It makes you feel shut in — like in a trap. Little Strang — huh!" He snorted with distaste. "I call them 'stranglers'! And to think the people stay in those miserable stone houses all the year round!"

He spoke with an accent which Fal sometimes found hard to follow and he had to give conversation a lot of attention, for Frekk turned out to be more talkative than was to be expected after yesterday's encounter.

Perhaps Frekk guessed his thought for he said, "I'm not used to the company of strangers. Aurëlund is a great forest, and we forest people seldom go beyond it." He smiled apologetically, obviously wanting Fal to feel more at ease with him. Whenever they saw a bird or heard a strange cry, Fal would ask Frekk what it was — Daisy had said it was his special interest — and the hunter seemed pleased to tell him. He also told him some of the remarkable things which the wild creatures of the moors did: the drumming of the snipe, the pretence of being wounded when a grouse fears discovery of its nest, the merry games of otter and hill-fox, the eerie gathering of the curlews under the stars at night.

"But moors are uncomfortable places to get around in," he said, "all right for these woolly folk" — a group of beady-eyed upland sheep were watching their progress suspiciously — "but lonely places for man. Don't you hear how all the cries of the birds out here have the loneliness in them?"

Once they saw an eagle wheeling over the broad valley which led out of the hills and over the flatter moors, and its fierce shriek also had that wild, lonely quality. But, looking at Frekk, Fal wondered whether Aurëlund was going to be so very different, for there was a starkness about the hunter which he thought fitted in rather well with their present surroundings.

In the afternoon they stopped for a snack of rye-bread and cheese, but Frekk said they would eat better in the evening if they could find enough dry heather to make a fire. If not, it really might be raw rabbits!

As they looked down from the hills over the thirty or forty miles of wild moorland which separated them from the forest they saw that the sky before them was blue. Frekk smiled and said, "Then we should be able to dry out a bit this evening. A wet night on the moors is even worse than a dry one!" He smiled, a little more broadly than usual, and as they strode along began adding words to a little tune that he had been humming:

Where curlews cry
and boulders lie
among the springy grass,
where echoes die
unanswered by
a friend with time to pass
to walk with me
contentedly
across the lonely moor,
I will not stay
for one more day
than need makes me endure.

Let's back to tree
where merrily
the squirrels leap and bound,
where forest folk
in leafy cloak
with antlered deer are found.

Through reedy marsh
the journey's harsh
when boots get wet and chill;
no shelter from
the rain and storm
upon the moorland hill.
The heather pricks
its twisted sticks
into my body sore;
with sigh and frown
I lay me down,
and sleep's kept from my door.

Let's back to tree
where merrily
the squirrels leap and bound,
where forest folk
in leafy cloak
with antlered deer are found.

That evening there was a fire of twisted heather-sticks and a roasted rabbit for each of the travellers. Fal drank from the tiny stream that gurgled its way through the moss and felt refreshed and happy. Frekk's face had also lost the tense expression which had made him look particularly odd and suspicious in Little Strang, and Fal thought it might be time for some more music. He undid the straps of his harp-case and took out the finely carved instrument. With the tuning key which he kept on a leather thong round his neck he checked the strings and was about to begin playing when he found the hunter kneeling by his side, peering closely at the intricate patterns.

"Who made this?" he said, "Dwarves?"

"Nobody knows. It was with me in the boat when I was found as a child."

"What is it made of?"

"Ivory, so they say."

To Fal's surprise Frekk suddenly leaned forward and with a quick movement rapped his knuckles against the hollow sound-box, making all the strings ring. Then he ran his finger tips up and down over the patterns, carefully, as if tasting the ivory through his fingers. In the Forge such behaviour would have been considered outrageous, and Fal had to make an effort not to snatch his harp out of the hunter's reach, but he guessed that to have done so would have deeply offended his companion.

"No," said Frekk, "not ivory; ivory is from tusk teeth of big animals. This is from leg bones. This is dragon bone." He went on stroking the harp for a while, apparently lost in thought. Then he sat back and said, "Play your dragon harp, it's good."

Fal played, without singing, some of the midsummer dances of the Forge, a choice which avoided any turns of phrase involving magical influence. Yet when he had finished he found Frekk watching him, smiling. "Play some more," he said, suddenly grinning. "I like it."

He untied the blankets from his pack and rolled up in two of them by smouldering fire, listening while Fal played a long, slow dance. When it was finished, the hunter was fast asleep.

The next morning they were up early, and Frekk was in fine spirits. "Tonight you shall sleep under the eaves of Aurëlund," he said, and when he sang his song about the squirrels and the antlered deer, Fal joined in, adding a verse of his own at the end.

> The cobbles grey
> where townsfolk stay
> we've left and feel no loss;
> one trail we share
> with fox and hare,
> though paths go criss and'cross,
> where eagle flies
> and curlew cries
> and brooks run through the moss.
> The soft green leaf
> soon brings relief
> 'mid birches silver gloss.

Then they sang the chorus so loudly together that the grouse rose squawking with alarm out of the heather. Frekk laughed.

"They are foolish birds, these heather-creepers," he said. "But Mister Harper, you still haven't told me whether it's just Aurëlund you want to see or whether your journey lies still beyond!"

"I'm looking for Lune," Fal answered, "to see if there's anything left of Gelmindel — the city of the fair fountains."

"Fair fountains where the dragons dance and elven maidens sing; Bold knights at arms with sword and lance give homage to the king," said Frekk. "I see. At least, maybe I see. At any rate, there's something in the Forest of Aurëlund you can have a look at first — and maybe try your harp out on that!"

His face puckered, and Fal was left wondering at the shrewdness of his companion, for the hunter would say no more of it for the moment but turned the talk to other things.

That night they camped on the edge of the forest, just where the trail passed in between the trees, and there were signs that fires had been lit there before.

"Tomorrow we shall come to the Starwell," said Frekk, "it's a holy place for the hunters. From there your path is easy to find. Mine goes further east, deeper into the forest."

The next day Fal was taken on winding paths through a sea of green bracken from which alders and birches rose into a second green sea above them. They were forever crossing streams, and the path was always dividing or being joined by other paths. Fal doubted whether he could ever have found his way alone and began wondering whether he would ever find his way back. The trails, when they were visible at all, were very narrow, probably made by animals, so he had to follow along behind Frekk's enormous pack and there was little chance to talk.

About mid-day they stopped by a brook to finish the remains of a roasted hare from last evening's supper.

"Yes, there are wolves," Frekk said, in answer to Fal's question, "But most of them go north into the Waste in summer. Anyway, it's only in winter that they're dangerous, when food grows short and tempers thin. You'll have more trouble from gnats than from wolves once you're out in the Waste!"

"Am I likely to meet any men?" asked Fal, who didn't think gnats were worth worrying about.

"There are only us hunters in Aurëlund. You won't see any if you stick to your trail, which I'd advise you do if you don't want to get lost. I'll show you tonight when we camp. Come." He shouldered his blankets and once more led the way.

The sun was still in the treetops when towards evening they came to a spacious clearing. It was a fair place, the short grass a fresh radiant green as if animals grazed upon it regularly. The trees and bushes which formed the further edge were hung thick with blossoming honeysuckle and the still air was already heavy with its fragrance. Pink foxgloves flowered in profusion among the trees and close by where they stood ragwort made splashes of strong golden yellow. Yes, a fair place. But strangely over quiet. Not even a bee or buzzing fly broke the silence.

Fal turned his attention to the dark stones which formed a ring in the centre. "Come and look," said Frekk quietly, "it is the Starwell."

The gnarled stones were hardly more than waist-high, each some fourteen or fifteen feet from a slab of the same rock which lay flat in the middle.

"We only lift the cover at the beginning of spring," said Frekk. "Many hunters come every year — women and children too. Some say that from this well flows all the life of Aurëlund. We take out water only to bless the people."

"Do you sing?"

"We sing, yes, and we dance — to Istra, mother and giver of life."

While Fal gathered wood for a fire at the edge of the clearing, Frekk went off alone into the forest to find their supper. By the time he returned there was a good blaze going. "Two rabbits for tonight, two for you tomorrow," he grinned. "Save your bread and cheese for the Waste."

As Fal helped clean the rabbits, Frekk said, "There are many trails in and out of this clearing. It's a meeting place and a parting place, you might say. From the north end the path runs straight. It was an old road once, a long time ago, and in some places there are cobbles under the earth. You can easily find them if you dig around. We still call it the Lune road, though I don't know anyone who's followed it right out over the Waste to see where it ends. It's not an easy thing to do. You will see."

When they had eaten, Frekk wrapped the two remaining rabbits in large coltsfoot leaves and stuffed them carefully into Fal's pack. Then he said, "Play the tunes you played at our first camp on the moors. They'll sound good here." He rolled up in his blankets and watched Fal tuning his harp.

As he played he decided he would ask Frekk more about his people, the hunters of Aurëlund, and their customs and beliefs. But, as before, by the time he finished playing, Frekk was sound asleep.

TEN

When Fal awoke, the clearing was grey with the first light of dawn. He yawned, stretched, and rolled over — then sat up straight in alarm. Frekk had gone, so had his pile of new blankets.

For a moment he was confused and hurt. But then he realized that Frekk was not a person for farewells. He had probably said all he wanted to say on the evening before. He was going to miss Frekk's company; but it was too late to do anything about that now. He stood up, cursing his own stupidity, folded his own blanket and cloak and walked through the trees to the stream where they had cleaned the rabbits. He washed himself and drank deeply from the cold, clear water. Bread and bilberries would be enough to begin the day with.

Then the sun was touching the leaves above his head and it was time to be thinking of going. Should he really 'try his harp out' on the stubby, grey stones of the Starwell, he wondered? How much did Frekk know — about the nature of his harp, about Lune, — about the Starwell?

"Why on earth didn't I ask him?" he sighed; though he consoled himself with the fact that Frekk had not been an easy person to question.

"Well, let's try it, then!" he said aloud, though somehow he could not find the right mood. He sat stroking the ivory, or bone, of his harp thoughtfully for a while, as Frekk had done, then said to it, "I wish I could solve *your* mystery! But that's my mystery, too, and there seems to be no way of doing that."

He was still for a moment, then very quietly began to sing.*

> Times will come, times will go,
> the patterns run, the patterns flow,
> where rocks crumble mountains grow.
>
> The tunes are long, the dance is slow,
> the patterns drawn by heels and toe
> are never done while star worlds glow.
>
> What blossomed once its fruits still show;
> the pattern weaver seeks to know
> where to reap, where seed to sow.

---

* For musical accompaniment, see Appendix, page 320.

The words were a statement, but the melody a delicate, searching invocation, and the result was startling. The lively colours of the clearing faded again to the grey of dawn, but quite lacking that quality of awakening which is so abundant in the early morning. It was a greyness of death, of the draining away of life, and it touched him as strongly as it touched all the trees and flowers around him.

"Go away, leave us alone!" cried a voice in his mind. "We cannot show, you cannot see. Leave us in peace. Go!"

He staggered with nausea at the sucking withdrawal of life both in and around him. His fingers fell numb from the strings and he fought not to lose consciousness. At last he managed to put the harp back in its covering and fasten the buckles.

Gradually the colours returned, the sun was shining again.

"Very well," he said. "It's anyway my only wish to get to Lune, to find the Fastness. That is what I seek."

He shouldered his pack and walked slowly towards the northern edge of the clearing.

———

The moment he passed between the cascades of honeysuckle and began walking northwards, his heart lightened, as if a burden had fallen from him. The forest seemed lighter, too, more open than on the day before and nearly free of brambles or other undergrowth, but carpeted here and there with springy grass, wood sorrel, and moss. Giant beeches grew out of the wild lawn with broad, silvery trunks and heavy root limbs. And along the path itself was an abundance of blossom: white umbels of stout hogweed and fragrant meadowsweet, a multitude of frail blue harebells, purple vetches and stiff, yellow hawkweeds. While all around was the hum and buzz of insects, of furry bumble-bees, fat black and orange muscid flies, a whirring beetle, and elegant hover-flies stood motionless, wings all a blur, in a sunbeam.

Fal, too, was so full of vigour that it was well into the afternoon before he allowed himself a short rest and a bite to eat. He stopped at a sunny spot where a stream ran close to the path. Ferns and feathery grasses grew on its bank, and the raspberries ripening by the path gave an added relish to the meal.

As he ate he listened contentedly to the friendly sound of the brook as it leaped and spiralled along over its many stones. The Starwell and its grey mysteries seemed far behind him. The world was full of sunshine now. And a voice whispered to him out of the splashing water.

"Sing to me sometimes on your journey," it said. "I'll be watching over you."

"Oh, how stupid of me!" he answered aloud. "It's you I should have sung to this morning, not to that ring of dark old stones."

He took his harp and sang, making up both tune and words to suit his mood.

> Where grass grows tall by woodland stream
> the world is caught in summer's dream
> of berry red, of mosses green,
> of cobwebs bright with rainbow sheen.
> From harebells velvet bees appear
> to bring their queen the summer's cheer.

And as he sang, a wonder happened, though at the time it did not seem strange to him. For there, in the grass, sat Feather, her gown embroidered full of bees and wild flowers, her eyes dark and deep, but very happy. Yet even as his singing ended, so also had she gone, and he woke, as if indeed from a dream, amazed. Then he went on his way full of joy, not pausing again till the light was fading, late in the evening.

The forest was as full of life in the growing darkness as it had been in the day. As he slept an owl was whooping in the branches just above his head, mice squeaked and scuffled close to his ear, and from the direction of a thicket in the now dense woodland a larger animal sniffed and wuffled. Glowing green eyes approached him doubtfully, peering first from one side then from the other. Invisible nostrils inhaled images of his life and character as they tested the air around his pack, his harp, his cloak and blanket. He slept and was not aware of them; nor did he see the shadowy forms of the deer as they passed him along the trail. But in his sleep he dreamt of them, heard their thoughts in speech he could understand, and felt their warmth.

And at the end of his dreams he saw a world of swirling mist, where a stag stood tall and black, with massive antlers, blocking his path in a grey land. It stared at him from golden eyes. "Come, then," it said. "Why do you tarry?"

When he woke, the sun was shining in the trees above him, and he knew it was indeed time to be on his way.

He strode on, puzzled but contented, not daring to sing again lest the wonder of the afternoon before should fail him and bring disappointment to his cheerful mood. But he thought often of the twins, trying to imagine them as part of the daily life of Gopley Farm.

Towards evening the forest changed again. The trees had become much smaller and the ground was all carpeted with heather. Soon it would be blossoming, and he wondered whether he would see the riot of its colours when he returned.

He was beginning to think of stopping and calling it a day when he saw before him two cliff-like outcrops of rock, between which the path ran dark and narrow as through a high doorway. He went on up the hill slope to the moss-encrusted towers and walked through the gap. On the other side he emerged into a different world. The forest had ended abruptly, and before him lay a stony plain, boundless and open to a vast blue sky. He had come to the Waste.

———

He could have been standing on a low cliff overlooking the sea, for the forest swung out slowly northwards to left and right, as on the shore of a bay, and the heather ran down a short tumbled slope to what might well have been the dried out bed of an ancient ocean. Lichens now covered the rocks and between them, close to the forest's edge, were clumps of stunted foxgloves. Creamy-coloured moths fluttered around the heather, already blossoming here and there in the open, and there were some large black flies. Otherwise there was no sign of life.

From where he was standing the path ran straight across the plain, raised on a dike or causeway some eleven or twelve feet wide, as if to avoid the incoming tide. But there was no sign of water. For miles he could see the road running into the north until it was lost in the haze which shrouded the horizon.

He stood a long while as the sunset flamed and slowly softened into grey, wondering what it could all have been in some long forgotten age. The road, where had it once led? And who had made it? He had never heard of elves — elves of Gelmindel or of anywhere else — making a great work of stone like this causeway. He had heard stories of the colossal builders of old, the giants, but remains of their bastions were unknown, and nobody seemed to remember who they were or where they had gone.

"It would certainly be a help to have giant's legs to get across this," he smiled. "But tonight I'm keeping to the forest!"

He retraced his steps between the rocks and walked back a half a mile until he found a narrow stream. There he made a camp in the heather under the birch trees. When he had finished eating, there was still half a rabbit left for the next day. After that it would be hard bread and cheese. He washed out his leather water flask and refilled it to the brim. The Waste had looked very dry — dry as a bone.

———

He was light-headed with excitement as he stepped out over the flat plain. The causeway was going to make easy travelling, for, in contrast to the rough, barren land around it, its surface was quite smooth. Only a sparse line of moss showed here and there between the flag stones which still fitted together so well that there was no danger of stumbling. He knew of course that the mountains which stood above the horizon were much further away than they looked and it would take several days to make the return journey. But the weather was mild and very still and his mood so over-flowing with high spirits that he sang loudly for much of the morning and would have skipped along but for the encumbrance of his harp and pack.

The second day was very different. He woke with a searing headache and at once felt unbearably alone and dangerously exposed. The world tipped and reeled. He sat up and struggled to gain control. He thrust down an irrational urge to get up and run back towards the forest. It was an almost audible command. He fought and mastered it until the pressure broke and left him, trembling still as if a fever had possessed him during his short sleep.

He stood up and looked about him. There was no sign, no movement or feeling of attack. He was puzzled and frowned apprehensively. Did the causeway have its own invisible guardians? He would have to struggle against them. Whatever the Fastness was or had been, he had to see it and explore its mysteries. He would not go back.

Lacking in appetite, he ate a tiny breakfast and trudged on. Haze and mist blocked his view for less than a quarter of a mile in any direction and it began to get strangely warm. All trace of the the previous day's optimism had deserted him.

It was about noon when he noticed the stony wilderness around the causeway showing signs of green. It appeared in flat, even patches, and he at first thought it was grass reeds. That meant water, and he wondered whether there would somewhere be enough to drink or whether it would all be stagnant and foul.

But the whole plain around him was turning dark. The darkness moved, as if an angry, oily sea was flowing everywhere between the rocks. He looked and saw that it was not water but rather a black smoke. It was rising out of the ground.

All day he had felt totally unprotected and vulnerable in this bare emptiness, and the feeling was growing violently. There was no escape! Terror flooded him, overpowering beyond all rhyme or reason. His mind clamoured wildly for retreat. Turn and run, get away, just get away from this nameles, shapeless horror! He called out in anguish. So this was why no traveller ever came back from the Waste — the black terror, the engulfing dread! And no-one had said, no-one had warned him! Yet even as he turned and began stumbling back towards the forest he remembered the Starwell: he had failed there, too. Yes, already failed. He could not fail again.

He made himself stop and stand still. With a great effort he swung his pack off his shoulders and climbed down the slope. He would look closer at this writhing black mist between the rocks.

As he descended, the darkness rose everywhere as if to meet him. Then he saw — and felt — what it was: thousands upon thousands of tiny black gnats whining about him.

"You have come so far to feed us. We will drink you," they sang, "we will drink you quite dry." Then they covered his hands, neck, face, and eyes, stinging, biting, blinding.

With a cry he staggered back up the embankment, but the gnats rose with him like a cloak, all obsessed by one greed and desire — for his blood.

Wiping the hungry plague from his burning eyes with one hand he managed to jerk the blanket free from his pack with the other and wrap his whole head and shoulders in it. Then, with his hands plunged into the folds, he knelt down, resting his elbows on his pack and gasping for breath, trying to recover from his shock and panic.

At last he decided that the only way was to go on, all wrapped up. Without unmasking his face he felt for his shoulder straps and struggled into his pack again. Then making a peep-hole just large enough for one eye to see where the road went and keeping his hands well wrapped in the blanket, he stumbled on.

That night he went to sleep hungry and thirsty, for he dreaded baring his hands and face to eat. So he lay on the hard stone under the stars all enswathed from head to foot, and it was the worst night's rest he had had since leaving the Forge. Not till early morning did the torment leave him, for his eyes, nose, and mouth were swollen and burned horribly. But then he slept deeply until the sun was well up into the sky.

It was a bright, warm morning, and the first thing he noticed was that the gnats had vanished. That at least was an unspeakable relief, but he guessed they would emerge again in the afternoon. The mist had gone, too, and in its place the mountains in the north stood out clear. In the centre of the range and now clearly closer than the other peaks rose a sullen, flat-topped giant of dark rock. He would reach it by the evening, he thought, if the gnats did not slow him down too much.

By mid-day the whole line of peaks formed a majestic spectacle no more than twenty miles distant. But there was still no sign of foothills or indeed of any alteration in the monotony of the plain ahead. Not until the flat-topped mountain blocked out the northern sky, no more than four or five miles away, was there any change. Then the level of the stony desert rose to meet the causeway, so that the road ran flat, and all about it were strewn blocks of stone. Cracked and weather-worn they were, but who could say that they were not from the ruin of some ancient city? Yet not one stone rested straight upon another and nowhere could shape of wall or pillar be made out.

The road had also become increasingly broken and Fal had to take care where to tread. So it was that he was taken by surprise to find a cliff towering before him, totally blocking his way. The road had ended.

On a grass green a few goats were grazing. And there was a cottage, turf covered on either side to the very ground, built right against the rock. And behind the goats, close to one of the massive buttresses that ran far up the jagged cliff, someone was standing, still as an ancient carving, worn and gnarled. An old woman it was, maybe, though tall and gaunt, and her hood was raised over her head.

He approached her, and her eyes were downcast, or closed perhaps, yet there was a vigilance about her as if she viewed him with the power of some other vision.

He became conscious of his own face, swollen still and smarting so that his lids too were half shut. She looked up then and stared at him with cold, grey eyes.

"What do you seek here, wanderer?" she said.

"I'm seeking the Fastness of Lune, old mother," he answered and felt that he was dreaming.

Out of the folds of her grey robe a hand appeared and pointed a finger sideways, towards the door of the hovel. She seemed to turn to stone again and an awkward silence fell.

He felt himself slipping more and more into a dream, but he followed the direction of her finger and looked at the door. There was something odd about it; it did not fit to the humble exterior of the cottage, perhaps that was it. It was too broad and rounded, too richly wrought for such a simple croft. The woman stood motionless as he took in the details.

Two enormous bronze hinges, well polished, ornamented the heavy door with golden spirals. The shiny metal flowed out across the dark wood like a lazily moving liquid. Knobbly bolt-heads held the hinges in place, standing out here and there like islands in rivers of gold.

He was drifting, and the woman's voice startled him.

"This is the Fastness," she said. "I am the mistress of Lune."

ELEVEN

The cottage was roomier inside than the outside suggested, the more so as the back wall was sunk several feet into the mountain-side. In the middle of the one large room a broad chimney tapered upwards between the beams and rafters of the roof. Its heavy copper funnel rested on four pillars of slate-like stone, clean on the outside but black with soot towards the smouldering peat. A pot leaked appetizing smells, and around the fire were chairs, shiny and dark with age, and a settle, its high back to the door.

Fal found himself seated, dazed and still half dreaming, staring at the glow of peat. Exhaustion and disappointment had combined to throw a dulling blanket over his mind. How long had he been sitting there staring? He made an effort to pull himself together.

"Thank you, old mother," he said.

She did not reply, and he looked up at her. She was not a young woman but he had obviously been mistaken about her age. Strange. Now she was smiling. Was it amusement at his miserable appearance? She had thrown her cloak off to reveal golden hair, streaked with grey, plaited and twisted into a heavy bun. Her gown was black but embroidered round the neck in many colours.

"I am Rymon," she said. "You are welcome to stay here — but you must eat your broth or you will not get strong again. It's not often that a harper comes this way to entertain us!"

He noticed that his own cloak had been carefully folded over a chair, and his harp was lying on it. He also noticed that she had said 'us'. But his desolation at finding a mere peasant croft instead of at least the remains of the magic fortress of his dreams had dispelled all the longings and curiosity which had brought him on this long journey. The woman must have seen the misery in his eyes for she stopped smiling. Her face was strong and rather uncomfortable but not altogether without kindness.

"You think my house could be just a little grander, is that it? Well, be glad there's anything here at all. A hot broth and fresh bread can be worth more than faery towers when needs arise!"

He knew he should be grateful, but the shock was still too great for him and he was not yet ready to be consoled. Faery towers? Yet Rymon was surely no crofter's wife, picking a living among the ruined stones and mossy tumbles of a lost city. There was something about her of Sulthind's mother: the level gaze, a trace of the same inner power, maybe, but there was no sense of threat or malice. Who cared who or what she was?

He was sick and weary, and he was drowsy with the warmth of the fire. He felt himself drifting again. There was after all a lot to be said for homeliness... gnomeliness... luneliness...

He slept deeply, without dreams, and when he awoke it was well into the next day. He was lying in a wooden bunk. Rymon had milked the goats and was singing softly as she prepared a late breakfast for him. She showed him the little washhouse outside by the stream and told him to look in the hen roost for eggs. The chickens were already scattered around the cottage, pecking in the turf and clucking contentedly to one another.

So began Fal's stay at Lune, herding Rymon's goats, fetching water from the pool which the narrow falls had rounded out of the rocks, cutting peat and old ling for the hearth. In the evenings he sang to her while she sewed or spun. Sometimes they talked, but he asked no questions, fearing perhaps any further disillusionment. For her part, Rymon wanted to know this and that about his life at the Forge, but on the whole she already seemed remarkably well informed, both about the Delming and about places little more than names in travellers' yarns to Fal. She told him that in a few weeks her husband and daughter would be coming down from the farm, which lay, she said, on the ledge near the mountain's hollow top. They would go up together to help bring down supplies for the coming winter.

"Strange," he thought. "Tholaiwin never mentioned a farm up here. I wonder if she knew of it?" He was aware that Tholley had scarcely mentioned anything, of course. "If only I'd waited till she came back! I might have saved myself this useless journey, just rushing off without the faintest clue!"

He spoke to Ragwort, the yellow-haired lord of Rymon's goats. Ragwort regarded him glassily through long, slit pupils and burped noisily.

"Yes, my lord," he sighed, "I deserve all your comments, I'm sure, but what next, that's the question? Home again soon or wait to meet the family?"

He realized then how lacking in curiosity and interest he had been since, half blind with exhaustion, he had staggered up the last stretch of the causeway only to find that the Fastness was a turf covered hovel against a bare cliff.

"Well, I'm going to ask a few questions tonight, Sir Rag-and-Bones, you see if I don't," he muttered. But even as he spoke he heard a sound behind him. He swivelled round. It was Rymon, smiling down at him in her strange, amused fashion.

He rose to greet her, but she said, "Have a care now, Master Fal. Standing up with your back so close to Ragwort is a temptation he might not..." Fal felt a jarring thump and he was sprawling in the grass at Rymon's feet.

"Come," she said and laughed for the first time since his arrival. "It's a fair evening. Let's take the lord and his ladies for a walk along the mountain's edge."

Then at last he spoke to Rymon of his quest, and she in her turn told him about her upbringing in the Waste. Like her mother and many that had lived there before them, she was the guardian of the mountain and its hidden secrets. "But no-one has ever unlocked those secrets," she confessed, "so they have been guarded even from the guardians!"

She seemed to think that his quest was part of her own, but Fal thought that if her cottage contained any secrets they must be well hidden indeed. The misery of his first disappointment was clutching at him again.

But she was still talking. "Now look, young harper," she said. "See this plant growing on the bank? No, no, — here, look, among these mosses."

The goats had caught up with them and fell to cropping the turf around the path. Rymon bent stiffly to where a whorl of leaves, covered with tiny red bristles and sparkles of dew, was growing between the rocks. "What plant is it, lad?"

"I don't know, lady; it's not a plant of the south. I've never seen one before."

"It's a fly trap," she said. Ragwort bleated, and her bony fingers rubbed his head hard between the horns. "It eats flies that come to drink its dew. If it didn't it would die. Yet it also has a root to gain moisture, and it sometimes sends up a spike to bear blossoms and seeds. See now, a fly has settled. Watch."

There was no sound except the chewing of the goats and the occasional patter of droppings on the turf. As the fly drank greedily, the red bristles curled in to embrace their victim.

"That's how I view the problem," she said.

Fal frowned. "I don't understand," he mumbled.

"Why then," she exclaimed, a little crossly, "how can anything be clearer? The leaves feed the roots, the roots feed the leaves, and it all feeds the flowers and seeds! When north and south are severed, each must in the end wither and perish. When did your famous Golden Tree last blossom? Eh? Tell me that!"

"I see," he said. But he wished she had chosen a different plant for her explanation. "Which do you see as the trap, the north or the south?"

Rymon laughed, suddenly and loudly, her face creased for a moment with mirth. Ragwort bleated and stamped his foot. "Nay," she said, "I see you'll be taking me for the old Hag o' Mountain herself! I chose that plant because I thought you might never have seen one before, and I was right." She looked at him slyly for a moment and added quietly, "But the south is the fly trap, of course. Does it not lure the riches of the world into the Forge's treasure house?" She laughed again, more gently, but her gaze was veiled now and he still felt puzzled by her image.

"Are all harpers so slow to understand!" she said. "Then let's talk about these bilberries that Ragwort has discovered. They enjoy the light of the sun, and the leaves pass it on, both to berry and root. What once flowed through Lune and through the Delming was passed from one to the other, back and forth from north to south and from south to north, ever increasing the power of each, each living in balance with the other. That's how it was. But how did it work, how was it controlled? How can the power be made to flow again? That's the knowledge that has been lost, and without it the withering and wasting of the world will go on and on. Slowly, maybe, so slowly that in the end people will forget and not even believe what's been lost. But you know, lad, and so do we guardians. We have sought the knowledge ever since Lune faded and the Waste grew up around."

"How do we seek it?" he asked.

Rymon drew a sudden breath, and for a moment he thought he had asked too much before times. But her face relaxed again and she leant a little towards him. Briefly, her eyes took on an eager, excited look, but she smiled and whispered, "Let's return now, the supper will be cooked. When we've eaten I will show you."

———

While they ate, Fal speculated wildly. What was he about to learn from Rymon? he suspected some ancient book or maybe stone. But she had said the mountain's secrets were still hidden, even from her, or had he misunderstood her? He did not think so. And why should she reveal them to him?

"Let me tell you the story of Lune," she said suddenly as she ladled him out some more of the thick barley broth. "There are many old tales, but only the guardians know the true story." She sat down on the settle again and pushed her empty bowl well away from her.

"The mountain once had a shape quite different from what you see today. Oh, it wasn't always low and spread like it is now. It was young and tall and crested with silver. The pride of the world! But that was long, long ago. Dwarves lived in its depths, a whole people of them. They had a king, but over them all ruled Varya — goddess-queen, lady of wonders — who knows what she was? It was she who first gathered the powers together — from the stars of the deep above, from the depths of the earth below. She gave life to all the world, as a mother gives life to the child in her body. And the dwarves were her helpers — servants, workers, and messengers — and they loved her above all. She was the real ruler of Lune, for the people in the city outside were a fey and foolish folk, living at the skirts of the mountain with scarcely more understanding than the chickens and goats that live by it now. They had their own king and queen, of course, who had a little power of their own; enough to keep the town pretty and the beasts that lived in it tame and stupid.

"In time they grew jealous of the mountain goddess, the mother who gave them their life, and by some bungling magic they managed to check the flow of power, which was her precious gift to them and all the world. Beginner's luck it was, for of certainty they were but as ants beneath the paws of a mountain-lion compared to Queen Varya. Yet even ants can sting — as can the tiny flies out there in the Waste — and when they all work at it together they can damage a man and send him off raging. So the lady of the dwarves left Lune, and its flow of power was turned back. The mountain boiled and fell in on itself. The empty-headed people of the town were destroyed by their own folly, but it wasn't only they who suffered.

"The whole world changed, ay, the whole world. And since then we guardians have striven to unknot the web of secrets which the mountain hides. As long as we worked alone we got nowhere. But I've been luckier than the others. Visitors have come, visitors with skill and untiring hands. And they wanted to stay. Maybe you'll help us, too. Come on! You've had enough supper. Bring your harp with you, some music will be fitting."

She thrust a taper into the fire and lit two candle lanterns. Then she went into the larder at the back of the cottage and dropped a few spare candles into her apron pocket. Fal still did not realize what she was going to do but stood watching her, waiting for her to return.

"Come along, then," she called, "you must come with me!"

Puzzled, he followed her into the recess. She moved a latch at the top of a cupboard and the whole unit swung out towards her. Behind it was a door, the twin of the front door of the cottage, its spiralling hinges flickering and flowing in the candle-light, the door of the mountain. She thrust at it triumphantly, and it swung inwards. It was the beginning of a tunnel.

"The way to the halls of Queen Varya's dwarf-kingdom!" she whispered, as if fearing to be overheard.

He had to stoop a little to avoid scraping his head on the roof. The tunnel ran quite straight and was evidently very long. His back began to ache. The walls were smooth but unpolished and did not look like part of anyone's kingdom. Where was this woman taking him? He was feeling trapped and confined and was not at all enjoying being inside a mountain. Surely it could not go on like this for ever!

The tunnel opened into a large space. He heard it in the sudden change of sound from Rymon's footsteps before he saw it, for it was dark and she was blocking his view.

She stood to one side and held up her lantern. His eyes strained to penetrate the gloom. All he could make out was a long table in the centre. He walked over to look at it. It appeared to be of polished black stone, but it could have been dark blue or green. Around it stood benches of the same stone and at each end a stone chair.

Rymon said nothing but was apparently waiting for him to pass some comment. He would look around first.

Wheelbarrows and mattocks leaned against the wall and there were several piles of rubble, neatly stacked, waiting to be carted off. There was no sign of the workmen, whoever they were, nor was there any sound to suggest their presence in one of the three tunnels which led out of the far side of the cavern. He looked at Rymon enquiringly.

"They're helping with the harvest," she said, "at the farm, somewhere above our heads!" And, after a pause, "The tunnel on the right also leads up there." Her eyes gleamed. "There are five hundred and seven steps up to the first level. Other halls and chambers are there but they haven't been properly cleared yet. Then the stairs go on. Another three hundred and thirty-eight steps to the second level — but that is still closed off." Fal thought her eyes hardened a little and once again he was reminded of Sulthind's mother. But she hadn't finished.

"Another eight hundred and forty-five steps lead to the top." She began walking towards the dark openings. "The tunnel on the left leads to the back door. It's in the middle of a cliff. That's where all the rubble is being taken."

He looked more closely at the mattocks and barrows. They were small, almost like children's toys, but very sturdy. "So it's dwarves," he thought.

"And the third tunnel," Rymon continued, her voice trembling with excitement, "there we have uncoverd something very unusual. Come along, it's a solemn place, and I would have you play some music as we enter it. Who knows how long it is since harps were played in this hall! The stone hungers for melody and song."

Fal thought his hostess was making a little too much of these old caves, but he wanted to please her and played a tune which the dwarves of the Delming sang to their children. She took his lantern, and as she turned to lead the way through the middle door, he caught a glimpse of a strange, almost crazed look in her eyes. Maybe she really is half mad, he thought.

The tunnel was short and soon opened into an octagonal chamber. In the middle stood what appeared to be a round table of polished metal that shimmered golden in the unsteady light. It was rather like a giant, flat-topped toadstool, the metal of its underside sloping downwards towards its one stumpy leg. There was nothing else in the room.

Rymon was offering him his lantern back, so he brought the tune to an end. He walked closer to the golden toadstool and examined it closely. In its centre was a deep hollow or built-in bowl surrounded by a rim of some darker metal, but he could not see into it without leaning over the tabel and he was reluctant to touch it. There was no ornament or patterning anywhere. The whole thing was quite plain, beautifully and perfectly wrought but, as far as he could see, without meaning. He had no idea what it might have been for.

"We don't yet know how to use this — this table," said Rymon, "but we believe something is missing from the bowl. Whatever it was, we are sure this lies at the very heart of what we're seeking"

Her candle was guttering and producing smoke and she had knelt down
on the floor to change it.

"Put your hand on the table!"

He had heard a woman speak. It was not Rymon, nor did she appear to
have heard it.

"Your hand, put your hand on the table!"

It was Feather's voice surely, but how...?

"Quickly, your right hand, she will want to go soon."

He put his lantern on the floor and laid his hand on the cold surface of
the metal. A slight tingle flowed up his arm, nothing else. Why? Suddenly
his harp began to feel warm, then burning, burning fiercely through his
tunic into his heart, burning fire!

Rymon had stood up and had walked over to the wall where she stood
pointing at a worn, unintelligible inscription. She was saying something,
but he was not listening. A deep tone, a powerful resonance, was sounding
from the table, throbbing through the enclosed space. She must have been
unaware of it, for her lips went on moving though her words were
completely drowned in the music of the mountain.

The table was getting hot now, but Fal's attention was being drawn to
the hollow where a sphere of spinning light was flashing above the bowl.

Then it was gone, the light and the tone of power. He lifted his hand and
stepped back. For a moment he thought the candles had gone out till his
senses began to readjust.

"... too faint down here, and we can't decide whether it's some ancient
writing or only ornament." Her voice was droning on. "Come, replace
your candle and look."

Trembling, he managed to light a fresh candle and push it onto the stub
of the old. He tried to concentrate on the inscriptions but he could make
nothing of them. Suddenly, Rymon stood up and turned to go. At the same
time Fal became aware of a feature of the chamber that he had not noticed
before. In the wall behind the golden table there was a door.

It was low and unornamented except for a dull iron lock. He walked
towards it.

"That way is barred, the door is locked," said Rymon sharply. "Come,
you have seen my treasures! They are full of riddles but we cannot be far
from solving them." She smiled fiercely. "Tomorrow we shall go up on the
mountain and help them bring down the harvest."

———

That night, as he slept in his bunk at the men's end of the cottage, he had a
dream. At first he thought he had woken, out in the open air, for all above
and about him shone the stars. For an age he lay and watched them as they
moved, regrouping themselves, forming patterns: some yet to be — in a far
future age — others constellations from the past, never to be seen again.

Slowly he sat up and looked around. Trees stood out on the horizon against the stars. Grasses and meadow blossoms whispered as the starlight rippled down into them, a hundred thousand rivulets of molten light, sparkling and glowing: here with a sudden blaze of sapphire at the tip of a leaf, there an explosion of gold, everywhere plumes of silver and a rapid pulsing of amethyst. Yet above him still the silence of the night and the glitter of the stars.

A ring of solemn dancers moved into the meadow, kicking up the liquid colours, splashing out the rainbow dew into the black night as they brushed the summer grasses. And as they danced, from the ground in the centre of their circle another light began to shine.

"The coming of the bride!" — was it a voice or a thought speaking in his mind? The light grew, a resplendent sun rising out of the very earth. It grew, engulfing the dancers till they seemed to be floating and flying in the radiance. It paled the stars until he too was caught up in it and carried aloft in its blaze.

Again the passing of immeasurable time till, when the wonderful light faded, it was like the waking from a dream — the emptiness and the loss. Yet still he slept and dreamt. But the clearing where he sat was an ordinary forest clearing, and it was daytime; the trees were green and the sky fresh and blue, and in place of the dancers there was a ring of sixteen standing stones.

TWELVE

The giddy zig-zag climb up the side of Lune took the whole morning, for they did not journey alone. The goats came, too, drawn by promise of better fare, Rymon said, and Ragwort did not forget such matters in the space of only a few months. They had been up in the springtime at ploughing and sowing, and again at haymaking.

Fal was glad of the frequent stops to allow one or the other of the little herd to catch up, for it gave him time to look around. As they gained height, more and more of the Waste became visible. First, the causeway running as straight as an arrow towards the distant blue of Aurëlund, misty in the warm sun of autumn. Then, on the horizon, more and more mountains became visible, enclosing the Waste to the east and west so that the impression of a dried ocean bed became even stronger.

As his feet plodded a steady rhythm up the rough path, a song formed itself in his mind. Ragwort's bell was part of it, so was the stillness which stretched out around him, but there was something else, too; something he felt he should remember if he could only bring it more clearly into his mind.*

> The grey eyes of the stone-lands
>   sing of more than whispering dreams;
> the silent seeds of winter
>   know best what summer means.
>
> Beginning, once, and centre,
>   the mighty land of Lune,
> where bare rock reigns and silence:
>   crystal mountains of the moon.
>
> Listen, and learn the story
>   of how the land shall wake again!
> The stone has not forgotten
>   who shall end its ancient pain.
>
> The Tree once more shall blossom
>   and the golden light shall run,
> bursting up the pathway
>   like the fires of the sun.

* For musical accompaniment, see Appendix, page 321.

Rymon had stopped above him on the path, her hand resting firmly on Ragwort's head. The jingling of the bells stopped as the procession piled up behing him.

"Whence comes this rhyme?" She spoke with a mocking smile, but there was a hardness in her eyes.

"I've just been making it up. It seemed to come to me — out of the rocks!"

She stood staring down at him and for a moment she was again the strange figure he had first met when he had arrived, exhausted, from Aurëlund. She was about to speak but checked herself. Instead she half turned and, pointing upwards, said, "A dozen more steps between these rocks and you'll see the pastures of Lune!" She released Ragwort who, with a grunt, at once pushed past her and disappeared through the gap.

Whatever he had expected the farm to be like he forgot the moment he looked down into the hollow where the fields nestled. There was of course a cottage, similar to Rymon's house, a threshing floor with its yellow sea of chaff, and barns. There were ponies tethered by a barn door and there was the startling green of a cluster of birch trees. But he had thought that this would be more or less the top of Lune and was quite unprepared for the immense cliffs behind the farm, sheer and threatening.

"I thought this was near the top!" he gasped.

"It *is* the top as far as we're concerned! There's no way up there except for eagles and ravens. Our way lies down now, Falimbravel, to see what those folk of mine are doing. Not started eating without us, I hope. I did say the first day of the new moon!" She hurried forward, muttering, past the goats who were already giving the uncropped grass around the path their undivided attention. The ponies whinnied in greeting and the door of the cottage flew open. Two people were standing in the doorway waving — they were dwarves.

Fal walked carefully down between the last jagged boulders onto the level of the fields. He was still overwhelmed by the contrast of the cosy-looking farm and the starkness of the cliffs and was trying to adjust to the fact that he had formed too simple a picture of the structure of the mountain. He had reckoned that the farm would be on the edge of the old crater, but now he saw that Lune was more colossal and even more alien than he had thought. The fields lay in a broad, well protected pocket on the south face. The hollow summit, whatever it contained, rose almost vertically above them, wild, inaccessible, and inhuman.

But there was a clamour of people coming along the path curious to meet him. The dwarves had been joined by a homely looking man, round faced, with simple, childlike eyes, and a girl, some fifteen or sixteen years old. They both had the same pale, flaxen hair and the same freindly smiles, and both wore brown homespun, worn and grubby.

Rymon had just been telling them about the visitor. "... and this is my husband, the Lord Osmarin, and Ristilian, our daughter. They have the dinner all ready. Come!"

The two dwarves had hung back a little, out of courtesy maybe, but Fal thought they were eyeing him rather carefully as if they were even less used to strangers than their masters. They certainly looked different from the dwarves of the Forge — less sunny, even just a little sour, more part of the rocks — more dwarvish, perhaps, he thought with a smile, and quickly combined the smile with friendly nods in reply to everyone's greetings.

"You must tell us all about your journey, and about your home," Ristilian was babbling like a brook. "We don't often get visitors here, you know, I expect mother's told you."

There was a squawk, and a crow flew off the thatch of the house onto her shoulder, where it stood bowing up and down at Fal.

"And this is Sooty, my pet crow. He's new too, or fairly new, anyway, he came this summer. I think he's jealous."

Osmarin coughed and said in a rather odd, sing-song voice, "Welcome to the fields of Lune. Our fare is simple, but you are very welcome." The crow laughed.

"Where are the sacks of grain?" said Rymon as she hustled them back into the cottage. "Not where those goats can get at them?"

"But mistress," one of the dwarves cackled as if enjoying a shared joke, "would we make the same mistake twice in one year!" He shot a quick side glance at Osmarin who was busy cutting up an enormous pie. "Locked in the barn they are, safe as mountains."

Fal was feeling warm after the long climb. The undertones of the conversation were making him feel uncomfortable, too; but it did seem a lot warmer here than down at Rymon's cottage. It should surely be the other way round, he thought.

"Young master is wondering why it's not pretty chilly today?" He was jolted out out of his musings and stared with surprise at the dwarf who had spoken. It was the one who had been silent till now. He was smiling, his head cocked to one side as if listening, and peering at Fal out of a wrinkled face with tiny eyes as dark and bright as polished garnets.

"How foolish of me," said Rymon, "I haven't introduced my dwarves!"

"This is Aurvang," said Ristilian, "Aurvang the Listener. He doesn't talk much; not like Amladorkaslagh — we have a job keeping him quiet — call him Slag, Slag Battletooth!"

Slag bowed deeply, displaying an ample shock of dark red hair, and grinned to reveal a distinct gap in his stubby, yellow teeth. Aurvang nodded a little and went on peering quietly at Fal.

"Young master plays the harp?" he said, adding a second question to the other. "Perhaps young master will play tonight? Dwarves like songs."

"My word!" Rymon exclaimed, "whatever has happened to this dwarf?

More questions in a minute than words in a day, or is he changing for the autumn?"

"My name is Fal... Falimbravel," said Fal.

"Master Falimbravel," said Aurvang, "I thank you."

Osmarin had handed the pie around in wooden bowls, and Ristilain poured a soup-like sauce on it. For the moment conversation lapsed, and the dwarves turned their bright eyes to the steaming content of their bowls. It was Osmarin who broke the silence:

Past the tending, past the care,
all the summer fields are bare;
patient now our doom we wait
by the ancient mountain's gate.

He spoke in the same dreamy sing-song as before, apparently to no-one in particular. Fal thought Ristilian looked embarrassed, but the dwarves went on eating. Only the crow paused in demolishing a crust, which it clutched between its claws. It squawked and shrieked wildly. Slag looked up and grinned.

"This bird will be the next lord of Lune," he said. "Think what wisdom it will speak once its tongue is loosed!"

If Osmarin had felt any barb, his face did not show it. Was he truly simple, perhaps? Fal returned to watching the crow, who, having reduced its crust to a row of beetle sized fragments, was busy killing each one with a solemn thrust of its beak.

"We didn't get Sooty as a baby or with a broken wing or anything." Ristilian volunteered happily. "Not like that tatty old raven they had in Vond. Oh yes, we don't always stay here, not all the time. At least, mother does, but father went with the ponies down to the sea last year to buy grain, and he took me with him. I expect you've never seen Vond, with all those wonderful bridges. That's where we met Slag — and Aurvang."

Osmarin stared vacantly at the door, Aurvang was eating; Slag grinned and showed his gap again. Fal appeared to be tongue-tied, waiting for Ristilian to go on. He thought he had never seen such a delicate face, made of pure enchantment, more elvish than the elves.

But Rymon frowned and cleared her throat.

———

With the new moon a change of weather was coming, and the dark rim of Aurëlund stood out clearly as if the journey to the forest would take but an hour or two instead of days. A grey sheet of cloud was drawing over the Waste. Soon the sun would be cut off.

Fal was bringing up the rear, bending under the burden which was his share. The dwarves were hopping down among the rocks in front of him and would continually stop without warning to examine some unusual speck or streak of colour in the dark stone. It was difficult not to stumble into them.

"Why is it warmer up at the farm, then?" he said.

Aurvang dropped back a little. "Be more sensible to live up there all the time, wouldn't it?" He whispered. "But the Lady Rymon won't allow that. Well now, it's very well sheltered, of course; but the real reason lies in the mountain herself. There's still some warmth here and there, you see, master; still a few veins of life in the joints of the Old One. But no more fire now, no."

That evening there were omelettes and beer to celebrate the bringing down of the harvest, and after supper Fal was asked to add music to the festival. The dwarves were very interested in the harp and its patterns and, though they peered at it closely, they made no attempt to touch it. Fal's songs were mostly of the elves of the Forge, for even the dwarves there sang music adopted from elvish ballads and only half-forgotten fragments of their own. He wondered whether Rymon's dwarves knew other songs and decided to ask them, saying that the music of the eastern kingdoms was famous in legend even in the south. They seemed pleased, and Aurvang went to fetch a little fiddle from his belongings. The tuning of the strings was strange to Fal's ears, stranger still the stark rhythms to which Slag sang. He at once realized that he had probably never heard a genuine dwarves' song before. It was as if the very rock was speaking in the fierce, harsh music.

> Jháldavél old
>   stirred in his sleep,
>   dreaming of delving the deep.
> Out of his dream
>   clad in bright mail
>   cried a dwarf warrior pale:
> 'Cousins, arise,
> come from your halls,
>   come where a kingdom now falls
> under the spear's
> merciless thrust,
>   lest what remain be but dust!'
> Jháldavél woke,
> gave a great shout,
>   calling his kinsfolk about:
> 'Dwarves of the East,
> great is the need,
>   Frekkir has urged us to speed!
> Came in a dream
> clad as for war,

pale as if living no more!'
Dwarves without count
whet deadly blade,
  weapons in ancient times made;
hammer and axe,
to fell-song and rune,
  chanting to grim-worded tune.
Up Mirrorwend,
round silent Lune,
  coming to Silver Hills soon;
songs speed the march,
dwarves tireless tramp,
  never once pausing to camp.
Driven by hate,
rank upon row,
  seeking the dwarves' ancient foe:
Witch-folk of ice,
thinner than bone,
  slaying the people of stone.
Painful the spears,
blue blades of ice,
  mocking to battle entice
those who remain
locked in deep hall
  waiting till ice grip them all.
Many lay slain,
Frekkir was dead,
  ice-spear had splintered his head.
Weeping and grief
hold back life's flow,
  waiting makes time's passing slow.
Silver belongs
where it is hewn
  under the light of the Moon;
not in the white
land of cold ice
  whence swarm these witch-folk like lice.
Jháldavél old,
beard grey and hoar,
  marching to save Frekkir's store,
laughing and grim
sought the Ice-King,
  longing to hear metal ring
blade upon blade,

iron cleaving ice,
  hammer in hand strong as vise.
Ice-King just mocked,
pointing his spear,
  sending out cold spells of fear.
Jháldavél's heart,
full of Earth's fire,
  made of strength ancient and dire,
could not be touched,
chilled by a spell,
  voice rang out clear as a bell:
'Leave Frekkir's hills,
icicle-witch,
  dwarves shall not help you grow rich!
Ghosts from the north,
plague-pack, be gone,
  in magic and strength you're outshone!'
Ice-demon laughed:
'Frekkir is dead!
  Rats to their holes all have fled!
Hasten away,
scuttle or crawl
  lest ice-men wither you all!'
Spears flashed aloft,
hammers were swung,
  dwarf axes shimmered and sung.
Jháldavél grim,
laughing at pain,
  blind but for taking his aim —
haft jerked and spun,
great throw unfurled —
  stood watching axe as it whirled.
Spear struck dwarf dead!
Axe clove the ghost,
  melting away all its host.
This the brave deed
Jháldavél bold
  died to save dwarves in their hold.
Sacred his axe
lies in his grave
  built of the silver they gave
out of the hoard
which he had won
  when the ice-ghosts were undone.

The room fell silent again. Osmarin was staring at his fingers, and Aurvang was shifting awkwardly from one foot to the other. Slag sat, hands clenched into hammers, glaring, waiting for the ice-demons to come and fight.

"Thank you," said Fal, and the dwarves at once felt that he meant it. They smiled. The manner of these two dour creatures was strange to him but he liked them, and a bond had grown that moment between him and them.

———

The next day he was back to his goat herding. The girl, Ristilian, was busy around the house, Osmarin began repairing the thatch for the onset of winter, and the dwarves had disappeared into the mountain to continue the labour of restoring what Slag evidently considered to be his ancient kingdom within. The sky was heavy and chill, as if the winter was ready to leap upon them.

Fal sat on the rocks watching Ragwort. A mood of utter desolation had descended upon him. Ristilian was a dream, but his heart ached for Feather whose presence he felt so close that he was puzzled not to see her sitting among the boulders, watching him. He tried yet again to concentrate on the problem of the mountain. He had not come here to find Ristilian. Rymon had shown him the secret caverns and what he had seen was without meaning. There was power there, he had seen that, but its nature and purpose were of a kind so hidden and forgotten that he felt no use could be made of them. Should he try a wakening song on the golden mushroom which the dwarves had found? He was not trained to control such deep energies and he did not feel that his next move lay in that direction. What about the door behind the mushroom, the one Rymon said was blocked. Would he find what he sought in there?

He began to realize that he had really no idea at all of what he was looking for, let alone what he would do if he found it. He felt increasingly foolish, and the misery which accompanied the feeling was growing intolerably.

He tried again to concentrate on what he did know, hoping to discover some pattern in it. Rymon herself had said something was missing from the mushroom table, yet it had spoken to him with a familiar voice, called out, drawn him into its energy and strength. And the door — would she allow him to explore further? He was sure she would not. He tried to think, but there was already a resonance, a sympathy, between him and that hidden heart of Lune and he could not get his mind away from it. His thoughts continually relapsed into vagueness. He understood nothing, and that was the truth of it. But the heart of Lune... it was calling him, defying him.

Suddenly he realized that the goats were indeed not his only companions. He glanced again at what he had presumably taken to be a stone, but he had not really noticed it before. It was Aurvang, sitting bunched up, knees tucked into chin, his wizened head twisted to one side as if deep in thought. His eyes were closed tight, their lids all screwed up, and his ears seemed to have grown out beyond his grey hair. They looked very alive whereas the rest of him might well have already half returned to stone. But under Fal's scrutiny the wrinkled lids snapped open and the dark jewels behind them sparkled. The dwarf looked very wide awake.

"Forgive me, Master Falimbravel, forgive me," he said. "I was eavesdropping, but only as a friend, master, who maybe can help, not as a spy."

Fal looked at the odd crature for a moment and felt that he must trust him. "I seem to have lost my way here, Master Aurvang," he said. "There are wonders and mysteries in Lune, but I don't know what I'm supposed to do about them or even if they are any concern of mine. I didn't come here to be a meddler."

"Dwarves recover dwarf-secrets," said Aurvang, "but there is more to Lune than that." He closed his eyes for a moment and looked as if he were turning to stone again. Then he said, "The Lady Rymon doesn't understand what she's found, nor will dwarves help her understand, — she wants power for herself. You're different, young master, but dwarves don't know yet, they can only point to what is not theirs, not explain it."

He peered again at Fal, scrutinizing him carefully. "Aurvang listens," he said, "Listens to the rocks, listens through the rocks — through wall, through stone, ever dark, ever alone. There are dangers in Lune, Master Falimbravel. They sleep, so Aurvang cannot hear their voices, but he hears their power. They are no concern of dwarves, and Rymon would do well not to face them. She must not unbind the door, lest that be lost which is gained."

"Behind the door, then," said Fal

"Aurvang listens to the heart of Lune. There are three doors. The inner door you have seen. Don't open it! But the other doors stand always open."

"Where? Which doors do you mean, Aurvang?"

"There's the back door. Not our little back door, another. You can't enter there. That's where the Black River, narrow and swift, comes out of the mountain. It hurries to join its mistress, the Mirrorwend. But before it finds her it is deadly and must be avoided."

"And the other door, the third?"

"That is the top door; that's always open, too." Aurvang looked glumly at Fal, as if he were giving him the most miserable advice in the world.

"Have you seen these doors?" asked Fal. "How do you know they're always open?"

Aurvang sighed. "Not seen, heard," he whispered. "Don't go, master! Yet if you don't you won't know Lune."

He looked so sad that Fal was half-tempted to smile at the glum old fellow in the hope of cheering him up. But a thought suddenly struck him.

"Does the Lady Rymon know of these doors?" he asked.

"No, master."

"Will you show them to me?"

"No. But I'll show you the way to the upper door. There's no danger to us dwarves in doing so, and your own heart tells me that your quest leads you that way. What you do then is yours to decide."

"When?" Fal asked.

Aurvang had shrunk into a ball of utter misery. "Tonight, if you wish. Before dawn."

___

The traveller had come to the edge of the forest and stook looking down over the Waste. He studied every detail of the awesome panorama. Lune stood out clear in the chill air, but Ilmarin was not one to be deceived by appearances. He knew it would be a hard and bitter walk across many dreary miles. And soon the wolves would be coming down from the north. He had heard about the swarms of biting flies out there in the middle of the Waste, but he smiled. The weather was too cold now for them to be troublesome.

Ilmarin was worried. He had had strange warning dreams and in the end had set out in search of his friend. But where was Fal now? The smith had spoken to the trees of Aurëlund and they had told him that he had passed this way. The stream remembered Fal's music and it remembered the vision of Fethilian. But that had been many weeks before.

He stared out across the causeway. His eyes were keen and probed easily into the distance. But Lune spoke confusedly. Ilmarin could not say whether Fal was still there. He was deeply troubled and smiled grimly as he stepped down towards the old causeway.

And it was getting very bleak outside the forest. There was a feeling of snow in the air.

THIRTEEN

Fal plodded up the third and longest spiral of stairs following Aurvang's lantern through the darkness of the mountain. For hours he had heard his own feet, but the dwarf moved noiselessly ahead of him. Rymon had spoken of more than eight hundred steps on this, the final section of the ascent. He had lost count three times now and had to guess at which number to continue. He had finally given up. It felt like thousands, and it was getting unpleasantly warm. Surely they must be coming to an end soon.

Aurvang had said nothing since he had woken him where he lay on his bunk. He was full of questions but sensed that the dwarf did not want to talk. In the end all desire had left him except the need to get to the top and end the torment.

Gradually, he became aware that he could see the steps better than before. A grey light was streaming down the staircase. It was all over, they were there! They were coming out of the mountain into a freezing dawn.

He had to bend nearly double to follow the dwarf out of a low doorway onto a shelf. He looked carefully over the edge. There was the farm, the cottage and the barns, not very far below. He decided to break the silence. "Has Rymon been up here?" he asked.

"No, she has never been here." Aurvang pointed into the recess behind them. Next to the door they had come through was another, equally low and unornamented.

"Is this the upper door?"

"No. But there is another staircase leading onto the top of the mountain. It is not so long as the last one. You must seek the door up there. Aurvang will come no further." He still looked very glum. "Farewell, Master Falimbravel," he said. "Aurvang hears that you are of the mariner kind. Dwarves do not like boats; but when times get bad, remember what is yours!"

"Thank you, Aurvang," said Fal, not understanding him but knowing enough of dwarf nature not to ask. "Thank you, and farewell!"

The dwarf looked at him and suddenly smiled.

> Though Dhulin came second,
> Motsognir was first;
> they keep us from hunger,
> from darkness and thirst;

make future and present
as sure as the past;
though Dhulin was greatest,
Motsognir stood fast.

I'm sorry if it seems a riddle to you; but was it not for the sake of riddles that you came on this journey? It is also a blessing!" he added with another quick smile.

Fal looked blankly at him. The poem seemed to require no comment. If it really was a riddle, the meaning was indeed deeply concealed beneath the obvious. Yet something within him, equally well hidden maybe, responded to the dwarf's probing eyes and he said simply, "I will stand fast, Aurvang. Thank you."

"I hope so, if you'll pardon the forwardness." Without further ceremony he turned and disappeared through the opening whence they had come. Fal was alone to face whatever decisions lay before him.

———

The fourth stairway differed from the others in being cut close to the cliff-face and had innumerable cracks and peep-holes through which light fell. This was fortunate as the steps had not been entirely cleared and they were often littered with rock-falls, unstable and precarious, up which he had to pick his way with care.

Then at last another portal, again leading into the open but this time not facing outwards from the cliff. Instead, it revealed the whole flat mountain top, some half a mile or so across, black and patterned.

Patterned! It was like the ocean bed of the Waste on a smaller scale, but darker and ornamented into a huge symbol. He stared down unbelievingly at the thousands of channels carved into the black basalt. It was a labyrinth, a gigantic maze! He strove with the idea that it was some monstrous whim of nature, that the stone had opened into chasms as mud will crack in a dry summer. But he did not really think so; it was too ordered, the passages too straight and evenly formed. It was surely no more a whim of nature than was the causeway itself. He looked again, at the high rim running round like a city wall, but dark and featureless. The broad, slab-like steps leading down from where he stood to a gateway of black pillars clearly formed the entrance. But what superhuman hand could carve out a maze as big as a city, and to what purpose? A test? Or a trap? And how did this relate to what he had already seen?

He stared at it for a long time, trying to discover the system in the patterns, but perspective made it impossible. The upper door, he felt certain, was out there in the labyrinth. But where?

"Well," he said aloud, "there's only one way to find out, I suppose. I'm not likely to find anyone sitting around up here waiting to tell me about it!"

He took out some bread and his flask of goat's milk for a quick breakfast, wondering how long the remainder would have to last. A sheet of unbroken cloud covered the sky, very low and grey. Tiny flakes of snow were drifting along against the stark background. He suppressed the sense of foreboding which was making him linger over his meal. He tried to enjoy the grandeur of the spectacle before him: the Labyrinth of Lune! But he was only playing for time, there was nothing to wait for. He found himself, quite unnecessarily, checking the straps and buckles on his harp case. He smiled at his own self-indulgence and walked down the steps into the maze.

He had never walked a maze before but he knew enough about the construction of such patterns to realize that it was useless to wander aimlessly about. You had to choose either the right wall or the left wall and abandon it only if you passed a landmark that you were sure you had seen before. This proved you were going round an island which was a self-contained unit. To be free of it you had to change to the other wall. The method was simple and foolproof, but it could take a very long time.

He went a short way in then made a ring of loose stones on the ground. If he came that way again he would change walls; for the moment he would follow the right. One way or the other it was going to mean a long walk.

Here and there the basalt walls had crumbled leaving gaps. By scrambling up the ruck of fallen stones he could have climbed into the next passage. But he was not looking for short cuts. Whatever was to be found here might be in the very section he missed. And would anything indicate a door? Maybe a rockfall would conceal it! Sudden panic rose in his throat. No. Aurvang had said the door was open, always open. He would see it.

Hour after hour he walked the maze, until he began to stumble and slide with weariness. More bread and milk. It was very cold now and the snow was beginning to lie here and there in fine drifts. Very cold. Black... and white... and the grey cloud.

There was a flurry of wings. He started violently. "Caw! Caw!" A crow. Sooty, standing on the wall. "Caw! Caw!" Was it Sooty? There were other crows. No, that was Sooty's way of bowing. The maze twisted into a right fork. "Caw! Caw!" Sooty flew to the left.

"This way, then," Fal said, "we're following the right wall at the moment." He walked on. At once he gave a cry of pain as Sooty landed on his head and gave him a vicious peck. Before he could retaliate, it had flown out of reach, back into the left fork. He was getting very tired. Against all sense and reason he longed to be led. "Do you want me to follow you?" he said.

"Caw! Caw!"

"All right, but only a little way. Only as far as I can remember." He made another circle of stones. He would memorize the route from here so that he could return and continue his own exploration.

Sooty bowed up and down excitedly before flying off to show him the way it had chosen, criss-cross, over broken walls, left forks, right forks, but never to a dead-end. Obviously the crow knew what it was doing. Soon he was following it blindly. He was lost.

"Caw! Caw! Caw!" It had stopped and from the top of a wall was peering down at the floor, bowing. He hurried to see what it was looking at. It was a crack which, through crumbling, had widened to a hole about two feet wide and more than three times that in length. He looked in. It opened, widening, into a pit. The crow had stopped bowing and was staring at him from close by. "Well, well," he laughed, "you surely don't expect me to jump down into that! Don't tell me *this* is the upper door!"

"Down there!" said the crow.

He froze. It was looking at him sideways out of one beady, glistening eye. "Down there, down there!" it cried hoarsely and cocked its head, waiting. He was suddenly reminded of the crow which had listened to him talking with Tholley in the woods outside the Delming.

"Where do you come from?" he said angrily.

"Down! Down there!"

He sighed with exasperation, lay down and thrust his head as far into the hole as he could.

At first he could see little detail and he blinked, trying to get his eyes used to the dark. It was at least twelve feet deep. There was comparatively little rubble on the smooth floor considering the size of the hole from which it must have fallen. He looked again at the rim of stone that pressed hard against his chest. There were several smooth, even polished patches. It was not a natural crack. It had once been a clean slot, fashioned with a purpose, but the ends and edges had weathered.

He studied the underground chamber again. It was about six feet wide at the bottom, and long, like a section of tunnel, but it led nowhere. He craned his head under to see the other end. There was a doorway in it, heavily ornamented with indentations and carving, possibly with writing, he could not see in the gloom. He did not doubt it was the door he sought, but it was strangely hidden; and there was no sign that there had ever been steps down to it. It was very puzzling.

He reckoned that by hanging on to the edge and lowering himself down as far as he could stretch, there would only be another five feet to drop. But then — the realization struck him with sudden force — he could not possibly get out again! He looked around wildly for large stones to drop down. He would need plenty to build a pile five feet high. And there were no crumbled walls in sight. "Down there!" shrieked the crow, "Down! down! down!"

Fal realized that this was probably the only real decision he had ever had to make, because of its utter irrevocability. But it was clear what had to be done, and he swung his legs out over the edge and lowered himself down.

As he fell he snatched at his harp so that it would not hit the floor, and at the same time landed with a heavy jolt. It was not too bad. He had managed to land on a rubble-free patch; there were no sprains or bruises. He half expected it to cackle or speak, but it just stared down at him.

"Aren't you coming with me?" he said, "you could ride on my shoulder, you know!"

It squawked and stepped back out of sight. It did not reappear, and he turned his attention to the carven doorway. The rectangular frame was covered in what was surely an ornate form of writing, but it had no meaning for him. It could be a welcome or a warning, there was no way of telling. He looked into the total darkness beyond the door... and the terrible truth struck him. He had no lantern! He had put his pack down when he had looked into the pit. It was still up there — with the crow!

Despair and irrational anger swept over him like a deluge. He wanted to scream abuse and curses at the crow. He called it back. The snow was drifting down silently, thicker now. But Sooty had gone.

He smiled bitterly at his own foolishness. What could the crow have to do with it, anyway? He only had himself to blame. Only himself... He had never felt so totally alone. And there was no possible way back to the surface. The pit was narrow enough at the top, but where he stood he could not even reach from wall to wall — and they sloped inwards.

He was beyond considering the situation from any further points of view. His despair had begun to dissipate and his anger remained only to strengthen his resolve. He would go on, not because it was his only chance of escape but because he had come here for no other reason.

He walked through the door. There was just enough light to see that the tunnel branched at once into two differnt ways. Another maze? He chose the right wall again and went on. After a few seconds he was in absolute darkness.

The tunnel was so narrow that it was easy to touch both sides. He paused to strap the harp to his back. He would follow the right wall but wanted to know how many forks or crossroads he passed. They were frequent. "That's the fourteenth fork now," he said. "Yes, I know. Why are you bothering to count? — I do it without thinking. Now it's the fifteenth. — Are you going to go on and on counting? — Why not? There's nothing else to think about. That's the thirty-seventh intersection and harp-thump number one thousand, one hundred and nine. You *must* mean 'heart-thumps'!"

He stopped. It was pitch dark and utterly silent. "I'm going mad," he said, "mad. I'm trapped. Trapped in my own mind. — You always have been. There's been no other experience, never, how could there be, outside your mind! Of course you're trapped."

He staggered and tried to lean on the wall for support; but there was no wall in that direction. He tripped and fell on his outstretched hands. "Who *are* you?" he cried. "Who are *you?*" he shouted back in a loud voice. "Stop, you must stop it!" he yelled. "Stop what? There is nothing else to do. Don't you understand? nothing — else — to — do!"

His voice echoed, and a small, saner part of him knew that he had enterd a cavern. A voice that was not his spoke, dry and thin, like a cold needle: "Idz ikder, plinterek theng?"

He immediately became quite still and very clear headed. Silence. Absolute silence.

Then a different voice spoke, deep and sluggish, overpowering and commanding: "Gulderum zashwerl, blashard! Kranmil gursh!" Broad, ponderous tones, engulfing, drowning... But the first voice cut him awake again like a knife-blade.

"Sallin?" it hissed.

"Sallin garp!" the heavy voice answered. "Wartong greep!"

"I can nearly understand this," he thought. "It reminds me of something very important, I'm sure I can understand it." "Of course you can," his mind answered. "There's never been a time when you couldn't understand *them*." But the needle sharp voice was hissing like a whiplash.

"Stishmin rifilsh, grestin greep?"

"Broltoom slandarem!" countered the other, its voice dragging with leaden indolence.

"If I can't understand them, I will at least see them," he cried out loud; and he knew for a moment what to do. "Tsellerk-i!" he called. "Reveal yourselves!"

A dim light began to shine. What it showed was at first so complex and confusing that he had to shut his eyes hard and open them again... Then he understood. The walls of the cavern were all mirrors, and the creatures in the middle were being reflected, in part or whole, innumerable times. It was not hard to sort out, no, not if you really tried... really tried!

They were dragons, both of them, but quite unlike one another. The first was sitting up very straight, like a cat, and it glittered as if its scales were of metal. It was very thin, and the thorns on its back, head, and snout were drawn out to wiry threads many feet long which waved and twitched continually, so that the monster appeared to be enmeshed in its own aura of shimmering hairs. He could feel, even at a distance, how the brittle thread sought to pierce him, bore into him, drying him out, making him all wire and pain. Its eyes were of pale blue flame, and a forked tongue flickered between its teeth so swiftly that it was hard to see. He wrenched his attention to the other dragon.

It was gross — rounded and dull — it might have been black or very dark red. It looked slow and heavy, but terribly powerful. Its eyes were watery, like pools, all pupil, as big as saucers. It lay with its chin resting on immense clawed forepaws, a wide grin on its face; not a smile, but a grin of bloatered self-satisfaction.

They were not looking at him, though he did not doubt for a moment that they were very aware of his presence. Nor did they look at each other but stared at the empty centre of the room. Uncountable replicas were reflected from every side, so that the whole cavern was a web of criss-crossing jerking threads through which hundreds of dragon eyes watched.

"Tsillerk-i!" He spoke the command again, at the same time carefully undoing the buckles of his harp-case, and added "Angsilu avai!" Literally, 'speak your wisdom', the ancient command to compel an enemy to communicate his intentions in known and comprehensible language.

At first there was no change, and he wondered if he should try the command again. His harp ready. He tried touching the strings and nearly cried out in pain: they needled up like wire into his fingers, hurting terribly. He knew it was the work of the thin, silver dragon. But it was the heavy dragon that spoke.

"I will drown him in my blood, dissolve him with my warmth." A rumble came from its throat. It may have been a laugh or a purr. But with a stinging flick of its wiry tentacles the thin dragon spoke, and he gasped with agony.

"I will dry him into crystal threads and make him part of me. He shall share my limitless pain."

"I can bear the heavy one more easily," he thought. "I can't stand this pain; play to this one first."

"Hardly begun, not even touched, then stand it forever," the cold voice pricked deep into his mind.

"No, stop, no, no!" he cried as the delicate threads grew and quivered towards him. Making a terrible effort to thrust back the searing pain as he touched the strings, he began to play a rocking, lilting tune. The threads coiled away from him and another rumble came from the dark dragon. He was sure it was a laugh this time; and as he played, the thin dragon began to shrink. The pain faded and he experienced a thrill of triumph. But as the creature dulled and the threads twisted back against its body, the other dragon grew. It swelled and spread, pulsing with power. The room darkened as energy gushed tangibly towards him, warm and liquid.

For a moment the sensation was pleasant, deliciously washing away the agony of the threads in his nerves. Then he felt his mind being diluted, drowned in the smothering torrent. He cried out and changed his harping to a clear, rhythmic melody, with dissonant harmonies which cut the air like tiny bursts of lightening. At once, the flowing ceased, but the silver dragon was already there, tall and menacing, its slanting eyes flaming with bitter ice-blue.

"The balance, the balance!" he muttered. "I cannot fight them without upsetting the balance! I cannot do it! I cannot do it!" he turned to run, full of a wild, instinctive fear, and a thousand reflected dragons reared threateningly towards him. There were five doors behind him, he had come through one. Which? Must guess, take chance. Run.

He plunged into a tunnel. It was the wrong one, it sloped sharply downwards. He heard a dry swish and a snarling roar as the dragons surged after him. How could they get into the narrow tunnel? Against reason, but yes, coming! He could hear them, see them! Light flickered around him, he expected to feel them now. No, please, not feel them! Please!

His terror grew to an insane panic. The tunnel was polished all around like a mirror, too, and he could see himself, left and right, fleeing from the dragons: two others of him, then two more, and more again, all gripping white harps.

Sometimes the passage branched, but it did not matter which way now. Just run, run, always down. Down stairways, down tunnels, running, sliding, always down, mad with fear. Yes, he felt the needling threads now, their unbelievable pain. He felt the drowning, too, washing out his mind: both at the same time, stronger and stronger. He loved it...

He loved it! Then why was he running away from them?

He stopped and turned, trembling with anticipation, with the lust of being devoured. The tunnel had just opened into another cavern, and the dragons were already on either side of him, on opposite sides of the doorway. He looked from one to the other — solemn, magnificent creatures, gods. And he the privileged victim, the fly in the trap of heavenly dew, to be devoured, to share their divine life, their immortality. He was laughing insanely, laughing in an ecstasy of joy.

The dragons had been watching him fixedly. Now they began moving in towards him. He backed away from the tunnel entrance, he wanted to see both his gods at once. He knew there was no escape. Besides, it was the last thing he wanted. No, but to extend the pleasure of waiting a little longer, then the utter fulfillment, the inexpressible, beyond words, beyond thought, beyond all possible desire.

His legs bumped into something behind him and for a second the spell was broken. He looked round and felt anger, rage, at the interruption. What was it? A wooden post, and tied to it a boat, like his own, but without mast or sail, moored to the edge of an underground lake. He stared for a brief, crazed moment as a memory thrust his irritation aside: "You are of the mariner kind... remember!" He knew now that he must indeed be mad. This low jetty — it was the quay-side of the Forge. This boat — it was *his* boat; the patterns, *his* patterns — here! How could it be, how, except in an insane world?

The dragons were nearly on him now, their heads swinging down. Involuntarily, he twisted his legs over the gunwale as he had done thousands of times before. He unlooped the rope and pushed himself clear. At once he was himself again, Fal, free, bound to no one. "How could you think they were gods?" his mind spoke. "You commanded them and twice they obeyed you. You played to them and mastered them. How can they be gods?" But he thought of the balance, the balance he could not achieve. "You have only learned what you still lack. And that is a great gain. Now go!"

He looked around for oars, but there were none. The boat was empty and unfurnished. It seemed to be caught in a current and was moving out silently into the centre of the dark lake. The dragons stood, quite still, like colossal statues, staring emptily after him. They grew slowly smaller until they were only glowing hieroglyphs against the distant wall while he was borne away further and further out into the blackness.

Swifter and swifter. He could feel the current beginning to tug, hear it sucking at the keel. But there was another sound, faint and undefined at first, now growing clearer. A trembling of the air growing to a thunder as the cavern closed in on him.

He was swept into a narrow tunnel and once more he was in total darkness, alone with the growing roar, deafening in the narrow space. Then out into a larger darkness, the sound broadening into a wider spectrum of terrible thunder. Suddenly he knew what it was. A waterfall, a huge and deadly waterfall, and he was rushing helplessly towards its brink!

Even as the thought struck him, the boat shot free into the throbbing blackness and he was thrown over onto his back. He cried out as for seconds the boat hung in nothingness, but he did not even hear his own voice. Then the boat hit the bottom, and Fal's world went out and was no more.

FOURTEEN

The day of Fal's disappearance from Rymon's cottage had been one of gloom for all those who remained there. To say the mistress was furious would do little to describe the dangerous heat of her anger and frustration. Slag had shrugged his shoulders. As far as he knew, he said, the harper had gone off by himself exploring; where, Slag did not know. True enough maybe, but Rymon was far from satisfied. Aurvang had withdrawn into himself and took no part in the long exchange of speculations and accusations. This was quite usual and attracted no attention. Twice Rymon had gone by herself into the mountain and stood, her hands pressed hard against the closed door, as if she expected it to burst open and bring her doom upon her. And the tension in the little community grew as before a storm. Even Ristilian stopped talking and went silently about her tasks. Sometimes she paused to look at Aurvang where he sat in the corner bunched up, listening. Work in the mountain had stopped.

"I wish I could listen," Ristilian thought with a sigh, "instead of always babbling. Perhaps then the harper would have liked me more and not gone away."

The only one who seemed unaffected was Osmarin, who continued cutting turves for the roof, a bland look on his face. But at moments of strain or crisis Ristilian never felt his serenity to be helpful. Her mother despised it, she knew. Yet she felt closer to her father than her mother, especially when she was alone with him up at the farm or on a journey. But this year, with the two dwarves around, it had been different; especially with Slag. He looked on Osmarin as a simpleton and was bold in not concealing his opinion. Not that her father cared. She sometimes wondered whether he even noticed. Many a time she had longed for him to speak out and defend himself. But what would it lead to? Perhaps he was right. If he had any reasons for behaving as he did and was not merely foolish, as Slag believed, they would be good reasons, she was sure of that. Yet it all made her more aware of her own loneliness.

How she longed to get away from Lune, from her mother's obsessive guardianship, as she called it, of a black, dead mountain. Back to Vond, maybe, or somewhere else where there were people. She doubted whether her father was in any way simple, but if he was, then her mother was crazy. It was easier to believe that. How could you guard a mountain when nobody else wanted it? And now she was going to give it to a couple of dwarves and crown one of them king of Lune! Crazy, that's what she was, totally crazy. She had been in the mountain today and come out muttering to herself. Then she had bolted the inner door of the larder, the one that led into the tunnel, as if she feared being drawn back into the dark. Perhaps the wits of anyone would crack if they spent their whole life up here in the Waste, she thought.

But by the third day everyone was returning to normal. Aurvang had stopped listening and had even suggested to Slag and Rymon that the work of clearing the dwarves' hall might continue. She had agreed with a shrug and left the inner door open when the dwarves went in. Ristilian watched the goats. She kept a look out for Sooty, too. The crow had disappeared on the same day as Fal and had not been seen since. She heard two ravens and the distant scream of an eagle, but no sign of Sooty. She was thus more watchful than usual and saw the traveller coming up the causeway long before he saw her. It was not Fal. Fal did not have a russet cloak, nor a white tunic; nor did he walk so briskly. And this stranger was golden haired and went bareheaded, his hood thrown back, as if in contempt of the chill which had settled over the land. And even before he spoke she knew she would die for him if need should ever call.

Ilmarin smiled sadly when she told him that only two days before Fal had gone off by himself and that they could only suppose he would soon return. And she reddened when Rymon and Osmarin, who had come out to meet the stranger, bade him enter and stay with them — as long as was his need.

When Rymon understood that her visitor was the master smith of the Delming she made a great fuss of him. And when she realized that he had travelled alone to Lune in search of his closest friend, she was angry with herself for not being more helpful to Fal and making more of him — instead of setting him to tend the goats.

Slag Battletooth asked him if he was then the new Lord Dringskel, whose family the dwarves of Vond had revered for generations. When Ilmarin agreed that Dringskel was the name by which the dwarfkin knew him, Slag and Aurvang bobbed up and down like buttercups in the wind; but soon the Listener looked troubled. At last he could bear it no longer.

"Lord Dringskel," the poor dwarf said glumly, "Aurvang is a listener and no talker; but if it's Master Falimbravel that you're seeking, you won't find him anywhere near Lune!"

"What!" cried Rymon, "you miserable... you stunted stinking little goat's dropping! You mean to say you know something of Master Fal and haven't told us?" She had leapt up from the table, the heavy copper soup ladle clutched murderously in her hand. Slag gasped. He had always known that the Lady Rymon had a dash of the battle-dragon in her blood. He hoped desperately that it would not come to blows in front of the Lord Dringskel. But Aurvang had his answer ready.

"Nay, lady," he said, resigned and glum, "I can tell little of him, except that he's far away — and that he sleeps! If he woke, I could listen to his story. But his sleep is deep and very dark, lady, there is nothing for Aurvang to hear."

"Good dwarf," said Ilmarin gently, "do you mean that he is dead?"

Aurvang sighed heavily. "Not dead, lord, though near to death maybe. Yet already he's been found by a friend who understands well the care of those in such a need."

"A friend?" snapped Rymon. "A friend of yours or a friend of his? What friend? Why do you always have to talk in these cursed hints and riddles? Say what you mean!"

"A friendly person, I mean. One of a friendly disposition, lady. I cannot say who it is, except it's someone I have never met. As long as Master Fal sleeps so deeply, I cannot tell. Nor can I hear where he is, only that it's far away — nor even how he got there." Aurvang glanced pathetically at Rymon, then at the other faces in the room. Even Osmarin was watching him with alert interest. Ilmarin smiled.

"If Fal lives, then I shall seek him," he said. "And as you're a listener, perhaps I could persuade your mistress to let you come with me for a while to help me in my search?"

Rymon smiled venomously. "An excellent plan," she hissed. "Though unfortunately, as long as Master Fal sleeps, our worthy dwarf isn't likely to be of much use to you, if his patchy explanations are anything to go by. And as Fal appears to be in good hands, perhaps my lord Ilmarin will do us the honour of accepting our hospitality for a space. In the meantime the dwarves can go on with their work." She cast a razor edged glance at the Listener. "My lord might like to see some of the ancient places which have been uncovered."

She smiled at Ilmarin, while Slag sighed audibly as the ladle was returned to the soup pot.

———

The next morning a solemn procession entered the hall of Lune. In the tunnel six lanterns swung to different lengths of stride through the darkness. In front, proudly leading the way, was Rymon, Osmarin at her side. Behind them their guest, the elven-smith, followed by Ristilian, her hair glinting as golden as his, eyes soft with love, a wrinkled dwarf on either side of her skirts. It was a festive moment for Rymon, a moment of which she hoped much. So did Ristilian, though if her hopes coincided with any of her mother's, she had no way of knowing it.

Ilmarin made admiring comments to the dwarves about the clearing of the hall and the restoration of the great table, but the procession was led on, and soon they stood around the golden mushroom.

No-one spoke. The smith did not need to touch it in order to feel its power or to perceive its ancient use. But he was pondering other things. What had Fal made of all this, and what had led him off secretly so nearly to meet his death? He needed to know more of these matters before he spoke. And he was puzzled, too, by this Mistress of Lune. He liked Osmarin and Ristilian and felt easy with them. But he touched on something hidden in Rymon which worried him, yet it was still too concealed to be named.

At last she could wait no longer. "What do you say, my lord? Is it not an ancient and rare treasure?" She tried to speak calmly, but Ilmarin caught the fever of anticipation just below the surface.

"Indeed, lady; yes, a treasure indeed," he said. He had seen what the table was; an instrument so structured and so placed as to focus the energies of the mountain, possibly of the whole Waste. But its centre was missing, the centre where the energy had been controlled and made available to the masters of this place. Missing, or maybe faded, he thought; for it had not been made of metal. As he looked he knew what it had been — and how it had been made. It was amazingly simple. Again he wondered what Fal had managed to discover.

Once more Rymon broke the silence, scarcely able to keep her impatience down. "Something is missing, wouldn't you say so, my lord?"

"The bowl is empty. Yes, something is missing," Ilmarin agreed. All five faces stared at him expectantly. He glanced at Ristilian, noticing how lovely she looked in the light of the lanterns. She caught her breath, nodded and smiled.

"Please help us, Master Ilmarin," she said.

"We have searched very carefully," said Slag, "most thoroughly; unless, of course, it lies behind the door." He glanced quickly at Rymon, expecting disapproval. But Aurvang came to his rescue.

"Not behind the door," he said. "Not here at all. Aurvang would hear it when he listens."

"Perhaps," Slag continued, relieved and encouraged, "perhaps it was not made of anything so permanent as metal or stone?"

Involuntarily, Ilmarin looked again at Ristilian. It bothered him to be so pressed and he needed to see whether she still looked as beautiful as she had two minutes before. She smiled and her eyes shone towards him.

"It was made of light," he said.

———

Long indeed was the sleep of Falimbravel through the cold white months of that winter, and anxious were the eyes that watched over him. Dreamless he slept, and if his mind wandered from his broken body, no knowledge of it remained with him. Only when the mending was nearly complete did he begin to mutter and groan in his sleep, and the old couple who nursed him nodded and smiled across at one another, for they knew the long battle of their labours was nearly won.

And then in his sleep he began to dream, and he was back in the caverns of Lune, by the lake, looking for his boat. Long he sought it, in and out of dream and troubled sleep, and always in vain.

Then at last to the shore of the dark water there came a dwarf, wildly dressed but with a golden circlet round his head as if he were a king. And it seemed to Fal that he was in an ill humour. His eyes were hard and black, and in his hand he carried a staff of shining black wood.

He stood and looked around but appeared not to notice Fal where he sat by the rocky beach, huddled up, miserable and utterly weary. Then the dwarf turned to the doorway through which once the dragons had come, demanding worship.

He struck the stone with his staff, a resounding blow which echoed like thunder in the depths of the vast cavern. Fire shot up around the gate and resolved itself into a burning, flickering script. Fal could not read it; indeed, he was too tired and resigned even to try. But the dwarf pointed at the flames and called out in a loud voice:

> Born he was mid ancient fires,
>   with us, with you;
> born his form of mighty sires,
>   like us, like you;
> to music of the heavenly choirs
>   slowly he grew;
> lost and damned in Fate's dark mires,
>   hollow, untrue.

Then he reached into his tunic and brought out a scroll. "Even as I thought," he cried. "The gateway proclaims it. And to this word I shall add another, and it is from the Portal of Chardec, where I am king. So shall the two words flow together and strengthen his condemnation."

Fal sighed as the wild king unrolled the parchment. He did not want to hear all this but could not find within himself the power to avoid it. Again the dwarf called out:

"And this gives cause to anger among us that, although born with us amid the fiery waters, he looks now upon the rivers and clouds, the lakes and torrents, and does not greet them as sister and brother; yea, as blood of his blood. While we, who live where form is slow or permanent revere them even as the eyes of our Lady, our Mother and Queen. Truly, man is a bane, to himself and to all. He remembers nothing, knows not who or where he is, yet grows ever more proud and harmful, powerful in destruction, while yet a prisoner to his own folly.

"You guardians of the burning arches, hearken: shall such a one pass here?"

Fal groaned. "It's not true, not true," he mumbled. "This is not a fair judgment."

The dwarf spun round. He had heard him. As if pronouncing a malediction he lifted the black staff and chanted in a monotone:

Fangs in the brain,
sting-tail in tongue,
giver of pain,
heart of dry dung,
betrayal in limb,
outcast of Earth,
dour and grim,
bringer of dearth:
Where are the crossroads,
where the choice?
Where now the shining one
with joy in his voice?

"Do you come only to accuse me?" cried Fal. "Do you bring no help? For help I need, not curses."

"Help can only come to you when you acknowledge the truth," shouted the wild king angrily. "So long as you wander, lost in your self-pity, no help can be given and none be found."

"Anything else?" said Fal miserably.

The king took a slim, leather-bound volume from his tunic and opened it. "Hear what the Oracles say of man:

"Day by day we shall see him growing in arrogance, congratulating himself on the cleverness of his ideas, on the detail of his observations be it of star or stone, of leaf or worm — and the idiotic interpretations into which the ravings of his brain have trapped him. He will live in a world of deceptions; yes, in the end he will create his own world utterly, a world of shadows and illusions. Then he will pass us by as but a dream of his infancy, while we see him stumbling ever further, as it were down a maze, a maze of mad mirrors."

"You can't believe this to apply to me," said Fal.

"It has begun to apply to you," shouted the dwarf, "to you and to all mankind. It must either be fulfilled or it must be prevented."

"How can it be a true oracle if you think it can be prevented?" said Fal, but he knew he was on dangerous ground. "It might be the destiny of the world to live through this terrible thing; who knows?"

The dwarf walked over and looked at him. His face looked less harsh and wild than from a distance, and there was a sadness in his eyes. Then, as Fal drifted into sleep again, the dwarf seemed to grow, beyond the cavern, beyond the world, beyond the stars.

———

He woke once more in an underground workshop. Everywhere he looked dwarves were busy: etching and engraving, polishing precious stones and metal, inlaying and hammering. He walked around looking first over this shoulder then over that. They were apparently too engrossed to notice him.

"I'm dreaming again," he said aloud. He felt happier about it this time. He even felt at home amid all this concentration and bustle. "I'm dreaming, you know," he said experimentally into the ear of a nearby craftsman. As he expected, there was no response. But his eye was caught by the tiny writing which had been engraved onto plates of gold. Six finished plates were laid out side by side while the dwarf was working on the seventh. It did not appear strange to Fal that he could read the script or that the words were of a language familiar to him. It seemed to be a story.

Suddenly, in one instant of vision, he knew that all these dwarves were working together preparing a book: inlaying illustrations with gold leaf and silver foil, preparing the leather binding, the boards and end-papers, ornamenting the clasps with a hundred wonderful jewels. The plates were for printing, and the writing ran backwards. He had failed to notice this at first glance. But far from being hard to read, he found that the words seemed to speak to him with a life of their own. He wondered what story it could be that was of such importance to these earnest craftsmen.

Already he had quite forgotten that he was dreaming and had begun to read the first plate:

'At this time many of the people of Chardec came to the west, even as far as the kingdom of Andravel, where the mountains were young and tall and full of grandeur. As craftsmen they came, teaching the art of writing with scripts and runes and the inlaying of them in flowing gold and copper. They would not work with silver or any other white metal, and for this and no other reason did they become known as the Red Dwarves. The name was well given, for, as was later discoverd, they had a wonderful knowledge of fire and flame, the like of which had never been seen. But these skills they would not teach.

'Yet they assisted Andravel in the Great Hunt; and it is mostly agreed that, although Andravel himself took more risk than any and himself succeeded in finding the caverns where Skelgrist dwelt, it is equally true that the mountains would never have become his and the dragon would never have left them without the help of the dwarves of Chardec.

'Then Varya sent to Andravel a gift of jewels: a round stone which shone by night or day alike with silver moonlight and with the gentle colours of the moon-rainbow; and with it three times twelve sapphires of deepest, clearest blue. It was reckoned to be a handsome and royal gift, worthy of a king newly come into a great kingdom, and worthy too of so godly a queen as she who gave it.

'He took the Moonstone and the dark sapphires and went aside with them into his halls. The one stone he laid in the middle of a table and worked long, laying the sapphires about it, till they made a pattern which he deemed perfect. Thereafter he sat long again, absorbed in contemplating what he had done. And when at last he arose he appeared to his ministers and to those others who had been waiting there much grown in wisdom. He had become solemn, and they stood in awe of him.

'Then one of them suggested that the jewels might be set thus in a shield of gold, but Andravel shook his head and swept the stones together. His ministers feared that they had given offence, but Andravel was not angry. He went aside again and sought new patterns, saying that the stars had many gateways, each leading to a different land. "For still it is in my mind to be a wanderer," he said, "though not maybe of the same kind as were our forefathers. This is now our kingdom; yet the mind seeks wisdom and will gather it wherever it is to be found."

'But Skelgrist came upon them suddenly, seeking his revenge, and he took Andravel and with him the jewels. And many of his subjects fled, to the north and to the south; and those that were left of the Red Dwarves returned to their own country.

'Thus passed another age, until, during the kingship of Laurin, the tree-maker came, even Bailor, who was neither dwarf nor elf; nearer, maybe, to the elves he was, yet beloved and claimed by the dwarves.

'Bailor sought out Skelgrist. Alone he went and without fear; and being neither furtive nor over bold in his approach he walked before it and gazed long and in silence into its face.

'If the dragon made any attempt to daunt him, he did not feel it, for though as but an ant before a bull in outer strength, there was no weakness in his mind where any attack could have taken hold.

'"Do you come to bore me with requests from the little people? Then you come in vain," it said, "for I will not listen. My mind is too full of thoughts far beyond your understanding. But, if you like, tell your king this: the time comes when I shall go, and with me many of my kind wherever they hold power. They shall let you take the things of the earth into your own keeping. But it will be a matter of less joy to you than you imagine. Look only for despair, disappointment, and a bane greater than all that has been before.

'"And on this too your king may ponder: that when man is ready, as soon he will be, we shall relinquish our ancient paths and enter into him, merging with him body and soul. Then shall he grow in influence from us and we from him, and you may at last face an enemy so terrible that you will long and plead for the old days when we guarded your treasures and kept them safe, even granting you, from time to time, a glimpse of our magnificence."

'Now when King Laurin heard Bailor's tale and the prophecy that had been given him, he grew silent, and it seemed to many that he was afraid and all the heart had gone out of his kingship. But he said it was not so, only he was pondering after his own fashion the dragon's words and seeking counsel in his thoughts.

'Then Laurin went out from the deep caverns and dwelt up above, high upon the mountain, whence he could see far into the world. And there he built a pattern of great stones and studied by their aid the stars for many years and lives of men. Solitary he became and ever more reluctant even so much as to visit the halls that lay in the earth. And he set at last Bailor to rule in his stead. Even then he claimed not to be shedding responsibility but rather to be accepting more. Some thought him crazed with age, but others, seeing the starlight in his eyes, held their peace and did him homage.

'Around his standing stones, on the high lonely greensward, Laurin planted a garden of roses. By day he tended them, year after year, talking to every bud and every opening leaf. Even amid the winter's snows he spoke with them and told them of humankind and of the need which was then yet to come.

Alone by night he watched the wheeling stars, which, it is said, opened themselves ever more to him, speaking of the mysteries which later are to be expounded in this book. And Laurin told Bailor the purpose of that garden, for he said that if evil would seek entry into man then goodness too must be offered him; and the silent red of the roses would contend with the dark dragon's blood, if man would accept the gift, and the dragon's might could be changed to wisdom and into a power for the good.

'And behold, as the ages passed and the stars changed, all the stone of those mountains became flushed with pink as the rose-red sought its way out into the hearts of men and women in the world beyond.

'But at last Laurin died, and a simple mound was made for his body amid his standing stones. Upon its portal were carved the simple words: Laurin, Watcher of the Stars.

'Anything else would have exceeded the wishes which he had entrusted to Bailor. But, in the greatest of the halls below, Bailor had made a tree of copper with a wealth of branches and broad leaves. It was gilded with red gold, and in its trunk were set copies of the Moonstone of Andravel and its many sapphires, clustered like the stars around the moon. And on the thousand leaves were inscribed all the teachings of the Watcher, the many stories which he told of the stars, and their meanings.

'"This wisdom will one day be needed by the Earth against her perishing," Bailor told the many small people that came to look in wonder at the Tree. "The Earth hears it and ponders upon it. Its memory shall not fade."

'Now when all this labour of the making of the Tree was completed and when its lore had been learned, and Bailor saw that the people had begun to grow in wisdom, he went again to the forbidden cavern. But, as he had expected, Skelgrist was not there, nor was there any sign that the dragon had entered that place for a long time.

'Then Bailor called the people before the Tree and spoke to them: "The dragon has gone from Laurin's halls, and I do not think that it will return. And you must choose from among you a king, for I can stay with you no longer. I have protected you, and you have been my friends, but I am not of your people; and, though friendship shall ever be between us, I must go and I must tread the paths that men tread, for I must seek your foe — the dragon, who is my foe, too."

'Then were the dwarves overcome with sorrow, for they loved Bailor dearly. And they begged him to tarry yet one year more, that they could choose their new king without haste and also prepare for Bailor's departure in ways that were worthy of their friendship.

'When Bailor consented they were very glad, and with a will they cleaned the hall where Skelgrist had dwelt, and made new feasting tables for it, that they could feast both their new king and Bailor before he went.

'And out of the bones of ancient dragons that Skelgrist had in ages past overcome and left as trophies in his hall, they wrought gifts for Bailor that he would not forget them. And when he smiled and said he would never forget, the elders became solemn and said that the ways of all humans would lead through deep forgetfulness, but that these tokens he would find ever and again beside him, albeit in different forms, and because of them he would at last remember.

'"I thank you — dear, good people — and though I deem your gifts unnecessary, I take them gladly and will treasure them as my very Self."

'"Even so it is intended," they said, and smiled.'

FIFTEEN

When at last Fal aroused out of his deep slumber, the awakening was long and slow. Dreams flowed within dreams, dreams of endless meaning and dreams of no meaning, dreams memorable and utterly elusive. Gone were the nightmares which had ended in his escape from Lune, gone even the greyness of the Waste; for now his mind was filled with landscapes of rare colour, with people kind and generous.

He smiled where he lay, and sighed. Into his dreams, at first from a distance, then nearer and stronger, came a voice. It was old, almost fragile, yet clear and lovely; and sometimes another voice sang, or perhaps hummed with it, softer and deeper. It was like the humming of bees. Gradually, as he came closer to full awakening, he began to listen to the words. This is what he heard:*

> The past you had forgotten
>   is growing every day,
> Through castles wrought of silverstone
>   and their dragon schools at play;
> To the greening of the golden world,
>   the young sun's rainbow land,
> To the vales the elves still call their own,
>   where fire-mountains stand.
>
>> Ride with the elf-queen
>>   out on the breeze,
>>   dance with a magic
>>   swarm of bees!
>> Oh, come with me!
>>   Come with me!
>
> In the mountains there are serpent paths
>   still hidden from your sight;
> Yet even the fierce giant kings
>   know dawn will end the night.
> The spirit of the rising sun
>   who is your oldest friend
> Will come again to touch your eyes
>   and make the long night end.

* For musical accompaniment, see Appendix, page 322.

> Ride with the elf-queen
> out on the breeze,
> dance with a magic
> swarm of bees!
> Oh, come with me!
> Come with me!

With the last chorus he rolled over onto his side, to face the source of the singing, and opened his eyes. He saw the two most extraordinary creatures he had ever imagined or known to exist. They were terribly old and thin, almost dwarflike, but with impossibly long, slender faces, very wrinkled and yet childlike. He blinked, trying to clear his vision. Were those really their eyes? They were unbelievable: large, oval and elvish, completely dark brown or black, but out of all conceivable proportion. They seemed to take up half of the pointed faces! Everything else about them was at first insignificant in comparison. The woman — it was she who had been doing most of the singing — had silvery-white hair, in two long hanging plaits, like a girl's. The man was bald, with mere wisps of hair on the sides of his head. Their ears were large and pointed.

They sat on either side of a leaded window set with thousands of fragments of thin white quartz, through which the sun glowed, and they were both looking at him intently. The man rose on thin, frail-looking limbs and walked over to where Fal lay. When he spoke, his voice had the warm, humming quality which Fal had heard in the song.

"I am Vigg, and this is my lady, Silfrintopp. Be welcome to us awake as in slumber you have already been this many a week past!"

Fal lay looking at this strange but gentle creature but was unable to speak. He was more used to dreaming now than to reality and found the will to form words lacking. Vigg smiled.

"Your dreams have been full of healing," he said. "But that is all past. Now you'll need food of a different kind. Come, wife, let's see if our guest can sit up against his pillows."

Fal struggled onto his elbows, but found he needed help to raise himself. "I am greatly in your debt," he managed to say. "I thank you."

Silfrintopp hurried off and came back at once with bread and honey. There was apple juice to drink, but he was only allowed to sip carefully to begin with. The food was delicious, full of sunlight, Fal thought, but he did not feel particularly hungry. He felt dazed and very contented; the pillows were soft, and he began to doze. With an effort he pulled himself back to wakefulness, but Vigg said, "That's good, sleep again. It will only be for an hour or two this time. And when you wake, you'll be feeling hungry. We shall leave the food by your side."

Fal slept at once and woke without dreams. He was alone and, though the food stood ready, he felt too lazy to do more than appreciate the smell and sight of it. The sun still shone through the crystal window and it drew his attention. He wondered whether the fragments of stone were arranged in a pattern or just laid haphazardly. Certainly the larger pieces were near the top, which was pointed, and the whole window was shaped something like a beech leaf. The sun glistened, and the white stones danced like snowflakes. They swirled and spiralled, then joined together. They were summery clouds in a still and distant sky. They broke again into a million raindrops flashing with colours as each took the sun's spectrum and glittered wildly in a stormy shower. The colours leapt together and a rainbow arched triumphantly across the turbulant sky.

He shook his head to free himself from the illusion and was rewarded by a piercing, iron-heavy pain. He put his hands to his head and felt for the first time the bandages. He frowned, trying to remember what had happened, but for the moment the many dreams and the wonder of the crystal window were too close and too absorbing. He must try to wake up. He also began to feel very hungry. Vigg had said he would. There was food and drink — fresh, clear apple juice. Who was Vigg?

"Where am I?" he said, half aloud. He looked around the room. There were furnishings, all carved of applewood, and a hearth with a sweet-smelling log fire. The walls were solid rock, but very clean and smooth, though at several places tree-roots came in. They looked as though they had been neatly trained down the wall to the floor, where they disappeared again. The window must be in a cliff, then. The roots had been cleaned and polished and made into a useful feature of the furnishings, for here and there they had pegs in them from which all manner of objects hung: shears, scissors, and trowels, all shiny and bright, a pestle and mortar, spoons and bowls, and platters, like the one from which he now ate. And there were musical instruments, a flute, a many-stringed fiddle and bow, and a large harp, standing on the floor. He wondered where his own harp was, for of that there was no sign. Nor were his clothes anywhere to be seen; he wore a linen nightgown, which his hosts must have provided, though it would have been huge for them.

He swung his legs down from the bed. It did not feel too bad. There were slippers, like two big puffs of thistledown, which fitted his feet perfectly as he wriggled his toes into them. The floor was covered with rushes, not strewn, but neatly woven into mats.

He stood up with determination and, feeling none the worse for the sudden effort, padded over to examine the window. The pieces of trans-lucent stone were unsmoothed and, though thin, of varying thickness. He could see the design now and could also see why he had been unable to discover it before. He had made the mistake of studying the lead outlines, whereas the pattern made by the stones came from their thickness and the varying amount of light they let in from the world outside. The darker pieces were arranged in a line down the centre and in veins running upwards and outwards from it. So the window really was a leaf, but a white leaf... or was it pale green?

He stepped back to look at the whole shape again. For a moment it seemed to tremble, as if hanging in the air, so full of sunlight now that its own green colour had been brightened almost beyond the point where the eye can grasp it. Then it was a rose-petal, of a delicate pink like the freshest summer sunrise.

The door clicked. It was the old lady. She brought a little crusty pie standing like a rocky island in a shallow sea of golden honey. It smelt wild and delicious.

"There," she said, "I knew it would go quickly once you'd eaten some of old Silfrintopp's bread! Come and sit down by the fire, young master, and try this apple-pie."

It really was delicious. He could not remember ever having eaten food which so thrilled the whole body with pleasure at every mouthful. And there was more apple-juice.

"I was looking at the window," he said. "Is it in the form of a leaf?"

"Sometimes it's a leaf, when it's not bothering to be anything else. Yet we're not really people of leaf, nor of root!" She smiled and nodded at the growing rack of pegs. "We're friends of the air, of sun, cloud, and wind. But while the snow lies and the frost is master of the land, we live where it's safe and snug."

He found her gaze strangely embarrassing. Perhaps she was aware of it for she turned away to pour him some more juice. As she moved, her gown rippled, as if carried by a breeze. It was of fine white linen, and he saw that it was embroidered with butterflies, moths, bees and dragonflies, with swifts and swallows, but so faded that many of them were hard to make out.

"You've told us nothing of yourself," she said. With a shock he realized that, unless he had talked in his sleep, they probably knew nothing of him, not even his name.

"Forgive me, lady," he said, "my head's still half full of dreams, and this strange house is like one of them. My name is Fal, and I'm a harper of the Delming. But how I come to be here I don't know, for behind all the dreams lies darkness, and I fear to probe too far into it."

"My husband will tell you how you came here, Master Fal," she smiled, "for that is part of his story."

Vigg had entered the room behind an armful of apple-logs, which he added to the stack beside the hearth. Even standing he was no higher than Fal, who was seated on a stool.

"Our guest is called Fal, husband," said Silfrintopp. "He is a harper from the Delming. He wonders how he got here," she prompted.

"Well then, Master Fal," Vigg began, "of your journeyings before you came to us I can tell you nothing, but very likely you'll soon remember them for yourself. As to your manner of arrival, it was by boat, a carved boat with neither sail not oar. It caught in the rushes where I was cutting them down at the river, for in our household rushes are needed for many things. A crow was there as well, riding on the prow. He looked very worried and kept hopping around until we got you up to the house. Then he flew off. We haven't seen him since."

"He was a pet crow," said Fal, "but he didn't belong to me."

He was remembering Rymon's cottage now, and the two dwarves; but Lune was still a darkness to him. He frowned and stared blankly before him. Vigg hummed a little then said, "You were holding a fine harp, your arms folded above it — to keep it safe, I expect. We decided to put it away till you awoke. A fine harp, a beautiful thing!" He went across to a large cupbaord, built into the corner, and opened it with a wooden latch. There on a shelf was his harp-case together with his belongings, all of which had been washed and neatly folded.

"Leave them there till you need them!" said Silfrintopp. "But you're looking quite pale again, Master Fal; you'd best return to bed. Don't overdo things to begin with — and the sun is setting, I see!"

Fal couldn't see, for the window was as bright as ever, and wondered how she knew. But he did as he was told, and the old couple left him in peace again.

As Silfrintopp had said, it soon began to darken; and as he drifted into sleep he watched the crystal window turn into the round face of the moon, huge and near, as if it floated there within the room, watching over his bed.

———

The next morning he felt stronger and decided to dress in his own clothes, though he kept the thistledown slippers on, for they were soft and warm. There was toasted bread and a steaming tea of wild herbs for breakfast, with ducks' eggs, soft-boiled and as golden as suns. His hosts were pleased both with his appetite and his appearance and thought he was well enough to look round their house.

The door from his room led first into the kitchen, from which opened three more doors, two of them into a warren of little chambers and tunnels, mostly used for storing apples and grain, and very dark. There was only one crystal window, and what few other openings there were to the outside world had shutters or rush curtains to keep out the cold. Here and there Vigg opened the shutters, and wherever he did so, bright sunshine streamed in.

He had fetched Fal's cloak and boots and said, "It's not too cold outside today. Put these on and come to the kitchen door. Let's see what the weather's like!"

The sun shone dazzlingly on the snow, and at first Fal was confused by the sudden onslaught of light and the cold, fresh air. He took a deep breath and smiled. In front of the door stood a row of beehives, like upside-down baskets, closely woven of rushes. Then began the apple trees, black still at the end of winter and spreading on all sides as far as the eye could see. The orchard was a veritable forest, but spacious and well tended, containing both young and ancient trees. Nowhere were they planted in rows but grew freely, each taking up as much space as its size required.

Between the dark trunks the crisp snow sloped away down the hillside, and since the sun stood a little to his left, he reckoned that they must be facing south. He wondered what lay beyond the orchard. How far was he from Aurëlund, from the Delming?

"The snow still lies thick," said Vigg, "but spring is not so far away. Swifts are getting ready for the journey now and geese are already on their way. You can see them in the window, maybe." He gave Fal a slightly mischievous smile. "Bees sleep longer than harpers," he said, "but they are stirring. They sing to each other of the coming of spring. Come and listen!" He put his ear to one of the hives. Fal bent down and followed suit. There was a gentle murmur, an awakening throb of activity.

"Hearts beat faster as the year begins to dream," said Vigg and hummed thoughtfully. But Silfrintopp called out from the kitchen, "Bring that young man in here out of the snow, husband; the swallows aren't here yet. Come and have some hot apple-juice!"

A wooden trough stood by the kitchen door, its ice thawed with warm water. Two black and white ducks dabbled happily in it.

"It will not freeze any more now," said Vigg; "the sun will do the rest."

In the late afternoon Silfrintopp declared it was time for music and began tuning her harp; while Vigg took down the broad, many-stringed fiddle that hung on the roots. The tuning was in some ways similar to that of the music of Slag and Aurvang, but the intervals had a wildness which Fal was unable to account for. Their songs were mostly about the seasons of the year, of growing and ripening, and they always seemed to have the hum of insects and the flutter of leaves or feathers in them. At times they sang of the Lady and Queen who came to them again in the spring, who came as an honoured friend and guest of their orchards. Fal mentioned Estera, and they nodded and smiled. So he sang some of her songs from the Delming, and the old couple became serious and wide-eyed. He was reminded of little Amba, the dwarf maid, and wondered how much his friends were worried at his absence through the long, hard winter.

Silfrintopp said she would gladly learn some of his songs of Estera, and Fal said he would very much like to learn some of their songs, too, and asked about the tuning which was strange to him. So it was agreed that on the next day they would begin giving each other music lessons, that the last days of winter should be of more joy and profit to them all.

———

That night he thought of the geese winging their way high above the snow. He looked at the window and, as if obeying his thought, the stones shifted in the moonlight and resolved into a landscape of hills and crags, crisp and silvery under the stars. He strained his eyes, trying to discover a line of geese moving acros the sky. He could see none. But dark shadows moved over the snow and drifted towards him. Heavy, maned wolves of the northern-most Waste they were, eyes shining yellow as they walked silently into the room and, so it seemed, passed by his bed and on into the night. Fal was himself wandering or floating over the Waste with them and watched as they joined others, already sitting rank upon rank in the snow, staring towards the distant forest, towards the south.

"She has not yet come! She has not come, she whom you await!" he cried. But already he was dreaming and slipped into a deep sleep.

The next morning, as he awoke, he at last remembered Lune and what he had met there. He remembered his failure and his escape, the darkness and the roar of the waterfall. But the horror of it had passed and the memories showed themselves calmly to him. And he remembered his quest and wondered what part his passing through the dragon maze of Lune should play in it.

———

He asked his hosts about Lune, and they listened quietly as he told them the whole story, from the entering of the upper maze to the plunging cataract below. He confided his thoughts to them about the nature of the balance between the two monsters.

Silfrintopp said, "To meet them so close, and as such a challenge, is surely a very great event in your story and so must surely be an important part of your quest. But really they are everywhere, those two. Are they not in life and death, in summer and winter, in sun and moon? They are in every living thing, in root and blossom, in blood and bone."

"Yet to confront them as you did is to struggle with them as part of yourself," said Vigg. "To learn to keep the balance there, that is a long path, longer than from the Forge to Gelmindel!"

Silfrintopp smiled very gently, and her kindness flowed into Fal like the warmth of a soft summer breeze.

"But how was it that I found my boat there, by the dark lake?" he cried, for that part of his story was still very dreamlike.

"Lune gives to each man his own nature," said Vigg, "or offers it at least. You did very well to accept the offer, and in so far your trials in the mountain were not a failure at all."

"But the boat!" Fal objected. "How could it have been standing waiting for me? Anyway, it would have soon rotted, floating untended in the water. And it was *my* boat!"

"Wife," said Vigg with a smile, "our guest looks well this morning, and the sun is warm. Shall we not take him for a walk down to the river? It will do him good to breathe the fresh air. The snow's begun to thaw, too."

"It will do us all good," said Silfrintopp. "But put on your boots, Fal."

Those slippers we made for you are not snow-shoes!"

———

The orchard was full of the exciting sounds which tell that winter is ending: trickling and gurgling under the snow, dripping and plopping as branches freed themselves to feel the sun again, and a robin scattering its silvery music. Here and there, where the snow had already grown patchy, crocuses were beginning to appear.

Vigg hummed to himself, muttering something which sounded like "dearly, dearly; nearly, nearly!" — or it may just have been the imitation of a bird song.

At the bottom of the orchard they came to a wall and a doorway. The two halves of the door had a wooden bar across them. Vigg lifted it up and flung them open.

"There!" he said. "That's gone! And here's the river."

Outside, where the land was lower and there were no trees to cast shadows, the snow had nearly all vanished. It was a marsh of grass and rushes through which the river swept, a growing, milky white flood hurrying eastwards.

"He'll rise more yet," said Silfrintopp. "The full thaw won't have begun in the Waste, not till the orchard lies bare."

"You wouldn't have got caught in the rushes today," said Vigg.

"You'd have ended up in the sea! Look, we pulled the boat right up to the wall, along here."

Soon, amidst a few last patches of snow, they found the outlines of a boat. Only a few rotting timbers were left to sketch the gunwales and ribs; of the planks only traces of spongy black wood, like the flesh of decaying mushrooms, discoloured and ground.

Fal stared in blank amazement, speechless, but Vigg said, "It is as I thought. The gift was all offered and all accepted. Of the husk little remains. Do you still think it was your boat?"

"Not the boat I had at the Forge maybe," said Fal uncertainly. "This was darker anyway. Yet..."

"Come," Vigg laughed, "Forget this now. Of such boats you have still a store in hand, and the boat at the Delming will be all the more yours because of your choosing at the dark lake!"

But there was a sudden movement in the sky.

"They are coming, they are coming!" cried Silfrintopp. "Welcome, dear ganders, good mothers, come!"

A wedge of powerful grey geese came hurtling down towards them and landed with a great noise of splashing and honking in the reedy shallows of the river. At once, they climbed out and began running, necks and yellow bills outstretched, gaggling and clamouring, towards the three watchers. Fal stood quite still amid all the commotion, while the two old ones leaped and danced with joy among them. They seemed to be singing something, but the sound of it was lost in the deafening noise as wedge after wedge arrived and joined in the honking, screeching throng. Suddenly, it all stopped and the geese, now in their hundreds, began rooting around for turf between the sedges.

"These are but the first!" said Silfrintopp, her dark, child's eyes wide with joy. "Many, many more are coming to help us welcome the spring."

_____

The world was busy with its preparations, and the excitement was everywhere; yet still the good time had not come, and much of Fal's days was spent in learning the music of the Old Ones of the Air, as they liked to be called.

Silfrintopp learned the music of the harpers' school quickly and effortlessly, but Fal had much more trouble in mastering the strange melodies of their songs. Every interval was a bit larger or smaller than his ears wanted to call 'in tune', and Vigg would not be satisfied with 'a bit'. Each interval would only speak of its true nature, he explained, when it was exactly itself, no more, no less. Often, Fal could just not hear what Vigg asked him to hear, and the old one was an unrelenting task master. But, at last, his ears began to distinguish, and his heart discover, what Vigg was teaching him, until, after many days, the old one began to nod and smile and hum as Fal sang and plucked the strings which he had spent hours tuning.

"You have learned much," Silfrintopp beamed. "My husband is a strict and thorough musician and very hard to please. Now you'll be able to hear the robin and thrush, blackbird and nightingale as they really are, not in the blurred and jumbled way that humans usually hear them."

"He has done better than I'd have thought possible," said Vigg. "If you wish, Fal, I'll teach you some melodies which will give you knowledge of the mysteries of the air: to calm storm and quicken rainbow, ripen fruit and harden nut. There's another tune, too, which has long been forgotten by your people. My heart tells me it's time these things were learnt again."

And so began another course of rigorous instruction, culminating in music which gave Fal a new mastery over his boat of patterns; not in the water, for that art was already his, but in the air. "So that your boat shall move freely according to your will and skill," as Vigg put it.

But spring was now close upon them, and the night that the instruction was completed the crystal window burst into a forest full of flowers: first of snowdrops, then crocuses, then a sea of daffodils, tossing and rippling in the breeze. Among them walked a girl, her hair flowing long and free as she scattered blessings all around her as a sower scatters seed. Her dress seemed woven of fresh green leaves and daises and she wore a crown of primroses. Nutbrown squirrels leapt around her as she went, making a path straight towards Fal. She held out her hands as if entreating him to join her and laughed, and the squirrels capered and skipped at the sound of it.

"Come!" she said. "Come, Fal, spring is here!"

———

He awoke with the sun streaming in through the stone window and knew at once that the house was empty. The fires had been allowed to go out, both where he slept and in the kitchen. The sound of a pipe playing wildly came through the kitchen window. He didn't pause to look. He dressed hurriedly and rushed out into the garden.

The whole orchard was in blossom, like a sea of snow bedecking the branches; leaves were unfurling everywhere, and the air was full of bees! Vigg was playing the pipe, and both he and Silfrintopp were dancing in and out of the trees, round and round, back and forth. Every trunk was being encircled and beswirled as they danced like whirlwinds, weightlessly, tirelessly, at a tremendous speed, round and round the orchard. In the choruses Vigg stopped blowing the pipe and joined in the singing.

> When the wind is blowing showers
>   from the Eastern Sea in spring,
> When the swallows come a-nesting
>   from the South on tireless wing,
> When the primrose and the daffodil
>   their eyes are opening,
> Then the orchard's full of blossom
>   and the bees begin to sing.
> All the bees begin a-dancing
>   in the paths of mother sun,
>   every busy, buzzy bee
>   does a merry dance of glee,
> Making honey, gold and runny,
>   is the sunshine people's fun
> When the orchard's full of blossom
>   and the springtime has begun!
>
> When the snow has turned to water
>   and the frost has lost its sting,
> When the hills are all resounding
>   with the thrush's summoning,
> When the elves bring back our Lady,
>   gladsome mistress of the spring,
> Bees will serve her and observe her,
>   this their queen who has no king.
> All the bees begin a-dancing
>   in the paths of mother sun,
>   every busy, buzzy bee
>   does a merry dance of glee,

Making honey, gold and runny,
   is the sunshine peoples's fun
When the orchard's full of blossom
   and the springtime has begun!

Dragonflies go zooming backwards,
   moonlight moths go spiralling,
Hither-thither, fox cubs squeaking,
   grunting bears dance in a ring,
Flying straight, the cuckoo's calling,
   back from distant wandering,
Vigg and Silfrintopp dance criss-cross
   when their trees are burgeoning!
All the bees begin a-dancing
   in the paths of mother sun,
      every busy, buzzy bee
      does a merry dance of glee,
Making honey, gold and runny,
   is the sunshine people's fun
When the orchard's full of blossom
   and the springtime has begun!

When every tree had been drawn into the weaving patterns and the dance was over, the two old ones came leaping back to the house. They were full of excitement, but not even slightly out of breath as Silfrintopp said, "Now, Fal, it has all begun again! Let's have breakfast together, and then you must follow the Lady's beckoning and continue your journey."

They sat at a narrow table by the edge of the orchard. There was stewed apples and honey, with large chunks of wheat bread, and cold herb tea. Silfrintopp had packed a bag with a liberal supply of bread, apples, and boiled ducks' eggs.

When he was ready to go, Vigg said, "Master Fal, this was a good time together, and before you begin thanking us for it, let us thank you, for we've enjoyed it greatly. Come to us again when you will; use the music you've learned here to find us, else you could wander for years in these hills and pass even within a yard of our front door and still you wouldn't see it! I found you this first time, but the next time you will find us. Those who are not invited never come to Vigg and Silfrintopp, not man nor dwarf, neither elf nor beast."

They told him to go south and a little west, taking the old forest track from ruined Gavelburg to Lunt Farm; then south, skirting Hallin Forest but not entering it, for the keepers of Hallin do not welcome wanderers. Then he would strike the River Westway, which would lead him across towards the Ironway and Gopley.   There were no dangers worth mentioning to one of his skills, Vigg said, but he should not linger nor should he allow himself to get involved with other folk's affairs.

And so at last Fal said his thanks and was escorted to the stepping stones of the Mirrorwend, where they exchanged farewells. Vigg hummed a little and Silfrintopp sang a blessing as he walked the giant stones, yet when he turned to greet them one last time from the other bank, the reeds were empty and there was no sign of them.

Only bees hummed around him and a mistle thrush sang.

SIXTEEN

The familiar chatter of the little waterfall was crisp and white in a shaft of moonlight. It glittered in all the colours of the rainbow as she moved. Copper-bright eyes blinked from the darkness of the silent forest, and the vixen longed to dash out and join in the game, but she did not dare... not yet. An owl glided low, clicking his beak in annoyance, and floated on into the dark.

The three children seemed to be playing with the moonbeams, leaping over the glistening stones as the silvery light flashed out to catch them. They laughed silently, they were part of the forest. It was more of a dance than a game, though to the vixen and the moonlight the two are the same.

Fireflies came to join in, expert in the dances of summer nights, careful to keep away from the cold, wet spray. The vixen's eyes sparkled with the thought of snapping at them. Yet the children were more interesting. A fox can run after fireflies, but only children enjoy both chasing and being chased.

Look at them! Round and round, over the water, behind the rocks, never stumbling. She wagged her tail happily. If she chased them, perhaps they would try to nip her tail as her mother had done! She would see; no harm could come of it. She began gliding through the shadows towards them. Then she flattened her whole body to the ground, pressing her throat hard on a stone. A woman was coming, *the* woman, the one who looked after the children. She glared sternly, she was going to spoil it, she always spoilt it. She took two of them by the hand and the game stopped. The third followed on behind.

The moonbeams seemed to steady and the fireflies returned to the forest; the people disappeared down the path. Only the owl was glad, and the vixen's eyes followed him closely as he circled the clearing, reclaiming it as his own.

Feather sat up and stretched. A little grey light filtered into her attic room, but it was still silent outside. It was time to be up and begin milking. She must have fallen asleep again and been dreaming; yes, dreaming — of her childhood, of Hallin, the forest of dark trees. She remembered the waterfall, but she had never seen the fox. And who was the third child?

She sighed, got up and went to the window. There was still no colour in the fields, the grass was all wet and grey. Strange! There was an old dog-fox digging for mice, poking his nose hard under the turves. She could hear him snorting to get the mice to move.

She dressed and went down the narrow staircase. The boards cracked and groaned. She knew why she had dreamed of Hallin. Fal was walking towards its eaves. At last he was on his way. It would not be long now.

Alone among his friends, Feather had never lost sight of him. She had followed his journey in the battered boat, she had seen Vigg drag it out of the icy water, and she had seen the wolves under the moon. She had watched — with sadness, and with joy. And she had danced with the Old Ones when the apple trees blossomed. Now she need not watch so often. She would look in the mirror later in the morning.

There were only six milking cows at the farm at present, so they would not take long. Then she would clean the pony stables, come in for breakfast, and begin making the cheese from yesterday's cream. As usual, Nonney, the cat, accompanied her.

They walked over to the byre together. No-one else was about. Gulmer and Tim had gone down to Brideswell, trading; the cow-hands, Crombel and Pombel, were a day's ride away inspecting herds. They would be away for another day or two, and Feather was enjoying the luxury of having the farm to herself.

Nonney shook the dew from her back and rubbed against Feather's legs purring. That's good! The cat had been behaving oddly lately. Feather opened the door to the cow shed and bent down to fondle the cat's head. But instead of going into the byre Nonney sat down on the doorstep and stared out across the fields. When Feather tried to touch her again she growled like a dog and would not move.

"Now, what's upset you, old lady?" said Feather consolingly. But she frowned and followed the cat's gaze towards the south. The dark cone of the Gop stood out against the grey dawn, its crown of forest black and impenetrable. Was something wrong with Tim or Gulmer? She did not think so. She would surely be quicker than Nonney to sense anything of that sort. She could use the mirror, but she felt certain it was not necessary. But the cat was spreading a mood of uneasiness.

It was not the first time that Feather had been left in charge of the farm. And cows were the most reassuring of companions.

"That's what the world needs," Gulmer had said when they had come to Gopley and established the farm, "herds of cows: calm, warm cows, right in the middle of things. There's more wisdom in a cow chewing the cud on a meadow than there is in all the schools of Vond, you mark my words. That's what they need up there in Vond, cows!"

They at any rate were behaving normally. They greeted Feather in chorus, shattering the stillness of the dawn. Nonney went in and began her morning inspection. As usual she prowled the length of the byre, lingering in the darker corners to read the chronicle of the night's events. The comings and goings of mouse, beetle, and cricket were her especial concern. Only when she was certain that nothing exceptional had occurred would she give her mind to the solemn business of watching and approving the passing of milk from udder to bucket.

But today she seemed to be watching not Feather's fingers but her face.

"You certainly are out to keep an eye on me today," said Feather.

Nonney stared. Feather's hands worked firmly on, but her mind gradually slipped into a dream. The cat's yellow eyes seemed to grow very earnest. They grew larger and larger, engulfing her, burning her, yet her fingers went on moving to the same rhythm with a will of their own.

Then the cat and the cow were gone. In their place a woman stood before her. She was proud and clear featured, not young, no, yet not old, but very strong. She wore a gown of the colours of flame, embroidered perhaps with many emblems, though they seemed imbued with life and flowed, twining and knotting into ever changing shapes around her. Red, too, was her hair which swept up as if the fire of her garment had grown to a whirlwind about her head. Her lips were smiling, but her eyes were cold with the blue of deep ice.

The vision faded, and for a moment Feather saw only the smooth, red flank of the cow she had been milking — how long before? Her hands hung limply by her side. And a loud whining sound was coming from the cat. Nonney was facing the open door, fluffed out bigger than Feather would have thought possible, and she was swearing, as cats do before a fight.

"Just what is going on today!" cried Feather. Nonney ran out with her, still yowling threats at an unseen enemy. They rounded the corner and came into view of the house. A silver-grey horse stood quietly on the grass, its bridle hanging loose. The house-door was open, and in the shadow beyond it something moved. Frowning, Feather stepped forward, but at the same moment the visitor came out towards her. The cat spat.

It was the woman of her vision, of that there was no doubt. But her hair was tied on top of her head, and she wore a black cloak which reached to the ground. In her hand she carried a small flat object of shiny silver.

"You cannot have that!" Feather's voice rang strong and clear. "That is the gift of Kereoma. It doesn't belong to you."

The woman had swung herself onto the horse and sat smiling down at her. "The gift of Kereoma will serve me at least as well as it has served you, I think," she said quietly, "and if not, then the knowledge that you can no longer use it to meddle in other people's affairs will have to be a second best." She spoke with a sweet friendliness and nodded. But at that moment Nonney leaped into action. She sprang at one of the horse's front legs and buried all her teeth and claws in it. Feather ran forward to grab at the bridle, but the horse reared and lashed out. The cat came free with a scream of fury. The rider tugged fiercely at the reins swinging the horse round and was off across the fields.

Feather felt rather than heard the woman's laughter as she raced away towards the south. She stood watching helplessly and hardly noticed when

Nonney scrambled up onto her shoulder, where she balanced, black tail twitching, her golden eyes fixed on the southern horizon.

———

Within two days of leaving the Old Ones, Fal had already come to the first trees of eastern Aurëlund: towering beeches, great kings and queens clad in silver and robed with copper, for the old leaves still hung, dry, on their boughs waiting for the new green to displace them. Around their feet wood anemones cautiously tested the air, sweetened here and there by the scent of the first bluebells. There were many squirrels and rabbits, and in the twilight he saw a long procession of deer, moving northwards.

He made his first woodland camp by a stream where the tireless singing of a nightingale kept sleep from him till after midnight. But, as Silfrintopp had promised, he heard the song with new wonder and understanding and listened gladly until exhaustion overcame him.

The next morning he was woken by the ringing laugh of a woodpecker just above his head. Birds were singing everywhere. He felt cheerful and eager to get on, but before eating any breakfast, he checked the tuning of his harp and practised some of the music which Vigg had taught him.

He thought too of Frekk, and wondered whether any of his people lived on the eastern edge of the forest. But all day long he saw no-one, only the beasts of the woodland's margin. Deer were everywhere, a large polecat stopped and stared at him, a snake was drowsing in the sun. And always the laughter and hammering of woodpeckers. The spring seemed to be carrying him along and he walked with an easy stride until by the evening, on the far side of a wide, unforested valley, no more than three miles distant, the outline of the Gavelburg stood out above the horizon.

The ruin of tired memories, Vigg had called it. From there, next morning, he would take another path and cut across a corner of the forest towards its southern edge, the path behind the burg. It had been a seat of power once; even the merchants of Vond had paid tribute to it. But now its walls were empty, its bulwarks a garden of bindweed, brambles and ivy.

As he crossed the valley its towers were already crowned with the first stars of the clear, mild night, and to his left a crescent moon was setting behind the trees. It was a peaceful scene; but he thought the place had an unsavoury feeling about it and he wondered who its lords had been and how they had maintained their authority. It was getting late. He would build a fire and camp down in the valley. He could look over the ruins in the morning.

He was about to turn aside when a glow of light appeared between the silhouetted towers. He looked up with surprise. Was there a fire in the ancient burg? Perhaps someone was there before him! The light stuttered, faded, then increased to a brightness which for a moment showed glistening green ivy between gutted windows and fallen roofs. He walked briskly on up the path and, although part of his mind knew he was being drawn to the castle against his will, he was more aware of feeling exhilaratingly self confident. He should have checked himself and considered what he was doing. Instead, he found himself studying the layout of the fortress. A chanting began, slow and ponderous; a drum boomed. Fal stopped in his tracks. What had Vigg meant by 'tired memories', he wondered? He said there was no danger on the journey for one of his skills. Anyway, his curiosity was thoroughly aroused, he could not miss seeing what was going on. And yet... The chanting became faster, trumpets joined the din. Someone screamed, shouting for help!

He began to run. He was being called — urgently. Vigg said his skills were enough. But wait, not the main gateway! That at least would be sheer folly. Rather one of the towers; safer to look down on it from above.

The staircase was crumbled, and he had to wait impatiently until a burst of flickering light showed him a way over the debris and ragged gaps. Then an opening... but the floor had collapsed, leaving only a stone apron. It was half overgrown with moss, even turf here and there. A small animal scuttled away into the shadows. The chanting was fast now and hurrying the drum along. Gongs clashed, rattles clattered. He knelt on the moss and looked down.

The hall was filled with shapes, themselves the source of the flickering lights. A pageant of ghosts, he thought, pouting his lips at the display; a solemn dance to the ancient music of the burg. Tall, featureless figures, man sized will-o'-the-wisps, strutted and paraded playing shadowy instruments from a distant past. He peered, fascinated, at the shimmering phantoms. It was difficult to keep his eyes on any of them for long: they appeared to fade and change, merge into each other. He fixed on one taller than the rest which held not a gong or trumpet but a glittering sword. He was using it to draw shapes in the air. Fal watched the patterns and tried to get a picture of them in his mind. He frowned. The symbols were definitely evil, weaving some binding spell. But on whom? It was surely not aimed at him, or he would have had to defend himself long since. He had unpacked his harp. He was sure he could rid the hall of the shimmering dancers in seconds if needs be, but for the moment he wanted to watch.

The dancers changed their grouping. They were bringing their attention to bear on the end of the hall. The figure with the sword had also moved, and Fal shielded his eyes from the lights below in an attempt to penetrate the shadows. What he saw made him catch his breath, for he made out a large table, of stone maybe, on which was tied the figure of a man! Not a ghost-figure, but a real man, struggling and still alive.

He decided at once. He must interfere in this ghastly ritual. He had not forgotten the Old Ones' warning about getting drawn into other people's affairs; but this was a matter of life or death.

He began playing his harp, and although it was drowned out by the spectral din from below, it was real sound and real magic. Gradually the army of dancers faded and only the tones of his harp strings echoed among the stones.

He needed longer to get back down the staircase than he had to come up, for it was dark now, and his nerves began jumping at shadows. Only the stars made a faint light in the hall as he picked his way carefully across it. An owl hooted. Something moved in the blackness by the main door, a stone fell. He tried to ignore it and worked his way round brambles and rubble to the far end of the old banqueting hall. Again a movement in the dark. He was definitely getting jumpy. What was it now? Perhaps an animal somewhere in the hall behind him?

But he had reached the stone table and ran his hand along its edge. He felt the warm wrist of the victim. There were leather straps which ran under the table. Not bad work for a crowd of ghosts. Fal drew his knife and began cutting the thongs. He was not sure whether the unfortunate man was unconscious or injured, but he spoke some reassuring words as he turned his attention to the tightly bound ankles. Suddenly the man sat up, rubbing his wrists.

"Well, well!" he said. "Enter the dashing hero! Fal of the Forge appears in the very nick of time to rescue the victim of unearned malice! Pretty good timing, too; and quite professional magic, if I may say so."

It was Sulthind.

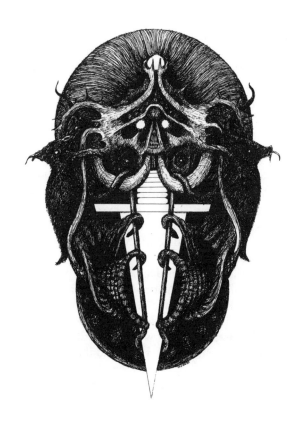

SEVENTEEN

When Gulmer's cowmen eventually got back to the farm they found Feather and Nonney sitting together on the doorstep, and the look of misery on the girl's face made Crombel break into a clumsy run.

"There *has* been trouble!" he called to his brother, who was not so quick on his feet. Neither of them was very nimble when out of the saddle, and they had already taken their ponies round into the stables. They were stocky men, ugly on the outside and as hardy as mules, but behind their rough looks they were gentle and good. Feather had known and trusted them since she was small, and she was glad when Crombel knelt beside her, full of concern, screwing his face up into a thousand wrinkles.

"What's happened then, lass, what's been a-doing?" he asked tenderly. Pombel stood looking down, his broken, blackened teeth showing through wide open mouth, his jaw slack with amazement. He had never seen Feather upset like this before and he was having difficulty taking it in.

She sighed and stood up. "Come and have some tea and I'll tell you. Cut some bread Pombel, the loaf's on the table."

The brothers exchanged worried looks but knew better than to fuss her. The kettle was full of hot water, and she made their jug of peppermint and honey without a further word. Then she sat down with them and told them the events of that terrible morning two days before. She had to tell most of it twice and her daydream in the cow-shed a third time for good measure. They sipped the hot tea and grunted here and there but passed at first no comment. Then Crombel said, "Seems there's more threads tangled into this cloth than were looked for, as I've heard 'em say down by the lake — or words to the effect."

"Yes, Crombel, there are; and now my comb for unravelling them has been taken, at the very time I need it most. Who knows what this means for Fal? 'Meddle in other people's affairs,' the woman said. What might *her* part in the affair be? Who can she be, anyway?"

The brothers sat frowning silently at their mugs. How should they know who the strange woman was or what her sudden appearance might mean! Then Pombel said, "'Tis putting faith in magic trinkets has led to this, mistress, and I hope you'll not chide an old friend for speaking out. People are people, and trinkets are trinkets; I don't know if you take my meaning. Whoever this woman is, she'd have kept clear of here if it hadn't been for this mirror of yours. What help it may have been to you and that young Fal I can't say, one way or the other, but it's this ginger-headed woman who's got it now; and she means no good with it, that I'll be bound."

"Now, now, brother," Crombel interrupted. "'Tis no use worrying about what has been any more than what is or will be. The question is, what's to be done? For that there Fal's like to be in no small danger, I'm thinking, from what Feather's been telling us. Though why is beyond me, I must say. Somehow I fancy there's more to it than magic trinkets, though. Something that Fal's found out on his journey that she'd like to know, could it be, I wonder?"

"Then why don't she just go an' ask him proper?"

"Ay, why not?" muttered Crombel, and fell to frowning into his mug again. Feather sat staring vacantly at Nonney, who was sitting on her lap being fondled absent-mindedly. Never before had she known a cat to be quite such a comfort.

Suddenly Pombel looked up, an expression of discovery in his eyes. "Talking of trinkets..." he began.

"'Twas you as was talking of 'em and calling 'em that," said his brother, "and you mind how disrespectful you get, talking of things as is beyond the likes of us."

"Ah, that's as may be," Pombel went on, not in the least put out. "But that boat now; the one the young master did leave in the barn. Have you looked at it lately, Feather?"

"No," she said, puzzled, "have you?"

"No, I haven't." Pombel pondered a moment. "An' I'm thinking it's a good thing you haven't or this woman now — she might've been drawn to that too, an' to taking a fancy to it."

"She'd 've 'ad a rare time getting it up on her horse, I'm reckoning," said Crombel. "Unless of course she'd 've brought a wagon an' team over the fields with her!"

But new thoughts were crowding into Pombel's mind and he was not to be daunted. "There's the river," he said, "she wouldn't need a wagon. Who says Fal's the only body in the world as knows how to sail a boat?"

"'Tis no ordinary boat," said Crombel sulkily. He could not follow his brother's line of thought.

"No ordinary boat? Think I didn't notice how little the sculls was worn? Ah! My fingers now... Let me tell you: when we had to carry that boat, my fingers did tingle that powerful I nearly had to drop 'old." He held out his hands as if to prove his point. "Of course 'tis no ordinary boat. But who says our Feather here couldn't sail — "

"Couldn't sail down the river after the red-haired lady calling out 'Have you forgotten the boat, ma'am?' Very clever, I'm sure."

"Please don't get cross, Crombel," Feather broke in. "Let him explain what he means. That's not what you meant, is it, Pombel?"

"It is and it isn't. After what you've said, I don't think the lady will be waiting around here anyhow. Yon cat wouldn't be behaving so peaceful if she was. No, she'll either be off back where she came from, wherever that is, or she'll be after finding that young harper — which shouldn't be too hard now she's got the mirror. One way or the other, the sooner someone gets along to warn Master Fal the better. An' if you reckon he's reached West Hallin, then we'd catch 'im down where the rivers meet, as like as not."

"You're right, Pombel," Feather nodded earnestly, "of course he must be warned. I might even be able to help him. Come on both of you, help me out with the boat. I must go at once!"

"'Ere 'old 'ard!" cried Crombel. "It's a case of 'we', I'm thinking, not just 'I'! What do you reckon Gulmer'll be saying if we just lets you up an' off all alone, with us standing up on yon bank calling out 'Have a nice time, hope you can manage the boat!'" He peered at her over his tea mug.

"I shan't have any trouble with the boat," Feather answered. The brothers exchanged glances. They knew that resolute tone. It meant her mind was made up beyond any likelihood of further persuasion. "It will just need steering downstream. I wasn't planning to go alone anyway." The brothers beamed. "I shall take the cat with me. She's been the most sensible one of us all. And now I understand her better I shall pay attention to whatever she wants to show me."

Crombel frowned and was about to object, but Pombel said, "She's right, brother. You and I are like to be little use against this lady, and we cannot leave the farm untended, one way or the other. And she's right about Nonney, too. But look, Feather — you say you've been feeling the last couple of days that Fal is in some dreadful danger. Now you're as like to be a-floating right alongside it, you might say. Are you sure you're doing the right thing?"

"Yes, Pombel, I'm quite sure. I'm bound to follow the mirror, anyway. And it went south, towards the Forge."

Crombel's eyes suddenly brightened. "I knew there was something wrong with all this," he said triumphantly. "I've got it now. Fal is meant to be coming here to collect his boat! That's what we've kept it shut up safe for. He said he'd come back this way to collect it! If you go a-floating off down the river with it, you'll be going in the wrong direction! Staying here — and keeping our eyes open — is the only sensible thing to do."

Feather shook her head slowly. "Fal's not coming here... I don't know why. Without the mirror... I can't see clearly enough. But he's heading down towards the meeting of the rivers; of that I'm certain. And the more we talk about it, the more I know that I must go to find him."

And so the boat of patterns began its journey back down the Ironway, with a black cat sitting large and motionless on the prow, and with a maiden at the tiller. Yet there was little need to steer, for the boat too seemed to possess a will of her own and glided swifter than the running water, as if she was eager to rejoin her master.

"Sulthind!" Fal gasped. "What on earth are you doing here?"

"You'll never believe it, but basically the answer to that question is: looking for you! Now just finish cutting my feet free, there's a good fellow, then I can get down off this slab of rock. They've had me on it since yesterday evening, stroke of midnight, and all that. But, I say... hold on... It looks as though we've got company."

Sulthind had swung himself stiffly off the table and was staring down the hall to where a shadow had moved into the starlight. A tall hooded figure stood facing them silently. It raised a hand and pushed the hood back. Golden hair glinted under the stars.

"Good evening, my friends," he said, "I too have been seeking Fal this many-a-month. Would you mind if I joined the party?"

"Ah, Ilmarin!" said Sulthind with striking presence of mind, "a very poor entrance. Scary, and too late to be helpful. Low marks. Fal's definitely the winner. Now if you'd both just help me find my pack — somewhere behind this table, I believe — we can all get out of this hall!" They went back into the valley and soon had a good fire going. Sulthind had some slices of fresh venison — Fal was much too bewildered to ask him how he came by it — which they roasted on sticks, and Ilmarin had gathered a few partridge eggs. Then it was time for explanations. Ilmarin had come with Aurvang to look for Fal along the Mirrorwend and had spent weeks wandering backwards and forwards in the Eastern Hills unable to find him. Aurvang had sunk into impenetrable gloom until two days ago, when he suddenly announced that Fal had left for the Gavelburg and that he was leaving for Lune! Ilmarin asked Fal where in fact he had been. Fal mentioned the Old Ones but was reluctant to talk too much about them.

"How stupid of me, how very stupid!" Ilmarin sighed, "Vigg — yes; Vindalfinor he is called by the elves. If I had only thought more instead of relying so much on poor Aurvang I might even have guessed it. It's known that he dwells by the Mirrorwend."

As he spoke, a most dejected, wretched looking crow walked into the firelight and stood, shivering, between Fal and Sulthind.

"And what have we here?" asked Ilmarin in surprise.

"We have here," said Sulthind, "the most miserable crow between the Silver Mountains and the bridges of Vond. Meet Cronk, my servant, friend, and messenger. Actually, I do believe Fal has come across him once or twice before. He spent last summer up at Lune helping in one way or another. Then he brought me up here with the story that Fal was mortally injured and in need of expert medical assistance. Didn't seem any better at finding him in the end than your dwarf, Ilmarin."

Fal felt himself drifting into a confusion of impossibilities. He made a quick grab at reality. "Sulthind," he said, "thank you very much. But what *were* you doing all tied up in the Gavelburg?"

"Ah now," said Sulthind, "you'll understand the answer to that one, Fal, as you're a fellow student, so to speak. You see, Cronk had been talking to some of the local crow population and heard about these phantom-fellows. Seemed to know quite a bit about ancient magic and so on; and as I couldn't find any trace of you, I thought I might just as well make use of the time and, well — invoke them, you know. Must have chosen the wrong phase of the moon, unfavourable planetary something or other. Anyway, it didn't work out too well, and Cronk seems to think it's all his fault, which of course it isn't. Worried that I might be cross with him. Utter nonsense! Glad your harp-playing's coming along so splendidly, by the way. Curious to know who you've been studying with. That music up there in the burg wasn't your usual style."

"I'm maturing, I suppose, as old Aren would say." Fal laughed, desperately hoping Sulthind would not pursue the question.

"Ah, I somehow thought you might be. As a matter of fact, I've been working at music a bit myself lately, hoping I should thereby — er, get a more appreciative feeling for the — subtleties of your skill."

"Well, I hope you get an appreciative feeling for what Fal did this evening up the tower! I only came in at the end but it seemed to disperse the crowd pretty satisfactorily." Ilmarin was frowning. He wondered whether Fal had noticed how they were slipping back into their old makebelieve style of conversation that had been such a feature of their friendship with Sulthind several years before. Fal could hardly miss that Sulthind was rather laying it on, no doubt to divert them and relieve the general tension. He was obviously beginning to enjoy Sulthind's company and looked as if he was getting more than a little intoxicated by it.

But Sulthind was offering round some more slices of venison.

"Actually," he said, "you might like to hear how far I've got. All very amateurish, you know, nothing polished."

He leant over to his bag and pulled out a bundle of clothing. He unwrapped what looked like a banjo, except that the fingerboard was plain and fretless. There were some old panpipes, too.

"Good enough for a beginner," he said, checking the tuning. "Belonged to a friend. Here's a ditty I made up on the journey. Nothing much to do in the evenings after dark, you know."

Ilmarin was thinking what a remarkably swift recovery he had made after his ordeal in the burg. Cronk had apparently recovered too. He was busy dealing with his third helping of venison. Fal was very ready to be entertained. He gave little thought to the fact that, according to Sulthind, this was the same crow that had led him to the door in the great maze. Ilmarin glanced at him worriedly for a moment, but he, too, was getting infected by Sulthind's buoyant humour.

The minstrel had finished tuning. "It's called 'Honky Cronk'," he said, "now, hold tight, here we go!"

He had begun strumming with a bone pick and tapping his right foot

energetically to the rhythm. It was so different from the picture of Sulthind
that Fal had carried in his mind for so long that he began to laugh almost at
once at his Honky Cronk Ballad!

Regarding your bill
along your sharp nose,
as every bird will
after preening its toes,
to ensure that no tick
or acarine mite
is creeping along it
to give it a bite,
you don't think to discover,
to see a great lump,
with one eye or the other,
a symmetrical bump!
So Cronk, good old crow,
gave a caw of surprise;
how should a bird know
why such swellings arise?
He was heard so to speak:
'Oh, what can it import
on the top of one's beak
to have grown such a wart?'
For a corvidious bird,
(I expect you will know
that's a damned clever word
for an ordin'ry crow)
both of meadow or hill
to suffer dejections
on account of its bill
growing fleshy projections,
is as rare, you might say,
as a lizard with wings,
or a banjo that plays
without fingers or strings.
But Cronk knew a crone,
for her wisdom well famed,
who once threw a pig's bone
— not very well aimed —
at a knick-knack collector
to ding on his head,
but it took the wrong vector
and donged Cronk instead.

For long he had sworn
his vengeance to wreak;
why droop all forlorn
when there's justice to seek!

Honkety cronkety
I know a crow,
in cunning unmatched
(though his forehead be low);
apart from his feathers
he has little to show,
but his beady eyes watch you
wherever you go.
Hi! Ho! Honkety cronk!
There's nothing to rival a crow!

During the choruses the crow joined in with loud caws, hopping round in circles and bowing, to the great entertainment of the audience. But it was only the beginning of the song. After a loud interlude of strums and crow-honks Sulthind changed the rhythm, tapping now with both feet at once in an extraordinary counterpoint of clicks and thumps on the stony ground.

Now the capable old maid,
who was crafty as Jack Pie,
to make sure she would be paid,
and winking slyly with one eye,
said, 'Look here, I'm not so simple
without right reward or fee
to cure every beaky pimple
twixt the Dodmoor and the Sea!
So what contract will ye sign
with a stroke of claw or bill
pledging payment to be mine
for deft removal of this ill?'

Clever Cronk said, 'I'll bring
in a casket of white
the knowledge of space,
aviation and flight,
condensed to a nutshell,
(just an image, you know!)
in a form safe from rival
or wizardly foe.

The casket is perfect,
unopened before,
no visible latch,
window, keyhole, or door,
but only a spinster,
in virtue complete,
could unlock its riddles
and rise off her feet!
The payment's a good one,
the best that I know:
knowledge of bird-kind,
or I'm not a crow!'

Honkety cronkety
I know a crow,
in cunning unmatched
(though his forehead be low);
apart from his feathers
he has little to show,
but his beady eyes watch you
wherever you go.
Hi! Ho! Honkety cronk!
There's nothing to rival a crow!

When the gullible old hag
heard this avian guarantee,
thinking greatly to enrich
her 'Witch's Guide' or 'ABC',
(she was writing on old batskin
soon to publish as a book)
under F for 'flight' or 'flying''
C for 'crow' and R for 'rook',
she was sure she'd made a deal
that would lead her to exceed
every previous appeal
of any witch-guide you can read.
So Cronk impressed his claw-mark
on a piece of batskin scrap,
while Delilah fetched her ointment
and her pointed witch's cap.
The salve was brewed from moonlight,
adding snake's blood flavouring,
with toadstool-juice preservative
and permitted colouring.

Delilah was an able crone,
as I have sung before,
although perhaps you'll not condone
that that's what magic's really for,
to cure unimportant things
like pimple, wart, or sty;
but it's magic folk that know the 'how',
you only ask the 'why'!

Honkety cronkety
I know a crow,
in cunning unmatched
(though his forehead be low);
apart from his feathers
he has little to show,
but his beady eyes watch you
wherever you go.
Hi! Ho! Honkety cronk!
There's nothing to rival a crow!

So this excellent crow
his bargain to keep
flies off as the crow flies
in tree tops to peep.
He knows of a rook's nest,
his stay will be brief
and polite his request,
for our Cronk is no thief!
An egg is the casket
of wisdom divine,
if you know how to ask it
for flight passerine!

Now the hag gave a howl
when she spotted his trick:
'You perfidious fowl!
Do you think you're so slick
as to swindle Delilah?
Try a swim in my pot!
You'll regret you beguiled her
when the gravy gets hot!
In the world there's no haven
can guard from my wrath,
you diminutive raven,

you'll end up as broth!'
But howl as she might
Cronk knew that he'd won:
he'd diddled her squarely
and justice was done.

Honkety cronkety
I know a crow,
in cunning unmatched
(though his forehead be low);
apart from black feathers
there's little to show,
but those clever eyes watch you
wherever you go.
Hi! Ho! Honkety cronk!
There's nothing to rival a crow!

EIGHTEEN

By the light of the rising half moon Feather saw the land fall away to the left and she heard the rapid waters of the Westway. Nonney had been sleeping the whole evening, the second of their journey, and was an eyeless ball of fur at the bottom of the boat. Feather swung the tiller over and staggered through the whirling currents where the two rivers mingle. The cat was awake at once, her front paws on the prow, peering beyond the water into the woodland on their left. Feather used a branch of an overhanging tree to pull them in, and there was a thump as the keel struck an exposed root. She tethered the boat and climbed out onto the bank. Somewhere an owl was hooting, and far away a vixen screamed. Moonlight patterned the ground between the trees. Nonney was rubbing against her legs and purring loudly. She seemed to approve of the choice of direction.

"Come on, then," said Feather. She untied the boat again and pulled it further along into some bushes, where it would be more difficult to see. But the cat was already padding ahead into the deeper shadows of the beech-woods.

"Wait for me," Feather called. She reckoned to bear left, following close to the banks of the Westway through the lighter woodlands where she thought Fal would be. But the cat had turned onto a path which was leading away from the river. She was hurrying along and Feather had to begin running to keep up. She was about to call out and demand a rest when Nonney suddenly halted and sat down. She had stopped purring and was turning her ears this way and that, listening intently. Then she was off again, bounding along so fast that Feather was frightened of losing sight of her. Again the cat paused, but this time even Feather's human ears could hear it. Someone was singing — up there on the ridge, behind the trees.

Nonney gave one last trilling purr then disappeared into the shadows. Feather followed more slowly, partly because the singer was now easy to locate without Nonney's help, but also because the voice was not Fal's. And it stirred a memory within her to which for the moment she could give no name. This is what she heard:

> Two wings high in the mountain sky,
> Four by stream means dragonfly,
> Four legs is mouse, four legs is hound,
> Six is the beetle-folk down on the ground,

Eight means spider where fly hangs bound,
None for the serpent who moves without sound;
Two is the king and two is the queen,
Ten is the wanderer out in the green.

She caught up with Nonney at the point where the trail joined a larger path. The cat had stopped short and was standing motionless before the shadow of an enormous wolf, which stared at her with glowing eyes. Feather gave a cry of surprise, but already an even larger shape was lumbering into view. For one bewildering moment it looked, in the moonlight, like a monster of extraordinary proportions, then it resolved itself into that which her memory had known it to be all along but which had played hide-and-seek within her mind: a great bear ridden by a little old woman.

At the sight of Feather and Nonney standing beneath the trees the bear stopped with a grunt. Its rider dismounted hurriedly, and seemed about to kneel down. Then she peered at them and started forward, crying, "Well, for one moment I thought... But isn't it the young Lady Fethilian? Down here in the woods, miles from home! And with only this good cat for company?"

Nonney had run past the wolf and was rubbing herself ecstatically against the old woman's skirts. Feather was smiling broadly — with relief and pleasure.

"Well met, old mother," she said. "You see, if you won't come to Gopley any more, you must be sought abroad, by cat and spell!"

"Nay, nay, lady," she answered seriously, "but it was not I that you were seeking!" And she peered at her again.

"Perhaps not, Tholaiwin; at least, not wittingly. But the paths have run well together."

"That may be so; but if you're looking for Fal, the way lies ahead — behind you, that is — for he couldn't have passed me on this path. Come, ride on Alfeng, for though you've grown a wonder since we last met, that wolf's as strong as a pony, and you're still only a slip of a maid — and as light as a feather should be!"

"You are looking for him, too?" She frowned. "Something really is wrong, then; not just the mirror being stolen, something more."

Tholley looked quietly at her in the moonlight. It was very still. The animals had all sat down and were waiting obediently.

"You mean you've lost the mirror, the mirror of Kereoma?" There was more than a touch of incredulity in her voice.

"It was taken from the farm, several days ago," she said simply.

Tholey smiled grimly and nodded. "Come," she said, "let's ride on, then you can tell me what's happened. Here, Alfeng, bear the lady for a while. Come, Bereldan! And Nonney, you go ahead to see that all is well."

She listened attentively and with unconcealed amazement as Feather described the events at Gopley. She asked no questions but once or twice appeared startled and muttered something to herself or perhaps to the bear.

"Who was she, Tholaiwin; have you ever met such a woman?" she asked when she had finished her story. Tholley smiled again, but there was a sharpness in her eyes which in the pale moonlight had the hard glint of tempered steel.

"Well, I suppose I have met her; though I never thought to meet her again. But if she has the mirror and is able to use it, which is likely enough, I fear, the less we talk about her the better. Let's see what Fal has been doing and then get back to the Forge. Even the mirror of Kereoma can't look into the heart of the Delming unless we permit it. All of us will have a number of things to talk about then!"

They rode on without further conversation, but Tholley muttered incomprehensibly and began scratching Bereldan between the ears. The forest was silent and the animals moved almost without sound. Strange words kept forming in Feather's mind. "I never knew light could be so silent," she thought, "it's usually so loud." And later, "This quiet music is the best song of all. Why have I never heard it before?" And voices out of the forest seemed to answer.

"Because you've never been among us in the moonlight. Greetings, lady!"

"It comes of riding wolves, you know." Laughter rang around her, the laughter of many voices.

"Because you're our Fethilian, and it's springtime."

"It isn't far to Hallin now. Come! Come and dance with us."

The laughter rang like a hundred little bells. She glanced at Tholley, but she still seemed completely preoccupied with her own thoughts. Feather was about to speak and ask her who was talking to her so, but she looked up suddenly and said, "Quiet, lady, we are coming somewhere!"

Nonney had disappeared in the shadows ahead. Someone spoke — a voice unknown to her — and there was an acrid smell of smouldering wood. As they entered the clearing, a man leapt up. Two others remained huddled round the fire. The animals stopped at once, awaiting further guidance from their mistress; but the man who had risen held a long bow and the arrow which was notched to the string was pointing straight at Tholley's chest. The two men by the fire had now also turned to face the newcomers and rose hesitantly. One of them was Fal. He stood staring stupidly, apparently in alarm.

Feather realized that she, Tholley, and the animals were still in deep shadow and that what little Fal could see of them probably looked very odd.

"Fal," she called softly, "it's Tholaiwin and Feather. Please ask your friend to put down his bow."

Still Fal and his friends did not move, but the bowman said, "Come forward into the light if you mean well, but not too far. And move no more than is necessary."

Tholley spoke quietly to Bereldan and Alfeng, and the little company moved into the moonlight. "That's far enough," said the bowman. "Fal, do you know these people?"

Fal's expression had changed to joy and bewilderment as he recognized the great animals and their riders. He stepped forward but the bowman quickly barred his way. Feather glanced at Tholley and was surprised to see how serious she looked.

"Come, come, now, good people," she said, "it's a sorry thing when friend endangers friend. We are no illusions or demons, whatever you may think. Fal, will you make your watchman acquainted with us?"

But the third man, who until now had stood quietly in the background, had already moved to the bowman's elbow. "These are our most trusted friends," he said. "Frekk, put down your bow!" It was Ilmarin, who now pushed back the cowl of his cloak as the hunter relaxed his arm. Feather dismounted and walked quickly to Fal. She took his hands in hers and felt them icy cold. Then she saw that it was not just the moonlight that made his face look tired and strained.

"I'm sorry Feather," he said. "What a terrible way to greet you! It's just that... we've had rather a bad time of it the last few nights since Sulthind left. Visitations, sendings! We were ready for anything."

"This arrow," said Frekk, "is not an ordinary arrow. Special power against magic. I'm very sorry, we're pleased to see you, yes, very pleased." He looked glumly at the animals, still clearly not quite sure what was happening. Then he saw Nonney rubbing at Fal's legs and grinned. "Good cat," he said, "who knows — maybe good wolf and good bear, too!"

"Very good wolf and excellent bear!" laughed Ilmarin. "This is Tholaiwin, the story-teller, and Feather, the girl from Gopley where Fal left his boat."

"And this," said Fal, "is Frekk, a hunter from Aurëlund, who tracked me all the way down here. To keep an eye on me, he says, because some of his people didn't like the look of the company I was keeping on the way back through his forest. He turned up suddenly when Sulthind disappeared."

"Disappeared!" said Frekk. "He's been around here all right — in all sorts of shapes and forms. I do not like that man." He fingered the head of the slender arrow and peered suspiciously into the shadows. "We've been besieged in this clearing since sundown. How did you get in?"

"The danger has turned away," said Tholley, "and I think it won't bother us now that we're all together, though it may try to listen to what we say. If you're not too tired, I think we should begin making our way southwards. We can sleep when the sun has risen, if we need, but we should move on. If the danger's gone from here it may mean trouble at the Delming; for behind all this is spite and envy, and they are nasty things to have around. And Frekk, if you will come yet further from your home for a while, come with us. We may yet need your charmed arrow and I don't advise you to travel alone at the moment."

Frekk seemed to hesitate, then he nodded. The friends gathered their belongings and followed Tholley out of the clearing.

———

Fal walked beside Feather and Alfeng, while Tholley and Bereldan took the lead. Frekk insisted on guarding the rear. Little was said. Tiredness weighed them down and Tholley stressed the possibility of their being watched and overheard now even from a distance. They would all want to tell one another many things, she said, but it would have to wait till the Delming.

By the time the peculiar cavalcade had reached the Westway and the place where Fal's boat was hidden, the sun was already sparkling on the water. Tholley had some oatmeal and some fresh eggs in her pack, and they soon had a fire crackling. Even the first sizzling pan of eggs and bannocks went a long way to relieve the tense atmosphere.

"Let's rest here for a while," Tholley said. "The sun's warm and kind, and this is a wholesome place which Fethilian has chosen. Later on we must split up; some in the boat, some with the animals. In the meantime, as no-one seems very talkative, I'll tell you a story; and if anybody else is taking the trouble to listen, then I hope they enjoy it!"

She winked and hummed to herself for a while as Fal and Ilmarin were finishing their breakfast. The others had already made themselves comfortable. Frekk had apparently decided that Bereldan was not only a good bear but also a useful one, for he had his head cushioned on her haunches. Then the story began:

'There was once a monster — oh, a very long time ago it was — and his name was Bel. He was a lot bigger than the monsters you hear about nowadays. In fact, he was so huge that very few people ever realized he was a monster at all, for they never saw more than a tiny part of him at once. If they saw an eye they might think it was a lake, a nostril they might take to be a volcano, and the gaps between his claws they thought were valleys.

'Bel so rarely moved, a whole lifetime of men could pass without even so much as a twitch, for he was a contented and dreamy creature. Sometimes he smiled and sighed, and people would think there was an earthquake; or he would snort and growl in his sleep, and there was a wild storm.

'You might be wondering how Bel could afford to be so dreadfully lazy. Well, there are two reasons for that. The first is that in those days the clouds were made of nothing but milk and the dew was all made of honey, so Bel could get plenty of food without having to do very much about it. Once he had lain down so that a river of milk and honey poured straight into his mouth, and there he had stayed for ten thousand years! He kept his eyes open so that he could see what was going on in the world, but most of the time he drifted off into his dreams. The fact was — and this is the other reason why Bel was so lazy — yes, the truth of it was that all the different desires of people all over the world made him grow! The hopes of lovers, the plans of kings, the ambitions of soldiers and of scholars, all the longings in people's hearts, whether for good or ill, selfless or selfish, made him stronger and mightier.

'But one day his dreams were cut short with a bang. People and animals never disturbed him, for they were smaller than fleas to him; but now, right in front of his nose, stood the old earth-giantess herself. Her hair swept out long across the clouds and her eyes were shining like the sun; and she wielded a club as big as Bel's head.

'"How much bigger do you intend to grow, Bel?" cried the giantess. "When is enough, enough?"

'Bel snarled and twitched his back irritably, for he was not used to being disturbed; and three kingdoms, seventeen princedoms, and thirty-one cities perished in five seconds. "Never enough!" he roared, and an earth-quake reduced several empires to rubble. "Not till I am all the earth and all the earth is me. Then you can come and ask me again."

'"You lazy good-for-nothing! If that's what you think you'll have to fight, for such a thing may never, never be" shouted the angry giantess, and a crackle of lightning burst from her fingers and struck Bel right on the nose.

'"Ow!" he cried, and his tail lashed, sending the biggest range of mountains that the world had ever seen scuttering into the sea. This uncovered a few dozen volcanoes and flames gushed out of the earth right up to the sky. But that was only the beginning, for the fight had only just begun.

'Nearly all the world was destroyed that day and most of what was left was burning with fire. Never had there been such a dreadful battle before and there never has been since; though one day it will be even worse.

'But fierce and powerful as Bel was, he began to weaken and at last the giantess got the upper hand. And then, when he had only a fraction of his former strength, though he was still very great as monsters go, the giantess called out, "Give back to the earth what you have stolen, thief! Let bane be blessing, lout be life!" And she hit him so hard that his head flew right off. Up to the stars it went and there it stayed. Yes, it has been there ever since, staring down to see what has become of the earth without it, for Bel's head became the moon.

'Slowly the raging fires died down again, and from the rest of Bel's body life spread out over the earth; new forests grew and flowers blossomed as they had never done before. His back broke into a long line of mountains; glaciers grew from them, and it was the first ice of the earth.

'The giantess was pleased, for she reckoned she had saved the world. Be that as it may, things changed from that day on, and the clouds of creamy milk and the dews of honey were never seen again.'

Tholley chuckled. Her listeners were all sound asleep in the warm morning sun.

"Nothing like a bed-time story after breakfast," she sighed. She nestled her head onto Alfeng's belly and she too fell into a deep slumber.

––––––

By the time she woke, Frekk was already drying himself with handfuls of grass after a quick plunge in the river. The animals had been watching him with much interest. Only Alfeng had been in the least tempted to join the hunter but even he declined the invitation to battle with the chill water.

"The sun is on your side this morning." Frekk laughed. "Come on, you do not fight alone! And it will warm you through and through."

Tholley rolled over on her back and laughed at the blue sky. Alfeng tried to sit on her chest for protection.

"The sun's fought well enough already," said the story-teller. "He's chased away the phantoms of the night. Let's hope they stay away.

Over a small breakfast they discussed how the party should be split. Fal, Feather, and Ilmarin would go in the boat, while Tholley went with Frekk and the animals along the bank. It would be best, she thought, if the boat always stayed in sight of them; so when necessary Fal should steer into shallow water and wait for the others to catch up. Fal woke at this point and said that was fine. Feather and Ilmarin both claimed to have been listening all along and said they had not been asleep for ages. So it was agreed, and they set off once more, southwards along the Iron-way.

The journey was pleasant, and tongues began to loosen as the day wore on, for it is hard to be always mindful of a threat if there is no sign of it. But they did not forget Tholley's warning to speak of nothing they had experienced or learned that winter, nor to discuss any plans they might have for the future. She had looked sternly at Ilmarin when she said this, which Fal thought odd and which made Feather wonder, for she had a feeling that it was not only Fal who had a secret that might surprise them all.

But their talk in the boat was of the things about them, the things of the woods and the water, of the sunset and, later, of the stars of the springtime.

It was late into the night when Tholley called a halt. She said she was sure there was no danger now and they could rest without keeping watch. Frekk wanted to argue about this, but Tholley insistad that Nonney, Alfeng, and Bereldan would be sure to warn them sooner than human senses ever could, and Frekk agreed that this was likely enough. So, after a meal, they all slept around the fire, and only Nonney stayed in the boat to guard it.

———

It was nearly three days before they came to the lands around the Forge, for they had to take the boat down to the lake and then westwards along the shore. But long before they reckoned to see the town they could see the fog.

It covered half the horizon, lake and land alike, a long featureless cloudbank lying dead and stifling, cutting off their view of whatever lay within it or beyond it.

"We are in for trouble there," said Frekk.

"The people of the Forge may be having it already," said Ilmarin.

NINETEEN

"There are various kinds of sorcerous mists and fogs," Aren explained learnedly. "Some are merely intended to protect the adept from the over-curious gaze of the ignorant. Such fogs do but extend the wizard's mantle, so to speak, only they are woven with spells instead of thread. Others are sent to weaken and numb those over whom the sorcerer wishes to obtain influence, thus facilitating his task considerably."

He coughed and studied his audience carefully. He took a poor view of inattentiveness; but though some faces may have shown the first signs of fatigue, no-one's mind was wandering.

"Well then," he continued, "those are the — ah — basic fogs, you might say. After them come the specialized fogs; fogs, that is, for a special purpose. Some, for example, are sent to cause wanderers to go astray, whereby they may perish by cliff-fall or in mire. Other fogs engender pestilence, plague, leprosy, madness, boils, fever, rheumatics, or blindness. Others bring phantoms, wraiths, ghosts and cruelties, horror and fear." He gazed thoughtfully before him, trying to think if he had missed any-thing out.

"And which of all those fogs might this one be?" asked Tholley.

They were seated before the ancient forge-stone: men, elves, dwarves, and animals. Through the southern windows the sun was shining with unnatural brightness, for Ilmarin had succeeded in banishing the fog from the courtyards, and the light reflected strongly from the bank of whiteness all around. In the streets of the town those who still went about their business stumbled, half blind. No natural fog this, but a choking fume, clutching at eyes, lungs, and mind. No door or window shutter could keep it out, and people sat huddled round the damp, smouldering fires in their hearths closer than at the dead of the year. Many who had relatives out at Fyrwell had made the journey there just to be rid of the despair and misery, and this was the springtime, two weeks past the feast. And others were talking of following them.

"Maybe it's all of those," Aren mused. "It is too early to be sure. No plague or raving madness has as yet beset the town; but it could, no doubt. At any moment it could."

On the day before the workers and masters had gathered together as if for a patterning. There had been song and music of harps; the power of the stone had been invoked to claim what was its own, and within the walls of the Forge the six courts were clear both of visible and invisible intrusion.

Now all could speak and speak freely.

Before them, just inside the south doors, stood Fal's boat. It had been brought up from the lake as soon as they arrived, for they felt it would be unsafe to leave it out in the fog. And Ilmarin said he wanted to be able to see its patterns.

Next, Fal was asked to tell all that had befallen him. He had been away almost a year, and the telling of his adventures cut well into the afternoon. Tholley asked a lot of questions about the crow which had turned up at Lune, and the dwarves were beside themselves to hear that an ancient hall had been discovered in the middle of the Waste — and that two dwarves were doing most of the discovering. Fal's terror in the labyrinths was more like a wild nightmare than reality to most of his listeners, but others seemed to think there was something that might be learned from it which could yet be of value in their present predicament.

"Pardon me, Master Fal," said one of the dwarves suddenly. It was Skelfir, one of the two brothers. He stood up looking very sheepish, but Fal thought he detected a slightly mischievous twinkle in the dwarf's eyes. "Pardon me, but I think I know what you mean about the balance; and I've just made up a couple of verses about it. Not the sort of thing that harpers would compose, but dwarves have strange taste in poetry at times."

"Well, come on, then," said Ilmarin. "As there appears to have been a dwarf kingdom at Lune once, I expect you'll be wanting to make up some pretty lengthy poems about it before long."

Skelfir looked embarrassed. He had just caught the frowning eye of Celbring, the master of the dwarves' house; but everyone was waiting for the poem. "I only mean about the fact that there were two dragons," said Skelfir nervously. "It is a bit unusual when you come to think about it."

"Very unusual," said Tholley. "Yes, you'd expect the painful dragon to be there in the cold, barren north; but the fat, over-comfortable one did seem rather out of place. Something of a surprise, I must say. And it was the two together that very nearly brought about Fal's undoing."

"That's it," said Skelfir, "that's just it, the two together. But I'm wondering whether we haven't got two here as well at the moment!"

"Now then, Skelfir," said Melauriën, "don't make it worse by talking in riddles! What about your verses?" She sat in her own carved chair, which had been brought down that morning for the hearing of Fal's adventures.

"Very well, but it could be improved on given time, I expect." Skelfir looked for a moment as if a doubt had entered his mind, but he took a deep breath and chanted:

> The Delming by the lovely lake
> has summers fair and long;
> its opposite is in the Waste,
> a drake of pain and prong.

A warm worm too lives in the north,
down south's a chilling fog;
the rune of balance is complete,
or I'm a flying frog!

He sat down on the bench again rather suddenly amid the cheers and laughter of the other dwarves. Theck took off his own wide-brimmed straw hat and pushed it down hard on his friend's head, which helped to cover at least part of the poet's brightly blushing face.

"Do not laugh at this excellent dwarf!" said Tholley. "He has spoken well and he's quite right. We've always thought of the lake and the Waste as two opposites, so distant and different that there could be no connection between them. But even without the fog we must see that each contains each within it, and each balances and belongs to the other. Perhaps when we've thought more about that, we shall begin to understand what Lune is and what it can mean to us."

"The Portal of Sorrow has rusted into its frame," said Fal. "We've cut the Forge off from the north."

"And cut the north off from the Forge, too. Don't think of opening it now, with the power of the fog all around us. But what else did you learn on your travels, Fal? The story's not finished, and it was more than the dragons of balance that Sulthind wanted to know about, I'll be bound!"

"He was desperate to hear about the Old Ones, who had healed Fal and sent him on his way," Ilmarin put in; "and he seemed determined to keep us away from Gopley. But Fal wouldn't tell him much. That's when he began to turn nasty. Then he suddenly went off."

"Only don't say he disappeared!" said Frekk.

"He went the same morning that Feather's mirror was stolen; isn't that so?" said Tholley.

"Who *is* the thief, Tholaiwin?" Feather asked. "You said you'd seen her before; won't you tell us now?"

"To have seen her before and to be able to say with certainty who your visitor at Gopley was, is not necessarily the same. I'll tell you what I think in a while, but let's hear Fal's story out first, for the answer to your question will have to be more than one word. Come on, Fal; what happened when your boat left Lune? Tell us more about these Old Ones."

And so Fal came to his stay with the ancient friends of the air, Vigg and Silfrintop, of how they saved his life, how they nursed him, and how they taught him the secrets of their music. And in the telling of it a contentment came upon him and he knew that the Old Ones were his friends and he would ever find them in all the things of the air: weather and seasons; dawn, rainbow, sunset; and in the song and flight of bird and insect. When he came to tell of the power of their music, the eyes of his listeners widened with wonder, and both elves and dwarves became very solemn.

At last, when it seemed he had come to an end, Aren said, "Do we understand you to mean that you're now a master of wind and weather? That by the melodies you have learnt you could — dispel this fog, for instance?"

Before Fal could speak, Tholley answered for him. "This fog is no part of the weather Master Aren, as the bright sunshine in your courts testifies. It comes of sorcery, and to challenge the will and mind behind it with the gentle magic of the bee-folk could be very dangerous."

"Perhaps the rest of us together could do something without Fal rushing at an unknown enemy and with his new skills as yet untried," said Melauriën.

"It must surely be these very skills that Sulthind was after," said Ilmarin.

"Then it was lucky you didn't try using them against him in the forest," said Tholley, "and it's all the more reason for not using them now. The Old Ones also taught Fal how to control his boat in the air, as he was telling me last night, and no doubt Sulthind would dearly like to learn to fly! You've brought a great treasure with you, Fal. Very few have ever seen Vigg and Silfrintopp, fewer still have learned from them; and for anyone to gain so much from them as you have done is unheard of."

But Fal was remembering his rejection at the Starwell, the stone circle of Aurëlund; and he thought of the dream he'd had of it later when he saw the dancers in the field of colours. He said, "There are still some things I don't even begin to understand."

"And as many mysteries as the stars in heaven," Melauriën quoted. "But doors are made not only to be closed but to be opened, and what you have learned may, with wisdom, provide a key to open them. Such knowledge could one day change the world."

A silence fell. Everyone imagined the coming years in different ways. Some saw the Golden Age founded anew, some the realms of elf and dwarf once more in splendour as of old, while others saw it choked with fog and pestilence unless challenged by Fal's new powers.

Their dreams were broken into by Feather's gentle voice. "The thief, who was she, Tholley?" She glanced up at her, pursing her lips. She cleared her throat and seemed to be seeking the words to begin. Then she said, "Well, my thoughts are likely to seem strange and uncomfortable to you, but they are these: Fal told me last night a bit about the meeting at the Gavelburg and some of the things that were said in chatting with Sulthind — the odd sort of mood that came about, and so on..." She frowned and paused. "And he disappeard on the same morning that the thief appeared at Gopley."

"But it was a woman," Ilmarin interrupted. "And on horseback, too. What could that have to do with Sulthind?"

Tholley sighed, as if the subject were an unusual burden to her. "The woman," she said, "was described in some detail to me when the Lady

Fethilian and I met in the woods along the Westway. She had seen her first with the inward eye before she saw her outwardly, so she could describe her in two different ways, on two different levels, so to speak."

"And you recognize this woman from the descriptions?" said Fal.

"I do," said Tholley. "Her name is Grindassil, Sulthind's mother."

A hubbub broke out. Everyone seemed to be speaking at once. Melauriën clapped her hands and asked for silence.

"Let Tholley finish," she said. "Tholaiwin, we all know that Grindassil has been dead for years. Please explain what you mean. Or do you doubt that she died?"

"No, lady, I don't doubt that she died, and that's just the trouble. Feather saw her as she was a long time ago, thirty or forty years maybe. And that's what worries me. It's said that her son killed her in the end, and I think the story's true. But when sorcerer overcomes sorcerer, the victor can sometimes save a part of the power of the vanquished one; perhaps all the power if he's strong enough... and sometimes, but only when great skill is present, even the phantom of the victim can be preserved and used — either as a servant or as a body for the sorcerer to use at will."

It had grown very still in the Forge. The sunshine seemed suddenly blatant and hostile.

"Then we have an enemy indeed," said Melauriën quietly.

"Unless I'm wrong, we have, and one maybe who could use Fal's knowledge to enliven the world and bring about a new Golden Age — with the sorcerer in its hub, controlling and ruling it!"

There was a long silence. None of them had ever thought in those terms before. The island in the lake, and those who lived on it, had at the most been an object of their disapproval. Danger was not part of the Forge's experience of life. For many hundreds of years the Delming had lived by trading and by the arts of making: the skills of hand and the skills of mind. But they were only the gentler arts, Fal saw that now. The power of the forge-stone was used to make things of daily life, bowls for enlivening seed, pendants for lengthening youth, wands for the blessing of house and field. For all the ritual and solemnity of the festivals this was a place of homely magic, different indeed from the power and cunning which he had met at Lune and in the woods by the Westway when Sulthind had tried to subdue them with the terror of illusions.

Still no-one spoke. Melauriën was frowning at her hands folded in her lap, as if she disapproved of them. Ilmarin was watching Tholley and waiting for her to continue. Aren looked incredulous, the dwarves and elven-apprentices disturbed and bewildered.

It was Ilmarin who spoke first. "What do you think we should do, Tholaiwin?" he asked.

"Eh? Do?" The old woman seemed surprised at the question, or maybe she too had been deep in thought. "Do? Why, there's nothing to do! Just live on, that's all. That's doing enough for the moment. There's no danger that anyone could steal Fal's knowledge from him, you know," she laughed. "It's not something you could tell to anyone in a few minutes, as I myself feared it was at first. Fal took many weeks learning those melodies of power, and very hard work it was. Such knowledge can never be stolen, it can only be taught! And if Sulthind was hoping for lessons then he's going to go on being very disappointed."

"But Mistress Tholaiwin, the townsfolk are being suffocated, stifled by choking fumes! Why — we are besieged!"

"And yet you say there's no danger!"

"You suggest we just go about our daily tasks — as if nothing was happening!"

"What if Sulthind were to capture hostages and *force* master Fal to teach him!"

Tholley spread out her fingers as if stroking the air. She pursed her lips and looked down. Her animals stirred, sighed, and shifted position. Nonney was no longer with them. She had stubbornly refused to enter the town and had slipped away. Feather was sure she would make her own way back to Gopley. Perhaps she had done the most sensible thing! Fal was longing to get away from this endless discussion. But order had been restored and Tholley was about to speak.

"Good people, listen to me. You're not sorcerers, you're workers, craftsmen, all of you, and Fal's skills weren't taught him for the wielding of weapons, for the crushing of foes."

"You have called the Old Ones the bee-folk," said Frekk, "and bees can fight and be terrible in their anger when foes tamper with their nest." Fal could see from his tight smile that he for one did not intend to follow Tholley's mild advice.

"That is so," the old woman replied, "And even the good Lady Bereldan has been known to flee their wrath!" She chuckled and poked the bear gently with her toe. Without waking she grunted and rolled over onto her back anticipating further attentions. "But where are your stings, dear friends? Charms over wind and wave will not wash the island away, and even if they did, they would do little harm to our enemy if my guess about Grindassil is correct. I'm but a wandering singer of other folk's tales and no sorceress, yet I've gathered some wisdom in a long life. And I say this: that to fight sorcery with sorcery cuts wounds into the heart of the earth and brings her endless suffering. And do not bees die once they have stung, Master Frekk?"

The hunter scowled at the floor. He knew there was sense in what Tholley was saying, but it still made him angry to hear this old animal tamer preaching what seemed to him the weakest possible path.

"And yet this wisdom of the Old Ones was not only of weather charms!" It was Feather who spoke. "There was talk, too, of the boat and of another use of the patterns carved on its wood." She nodded to where the boat rested, dry and rigid, between its props.

Now that's what I call a really sensible idea! said Melauriën, emerging suddenly out of her gloom and sitting up very straight. "If we're to try just living on as if the fog weren't there, we could at least apply ourselves to the making of the new boat, Vigg's boat, the traveller in air!"

"It could be tried," said Ilmarin. "And I agree with Tholaiwin. We must go on in our own direction; that's the only way to fight and still be true to ourselves. Don't you think so, Fal? It would be a marvellous challenge to us all and give us plenty to think about!"

"It could be tried," said Tholley, "but what you would do with it when it was made is another matter. Are there any more journeys to be undertaken in the near future?" She smiled and looked round at all the company. Ilmarin blushed.

"I am betrothed to Ristilian," he said, "the daughter of Rymon and Osmarin. I've promised to return there as soon as I can — to the wedding!"

Fal looked at him in utter amazement, and Feather thought, "So this was his secret! He was wise not to tell Sulthind, he would have been jealous... " Melauriën looked completely stupified but at last managed to say, "It's splendid news, son! If the boat can be made big enough for a wedding party, maybe more of us will see this Kingdom of Lune before the summer is out!"

Bereldan was awake and tugging at Tholley's skirt with her teeth.

"Let's celebrate the Lord Ilmarin's announcement with a meal," said Tholley standing up. "Bereldan is reminding us that we've fasted for many hours. It's time to eat." She laughed and mauled the bears ears. The conference had ended.

TWENTY

The new boat was planned by Ilmarin, Fal, and Aren, and by noon three days after the conference all the details of the design had been agreed upon. It was to be half as broad again and a little longer than the old boat and flat underneath.

Aren's part would be the making of the hull, which was to be woven of fine, light wickerwork. The gunwale was to be even larger than that of the heavier water-boat but it was to be hollow: a sealed trough of poplar, a tree which has a love of every wind and breeze and of which there were some well-seasoned planks in the wood store. Ilmarin's elves would see to the carving of the patterns which, according to Vigg's instructions, were to be modified from the old ones. Ilmarin himself would cover the wood with gold leaf for the sun, inlaying the patterns with silver for the moon.

The prow, carved into the likeness of a hawk, hovering, was to be of the finest white birch. This would be the work of the dwarves, who would care for the inlaying of the silver feathers, make the beak, half open, of copper, the claws of iron, the brain alloyed of grey lead and quicksilver, and the heart of yellow tin and gold. So were the wandering stars, the masters of movement represented. For the earth and the white stars a transparent rock-crystal, with thirteen facets, belonged in the forehead between its eyes which, for the golden stars, would be of dark topaz.

The trough of poplar was to be lined with undyed linen and would be filled with fresh ripe grain. This had to run, according to Vigg's description, uninterrupted around the whole boat. The life of the grain had to be awakened, but in a way that avoided germination, and then harmonized with the patterns of the gunwale. For this all the Forge would be present, with the boat lying up on the stone, and Ilmarin working with the music of Fal's harp.

Vigg said that the life of the grain would last twelve months from the day the trough was sealed, irrespective of how far the boat travelled or how often it was used, unless some intolerable strain was put upon it, such as the attempt to travel during an eclipse of the sun or moon, or during an earthquake. He had been disturbed and surprised to learn that there was no-one at the Forge skilled in prediction and told Fal that if ever the boat began behaving strangely he should set her down at once and wait for a while before continuing the journey. Travel at the solstices would be easier and quicker than at other times of the year, and Vigg seemed to think that, if used properly, the boat might greatly benefit the land over which it passed. "The earth will smile and shine with pleasure at the touch of the stars in proper measure," Silfrintopp had said.

Fal now began practising in earnest the music he had learned from the Old Ones, and as he worked the fog began to thin around the walls of the Forge until, after a few days, the inner streets of the Delming were clear of the white scourge and people could at last be heard laughing and calling out in them again.

By then the gunwale of poplar had been cut and smoothed and warped to the shape of the boat ready for carving. The trough and its lid were everywhere carefully matched and lightly pegged together. As the elves began their painstaking work and the patterns began to appear, the whole town cleared of fog as far as the outer walls, leaving it as an island in a sea of silent whiteness. At last the wickerwork could be bound to the wood and the leaf of gold smoothed into the patterns.

Then messengers were sent to Fyrwell to tell those who had fled there that the fog was lifting and to bring good grain in as soon as it was ripe, both for the boat and for the making of bread, for the harvest all round the town was mildewed and rotten.

This was a time of waiting, for the grain would not come until the midsummer sun was five or six weeks old, even though the sky beyond the fog was blue and warm and the corn turning gold without hindrance. By then even the hawk would be long since finished, though dwarves do not work swiftly when given the choice but like to pause often and listen to what the depths of the earth are telling them. Yet the hawk was 'ready to fly', as they said, a full two weeks before the corn was brought in, and mounted on the prow, its feathers delicate and glittering.

Fal began working again with the apprentices of the harpers' school and Feather was accepted into it as a welcome guest, for she brought with her many songs of Hallin, which all desired to learn.

Aren was embroidering a canopy of stars which he wanted to fix on four poles as a shelter for the travellers. This was not part of the original plan, and he was not sure how top-heavy the boat would become through this addition; but he thought there should be at least some sort of covering included as a protection against rain or too much sun. It showed the stars with plants and flowers growing down from them towards the earth, with their roots weaving in and out of the constellations. Aren had designed the resulting patterns to harmonize well with those of the gunwale, thereby reinforcing the intentions of the boat, as he liked to call the energies which Fal was to control. He seemed very pleased with the idea of flowers growing down from the stars and kept smiling to himself like an old tom cat by the fire. He was sometimes to be heard muttering comments such as "Quite an elegant addition!" or "Exceedingly appropriate!" and "A most propitious idea, to be sure!"

When all was finished and the boat was standing in the Forge complete

— waiting to take the grain, as Aren said, as if she were the hundredth and not the first aerial boat which he had helped to make — she did indeed look not only elegant but quite magnificent. Both elves and dwarves would daily spend much time walking round her and talking in whispers about the perfect workmanship with which the magical harmonies were revealed.

At last the harvest arrived and the Forge could be prepared for the final patterning. First the whole room was yet again swept and purified by the burning of herbs and fragrant woods, and appropriate symbols were drawn on all the doors. The grain was brought in by two men who carried it in an enormous wooden bowl. They viewed the aerial boat with wide eyes, one forgetting to address the master smith, so that his partner had to kick his ankle to remind him to begin the greeting in unison.

"Our hearts are full," answered Ilmarin, and the dark eyes of his apprentices sparkled with amusement. The men accompanied him, still holding the bowl, while he shovelled the grain into the gunwale with a silver trowel. When it was done, they bowed and withdrew — to tell the waiting townsfolk with baited breath the strange things they had seen: a boat made like a basket, with a rim of gold, and all under a splendid canopy fit for a king or queen.

"There was a hawk of silver that snapped its beak at me as I went past," told the one.

"Its eyes bored right into me," told the other, "and it hissed when I went too near."

"There never was such magic things going on in the Forge as today, fog or no fog," said the first.

"Ah then," said a woman in the crowd, "the fog will all have gone by tonight! You see now, by the time they come to the end 'twill have all disappeared."

"Times are changing," said a child; "they must change sometimes."

"Maybe the Tree will flower again, then," said an old man. "What do you say? I say it will!"

He was wrong, and the child went unchallenged, but the woman was right, for as Ilmarin stood before the forge-stone that afternoon and the light of sun, stars, and moon danced with the light that comes from the depths, the land was cleared of its burden and the people were free again. And the light which wove round and round the boat sent forth such a dazzle as had never been seen, not even in the Forge, in all living memory. So fierce was the running and pulsing of the wild light that the dwarves often had to shield their eyes, and even old Aren was hard put to keep his mind on the patterns and help hold them steady. The sun was sinking low towards a clear horizon by the time the whirling radiance came to rest and the dwarves, with much stamping and clapping, shouted that the task was done and well done.

Then the south doors were thrown wide and the apprentices commanded to carry the boat out into the court of the Golden Tree, to show what had been made to the townsfolk who thronged the gates and walls.

Light as the great basket was, the apprentices were at first unable to move it, for their arms numbed as they raised them to touch it, and it was several minutes before the new-born energies quietened enough for the boat to be brought out and set down on the white tiles of the pointer.

Then the people forgot their vigil and stared dumbstruck in wonder. For they could see what the dazzled eyes of the artisans could not: a marvellous glow under Aren's star canopy, as if the light of dawn was filling the strange craft from side to side and the sun itself were the boat's gentle passenger. They gasped and sighed but none dared speak. Yet even as the flat hull touched the stone paving the light faded, and at the same time the last rays of the setting sun were cut off by the hills, as if morning and evening had become one again and had withdrawn from the world, their task achieved.

But Ilmarin was leading Fal to the boat and helping him step in over the rail; and as Fal stood behind the silver hawk with its glistening, outspread wings he waved and smiled shyly at the people. And they, who had been oppressed by the fog so long and who had lived pent up in the misery and fear of it, exploded with joy and yelled "Hurrah!" and "Fal for the Forge!" and much else that was lost in the roar of their exultation; for the fog was gone, and they had seen the ancient magic of the sun, yes, seen it with their own eyes, victorious, yet carried by their own craftsmen.

Before the hubbub died, Fal sat down on the bench which ran behind the prow and began playing the music which Vigg had taught him. He had practised the flowing music for many weeks now, imagining the patterns running in a stream of gold all about him. But now that the moment had come a more urgent rhythm leapt into the melody as of its own volition. Light glowed once more above the boat, and the rippling on the golden rail swept around her like a rushing shoal of glittering fishes. With a shudder she lifted into the air, first only an inch as if to feel herself safely free of the ground. Then, as the music steadied to an easier pulse, she floated up as light as thistle-down into the beams of the rising moon, and the crowd sighed again with wonder. Theck, on some strange impulse, reverently removed his hat and stood, unabashed, with his glossy pate revealed to all. But no-one had eyes for him, for Melauriën had stepped towards the boat, her hands raised.

"I name you the Bee Song!" she cried. "Blessed is this night in the history of the Delming." And she turned towards the tree where it stood, silent, heavy with leaves: "Of the Delming of the Golden Tree!"

There was a sound of grinding, rending metal from within the Forge, harsh and dissonant and as the mistress of the city leapt round to face the open doors, the elves clapped their hands over their ears in horror. It lasted three of four ghastly seconds, then there was a resounding clang, which echoed cruelly round the walls of the courtyard and out into the empty streets of the town. Ilmarin had run in and stood now before the stone looking beyond it in baffled amazement at what he saw. The doors on the north side which led through to the dwarves' hall had sprung open, but it was not from them that the crash of metal had come. At the far end of the tunnel the iron gates of the Portal of Sorrow which, for more years than any had counted, had been rusted together, had burst asunder and been hurled in against the walls. And from the north a path of starlight, like flowing quicksilver, came racing towards the town, in through the market place and through the dwarves' court, engulfing the stone where Ilmarin stood, his hammer of office raised as if to ward off the uncontrolled insurgence. Behind him the crowd in the elves' court was lit as if by daylight, so bright had the Forge become; and the Tree rustled and then shook its leaves with a roar, swaying wildly as if struck by the sudden force of a gale.

———

On the next morning the air was so clear that the outlines of the island stood out with almost unnatural sharpness as if it had been drawn closer to the mainland. But still Sulthind made no move.

"If he'd wanted to attack us openly he would have found it easier while the fog held. He'll be puzzled now and very disappointed that he can't use the mirror to spy on us. He might try some new disguise; or maybe one of his servants will be sent." Melauriën's face puckered as if she were remembering something disagreeable.

"Do you think he's frightened to come himself? He didn't seem terribly put out when Fal rescued him from the ghosts of Gavelburg," Ilmarin objected.

"You'd have been impressed by his coolness and presence of mind," Fal agreed.

"Maybe," said Tholley. "If there *were* any ghosts at Gavelburg!"

"If there *were* any! By the Tree there were! You should have just seen them!"

"I only heard the din they were making but Fal actually watched them dancing, didn't you, Fal?" Ilmarin wondered what Tholaiwin was getting at.

"Oh, I don't doubt it," said Tholley, "I don't doubt it at all. But to my mind Sulthind was a bit too cool when you rescued him and so over played his part. Did it never occur to you, Fal, that the whole display might have been put on for your especial benefit? Sorcerers can be pretty good at producing entertaining illusions, as you know from the night we met in the woods up by the Westway. What makes you think the show at the Gavelburg was anything different?"

Fal was indignant at the suggestion that what he had secretly regarded as a rather brave and accomplished rescue might have been nothing better than a near disaster — that he had fallen headlong into a trap!

"But what on earth for?" he asked belligerently. "He could have just come up to me and started speaking! Why all the melodrama? Anyway, he *said* he was looking for me, there was no secret about it."

"No," said Tholley, "there wasn't. Not after he'd got you to rescue him. You see, Fal, if you have an enemy or someone who at least regards you with mortal suspicion, as Sulthind knows you did him, there's no quicker way of winning him over than by appealing for his help. Your direct enemies can become your friends if you give them enough chance to be admired."

"Then he was wasting his time! We became quite good friends again for a while, it's true, but for the little he gained from that he might have saved himself the trouble."

"And he might have gained a lot more if there had just been the two of you and he only had the one old friend to work on," Tholley replied, "but something went wrong in his calculations. You said he seemed a bit put out when Ilmarin turned up and that his good humour seemed a bit strained as if he was having to put too much into it. I reckon he was. My guess is that he'd have — well, let's say he might have found things easier if you hadn't had Ilmarin — and Ilmarin you — to remind each other of your sanity. I'm not saying that alone you'd have become such good friends that you'd have ended up teaching him the music of the Old Ones. It's not very likely, of course; but it is just possible!"

Fal was finding this all extremely uncomfortable, for he could see the strength of Tholley's argument. If he had been at all proud of coming through Lune and its deadly mysteries or of bringing the wisdom of Vigg and Silfrintopp back to the Forge, he now felt thoroughly deflated.

"I hadn't noticed how conceited I was becoming," he said.

"Oh, we live and learn, son," said Tholley, giving him a quick glance, "we all do. And who knows what his next move will be? Something quite unexpected, you can be sure, and then we might all fall in it. That's what he no doubt hopes, at least. I wonder what *he* would like us to do next?"

"That's what I was wondering," said Melauriën, who had been tactfully looking out of the window over the lake. "The art of sorcerers always depends in some way or another on the ignorance of the victims. I wonder whether he might not have taken Feather's mirror to prevent any attempt to spy on him rather than to use it himself. Grindassil surely had means of looking afar, and I don't doubt her worthy son learned them from her. But let us set skilled eyes to watch on all the gates, that only known faces come and go."

"And let the hunter from the north be ready with his bow lest any talking crows should try to perch on the Golden Tree!" Tholley laughed. "In the meantime let's live on and do what's needed without giving too much thought to the island. Fal, the Bee Song must be mastered before she can take passengers on a long journey. Take her out daily and learn her ways. Ilmarin says that without the canopy she'll just pass through the dwarves' tunnel; so, by their leave, take her out that way and keep to the north of the town. And if you're taking passengers to the wedding, begin practising now with at least one."

"Don't go out alone," said Melauriën; "nor indeed should any of us leave the Forge without company. For all else, chenailië! — Think of joy!"

———

Then it was time for making the wedding gifts which Ilmarin was to take with him. A long cloak of silver-grey was woven for Ristilian by Aren and embroidered by Melauriën. It showed the Golden Tree, large and splendid, in full blossom on the back, extending its branches over the shoulders to form a necklace of leaves and flowers in front. The elves made a wooden casket, of white rowan, carved with ivy climbing delicately up its legs and completely covering the box. From the spiky little three-pointed leaves around its feet to the larger, heart shaped ones on the domed lid no two leaves were the same, and the elves took great delight in it, as they do in the living ivy, for much the same reason.

From the dwarves there were twelve insects, which could be kept inside the casket, made of metals and precious stones, of the most exquisite and lifelike workmanship down to the veins on the wings, the segments of the antennae, and even the faceted, jewelled eyes. This took nearly a month and would have gone on much longer, but Ilmarin had insisted that it was not essential for each wing and jointed leg to work with its own natural movement. Even so, several of the dwarves managed to incorporate some unusual features into their designs.

There was a heavy ladybird of gilded lead, with twenty-two inset spots of rock crystal, and a handsome, glistening blue-bottle made of steel so tempered that it shone royal blue. Its eyes were of rubies. There was a great grasshopper of bronze with glazed, unseeing eyes of turquoise; a silver-winged moth with feathered antennae and a body of clear blue beryl; there was a vicious horse-fly of iron with eyes of flaming emerald, and a copper stag-beetle with heavy jaws that snapped ferociously when picked up. The eyes of a dragonfly of finely patterned silver were globes of yellow topaz; and a pompous-looking queen bee of soft red gold had eyes of garnet. A firefly had a body of moonstone which glowed brightly in the dark, and a butterfly with a head of radiant sapphire had wings of inlaid violet opal. There was another beetle, a weevil with a long nose, of green copper with rows of tiny diamonds set in its wing-cases. And, most remarkable of all, a fat, self-satisfied cicada of brass with a head of polished flint which, when held on the warm palm of the open hand, sang with a metallic, ringing purr. The dwarves refused to say which of the twelve each of them had made, or whether they had worked together, and when asked how the firefly glowed or how the cicada sang, they would smile and politely pass the question on, saying, "So-and-so might know. Please ask him."

The elves of the Forge found these insect presents ill-chosen and would have said so had not their master warned them against it. One of his apprentices, Ferwinor, retorted that there was more wonder in the deep eyes of any one pond-hawk, as the elves call the dragonflies, than in all the clever works of dwarves; but Ilmarin pointed out that the dwarves might say something similar of their carved box of trunk-chokers, which is one of the many dwarfish rude words for the ivy that they so detest: for "it has little root and covers good sense and rotten thought alike with never ending leaf, like the conversation of a chatterbox," as they say.

"And did they say this about our work?" said Ferwinor, reddening.

"I doubt it," said Ilmarin sternly, "but very likely they would, and much more, if you were to mock their craft. And it's such talk, Master Ferwinor, that led to the estrangement of the Kingdoms from one another to the west of this land. Maybe their gifts are not so unapt as you think, for was not the one dragon which Fal met in Lune very insect like? Insects too are akin to thought, sometimes crawling, sometimes shimmering and soaring like the pond-hawk's wing — and sometimes like a hornet's sting!"

"The other dragon was toad-like," said Darriel, an elf with far more good humour than her brother, "and it's said that dwarves hate toads even more than ivy. Shall we not carve a good fat toad to keep inside the casket? Then perhaps he'll gobble up all the loathsome insects!"

Ilmarin smiled, but Ferwinor turned away, frowning.

———

Ilmarin had been planning his own gift ever since he had left Lune in search of Fal. It was to weave a ball of light to fit into the empty bowl of the toadstool-table behind Rymon's hall. He was certain that from there, deep inside the mountain, the life of ancient Gelmindel had flowed. Fal in his turn believed that by taking light from the Forge to Lune they might correctly counterbalance the energy which had rushed down from the north when the Bee Song was named; though whether it had come from Lune or elsewhere they could not say.

Now it was the first new patterning since the bursting of the Portal of Sorrow, and though the inner doors, both north and south, were sometimes closed, the ancient iron gates remained always open. Indeed there was none in the Forge who would have suggested trying to close them.

So Ilmarin wove with the light running through the dwarves' court into the stone and he quickly learned, as if from an old, barely forgotten instinct, to use it and blend it with the fire which was the Delming's own. The power between his hands was greater than ever before but, strangely, easier to control.

"The light is full of new exciting possibilities though the old fury seems to have gone out of the stone," Aren commented later. "Sense and clarity have come in; like the mind of an old man when the wildness of youth leaves him in peace at last!"

Over the ball of light which he had made Ilmarin gained such a mastery that he could diminish or enlarge its size at will; and after some experiment with various vessels he enclosed it in a solid jewel, a perfect adamant, clear but unfaceted, as big as the tip of a man's thumb. It was cushioned in a tiny casket of gold, an old heirloom, given by Melauriën, and put in a plain leather purse which he hung about his neck.

This was all Ilmarin's gift, for it was not the custom of that land to give rings in marriage.

———

And now it was decided that the wedding should be held twice: first at Lune, then at the Delming, for Melauriën thought it best that she should stay at the Forge and govern it, protecting it, too, if needs be. Tholley and Frekk, who had struck up a friendship together, were to travel ahead on foot or on beast-back, for to everyone's surprise Frekk had also found a new and inseparable companion in Alfeng, who followed him around everywhere as if the hunter had raised him since he was a milk sucking cub.

After nine or ten days the Bee Song would follow, taking Fal, Ilmarin, and Feather. Some hinted that there might be another wedding at the Delming before long, but Fal said he would not think of such matters till his quest was over.

"Yet that may be soon enough if Ilmarin's gift brings life back to the north," said Melauriën.

"Who knows what the old fire-mountain will make of Ilmarin's gift!" said Fal. "There's a will in Lune, ancient and strange, which may need more than the light which Ilmarin brings to change its mind. Let's wait and see!"

TWENTY-ONE

In due course Frekk and Tholley set out, taking a more direct route than Fal had done the summer before. They would head due northwards all the time, going overland to Gopley, and would then follow the old hunters' trails through the Iron Mountains thus avoiding the westward road through Little Strang. Frekk was especially keen to do this as he seemed to remember the grey town with unabated distaste and still talked about the 'stranglers'.

In the end it was nearly a fortnight before the Bee Song was made ready for the journey, as it had been raining heavily for several days and Ilmarin decided to wait. At last she was loaded with a small cargo of apples, pears, walnuts, wheat flour, and even some grapes to help towards the feast. They estimated that Frekk and Tholley would arrive at Lune before them, even allowing for the hunting of a small deer in Aurëlund, which would be carried on a pole between the two people. Feather would want to stay a day or two at the farm, and Fal had no intention of risking the Bee Song on the crags of the Iron Mountains. They would have to go round.

Their departure was arranged for the early morning, and though the townsfolk were now accustomed to seeing the aerial boat pass in and out, they were in a festive mood waiting for the wedding party to appear.

"Return soon, Lord Dringskel," called Fidda, a dwarf maiden, standing in the northern court with her dark-eyed cousin, little Amba. "The people of the Forge are skilled at preparing feasts, too, you know!"

"That's right," said Aren, "be sure to return by the feast of Estera, for the Tree will surely blossom next spring."

"I believe so, too," said Ilmarin earnestly. "I've felt the changes in the earth as her light flowed through my hands. Yes, the Tree will certainly blossom again. But we plan to return even before the winter snows come, if the Lady Rymon will give us leave, and bring Ristilian to the second feast. The next Praise Song will be one the Delming shall never forget!"

Then he joined Fal and Feather in the waiting boat and stood, his hands raised at once in greeting and farewell to the folk who thronged the gate. "The Tree will blossom again!" he called in a loud voice; and the people echoed his words with a shout, passing the news on up the streets to the market place where the shouting turned into a sustained roar: "The Tree — the Golden Tree will blossom again!"

"Now go, my children, go, before this shouting grows so loud that it sounds afar to other ears! Be gone, and return soon!" Melauriën kissed all three tenderly, and at last the journey began — out of the North Gate and through a jubilant crowd which seemed intent on sinking the Bee Song beneath the weight of asters, michaelmas daisies and wild gladioli which they cast upon it.

———

They moved slowly at first, but once all the shouting and waving was behind them Fal increased the pace as much as he could without strain and kept it steady: about as fast as a man might run in a leisurely fashion. Once speed and direction had been fixed, the harp could be put aside and there was nothing to do but sit and watch the land glide past.

As the Delming gradually receded behind them the morning sun stood like an emblem over the lake in a clear blue sky, glittering on the spires of the Forge. "The town belongs to the sun again," Fal thought, and then, musingly, "I wonder where I belong!"

They had left at sunrise and planned to go for most of the day before making their first longer stop, near the woodlands around the Runeway, the river which joined the Ironway from the west. If it was a fine clear night they could press on, arriving at Gopley the next morning. Only Ilmarin had been in those woodlands before but he assured them that there were plenty of sheltered and well watered valleys there among the hills, which would be excellent for camping should the need arise.

By the late afternoon Fal could already see that the hills were higher than he had expected, and when they set down for supper in a pleasant valley below the forest he began having doubts about their choice of route, for the trees looked very tall and there was no road between them.

"It might be safer to go round and cross the river at the falls you were telling us about," he said. "I don't fancy getting the Bee Song tangled in these tree tops."

"How high can you take her?" asked Ilmarin. "Are you sure we have to stay so close to the ground?"

"She didn't feel particulary steady when you lifted her up to have our last look at the Delming," said Feather.

"It was more likely me who wasn't very steady! You may not have realized it, but I'd never taken her up so high before!"

"It isn't very far round to the falls," said Ilmarin. "It might be more sensible to keep to the flatter land until our charioteer has had a bit more experince in the daylight. You know what the dwarves say?

"Only a fool will rush to seize
the thunderbolt by wrist or beard;
in wisdom does he truly act
who waits until the sky has cleared."

"I've never heard that before!" said Fal, amazed.

"He just made it up to tease you," said Feather, "can't you tell?"

Ilmarin laughed. "Anyway, there aren't likely to be any thunderstorms tonight; but there'll be precious little moon, either, and none at all till just before dawn. But the falls should look fine by starlight; a sight worth the extra distance, I can promise you."

Fal was not too keen on the idea of waterfalls, but the choice of route was taken out of their hands, as they were soon to discover.

By the time they were ready to go on, dusk was deepening around them and the evening star was flaring white in the west. In the east many smaller stars were visible and more were appearing every moment. They climbed back into the boat and Fal began the music for lifting her. The golden radiance, which easily went unnoticed in the full light of day, began to flow and shimmer around them, and she floated up. At once the path of liquid starlight shone out beneath the Bee Song, running straight up into the valley. A mile ahead it could still be seen sparkling in the tree-tops and here and there even flashing on a distant ridge. Fal held the boat steady, not yet moving on nor setting her down again.

"Just look at that!" he whispered; "behind us, too — it runs back down towards the lake, though there was no sign of road or track by day. Did we travel up the path by chance, I wonder? Or does the Bee Song create it as she goes along? Let's see!"

By turning the hawk he guided them some fifty yards away to the left, but the path stayed where it was. It was losing its brightness but it certainly had not moved.

"The path will fade without the music," said Ilmarin, "and I don't really think we could have followed it by chance. More likely it's the way the Bee Song chose. You were only guiding her roughly towards the north."

"Vigg said this was an old way of travelling which had long been forgotten," said Feather. "Perhaps the path was once created for it — or even by it through many years of use. And didn't he say that the passing of the boat would awaken the earth? Something about the earth 'smiling with pleasure'?"

"It was Silfrintopp who said about the earth smiling," said Fal, "but you're right. And the Bee Song certainly feels quite different now we've left the path."

"There you are, then!" said Ilmarin. "It sounds as if the boat knows what it's doing."

Fal steered back to their camp, and the glistening light, which had become dull and hard to see beyond a stone's throw, blazed up once more.

"How does she feel now, Fal?" Ilmarin asked.

"Full of life and — yes, steadier, I think."

"Then my guess is that the path of starlight is the safest place in the world for her. How about trying the first ridge? We can always turn back and wait till the morning if you're worried."

"We can try," said Fal, trying to sound more confident than he felt, for in the dusk while they were eating supper he had judged the larger trees at a hundred feet or even more. That was about the highest he had ever taken the Bee Song and he would need to go another thirty feet higher still to make a safe clearance in the dark. Yet the tree tops above them shone with light, they were easier to see than by day, and the boat had never felt so full of energy. The thought flashed through his mind that the sunlight actually weakened the path: its nature was of the moon and stars.

"Bees don't fly abroad by night, but the Bee Song moves by ancient right," said Feather merrily; then she frowned, for the words had come suddenly to her without forethought.

But they were lifting rapidly, up towards the first trees, a-flame now with the silver light. They were as alarming as they were resplendent, vibrant with limitless energy. Fal staggered and for one terrible moment he thought they would crash, but the Bee Song responded with a knowledge of her own. If there was any danger it was because she was gathering so much speed now that the movement of air was making her buck like a boat on a rising sea. That at any rate could be disastrous!

Breathless with excitement he slowed her right down to a walking pace as they crested the first tree tops. He turned to speak to his companions and found them both staring, wide-eyed and incredulous, at the ridge before them. With a cry he followed their gaze, expecting to hear the crunch of branches on the hull. But they were looking beyond the trees immediately around them.

A castle, of black stone but outlined by the shimmering light, was rising out of the first hill top. The trees had gone, and the shining path, less dazzling now on the bare ground, ran right in front of the open gates. And from within light shone as from a thousand lamps or candles.

The Bee Song was gliding silently on to pass so close to the walls they could almost touch them. Then, as they approached the gates, men became visible, and yet more, standing in the shadows beyond the light: men in dull spiked armour, some with glinting swords, some leaning on spears with extravagantly barbed tips.

"They'll see us!" gasped Feather. "By the mother and father of all, how evil they look!"

They were in front of the guards now, only some eight or nine feet from the ground, and Fal was looking down into their faces. He had never seen eyes so empty and so utterly devoid of personality.

"They appear not to see us," whispered Ilmarin. "Set the boat down, Fal, I want to have a closer look."

"No, please don't," cried Feather, "I'm terribly afraid. There is no castle in these hills, Ilmarin, you know there isn't. Quick, please let's go on!"

"Then stop further down. We can't just sail off and leave a riddle like this unsolved."

Fal went a furlong or so beyond the dreadful castle, still in sight of the shining doors but far enough away to take off and escape should anyone come at them. Yet as they touched the ground the path faded, the castle wavered and thinned. For one moment the evening star shone through its massive keep, and then there were only stars and forest. An owl hunting down in the valley hooted derisively.

"I'm going to walk back there and have a look," said Ilmarin, "guards or no guards."

"I'm coming with you," said Fal.

"No you're not. You'll stay here and look after the Bee Song — and Feather," he added with a smile. "I'll call out if I need you, but keep the boat on the ground!"

He strode off into the darkness.

"You probably think I'm a terrible coward," said Feather, "but you mustn't put the Bee Song at risk like that. There's never been a castle here, it just has to be one of Sulthind's illusions. I do wish Ilmarin would keep away from it!"

"Sulthind's illusions usually do something, though," said Fal thoughtfully, "they don't just stand there... unless it's like the Gavelburg, to lure us in! I'm going back. Ilmarin was a fool to go up there alone!"

He began climbing out over the gunwale, but Feather had a strong grip on his arm and would not let go.

"Then we'll all fall into the trap," she cried. "He said he'd call out if there was any danger."

The owl hooted again. Footsteps were coming down the hill.

"It's alright," Ilmarin called out of the darkness, "Just as I thought: there's nothing there!" They could see him now in the starlight as he came towards them. "Just a bit dark up there; dark and very heavy. Full of brooding and watching."

"Pretty poor watching," said Fal, "they didn't see us even when we passed right in front of their noses! Lets all go back and have a look."

"It might be better to go on," said Ilmarin. "When I said there was nothing there I meant there was nothing to be seen. But there is a presence on the hill top, a memory of some ancient evil maybe, and we might just as well keep out of its way. My guess is that we shall see it quite well from here the moment the Bee Song lifts off the ground. Let's try!"

Feather was very relieved at not having to go back up the hill, and it was quite enough for her to see the grim towers materialize again as the path re-kindled beneath them. The sound of a dog or wolf-hound baying echoed from deep within the castle walls. A bell began to toll.

"I wonder what would happen if we kept the Bee Song aloft while one of us walked into it," Fal speculated.

"Well we're not going to try," Ilmarin laughed. "Do let's go on! If my guess is right, we could see some more wonders before the night's out."

As indeed they did. There were other castles and ancient houses, even villages with delicate gables and spires, all very strange and some very beautiful. They saw dwarves passing by in a large silent company, each carrying what looked to Fal like a burning lamp in one hand — though Feather said there were no lamps, just long flames coming from their finger tips.

Then by the River Runeway there was a warrior in finely pointed armour, holding a shield before his face and wielding a two-edged sword that looked impossibly big for him; and he was engaged in a combat against a great beast. Dragon-like it was, with a cruel beak as of an enormous eagle, and its feet were webbed and tipped with heavy claws. Yet fierce though it was, it seemed more intent on glaring at the knight than touching him, for its wild eyes sent out a light which wounded the warrior if its rays passed his shield and struck him. And the beast's body also shone like a jewel, for it was fashioned from layer upon layer of purple amethyst.

Fal stopped the Bee Song in mid air, for they were reassured from further experiments that the scene would fade if they descended, and they watched the contest for a while. But it seemed only to be an endless to and fro, neither doing the other any serious hurt, as if it were more of a ritual than a battle to the death.

As they went on, all the land around the path appeared to be peopled out of legend: a phantom world of light and shadow, it seemed, of beauty and of dangers without name or number, and they moved silently through it as through a marvellous dream.

"The path is showing us the world as it once was," said Ilmarin, "or maybe as people once saw it, at the time the path was created. Perhaps it's still like this, only we no longer see it so. Who knows?"

———

At last the hills ran down into the rolling grasslands between the Runeway and the Ironway. The land had become dim and shadowy, or maybe their eyes were tired from the sight of so many wonders; yet the stars were losing their sparkle too, and in the east a crescent moon watched them, heralding the dawn. But to the north the pathway still ran on in undiminished brightness as if urging them to follow its eager guidance without pause while Gophill loomed out of the plain before them, solitary, steep, and of unnatural angularity, crowned with a tonsure of dark oak.

The path made no attempt to avoid it, though it was the only obstacle on the whole of that wide plain, but ran on straight as if drawn up to the flat summit that rose, bare, just above the tree tops.

The Bee Song rose swiftly and easily up the slope and then lifted as if on a gust of wind to clear the trees. As they drew level with the summit Fal could see that the hill top was circular and surrounded by a grassy dike. In the centre of the pit, which was some forty yards across, lay a huge boulder. It looked as big as a house in the dark, though the path flickered and parted around it, so that it lay like an island of darkness in a river of light.

The boat slowed a little, as if gathering strength, then swung up over the stone. But as it did so other paths burst out from it in all directions, six-fold, with lesser paths between, to form a radiant star from skyline to skyline. And at that instant a mighty tone, or rather a chord of tones, rang out like a choir of gongs, so loud that the three friends clapped their hands over their ears and reeled as if struck by an invisible hand.

Their minds were numbed by the force of the energy which had rushed in one gigantic pulse through the Bee Song, and when they were able once more to look about them, the Gop was far behind, the stars had faded and all the fields were grey with dawn. And in the distance they heard the warm, homely lowing of cows.

TWENTY-TWO

Tholley had been to the farm more than a week before and had met with little difficulty in reconciling Gulmer to his daughter's wanderings.

"I'd been expecting her to go ever since Fal came here last summer," was his immediate comment. "She'll never settle down to being a farmer, that lass. Now Tim here, he's different: like father, like son." He even seemed to think that anything less than total involvement in mysteries and adventure — both rare and deadly — against unknown adversaries would be unworthy of Feather's nature and abilities. "It's what her mother would say, I'm quite sure." He smiled wistfully. "Ay, as a matter of fact that's very much what she was like too, before she took up with me!"

So the reunion was a joyful one for them all, both with Gulmer and his men and with Nonney, the cat. And the hearty everyday talk against the appetizing background of the smell of roasting was no small relief after that long night of magic.

But if Fal had ever thought that Gulmer was too earthy to be at home among the mysteries which were so important to him, he was mistaken. He found himself looking more carefully at the jovial cattle farmer. Gulmer obviously had the same idea, to take a closer look at Fal, and their eyes met, questing and questioning. For a moment Fal caught a glimpse of dark mountain pools, lonely but strong; then the water rippled and wrinkled with laughter.

"Well, young master," chuckled Gulmer, "I *am* pleased that you and Feather have taken up with one another, I must say. My daughter says you'll be staying no more than a couple of days and must be getting on; but maybe on the way back you could manage to stay a bit longer. You'll be needing a proper rest and a few good suppers after all that travelling."

Fal suddenly felt as if a burden had been taken from him and was very glad there was something akin between them that they had both discovered; and he felt that he had found a home. He smiled and nodded, and Gulmer, seeing his pleasure and sharing it, smiled and nodded back.

Much of that day was spent in sleeping, and the evening in discussing what had happened since Fal's last visit. He had begun telling them about Vigg and Silfrintopp, how they had rescued him, and about their strange house and orchard; and he had come to talk about the music he had learned there, when Ilmarin interrupted. He pointed at Nonney, who was wandering about the room looking first at the window then at the door.

"Fal," he said, with a puzzled expression on this face, "Nonney and I both feel we are being watched."

"I feel it, too," said Feather. "It's just as if someone had come into the room — someone with a very interested, listening mind."

"You may be right," said Gulmer. "Tholley warned us to look out for something of the sort when you were here. Tim, go and get some of that new cider that Pombel's been brewing, then let's have some songs — just some ordinary songs!"

Tim was if anything even quieter than he had been the summer before but he was clearly very pleased to see both his sister and Fal again. Ilmarin's presence seemed to be making it hard for him to talk, so Fal was doubly delighted when he joined in the singing. Fal had not forgotten his song of Gelmindel from their ride to Michel Strang by the Ironway and had since then often sung it himself. Now Tim entertained them with a much longer ballad that had a fine recurring chorus which they all learnt to sing together. It was the story of Istangelor, a prince of Dalf-Ender, who had once saved Hallin by slaying the beast that men had brought from over the sea — in a great iron bound boat without sails. This was the refrain:

Beneath grey skies Istangelor,
on shifting sands by foaming shore,
fought deadly worm from iron hull,
in stinging seas, ice-cold and dull.

Pombel and Crombel, encouraged by their own cider, also sang a few songs, one of a legendary cow that used to collect all the stars into her horns every morning and then shake them out again at night; and another of an extraordinary contest of wits between a hare, a beetle, and a fox.

The next day Fal took Gulmer and Tim for a flight in the Bee Song to visit what Gulmer described as a half-wild herd some twelve miles to the south-west of Gopley kept by another of his men, Talder, and his family. Talder had heard nothing of Tholley and Frekk and their recent visit and was therefore unprepared for the sound of Gulmer's voice calling to him out of the air as he sat dozing on his pony in the hot sun. He went very white and was quite unable to talk to Gulmer who wanted to know a number of things about the welfare of that section of the farm. Gulmer said that if he wasn't going to talk they would take a look round for themselves.

As they flew in over the large herd, admiring the massive bulls and the many yearling bullocks and heifers, Tim told Fal not to feel too sorry for Talder, for he was a dishonest man and had long been suspected of trading behind his master's back with the Runnings — the villages on the Runeway lakes — and even further afield.

"Still," said Gulmer, "I didn't really mean to scare him like that, I just thought a sudden aerial visit might help a bit with the respect, as you might say. We've been good enough to him and his folk over the years, but there's been little more than muttered sneers and curses in return. Very likely our little tour of inspection will be a turning point in his life! I'd been wondering how to tackle him for quite a time now. We'll send Crombel over next week to make a proper inventory of the year's breeding. Slammed the door on him last year, he did! I doubt he'll be quite so sure of himself after today."

"His family's alright, though," said Tim ruefully. "A real pity that Talder's gone the way he has; the others would have been good company."

"You can say that about quite a lot of folk around these parts," said Gulmer shaking his head. "You must have noticed on your way through the Strangs last year, Fal. A funny lot they are, for a start. Like folk who've lost something and don't know what. Talder's cattle are well looked after, that's one thing, and not so wild as I'd have expected; flying in close like that was a pretty good test. Maybe we'd better move out further now, though; they're getting fidgety, and we don't want to start a stampede. Ay, that's better... What were we saying? Ah yes, the people. It's as if their light had burned dim, you see, but it's happened so gradually that they never noticed it going, and now they're all grumpy and sour. They've lost something, but it was so long ago they don't remember what it was." He looked at Fal quizzically. "That's what your journeying's all about, isn't it? More than just the Tree and its blossoms!" Fal tried to say something, but Gulmer hadn't finished. "What would the Golden Tree be to Talder here unless something inside him caught fire again when he saw it? I reckon that's what you began learning in Lune, you know: your own fire had to be awakened. You had to wrench it free, first of the one dragon and then of the other. After that you were ready to learn what the Old 'Uns wanted to teach you, and not before."

"It wouldn't do Talder any good to face the dragons of Lune," said Fal; "but the sight of the Golden Tree might touch his heart."

"It might, if he ever went to the Delming to see it. There are Golden Trees in every buttercup if only the heart will see them. There's a gentle voice still that can speak out of every flower."

"Maybe if I can waken the voice in the land it will waken within people's hearts, too."

Gulmer smiled. "Maybe," he said. "And it might start speaking so loud that people won't have an ear for anything else! Very like it's all a matter of balance, as you were saying last night; all a matter of balance."

———

Ilmarin now thought it probable that the path which they had followed from the Delming would continue over the Ironway and on into the north. "It had no trouble crossing the Runeway," he argued; "why should it stop now?" Understandably, he was impatient to get to Lune, so Fal gave way and they all agreed to continue that evening when it was dark and the path would become visible again.

After supper it seemed to darken more rapidly than usual, and once more the feeling of being observed came upon them all. This time it was so oppressive that no-one even had the heart to suggest singing as a means of diversion.

"The sky's completely overcast now," said Feather. The atmosphere in the room had been too much for her and she had been standing at the door watching the grey cloud spread across from the south. Fal went to join her. "The darkness can only help us, and so will the breeze, but it looks like rain!"

They went back into the parlour and helped Pombel clear the table. They were all trying to think of ways of dispelling the gloom that had been settling on them like a muddy ooze. Ilmarin thought they should just gather their belongings together and get ready to go, and he was casting around in his mind for a tactful way of saying so. Then the air stirred about the house and in the kitchen smoke began coming back down the chimney. The wind sighed and rattled gently at the closed but unlatched shutters. Somewhere among the outhouses a door slammed.

"There's a wind getting up all right," said Gulmer and looked enquiringly at Fal. Then they all heard it — throbbing, tearing at the grasslands like a stampede of terrified cattle.

"Here, better latch them shutters," Gulmer grunted, pushing his chair back, "there's a gale."

But it was too late. It hit the farmhouse like a bone-splintering punch, smashing the shutters inwards — there were no window panes — and blowing out all the candles. For a second there was total darkness, and the bellowing voice of the storm was all they knew. A searing flash of lightning and they saw one another's startled faces, their lips parted to cry out. Then a second flash, and with it the rending crash of sound from the first, deepening into immense rolls which made the ground shake under them. Flash followed flash and the friends were thrown around on a tidal wave of light and beating sound, a drowning torrent in which tables, chairs, windows, and roof-beams were only a flickering and transient illusion.

Somehow Fal found his harp and staggered to the door: "— can stop this! Vigg taught —" But no-one heard the rest of what he was shouting as he struggled to open the outer door against the force of the gale. The moment he moved it, it was wrenched from his grasp and shattered against the wall, tearing the hinges from the wood and bursting the lock. What he saw then put all thought of Vigg's teaching from his mind: the barn, in which the Bee Song was being kept, was on fire.

In a moment they were all out of the house and battling with the wind to get to the barn. Gulmer had a key at his belt, and if they were very quick they would do it. Only a part of the roof was burning, but he knew that when they opened the doors and let the wind in, fire would engulf the building within minutes. The lightning crackled around them as if it was the end of the world.

Seconds later they had the Bee Song out and were rushing to move the heavy bales of hay, but already the roof was sagging apart in a rage of flame. Most of the precious winter store would be lost.

"Come on now, roof'll be down in a moment!" yelled Gulmer as he helped Crombel out with a double load of hay. It fell with a blast and roar of red heat. Then the rain began — with all the force of a tropical deluge combined with the fury of an arctic gale.

"Here's your good old north and south working together for you!" Gulmer shouted in Fal's ear.

"Even this rain won't put out yon!" shouted Crombel.

"'Twill stop it spreading though!" bawled Gulmer. "Get the boat and the hay against the north wall of the house!"

Soon there was nothing to do but stand in the soaking rain and watch the remnants of the barn burn. It would be hours before the flames died down and weeks before the heat cooled under the ashes; unless of course another gale scattered it. The force had gone out of this one now, and the rain fell almost straight. The lightning was miles away.

"I know it's a bit like shutting the gate when the bull's just jumped the fence," Fal said to Gulmer, "but I still want to see what I can do. There's some special music for storms, you see."

"All right by me," said Gulmer, wiping rain and sweat from his brow with the back of his hand. "There's nothing else for us to do."

Fal went back into the porch where he had left his harp. The sudden weather change had put some of the strings out, and the tuning needed some checking. Then, standing a little aside from the others, he began the music for dispelling violent rain. It was in four sections; by the end of the second section the rain should begin to stop. It didn't. The wind began to rise again and carry clumps of burning hay swirling across the yard.

"Hold on!" cried Gulmer, "that's no good!"

A flash of lightning crackled magnificently over their heads and exploded violently. Everyone ducked.

"Let it be, lad," said Gulmer, gently gripping his arm. "Let's just stand and watch the bonfire, make sure it doesn't spread, then we'll all go in and have a hot drink. There's nothing better to do tonight."

Tim had already gone in to fix the shutters and Feather to mop up the flood on the floor. Pombel had been making space in another outhouse for the Bee Song. The storm had blown over.

"He's beaten us, Ilmarin," said Fal desperately once they had the boat safely stowed. "Don't you realize, he's beaten us! If he could do this tonight he'll be able to do it tomorrow and the night after. He can stop us going on!"

"It's been a very warm day," said Ilmarin, "close and sultry even for the time of the year. Freak storms like that aren't unknown."

Fal looked at him searchingly; but Ilmarin was watching the barn burn — and thinking.

———

"But if we're not going to fight back we might as well stay here forever! Or at least until the Bee Song has been struck by lightning and reduced to ashes!" Fal was still in a dark mood after his defeat during the storm of the night before, and even the fresh butter and cheese, the brown bread and hot mint tea, did not give him the help and consolation he needed.

Feather smiled at him understandingly. "Fal," she said, "don't forget what Tholley said in the Forge: that to fight sorcery with sorcery wounds the earth. It was a mistake to do what you did last night, please try to see that. The Bee Song and its music have been awakening the earth; using music to fight with, that's just the opposite. Maybe that's why the world has become so barren, because people once misused their powers and turned them against one another. Tholley told us a story of a whole country being drowned under the sea because of the greed and cruelty of men of power."

"Tell me how I was being greedy or cruel!"

"It cuts wounds into the earth to fight with magic, and that *is* cruelty," Feather said.

Fal looked into her eyes for a moment. She was the girl who brought the spring to Vigg's orchards, the maiden crowned with primroses, the earth's own daughter; and he saw that she knew.

"Then why doesn't his island drown in the sea?" he asked savagely. "I wish it would!"

"We beat the fog by ignoring it," said Ilmarin, who had so far been careful to keep out of the discussion. He had been enjoying the late breakfast and was still feeling thoughtful. "Or rather by working together, not against the fog but for a better purpose of our own. I agree with Feather: we must leave the dark way to those who've chosen it."

"You know I agree with all that," said Fal. "But the question still remains, what are we going to do now? Set out during the day and take the long way round or wait and see what the weather's like tonight?"

"Neither," said Ilmarin. "I've been thinking. Hasn't it struck you as strange that the storm broke while we were all quietly indoors after supper? The Bee Song was protected by the barn, too. Just think how much more damage could have been done to us a couple of nights before, while we were gliding through the hills with nowhere to shelter!"

"That's just what I'm worried about," said Fal.

"Then why didn't Sulthind strike while he had the chance, while we were in the open, unprotected and tired out?"

"Because," said Feather, "we'd awakened the ancient power of the earth, and she was protecting us."

Ilmarin's eyes shone and he looked very elvish. "Exactly," he said. "The earth is greater than Sulthind!"

Fal sighed with frustration. "All right," he said. "But what are we supposed to do now, that's the question."

Ilmarin looked amazed. "Well, it's obvious isn't it? We just go on!"

"Stay on the path," said Feather, "and we're quite safe."

"But we don't know where the path is," Fal objected, "we lost it after it got light. We must have left it when we cut across to the farm."

"Oh, come on," Ilmarin laughed, "the only real damage done last night was to poor Gulmer's barn, not to your pride! We can easily find the path again. I wanted to have another look at that stone up on the Gop anyway; we just wait there till it gets dark then off we go."

"But if he's able to spy on us he'll know what we're going to do and he'll conjure up another storm before we've found it."

"He's not spying on us just now," said Feather quietly, "I should be able to feel it if he was, I think. My guess is that he's exhausted for the moment and he'll be having an even later breakfast than we are!"

Fal smiled at the thought of Sulthind having a late breakfast. For some reason he found the picture of a mighty sorcerer having breakfast at all quite out of place and rather funny.

"That's better," said Ilmarin, "you're beginning to look like Fal again! You were getting me worried. We'll have a picnic supper on the Gop this evening and keep an eye on the weather."

"Then we'd better go and tell Gulmer before Sulthind wakes up with a splitting headache and starts looking into his crystal ball!"

"His silver mirror," said Feather.

Fal gasped. "I'm terribly sorry, Feather," he said, "how stupid of me. Never mind, we might get it back for you before all is done."

"I hope so, but it's hard to imagine how."

"It's hard to imagine a number of things about Sulthind nowadays."

"I don't find them hard to imagine at all," Ilmarin smiled grimly. "But let's concentrate on the journey."

———

They had landed on the northern rim of the Gop where they could look down upon the dark stone at its centre.

"There are still so many things we don't understand about all this," said Ilmarin. "We can only hope that someone else doesn't understand them either, or maybe he thinks we do and hesitates to confront us in person before he's sure. This stone, for example: I guess that it was a key point in a whole system of forces which people once tamed and harnessed for their use; like the stone in the Forge, maybe, but more powerful."

"I don't think we should fly over it again for the moment, though," said Feather apprehensively. "Let's leave experiments till we're — well, a bit more certain of ourselves!"

"I wasn't suggesting we should. I was only wondering: it might be puzzling Sulthind that we've come back here, and that could be a good thing."

The twilight was deepening. All day the sky had been cloudless except for a tumbling bank of cumulus which had stood, stationary, in the south. For the last hour it had been moving slowly towards them, majestic and silent, and now, as darkness fell, it towered above the Gop, miles high.

"You know," said Fal suddenly, "it's hard to be sure in this light, but the clouds behind this white bank look darker than you'd expect them to be — almost sulphurous some of them. Just look over there! I suppose it might be a trick of the evening light."

"More likely to be a trick of our mutual friend," said Ilmarin. "Rather typical, I should say, creeping up quietly behind a mask of summery white innocence. A perfect idyll! I think it's time to try lifting off again."

As the Bee Song rose the path glimmered out around the stone and down through the trees. There was a moment's silence as the clouds sank down like a smothering blanket all about them, then with a snarl the storm broke loose.

The trees groaned and shuddered as the wind seized their boughs; and out of the gloom, only yards above their heads, the lightning broke. It leapt in one blinding sheet all around in an avalanche of stunning noise, and the three friends reeled beneath the onslaught. Then they realized what was happening. Amidst all the fury and violence the Bee Song was riding steady, as if on an island of tranquil air.

"She's holding!" Fal yelled delightedly, "she's holding it off!" But the others could not hear him. Branches were torn off and whipped past them like straw, and to the left the trees were burning, yet only a breeze rippled Aren's star canopy, and it carried a smell of summer rain.

"We'll be in trouble from the smoke soon if that fire spreads," thought Feather, but Ilmarin was shouting something and pointing to the stone. They took their hands off their ears for a moment but still could not hear what he was saying. But they could see.

The huge stone was no longer black. Even against the incessant flicker of the lightning they could see that it was shining green, like an enormous emerald: a glow at first, then a terrible brilliance. Soon it was so bright that it only registered as a searing whiteness.

"Don't look at it!" Ilmarin shouted, "it will..." But his words were lost in the bolt of light which broke from the centre of the Gop, striking up into the storm, numbing their senses and blotting out their minds. For the stone that crowned the hill was ancient and perilous beyond the dreams of any sorcery or science that the tinkering of later ages could devise and it would tolerate the presence of no power other than its own or that which called upon it rightfully.

Yet the friends recovered quickly, for the blow had not been aimed at them, and in the sudden silence they realized the storm had gone. The fire among the trees was, for the moment, even reassuring and homely compared to the fury of the elements. But the smoke was thickening all around them and would soon be a danger to any who lingered on the hill. While beneath the Bee Song the path glimmered, full of rippling life, like the careless mirth of a child. And in the centre the stone was again as dark as the night, silent and brooding.

"We must go on," said Ilmarin. "The smoke is spreading."

———

The silvery path led back across the grasslands very close to the farm where Gulmer and Tim, together with the two hands, were keeping an anxious look-out.

"I'm that relieved to see you all," Gulmer called out as they approached, "yon storm looked quite a show from here! Did you not get caught up in it?"

"We did, father," said Feather laughing, "but we were as safe as houses right in the middle of it all!"

"Safe as houses!" he exclaimed, casting a rueful glance at the remains of the barn, "let's not tempt fate with over-bold speech! But you'll be coming in for a hot drink before you go on? The kettle's been on the boil ever since the storm — er — blew itself out. That weren't half a bang at the end, must have blown the top of the hill off!"

He looked up enquiringly at the three smiling faces leaning over the gunwale, waiting for them to come down, desperate for more information. "Come on, then," he said, "Crombel and Nonney are going to stand guard while you come in and sit down."

"Yes, we'll come and tell you all about it, father, but I doubt we'll have any more trouble tonight. A hot drink and then we really must be on our way."

TWENTY-THREE

All about them the plain was dark and silent as they glided on beyond the Ironway. No star could penetrate the cloud, and for hours nothing but the path was visible, stretching as far as the eye could see in a silent and empty world. Later, both to the left and right of them, they saw patches of luminescence glimmering palely here and there as if the heavens — shining from the depths of time — were mirrored still in the waters of some lost, etherial marshland. But there were no more pageants of ancient legend. Only once, for a brief moment, did Fal see three gigantic beasts, reptiles from an age beyond all reckoning, their broad heads a-glow like lanterns as they raised them from the marsh to gaze at the travellers as they passed; or so it seemed, for when he touched Feather's arm and pointed, they were gone. Only a voice, like a note from a heavenly song, rang then through the night, a call full of longing, ancient and lost. The heart leapt in instant recognition but was yet unable to grasp its meaning; and even its memory was swift in fading,

"The land is very old," Feather whispered. "What is it that we have forgotten, that all the world contains?"

"And that maybe contains all the world," said Ilmarin. "Perhaps Fal will find it one day — his quest is but now beginning."

"We must all find it," said Fal, "for we're woven together in one great cloth, and though three shuttles bear us, yet the warp is one."

"Listen!" said Feather, "it begins to speak within us."

"Now we have heard it," said Ilmarin, "it will lead us on,"

Fal yawned and nodded. The cloud was breaking up and stars were appearing everywhere. All three of the weary companions fell into an untroubled sleep as the Bee Song sailed onwards under the rising moon.

———

When they woke, the sun was shining down upon them as they drifted over light and pleasant woodlands. No memory of their solemn conversation in the night remained and they were aware only of being very hungry. The rugged outlines of the Iron Mountains barred the whole of the northern horizon.

Fal did not think that they had left the path, the boat felt too steady and controlled for that; but when they passed through an open valley of bright green grass, closely cropped from the many small deer which they had seen in the region, he decided to set her down and spend the day there. Then in the evening they could see where the path would take them.

Ilmarin hoped that one night might be sufficient to clear the mountains if they began in the twilight as soon as the path became visible. He felt sure that the path, if it led on into the rugged wilderness at all, would not wind about through valleys following the easiest route but would cleave its own way to its own end, contemptuous of any barriers formed by cliff or crag. Even so he was not quite prepared for what confronted them.

As if borne by a strong breeze the Bee Song took them swiftly through the last foothills and entered a long ravine. The noisy cataract of swirling falls to their left was joined here and there by tributaries which tumbled off the cracked and boulder-strewn mountain sides. Where they crossed the path the water sparkled and flashed as if lamps were burning in the stony bed beneath its surface. Suddenly the valley broadened and ended in a round lake. Behind it the mountain wall swept up with harsh and savage finality: two thousand feet of split and deeply furrowed stone.

For one moment Fal thought the path sank into the lake, for the light had spread out in the water and shone as from a great depth. Then he looked beyond. Straight up the rock face it went, dimly while the glow of the lake was still before them but growing clear and strong as they approached.

The Bee Song lifted with a sudden movement, caught in a rush of power as if sucked by a wind from beyond the earth to the glittering worlds of the distant sky. Up and up she rose, and Fal felt such a wild joy surging through her that he was not sure he could have held her back even had he wished.

Feather muttered something and lay down on the floor, her eyes tightly shut, and Fal's stomach was dissolving into nothingness. He groaned.

"Don't look down!" cried Ilmarin. He was leaning forward, staring at the cliff like a mariner desperately seeking a place to moor his boat to a shore which is moving past too rapidly.

Then they were up, and the whole of the Iron Mountains were spread out in the fading twilight before them as the Bee Song floated easily along a bow-shaped saddle towards a rounded peak.

There were no more terrible cliffs. The southernmost ridge was the highest they had to climb and whenever they changed level they followed contours which were gentler and less alarming. Even so, the journey was spectacular and eerie enough for, until the moon rose, the mountains stood in a world of impenetrable shadows which fell away — sometimes on either side of them — as if to the darkest roots of the world or entrapped them in vast pits until they were led up another shining slope into a sky full of stars. And always the path ran, bright and straight, as far as the eye could see in front and behind.

"I wonder just how far it goes," Fal said. "How far does it show up, I mean? Can they see it in the market place in the Delming now because we're using it here, or does it only show up a mile or two in each direction from wherever we are?"

"I've been wondering about that, too," said Feather; "I'm glad it's not often more than a few yards *below* us, though, on this part of the journey!"

But they were already coming out of the high mountains and approaching easier country.

"There's something else that's been puzzling me," Ilmarin said after a while, "we should have tried it out, I suppose, with some of the less dangerous things we saw back in the hills of the Runeway. Were they visible to other people — people walking on the ground, I mean? Would a hunter stalking along all by himself in the dark find himself in the midst of a host of elves with drawn swords or in the path of a charging unicorn, shining like the sun? It could have given him quite a shock."

"Particularly if one of those evil-looking castles suddenly grew up all around him!" said Fal.

"The next thing we see," said Ilmarin, "we'll try it out. One of us standing on the ground while the others lift off."

Feather looked at him in surprise. "Maybe," she said. "Let's wait and see what sort of thing it is before we decide anything like that."

It was in the northern foothills that their chance came. They had been passing down a wooded valley, dark and shadowy still in spite of the moon which hung above the peaks to their right. Ahead of them the forest was full of radiance as of many lanterns, warm and inviting; and they became aware of a sound, a music so subtle that for a while it evaded consciousness, disappearing if the mind sought to focus upon it. At first Fal was reminded of the pipe he had heard in the woods the summer before as he had sailed up the river from the lake; but this was far richer and more complex, as if of many instruments, high and low, and was less alien, speaking more directly to the heart. He tried to identify the instruments that were playing, but whichever strand he listened to shifted and faded elusively, and he could only hear without trying to listen.

The path divided around a rocky mound on which a cluster of birches grew, but the light did not come from there. Beyond it the valley ended in a low cliff, not more than thirty or forty feet high, in which stood an open doorway, framed in heavy stone. Fal stopped the Bee Song in mid air and held her steady above the boulders which formed a rough avenue between the cliff and the mound. Was this really the way, then, the way to the music, to the wonderful light!

They hovered long above the glade, enraptured, as the music worked within them, stirring ever deeper memories; but the memories were like the separate threads in that magic polyphony, and Fal could never quite grasp them. Whenever he struggled to bring an image clearly into his mind, it slipped tantalizingly from him. He sighed, and Ilmarin nodded thoughtfully; Feather wept.

"It's so right," said Fal. "By the shape of the portal the path may be known."

"Hm? What's that?" said Ilmarin, "another saying of the dwarves?"

The door was indeed stangely constructed. The heavy stone lintel was in two parts, slanting slightly downwards from a central point. The uprights also sloped towards each other as they approached the ground, thickening massively and forming with the threshold a harmonious shape of five sides.

"I mean, you can see by looking at the door that whatever it leads to is very good."

"Our heart's desire," said Feather.

"All the best sunrises and sunsets we ever saw," said Ilmarin, "all woven into one."

"But that cliff is real rock," said Fal, "it's no illusion. I'm going inside!"

He moved the Bee Song to one side and set her down on the grass. The light faded, the music withdrew just beyond the limits of hearing, and the door disappeared without trace. Fal hesitated for a moment.

"Lift the Bee Song up," he said as he climbed out, "I'll stay down here."

"You've forgotten," said Ilmarin, "we don't know how. You're the only master harper round here!"

"I think I probably could," said Feather, "but if she got out of control I just wouldn't know what to do."

"Too great a risk," said Ilmarin firmly.

Fal ran his fingers all over the rock where the frame of the door had been. There was nothing. The cliff was cold, silent, and dark even though the sky was brightening with the approach of dawn.

"Let's change round, then," Fal suggested. "You two come here and I'll wait in the Bee Song."

Ilmarin shook his head. "Somehow I don't feel up to facing whatever or whoever is in there," he said, "Not yet."

"I don't want to go in without you," Feather said. "Let's try on the way back. Perhaps you can teach Ilmarin to control the Bee Song by then, and anyway, we shall have more time."

"I feel it's terribly important," Fal said, "it's calling to me."

"It will still be here when we return," said Feather gently, "the door's on the path, we couldn't possibly miss it."

Reluctantly, Fal agreed. He was disappointed yet at the same time exultant with the beginnings of a new hope. He sang quietly to himself as they went on. "The spirit of the rising sun, who is your oldest friend..."

"What's that?" said Ilmarin.

"From one of Silfrintopp's songs. I'm just trying to remember how it goes on."

"You're full of quotations this morning," Ilmarin laughed, "but don't forget, the path always disappears when the sun rises!" And he hugged him.

———

As the pinks and yellows of the sunrise swept magnificently into the north and the last valleys threw off the dull grey of dawn to regain their rightful green, the path faded and once more the land became indifferent to their passing. The power and the response had gone and there was only the familiar and predictable world they knew so well. Rabbits skipped and scuttled in alarm whenever the Bee Song mounted a crest, an otter paused to watch them before plunging into a stream, and an eagle circled above them for a while, following their path.

They set down on the bank of a narrow river running from west to east. Beyond it was the Dodmoor, which would make their way to the forest of Aurëlund easy whether the path ran on or faded forever into the ground. But Fal had joined Ilmarin in believing that it would stop only at a place of great importance, perhaps at Lune itself. Might this not be the very road to Gelmindel of which the legends spoke? Yet in the forest there were signs that it had once been paved; how did that relate to what they had just seen? People who needed cobbles and a causeway could surely not fly up cliffs! It was all too full of riddles, and though his mind crowded with possible explanations he could think of no evidence in favour of any of them.

The bright morning sun dispelled his ponderings, and the silence of the river was soon alive with the quacking of ducks, busily seeking food. The friends washed in the clear water, startlingly cold from the mountain torrents, and applied themselves to breakfast. The sun seemed to flash at them from the very earth itself, for the land was heavy with dew, and rainbows sparkled on every grass-stem and in the tiny spider-hammocks which hung like a mist an inch above the ground.

Fal agreed that there could be no harm in setting the Bee Song moving slowly northwards to find out whether she would travel unpiloted again while they slept, for there were no obstacles on the moor, and even if the path should end, they could scarcely get lost.

They drifted at a walking pace and it was late in the afternoon by the time they awoke, for the journey through the mountains had exhausted them all. They stopped close to the forest to eat again and to wait for the evening light, as Fal preferred to be certain of the path before trying to lift them over the trees.

Thus it was in the night that he came a second time to the Starwell, the circle of stones where Frekk had left him and which he had left in misery after failing to invoke the past. But now, as in his dream, he saw not the rigid stones but the revellers in their many colours, dancing the history of the heavens, the patterns of the stars.

Then the path followed the forest track he knew, past the stream where he had sung to Feather and seen her, robed in flowers. And he wondered again about the nature of that vision: had she also seen him, in the mirror maybe, as he sang? He turned to ask her, but since they had passed the Starwell she had slept, a happy smile on her lips, as if she were not fully asleep but in her spirit dancing on with the star folk of the stones. He bent down and kissed her, and she sighed and murmured in a strange tongue, "Enaith cernu ir astor!" — but she did not wake.

Ilmarin smiled. "She has marvellous dreams," he said, "do not wake her."

It was nearly dawn when they passed above the cleft of rocks that formed the gateway into the Waste. Fal took the Bee Song up as high as he could to look at the great panorama. As they had expected, the path led on to the raised causeway and ran, a glistening line, straight across the plain. Where it vanished in the north a shimmer of light lay above the horizon, a mirage under the moon, of walls upon walls, spire upon spire of white marble: the elven city of Gelmindel. And for a moment the ice-crown of the pointed mountain flashed its proud greeting to them as of old.

"A royal city for a wedding feast!" said Ilmarin. "Let's wake Feather now, for this is a sight that she must share with us."

Yet even as they flew towards it up the causeway, the dawn came and the vision faded.

TWENTY-FOUR

Their arrival at the cottage was a lively and rather noisy affair, with everyone talking at once. Slag and Aurvang in particular made a tremendous fuss at seeing Fal again and tumbled around in an astonishing sequence of somersaults when they saw the Bee Song in action.

"She is well named," said Slag gravely, when they had given suficient expression to their joy and admiration. "Though 'Bee Song under the Waxing Moon' would be a longer name such as dwarves love. And in our language, the tongue of the Eastern Kingdom, it also sounds well: Ghiad Anakîli Fiddakhâlvaur-kseh!"

It rattled from his lips like a little avalanche of pebbles. Fal smiled and nodded. "'Anakîli' must mean 'bee'," he said, "I can tell by the sound; but which word meant 'moon'?

"'Fiddakhâl' is one of her titles," said Slag, "but it does not mean moon. We often use it when we speak of her; she is sacred to us, and in our own language we rarely use her name."

Osmarin behaved in much the same manner as the year before, but Rymon seemed calmer and stronger — and perhaps more genuinely warm-hearted. Fal suddenly realized how little he had trusted her on his first visit. Ristilian looked older and more serious and she wept long with relief to be with Ilmarin again, but also with Fal, and he saw then that she had lived through a dark winter of fear lest they both should never return.

Frekk and Tholley, who had arrived some days before, had been hard at work helping to make a new outhouse against the cliff in which to keep the Bee Song. Frekk had been collecting and hauling stones of a suitable size whilst the dwarves trimmed and layed them. The three walls were finished but the low roof still remained to be added.

"That's going to be the really skilled part," said Tholley, "and we're all looking forward to seeing how they do it. You must watch the amazing way they trim the stones, Fal. They say it's obvious to them where the stone will split and where to lay the chisel. One tap and the rock just falls neatly apart! Their eyes must be very different from mine, that's all I can say."

"I expect they are quite different," Fal laughed, "if they're anything like their cousins at the Delming."

Aurvang overheard the last part of the conversation and gave Fal a dark look.

The roof-slabs, large slate-like tiles a half an inch thick, were stacked ready, and by the following evening the work was done. The dwarves spiralled the stones up, first wedging a row of tiles firmly into a deep groove which they had cut into the cliff face. They worked slowly inwards, going round and round the walls until they had made a dome, incomplete only at its apex, where there was still a small hole. This they closed with a spherical stone of polished white quartz, no larger than a man's fist. Slag said the roof was safe from any wind, not even the fiercest gale of winter would bring it down, and the overlap of the tiles was too great for any rain to blow beneath them. But Aurvang still looked strangely sullen.

There were shelved recesses inside which could be used for sleeping on, and the dwarves asked for the honour of being allowed to guard the Bee Song at night. They had woven the broad doors out of reeds in the most remarkable radiating patterns. Fal thought how interested Aren would be to see this perfect workmanship and he said: "Have you slept at all to have accomplished this in less than four days?"

"Our people need but little sleep," said Slag.

"That is so," Aurvang agreed, "at least with us rock dwarves of the north. It may well be different with other races." And he bowed.

Fal returned the courtesy. "It may indeed, good friends, it most certainly may!"

"The score is even," said Aurvang, bowing again.

"Enough of all this dignity, you solemn people!" Feather laughed. "Supper's ready. Make haste!"

———

The inside of the cottage had changed out of all recognition since Fal's last visit. The cliff had been cut away and the old inner door, which had been hidden behind the cupboards of the pantry recess, now stood in line with the whole back wall thereby nearly doubling the size of the house. The cupboards had all been moved to the right of the door which had been cleaned and polished till its flowing bronze hinges shone like gold. Rymon had apparently given up trying to hide the entrance to her dwarf-kingdom.

Fal discovered that there had been much talk since the arrival of Frekk and Tholley concerning his adventures, and also of Sulthind's strange and sinister interest in them.

"I'll tell you now frankly, Master Falimbravel," Rymon said as they discussed again the events of the past months, "I also once had ambitions of acquiring power like this Sulthind. I'm free of such desires now so I can speak openly of the matter. People who live alone on ancient mountains, like those who live on islands, often become strange in the end. It was my husband who talked it out of me after you and the Lord Ilmarin had visited us."

She sighed and ladled out another round of chicken broth.

"No, I shall give the dwarves back their kingdom. Slag and Aurvang will go off after the wedding and seek out more of their brethren. They say many are still living here and there in the Eastern Mountains and they'll be

able to persuade some of them to come to the halls of Lune. We shall move
to the upper cottage. There's the farm to work and the dwarves have
promised to go on helping us with it. Ristilian will be a great lady in the
lake town and will maybe come to visit us from time to time; but there'll be
no more Guardians of Lune!"

Ilmarin had not yet spoken of the ball of light which he had woven for
the golden table within the mountain, and Fal wondered how this would
affect Rymon's plans. It would now be more of a gift to the dwarves than to
her, he thought, and that could be an important step in bringing Lune and
the Forge closer together; but he wondered what Rymon would think of it.
The wedding feast was to be the next evening and gifts would be exchanged before it. Well, they would see. Anyway, it was going to be King
Amladorkaslagh soon with his wise advisor, the Lord Aurvang! That
would be interesting. But Ilmarin was talking to him.

"... after supper when it's dark. Be best in twos or threes, wouldn't it,
Fal? We couldn't go all round, of course, because it only works when we
stay right above the ancient path. The Master and Mistress should be
first," he said, bowing to Osmarin and Rymon.

"We shall be delighted," said Osmarin, and his cheeks reddened with
boyish pleasure. "I always said the gain would be a hundred times the loss
when I left Vond to wed the Lady Rymon, and I've been proven right again
and again."

Rymon gave him a quick, suspicious glance, but she, too, looked pleased
and full of anticipation.

"And after that we must return the honour," she said. "You shall
accompany us inside the mountain and see the halls of Varya's royal
palace. Ilmarin knows much of it, for some of the chambers were restored
in the winter months with his help, but Fal has only seen the work on the
first level. And there are still more to be cleared. But our industrious
dwarves have toiled enough and will fetch their kinsfolk before the labour
is continued."

The two dwarves nodded their agreement cheerfully but their mouths
were too full of bread and broth to speak. Suddenly an idea came to Fal, or
rather a question to which he thought he already knew the answer; but he
wondered...

"Slag, Aurvang," he said, "Tholaiwin has told you of my adventures and
of the perilous halls of the dragons which I passed through last year. Those
upper passageways, the hall of mirrors, and the underground lake, are they
part of the realm of Queen Varya, too? If so, there must surely be a way
into them from below! I mean, is it really necessary to go right up through
the maze?"

He immediately realized that he had indeed asked a difficult and embar-
assing question. Aurvang appeared to have an attack of cramp or rheumatics in the toes, and Slag, who had made a very bad job of swallowing his

last mouthful, was convulsed with coughing. Frekk was patting him between the shoulders.

"Nay, it's I who should answer that, Master Falimbravel," said Rymon bitterly when the confusion had subsided. "All the mountain belonged to the dwarves, even the great labyrinth, though that was built by the giants, they say, when there was friendship between them and the small people — though we know little of its purpose. Yes, of course there is a way in. Indeed, you've seen it yourself! The door behind the round table leads up into the halls of the dragons. I went there once, too, and stood before them."

Her face had become grim, her expression withdrawn. It was clearly not a pleasant memory. Fal's mind raced with astonishment.

"I did not worship them, do not fear. I had power enough to withstand them — just! But in the end I fled back down the tunnels and closed the door with a spell which has held good ever since." She sighed. "But I began making plans. I brought Aurvang and Slag from Vond to clear the lower levels and restore them to their former size. I thought one day to bring the dragons down into the hall, my hall, and I would strive with them — to win — or lose! I was tired of just living on and on, mistress of nothing! Then, if I won, I would begin increasing my power." She laughed, and the hardness passed from her eyes. "Nay, nay, I've made my decisions, I wish for no power, not any more. And if the dwarves want the upper part of Lune they'll have to deal with the dragons themselves!"

The company stared at her in astonishment. Slowly, old Tholley rose to her feet and bowed, first to her, then to Osmarin.

"You have won a mighty victory, my lady," she said solemnly, "and you do us a great honour to share it with us."

———

As it was nowhere near dark by the time supper was ended and the sun, though reddening, was still some way over the horizon — two thumbs' breadth, Frekk called it, measuring the gap with outstretched arm and squinting through one eye — Tholley suggested inspecting the inside of the mountain first and flying the boat only when it was really dark. This was agreed upon with some reluctance, but as none of them could hasten the oncoming of night it was clearly the most sensible way of spending the time. Ten candle-lanterns were fetched, and the procession filed into the tunnel, the dwarves modestly bringing up the rear with the animals, Bereldan and Alfeng.

The hall had been made ready for the wedding feast and although the walls had not yet been polished, it was a far grander chamber than Fal remembered from his earlier visit. With the combined light of the many lanterns he could now see into the high vault, all merely black shadow before. The patterns of the fine plaited ribbing baffled the eye and his mind began to whirl if he looked up at them too long.

Many brackets had been fixed into the walls, from which hung silver lamp holders, so delicate that they appeared to be made of gossamer, as if the dwarves had called upon spiders to assist them in their craft.

"We also have a small forge," said Slag by way of explanation, "in what is left of the lowest level. It runs below this hall and can be reached by way of some steps leading down from the back tunnel — that's the left-most of the three doors over there. We have extracted the metal ourselves; it is silver of a very high quality."

Embroidered cushions, the work of Ristilian, had been placed on the two stone chairs and on the benches, and five stone candle holders, complete with tall apple green candles, stood ready on the serpentine table top.

"Tomorrow there'll be much light and music at the feast," said Rymon. "It is fitting that today the halls should be silent."

Fal remembered her half-crazed eyes when he had first seen these dark, ancient places and was surprised at the ease and graciousness with which she now led them to the chamber of the mushroom table. It was just as he had last seen it, the hollow in its centre like an empty eye-socket, the black door behind it heavy and brooding.

"We're waiting to sting whatever you put into the bowl for us," said a voice in Fal's mind; "... and to swallow it as a toad swallows a firefly." And he felt once more the terrible pain of the two dragons pressing in upon him. Were they just behind the door?

He glanced anxiously at Ilmarin and for a moment their eyes met. The smith must have felt it too, for he was frowning and fingering the leather pouch beneath his tunic. But Rymon was leading them on. Ilmarin came to Fal's side as they returned to the hall.

"We may need to work on this together," he whispered, "you and I — and Rymon! She has more knowledge than you think. But one alone will never be enough."

They were being taken up the stairway on the right. After hundreds of steps they turned off into a narrow, pointed doorway which Fal had not noticed before. Perhaps it had been blocked with rubble; but most of his ascent to the summit of Lune was only part of a troubled dream in his memory.

Rymon explained that the gallery which they had now entered ran high above the banqueting hall, back towards the south wall of the mountain, so high indeed that the dwarves were sure there was at least one more level between them, but they had so far failed to discover how to enter it. Four square chambers led from the gallery left and right in pairs, and Aurvang thought they had once been armouries and treasure houses. They were unornamented and empty. Two more doors were passed, opening onto stairways and passages as yet still uncleared, then the tunnel ended in a broad archway, almost circular except for the pointed top. The surround, though cracked in several places, was polished and inlaid with beaten silver. Fal recognised the flowing, interlocking patterns as an old script of the dwarves, though it had been stylized and ornamented beyond legibility. But Aurvang smiled. "It can be read," he said. "The meaning is:

> Behold the Six, perceive the One,
> Six for the Moon and seven the Sun;
> Where hidden light's revealed in stone,
> The stars shine bright round Varya's throne."

"Come," said Rymon, "this is the best chamber in the mountain, and we're all very proud of it."

Behind the archway was a curtain of plain white linen, hanging in many folds. It parted in the middle, and Osmarin and Rymon lifted it to either side to allow the company to enter.

It was a spacious hexagonal room of many pillars all of which spread out at the top but were slender and quite straight where they met the floor. Most of them were around the walls forming an arched ambulatory, cloister-like, and so close together that a man might lay his hands on two at once and still keep his elbows near his side. In the centre, flanking a high-backed chair of the same white stone, were pillars of an even slimmer build which branched like saplings between the shallow domes into which the whole ceiling was divided. These domes were low enough to be examined with ease, one above the chair and six more surrounding it. All were thickly studded with gold and silver stars, set in polished blue stone, and appeared to be detailed and accurate maps of the heavens.

"In the dome above us," Aurvang explained, "are the stars of the north, those which can be seen in every night, at every season. Around them are other aspects of the heavens at different times of the year. But the Moon and the Sun, together with the five lesser planets, are set into the back of the throne. They would have come just behind the Queen's head."

Seven gems, of equal size but of subtly varying colour, were set into the back of the chair, while between them wove an inscription in the same style as that around the doorway.

"A place of wonder indeed!" said Tholley. "Can this also be read?"

"It is the true names of the Seven Planets," said Slag, "they can be spoken only among dwarves."

"Is this the very throne from which Queen Varya once ruled the north, do you think?" Fal asked — not without a little awe, for he was remembering the legends of the lady of power who had ruled the world before the fire rose within the mountain.

"She must have been taller than the dwarf-kindred then," said Feather, "for the circle of the planets is too high."

"That is so," Slag agreed. "Our stories do not say that she was a dwarf-queen but that she came from the stars to live among us. We also tell that, unlike a dwarf-monarch, she wore no crown but a shining necklace of white starlight. Yet some stories say that the necklace was wrought for her by the dwarves. Who knows?"

Fal said, "This must be a most sacred place for you, then, and we are privileged that you show it to us. Maybe good luck will one day bring you to find the star necklace, too!"

Aurvang grimaced, but Slag laughed, saying, "That would be a treasure great enough to cause war among the kindreds! Nay, as like we shall find the Lady Varya herself sleeping in her crystal tomb! But come, there are other chambers leading off from the Hall of Stars which you must still see, and to show our good will to the big people of Earth we make two of them over to them and to their children for ever. These rooms shall be kept ready for the Lord Dringskel and his bride, the Lady Ristilian, as often as they will favour us with their presence."

The dwarves bowed deeply to Ilmarin and Ristilian and led them through another curtained door in the south-east wall of the chamber. The company followed them. They came through a passage to a large room in which was a table and two chairs. To everyone's surprise Slag strode across the floor to what appeared to be two hinged wooden panels. He unlatched them and proudly threw them back. The twilight of the evening outside streamed in, dimming their lanterns; the panels were shutters!

"Men dislike being shut away from the Sun, we know, and with these two chambers, which are our wedding gift, goes the light of day. The furnishings are as yet simple and unworthy, but in good time we shall equip these rooms as well as the best in any lordly palace. The inner chamber goes with it."

Through a wide uncurtained arch the amazed guests looked into a delightful bed chamber. A broad oak frame stood upon legs which seemed to spiral out of the floor, and on four intricately carved pillars was hung an embroidered roof.

"The canopy is the work of the Lady Rymon," said Slag. "It shows the Queen wearing the necklace of stars. Around her stand the seven dwarf kings, one for each of the seven planets."

"Another interpretation would be the seven colours of the rainbow in the halo of the full Moon," said Aurvang. "You will observe that in each crown there is represented a jewel of a different sort."

The guests had knelt on the ground or otherwise contorted themselves to admire the picture over the bed, which was beautifully executed in many delicate colours as well as with thread of gold and silver.

"I thank you, dear people — my lady, good dwarves!" said Ilmarin warmly. "These gifts are a generous token of the bonds between us all. May they ever grow and be as strong and sure as Earth herself!"

———

By the time they returned to the cottage it had long been dark outside, although in the west the last red of the sunset still clung above the hills and in the east a glow of gold, herald of the rising moon, threw a line of distant mountains into dark relief. Everyone was weary, yet none thought of retiring before the Bee Song had been brought out and they had taken turns in viewing ancient Gelmindel from her.

"Have you thought what it would be like if a wall appeared from the past and the Bee Song was stuck in the middle of it?" Feather said as Fal, Frekk, and the two excited dwarves fetched the boat from her newly finished housing. The canopy and its four poles had been dismantled for the moment as the door was several inches too low for them.

"I doubt whether anyone would have ever built right on the path," said Fal, "though I suppose there could be an archway further away from the cliff, the entrance to the city or something."

"You might find yourself embedded in it then, with your head just sticking out — if you were lucky — and if you weren't, just your feet! No, really, Fal, if you couldn't move how would you bring the boat down?"

"Probably I couldn't! You'd have to leave me hanging there and live with the elves of Gelmindel till the time came for the mountain to burn us all to ashes."

But the Bee Song was ready, and the moon was watching them, waiting for the entertainment to begin. It was agreed that Rymon, Osmarin, and Ristilian should go up with Fal first while the others waited in front of the cottage. Fal took his harp and tuned it, then began the music to awaken the boat's golden patterns. In a ripple of light she lifted from the ground.

They all looked to see shining walls and palaces arise around them and so were taken off their guard when the moonlit waste was plunged into utter darkness. For a brief moment all that could be seen was the glimmer from the Bee Song's gunwale and the lanterns of those who, having but lately renewed their candles, had not bothered to extinguish them. The moon and stars had vanished.

Then the path leapt out beneath them, a white flame breaking like fire under the feet of those on the ground, so that they cried out in fear. It licked at the cottage door, and the hinges shone like molten metal and for a second writhed like angry serpents. Then the door burst open, and with a crash the inner door followed suit as the path sprang into the mountain like a ravenous wolf leaping at last upon its prey.

The cottage had disappeared. On the bare cliff was a carven archway, framing the inner door through which the path had gone, and out of that door a joyous sound came. It was music, happy but fierce, of loud and wild splendour, music of harps and pipes and cymbals and of a company of many voices. And above it rang out one voice, clear and alone, lovely and yet terrible, for its beauty was almost too great to be borne — the voice of a woman singing with her dwarvish folk.

Slag and Aurvang gave an agonized shout and dashed in through the doorway, their lanterns swinging wildly. But even as they did so the music began to fade, as if the festive company were removing deeper into the heart of their hidden realm.

Fal and his friends waited in anxious silence for the dwarves to return. But soon the music had completely gone and it was already difficult even to remember what it had sounded like.

"They heard it, too," Fal said at last from the boat, which he still held aloft, "though they were on the ground."

"We all heard it," said Feather simply.

"The path is stronger here," said Ilmarin, "this is its home."

"Maybe it's altogether an affair of the dwarves," said Ristilian, "the path, the whole mountain, even the very north itself!"

It was the first time she had spoken since they had entered the halls. She had seen their wonders with dull, heavy eyes, for her heart was sick with longing to be in the Delming, her future home, with its motley of people, its green hills, its many-coloured boats and its lake. But Slag and Aurvang came out of the doorway then. They were weeping.

"They are gone, gone!" wailed Slag, "their voices melted into the rock, we did not even glimpse them!"

"Yet we must rejoice and be glad, for we have heard Her, and forever and forever we shall remember that in the halls of Lune we heard the blessed voice," said Aurvang, and embracing one another the two dwarves wept anew, loudly and bitterly.

"Come," said Rymon after a while, "set the boat down, Fal. It is enough for tonight. In a few days we can maybe try again."

The moon and the cottage appeared once more, and, in a sober frame of mind, they all made ready for the night.

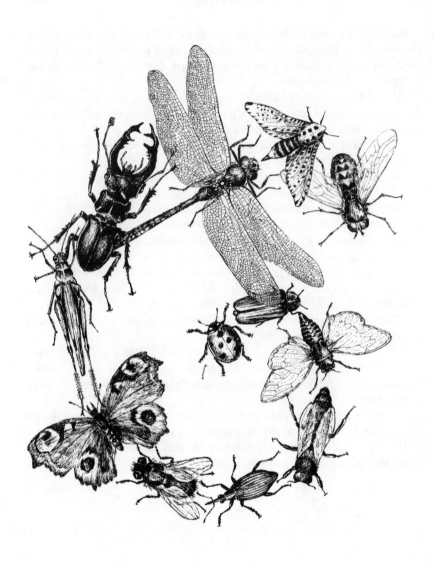

TWENTY-FIVE

As the dwarves had already presented their gift and Rymon had given the canopy, it was felt that present-giving was too much in the air to wait until the feast for the further exchange of treasures. So it was decided that they should share at least some of them straight after breakfast.

Frekk had brought a stone flask of water taken from the Starwell of Aurëlund. It was the custom among his people, he said, to keep this water to hallow weddings. It was to be sprinkled in the corners of the rooms, on the thresholds and window sills, and especially on the bed of the bride and groom.

"It carries the virtue of Istra," he said, "who brings the new life of the spring."

Tholley had a box of thin, dull metal ornamented with only a simple zig-zag pattern. The treasure was inside, not outside, she explained apologetically and opened it to show an enormous egg, longer than the hand of a man from finger tips to wrist. It was most wonderfully carved with the figures of dancers holding hands and spiralling about it. The company gasped in disbelief.

"A dragon's egg!" said Slag.

"The beginning of worlds!" said Aurvang.

"Nothing so magical, I fear," Tholley laughed, "and yet it's a rare thing, even in the far south, in the hot summery land where I came by it. There they have birds which stand higher than the tallest man, and their bodies are as big as ponies. They do not fly but run as swift as hares, and to be kicked by one can be dangerous. Yet they have large and tender eyes."

"And beautiful eggs!" said Ristilian. "How I long to see such birds and to visit those warm, exciting places! Do all their eggs have such pictures on them?"

Tholley laughed again. "No, lady," she said, "the birds are dull of mind and do not possess the wit to lay eggs with such skill. This carving was a long and careful labour of fingers practised in their art for many years — yes, through many generations, for it is an ancient craft."

Ristilian reddened. "Nevertheless," she said, taking a firm grip of Ilmarin's hand, "I will see those lands, and in these days of feasting, Mistress Tholaiwin, I bid you tell us more of the wonders of those people and of your adventures in their country."

Tholley said she would do so gladly and that if Ristilian did one day make a journey to the lands of the hot sun, the folk there would be well rewarded for their wonders by beholding the beauty of the frosty north.

Ristilian reddened even more — this time with pleasure.

"With my gift goes a tale," said Feather. "Long ago there was a lady of Hallin who dwelt in the City of the White Gates. When she was of age she married a silversmith of Dalf-Ender, the realm beyond the forest, and so went to live in Fram by the open sea. With her she took a necklace of eight stones which came from the hills where the four rivers rise, at the secret heart of the forest, and in which were imprinted — not by the skill of man but by the art of nature — the images of trees. She always wore it on her breast and was comforted by it regarding her loss, for though she loved the smith and his city the trees of Hallin ever whispered to her in her dreams.

"This was the time of the sacking of Fram, and although many perished she and her husband fled to safety and journeyed far by boat until they found the mouth of the Eastmorn. They sailed then through winter mists and bitter cold up the winding river and northwards through the lake until they came once again to the White Gates. But there she found misfortune had come before her and though she ran crying through the streets of the city, no voice answered hers."

"This is a tale of ill omen for a wedding!" said Osmarin.

"It would be, sir, if the story ended there," said Feather. "But the lady and her husband wandered on up the River Gard, and it is said that the stones she wore drew her on and guided her until she found the rest of her folk, living secretly yet in all their power. And she and the smith became at last great among them, both in worth and in happiness." She took out a round box of polished chestnut, dark with age. "The necklace was given to my grandmother at her wedding, many years ago. Here it is!"

The eight agates were mounted simply in thin frames of gold, and of gold too was the slender chain on which they hung. In each stone, as if growing in a world of blue, shifting mists, stood a magic tree, remote and silent, real yet unattainable.

"Thank you, dear Feather," said Ristilian, "I shall wear it at the feast tonight."

Then Ilmarin unfolded the cloak of the Golden Tree which Aren and Melauriën had made, and when Ristilian tried it on, the light of the elves seemed to shine about her and she was indeed very beautiful.

"Already we see a great lady of the Delming," said Tholley admiringly. "How they will welcome her and love her when she rides in the Bee Song through the city gates!"

Ristilian's eyes shone. "I can't wait to see the green hills by the lake and the Forge with its Golden Tree and shining spire," she said.

"My gift is wrought by the skill of the harper," said Fal, "but it should be sung tonight — and then thereafter as often as called for, as long as we are all together."

But already the festive mood had grown upon them and Ristilian stood lovely and resplendent before them.

"Please sing it now *and* tonight, good Fal," she said, "lest at the banquet I be too excited to take in all the words."

The company agreed that this was fitting, and Fal was soon persuaded. First he had to retune his harp to a more usual scale than that needed for flying the Bee Song, and then he was ready.

"It's a song of journeying, a song of the sea," he said. "It would go well with Aurvang's fiddle, but he can rehearse that another day if he is willing. Here it is:

> All waters of the world are one,
> though many are the boats that run
> above the deep: great craft and small,
> with lifting prow through calm or squall,
> boats strong or flimsy, slow or bold,
> on northern waters, grey and cold,
> or where the ocean warm and blue
> makes sailing easy, hardships few.
>
>> The seas of the worlds
>> are free from taint or curse,
>> the seas where sail the stars
>> through the wide universe:
>> They lead ever onward
>> by clear sky, wind or rain,
>> whatever the adventure,
>> the joy or the pain.
>
> All one the world's oceans wide,
> all one the wind, all one the tide;
> and when at last our boat finds land
> there may we meet a helping hand
> to pull our keel upon the shore
> where we must battle on no more
> until our roving heart again
> longs to be back on the ocean main.
>
>> Life is the conquest,
>> the distant shore the aim
>> whether we go swiftly
>> or stay limping with the lame.
>> Striving with the rigging
>> till hand and arm are numb,
>> self is overcoming,
>> and self is overcome.

So long the years, so long the night,
before the greying dawn brings sight
of countries where our dreams come true,
where we can shape our ship anew
and sit with friend we once thought lost
and know that it was worth the cost
to follow true the northern star
and seek new shores, remote and far.

   The greater the ocean,
   the less we seem to move;
   but we are fellow sailors all,
   as time to us will prove.
   Alike though we're among the strong,
   the timid, blind or dumb:
   self is overcoming,
   and self is overcome.

It was no silence that followed the end of the song, for so suggestive were the lilting melodies which Fal had matched to the words that for a while all the company still heard the breaking of waves felt the dipping and lifting of the deck, and tasted the salty tang upon their lips.

"Ay, the sea! The sea has a life of its own, a life that calls strongly to the heart. 'I never left you,' it cries, 'I have walked ever by your side! Come, return to me!'"

It was Osmarin who spoke and, as always, his voice had a far away, almost childish tone, but his eyes showed the hurt of a great sadness.

"I also have a gift," he said, "and as it was the sea that bore it hither, it follows well upon Fal's song."

He shuffled over to the curtains covering the nearest sleeping recess and fumbled for a moment at a cupboard over the bed.

"When I was a lad I travelled with a schooner my father owned, for he was rich even as the merchants of Vond go and he had many ships. A fine two-decker she was, called the Cloud Queen, and there was never a ship more worthy of her name. Several times I went with them but once it must have been for more than two years. We saw strange places and strange folk.

"Only one treasure did I ever bring back, for a ship like the Cloud Queen was too good to be cluttered with all the trinkets and oddities that sailors hoard, to my way of thinking." He was holding a linen wrapping tenderly before them. "It was the only treasure I would bring from Vond when I wed the Lady Rymon, too," he smiled as he unfolded it, "but now it is time to pass it on. It has been with me long enough. I give it to Ilmarin — it will look well upon him."

It was a long, slender dagger, almost a short sword, and it had neither sheath nor strap from which to hang. The hilt was of silver, burnished almost white, and crowned with a purple amethyst, simply faceted, so that the stone seemed too liquid to stay in its bowl. And, as if indeed flowing down from the jewel, curling patterns were worked into the hilt and spilled over onto the straight steel blade.

"The wonder of it is," said Osmarin, "that in spite of the big stone and the heavy silver, the knife lies so lightly in the hand that no matter which way it's turned, it balances perfectly and is ready for any move required of it."

The dwarves nodded appreciatively. They had seen this weapon before, but its worth was such that they were ready to admire it again and again.

"You give me a wonderful treasure, sir," said Ilmarin earnestly, "indeed your greatest, and you do me great honour."

"Not my greatest," said Osmarin. "My greatest treasure is my daughter, and with her goes my heart."

"Come, husband," said Rymon, and it seemed to Fal that she spoke more gently with him than was her wont, "our hearts will make sorry fare for the feast tonight if there's sadness in them, and without a deal of work there'll be no feast at all! Let's be about it now. I'll give each one his tasks so we may be the sooner ready."

———

By late afternoon all the remaining preparations had been made but by custom the feasting could not begin until sunset and the waiting was hard. The company sat in the cottage and went yet again through the sequence of the ceremony which they had devised.

First came the procession, with music, headed by Rymon and Ilmarin. The smith was to carry the jewel of light in its golden casket, but its lid would remain closed until they stood round the stone table when it would be given to Rymon as a token of the union of the Forge and Lune. After placing it upon the table she would open it for all to see. Behind them the bride was to come with Feather as her companion and then Fal as harper of the feast. Aurvang, Frekk and Tholley were to follow with the animals and would bring such foods as were not already on the table. Osmarin was to come last as master of the house to 'close the doors', a function to which both he and Rymon seemed to attach some special significance. Slag was already in the hall to 'sweep it with good intentions' and to welcome the guests.

Suddenly it was time. Aurvang came bustling in and said the sun was setting in a most propitious array of colours and was clearly dressed in all her finery in honour of the feast, so they must begin without delay. No-one wanted to argue with him and they at once lined up in their agreed order.

As Fal's harp began to sound, a serious mood came upon them all and they filed slowly into the mountain. Osmarin lagged behind touching the doorways of both cottage and cliff on left and right, above and below, muttering words which Fal took to be some kind of blessing.

The hall was all a-blaze with light. On the walls, on the table, round the edges of the floor, hundreds of candles appeared to be growing out of the solid rock, outlining the features of the cavern in white and golden flame. It was hard to believe that Queen Varya with her necklace of stars was not going to join them. Fal made a great effort to imagine the host of dwarves around her, the glory of their jewels, the gold and silver of their instruments; and he tried to remember the harsh resplendence of their music, as if the mere thought of it might draw them back into being.

But they did not come; or if they did, none there had senses fine enough to see them.

At the table Rymon, as mistress, welcomed the company and told them why they had met: for the wedding of Ristilian, daughter of Lune, and Ilmarin, son of the Delming. Then the smith gave her the casket, and she opened it and set it before her. But the stone was quiet and might have been made of jet for all the shine it gave, for its time had not yet come.

They all sat, and to begin with the dwarves served them, though they too had places set at the table, on either side of Osmarin.

The feast was simple but excellently prepared, and all fell to with a will. There was venison in cranberry sauce, fresh wheaten bread — a luxury in the north — with creamy golden butter. There were rye cakes with soft white cottage cheese, made of goats' milk, and there was barley beer, as potent as any wine, to add merriment to the solemnity and laughter to the tales and songs.

Then came the entertainments. First there was to be a story from Tholley, followed by juggling and games. The dwarves carried silver water-bowls round the table for the guests to wash their fingers and when they had returned to their seats she began.

"It is a tale from the south," she said, "from the same land as the carven egg; and yet it has a mood in it akin to the north and is well suited to be told at this feast.

"In the youngest age of the world there was a man. He was much better off than people are today for he had only to desire food and he would without effort find it. All that was on earth conspired to serve and feed him and the world was like a playground to explore and revel in. And yet he was lacking in one important thing, for the gods, who had carefully prepared a name for him, had decided to keep it safe until he was older and wise enough to possess it.

"For many years the man had no idea of this peculiar circumstance and turned his mind only to getting to know the countless wonders which the world showed him — its many weathers, its rivers and fishes, its trees and its blossoms. Music, too, was everywhere about him: there were the great songs of the birds and the little songs of the frogs and grasshoppers; but there was also the music of the thunder storms, of the rainbows, and of the stars. And all the beasts knew him and were tame in his presence, for he was their friend.

"One day he came to a chasm where he had never been before, and he was surprised to find it so barren that neither grass nor bush was growing in its poor soil. This amazed him even more than finding that the valley had an inhabitant, thin and lizard-like as he was, for in his dreams he had seen many strange folk but had never imagined that a place could be so waste as this.

"'My name is Shrimni,' the thin stranger said, 'What is yours?'

"The man looked at him and was bewildered, for though he knew the names of all the things that lived in the world, he did not know his own.

"'I am the man,' he said.

"'The man, *the man*!' cackled the thin one and did a wild dance to show how amused he was. His arms and legs flailed around like sticks in a wind, for he was as thin as a bone.

"'Why don't you leave this rocky place and come out into the world?' the man asked Shrimni. 'You are terribly thin! You can share my food for as long as you like.'

"'Imbecile!' shrieked the lizard-man, 'do you think I want to forget my name?' he did a jerky, hopping dance to show how scornful he was of a fellow who did not even know his own name... then he stopped and stared at the man for a long, long time.

"'I don't need your food,' he said at last, 'look how strong I am as it is.'

"He stooped and picked up a boulder, balancing it on his finger tips as though it were a pebble. The man was ashamed for he knew he could never pick up such heavy stones.

"'Is that... because of your name?'

"'Of course, of course!' Shrimni hooted, tossing the boulder down the valley, 'I don't need your useless food, but you need a name!'

"'Can you give me one?'

"'Give you one? That would be no good, no good at all! You must stay here in this valley until you find one!'

"The man glanced around at the rocks as if he expected to see his name just lying there, waiting for him to pick it up. He saw Shrimni smiling contemptuously and for the first time in his life he felt miserable and lacking.

"'That's a good start,' said Shrimni. 'Rule one: you can't learn till the right time comes. You've begun: Rule two: better late than never.'

"'I'm hungry,' said the man, 'do you eat stones?'

"Shrimni gave a piercing scream of laughter and began crackling up and down the rocks like a firework to show how impossibly absurd the man was.

"'First you want to learn, then you want to eat!' he bawled down from a cliff-top. 'Rule three: one thing at a time!'

"The man felt terribly tired and confused. A bony finger tapped his shoulder from behind and he leapt around. It was Shrimni.

"'Don't start getting jumpy,' he said quietly, 'or you'll have to be taught more on the first day than is good for you, and that will mean breaking rule number four.'

"'What's rule number four?'

"'The inquiring mind, eh?' Shrimni grinned, 'you certainly are moving fast! Rule number four is: don't get upset by what you can't avoid!'

"'I'm tired,' said the man.

"'Then go to sleep!'

"Shrimni turned and walked away, but later he came back with a razor and while the man slept he shaved the top of his head until it was as smooth and shiny as his. Then he took a sharpened adder's tooth and a bottle of nightshade ink out of his pouch and began drawing a sign on the man's head. It was only one sign but it was very complicated and took several hours to complete. Then he walked off and left the man sleeping.

"When he awoke the light of dawn was creeping down into the valley and it was very cold. He sprang to his feet and looked angrily around, for at first he could not remember where he was. Then fear entered his heart and he began to run, grazing his elbow, ankles, and knees in his haste to get back to his own green and lovely country. But when he reached it he discovered that it had changed in his absence. The light which had shone around all living things had grown dull, so that now he had to look hard to see any beasts at all, for they had become grey and brown, as drab as the rocks of Shrimni's chasm. And they hid from him.

"At first he could do nothing but grieve at his misfortune, but then he decided to build a house out of branches, for he felt lost and helpless in a hostile world. And he became lonely and felt cheated that his happiness had gone and he had gained nothing in return, for he still did not know his name. But he resolved never to rest until he had found it.

"'Then I shall go back to Shrimni's valley,' he said, 'and I shall tell him my name and I shall return to him the fear which he gave me, for it is his, not mine, and must be returned. And I shall take seeds from all the plants in the world and sow them in his valley until it is green and good and beautiful. Then the music and the light will come back and Shrimni will find the food he needs but does not want and he will have fulfilled his first two rules. I wonder how he will deal with the third and fourth?'

"And until this day the man has still not answered that question!"

The dwarves were highly delighted with this story and nodded and laughed when it was finished, but the rest of the company were made thoughtful by it and Osmarin looked glum, for he found the tale totally unsuited to the occasion.

But it was the dwarves' turn to take the entertainment in hand. They stood up, bowed and apologised for their being only two and thus limited in the scope of their performance, to which properly belonged a team of at least six.

"That's three pairs," said Slag.

"Or two trios," said Aurvang.

They commenced by leap-frogging over one another round and round the table in such rapid alternation that it was, after a few seconds, quite impossible to see who was who. Fal was just wondering whether Ilmarin was able to follow the rapid movements when the pattern changed. They were bounding now in enormous leaps from one side of the table to the other, right over the heads of the company. As they hurtled through the air they gave strange mewling squeaks, rather like the cries of seagulls. And though it was difficult to be sure, Fal thought he saw a light on their heads as if the tops of their caps were burning.

By this time even Ilmarin's senses were becoming overtaxed and no-one quite managed to see what was happening when at last the dwarves rolled into two quite round balls and began bouncing higher and higher round the table as if they were made of the purest rubber. Sometimes they were both up together, sometimes in alternation, but with each bounce the height increased until, near the roof of the cavern, there was a blinding flash and a bang and — they were gone!

The outcry of consternation which broke out round the table was at once mixed with the merry laughter of the performers. They were both sitting on their seats on either side of Osmarin.

"Why, how *do* you do it!" exclaimed Feather, full of wonder and admiration, "you're not even out of breath!"

"Ah, lady," said Aurvang, "it's different with dwarves."

Even Osmarin looked pleased and nodded approvingly, first to one dwarf then the other.

"Thank you, *good* dwarves!" Ristilian beamed. "May you one day see this hall full of bouncing, disappearing dwarves!"

Rymon laughed out loud, but the dwarves both rose and bowed deeply to their guests.

"And now," Ristilian continued eagerly, "we're going to play a game — the game I've made up specially for this feast. If Feather would pass me the covered basket I'll explain it to you."

She removed the wicker lid and the company saw that the basket contained a number of small rolls of cloth.

"Here are the twelve insects made by the dwarves of the Delming," she said; "we are going to pass the basket back and forth across the table. Everyone must take his chance and see what fate brings him; then he must try to explain the meaning of the insect he's chosen and say why it came to him. After that he must look for someone who hasn't yet opened a roll and pass the rest on. You see, it's a sort of game of omens, and we must interpret them."

The guests smiled and looked at the basket with anticipation. Only Osmarin frowned and at once sank back into his odd mood.

"I shall begin," said Ristilian, "and as there are twelve omens, the animals shall have one each, too. Frekk and Tholaiwin shall answer for them, if they will."

She chose a roll and unwrapped it. It was the gilded ladybird, and its crystal spots glistened brightly as they caught the light of the many candles. Ristilian hesitated for a moment, then she said, "This is easy. The ladybird's a homely insect and an omen of motherhood. And there's a saying, 'ladybird, fly away home' — which is what my dear husband and I shall soon do in the Bee Song, home to our new life in the green land by the lake. Here, husband, see what chance brings you!"

She handed Ilmarin the basket across the table. He stood up smiling, perhaps a little apprehensively, for so much talk of omens was making him uneasy, too, and selected a roll. It was the moon-stone firefly and the light of it shone through his fingers.

"It's the Bee Song that flies best in the moonlight," he said, "or — my heart that shines with light on this my wedding night!" He smiled at Ristilian and passed the basket on to Fal.

His was the cicada of polished flint.

"A songster from the south am I," he said — and then frowned. "But with a heart of stone!"

The company groaned in mock disapproval but was already watching Feather who was unwrapping the next insect. It was the queen bee of red gold. Feather appeared to be embarrassed and at a loss for words. After a few moments Fal came to the rescue.

"The bee is sacred to Mother Earth," he said, "and it's clear that she loves her daughter."

"Rather say that this bee is sent to remind me of our 'hive' at Gopley, and though the bees there give milk instead of honey they are dear to us nonetheless and will needs be tended. This omen strikes hard at my conscience!"

She passed the basket on to Tholley who quickly unwrapped an insect, clearing her throat as if about to make an important speech. It was the green weevil with its glittering diamonds.

"This insect's long and probing nose warns me that I'm too fond of poking mine into other folk's affairs. It strikes me hard, it too stabs at my conscience!" she exclaimed, clutching at her heart in feigned melodrama. "And as the Lady Bereldan lies at my feet, we'll open another roll and see what reproach the oracle proclaims for her." She unrolled a cloth and the enormous blue-bottle of steel was revealed.

"This queen, nay empress of blue-bottles tells us that she will settle on your nose and lay her maggots on it unless you wake up and perform some act of gratitude for the monstrous supper you've consumed this day!"

She nudged the bear gently with her foot and Bereldan sat up blinking in the candlelight uncertain at first why she had been addressed. Then she rose up on her hind legs, towering above the table, and to the delight of the company executed an elegant pirouette, after which she collapsed on the floor and went back to sleep, oblivious to the applause of her admirers.

Tholley had succeeded in getting Ristilian's omen-game away from its serious tack and she was sure Frekk would help her keep it in a lighter vein.

Frekk chose the opal butterfly. "Free as the pretty butterfly I'll roam the woods until I die!" he improvised. Alfeng was already sitting on his haunches eyeing the basket hopefully in case it hid an offering of fresh bones. Frekk opened a bundle for him and revealed the bronze grasshopper.

"You shall be a mighty leaper all your life, your legs shall never fail you!" he proclaimed, and Alfeng snapped loudly at the metal insect, narrowly missing the hunter's fingers.

Amid the ensuing laughter Slag opened the next bundle rather carelessly and was bitten by the powerful jaws of the ferocious stag beetle. He made a great show of exaggerated agony before he managed to prise the jaws apart and set the creature down on the table.

"This is to show that Slag is never at a loss to overcome even the most unexpected of foes, but also the rhyme drew it to me, for 'stag' and 'Slag' could not be missed even by such a poor poet as I!" And he pushed the basket over to Aurvang.

It was the dragonfly next, and Aurvang pointed out seriously that even as a dragonfly arose from the water and grew powerful wings, so he too had come up from Vond of the many rivers where he had lived a dull and ugly life to live in a hall of light and splendour. There was applause, and Aurvang, looking into the basket and seeing only two rolls left, realized that Rymon and Osmarin, at either end of the table, had not yet had their turns. He looked uncertainly from one to the other, for a moment undecided to whom he should give it. Then, leaving his place, he went up to Rymon and offered her the choice.

She took the silver moth.

"This is most apt," she said, "for silver is the metal of the moon and of the north. Yet Ilmarin also chose an insect of the night and that too is fitting, for the omen says that in this marriage an enduring affection between mother and son shall be found. But what of the last omen? Take it to my lord."

She returned the basket to Aurvang who had been waiting by her to carry it to Osmarin.

None remembered what insect was left in the remaining bundle, but whatever it was Osmarin rose to meet it as if it were a mortal enemy and unwrapped the covering slowly with a grim, white face. Out of the cloth flamed first the two emerald eyes, their thousand tiny facets sparkling maliciously. Then out came the heavy iron body of the horse-fly.

Osmarin set it down with a thud and pushed it from him. "Damned blood-sucking leech!" he gasped, and his eyes were filled with horror as if the creature were a ghastly threat to him and not a mere toy of stone and metal. "What day is this when omens shoot their poisoned darts at me yet show all honey to the others here!"

An appalled silence gripped the company for a terrible moment and none knew any word to save the situation. And in that silence a soft laughter was heard from the doorway behind Osmarin. Into the shine of the many candles, his face twisted with scorn, walked Sulthind.

Osmarin turned at once to face the sound, while the rest of the company sat lame with amazement.

"I closed the doors," said Osmarin, "how could you have entered?"

Sulthind stopped laughing and thrust his face forward impudently, his eyes wide in a pretence of startled indignation.

"You closed the doors! *You* closed the doors, you lime-faced mole!" Sulthind made a comic sound of pained commiseration. "Now I come to think of it, there was a faint odour of a little amateurish magic around one of the thresholds; just enough to discourage a senile tomcat on one of his off-days, I should think. Sorry if I've spoiled anything!"

He walked closer to the table, glancing quickly over its contents and around the circle of guests. Fal thought that his gaze lingered for a moment on the golden casket, but it was hard to be sure. Osmarin stepped out and barred his way.

"This is my daughter's wedding feast, Lord Lothur," he said, "and you're intruding upon a company of invited guests."

"'Lord Lothur' indeed!" sighed Sulthind with a tired expression. "Come, come, you know how I dislike that name, you are hurting my feelings. I've been Ilmarin's closest friend since we were infants, probably the invitation just went astray — lost in the fog or something quite silly. Obviously I'm invited, where shall I sit?"

With a contemptuous gesture he tried to push Osmarin aside, but the Lord of Lune, however unsuccesful he had been in defending his house with magic, had no intention of failing a second time in one day.

"Get out of my way, you bladder headed oaf!" hissed Sulthind. "Find me a seat or give me your own before the lightning sizzles your guts!"

Frekk and Ilmarin had both risen from their places, but whatever they had intended to do they were too late, for the unexpected took any immediate action out of their hands. Osmarin, with surprising force, hit Sulthind in the face with his clenched fist. Sulthind staggered back and at the same moment the two dwarves leapt upon him like wild cats. Frekk was wrestling with Alfeng on the floor trying to keep him out of it for fear of harming the dwarves, and Rymon was screaming something down the table, but in the ensuing uproar no-one heard what she said.

The dwarves were unarmed but were going for Sulthind's eyes with tooth and nail. Somehow he managed to hurl Slag to the floor, then, with his free hand, he appeared to punch Osmarin in the chest. Using Aurvang as a battering ram he shouldered Tholley back against the table, turned and ran for the door, the furiously scratching and biting dwarf still clinging to his neck.

Frekk had stopped fighting Alfeng now, and they both leapt after the retreating sorcerer.

If a wall of adamant had been built across the tunnel they could not have hit it harder than the invisible barrier which Sulthind had left behind. Fortunately the distance between the table and the doorway was too short for them to have been moving at great speed or they would have suffered grievous injury. As it was, they both reeled back, stunned and angry. The wolf leapt again and again at the hidden obstacle snarling explosively with rage until Tholley called him off.

"The Lord Osmarin is hurt," Rymon cried then, "help him from the floor!"

He had been half lying, supported by his hands and elbows, and as Tholley and Ristilian tried to raise him they saw that his chest was drenched with blood. He stared for a moment with blank, puzzled eyes at his daughter and then began to cough. A rattling, bubbling sound it was, and it struck despair into the hearts of those who heard it, for thus it is that a man will cough when he is on the very threshold between life and death.

"Help him sit up," said Tholley, "or he'll choke."

Rymon, her face a set mask of blanched bone, had walked to the door and was making signs in the air in front of the barrier, but she soon turned away with an angry gesture and came to where Osmarin sat, his breathing a gurgle in his throat. She looked down at him with hard eyes and yet when she spoke there was some tenderness in her voice.

"Fool, and fool again!" she said. "Why did *you* want to close the doors today? Why did *you* try to bar him from the table?" She shook her head and groaned. "Now I cannot even get at my herbs in the cottage — there are some that might yet have helped you. And Aurvang is caught out there with him! Maybe he's already dead."

Osmarin was sitting in his chair staring fixedly at the brilliant green eyes of the horsefly, and to those who stood around the cold emerald seemed to be awake, attentive and aware of him — waiting.

"Father, dear father," said Ristilian — and she was weeping — "father, look at *me* now."

But Osmarin's rattling breath had stopped, and the life had gone from him.

TWENTY-SIX

Slag Battletooth sat cross legged on the table of Varya's banqueting hall, a gnarled little body of pent up fury. He had been unconscious for nearly two hours and when he awoke it was to discover that Osmarin had been stabbed and lay dead, wrapped in Frekk's cloak, and that his dearest friend had been captured and possibly killed — though it was just possible that Sulthind would use him as a hostage to bargain with. To make things worse, they were locked in by a power on which neither Rymon's spells nor Fal's harping had the slightest effect.

"We thought before that he was after Fal's knowledge," said Tholley; "I say he's after that and more."

"He has the mirror," said Feather, "perhaps he wants the jewel of light, too."

"If he had that," said Fal, "he would need Lune itself before he could use it; and he'd want to rule Lune and the island! Maybe he only wants my knowledge so that he can travel quickly from one place to another.

"Flying the Bee Song releases the power of the path, too," said Feather. "Don't forget his defeat on the Gop!"

Nobody liked to mention that the Bee Song was outside with Sulthind, but the thought sickened every one of them.

"If he wanted anything at all except to vent his spite on someone why didn't he stay and challenge us instead of bolting off like a rat down a hole?" Frekk objected. "Surely he must have known who was here and what their powers are." He frowned and glanced first at Rymon, then at Fal.

"Whatever he wanted," Slag growled, "he was quick enough to seize a chance to barge in for it. The power over one can be a power over all."

"But needing to bargain shows that he's uncertain of Rymon's powers," said Ilmarin, "and though she cannot break the seal on the door, yet she has accomplishments which would surprise some of you."

Everyone turned to look at Rymon who was sitting, cold and silent in her chair, tearing at the golden casket before her. She leaned forward and closed its lid with a snap.

"A battle of power... in this hall..." — she spoke haltingly, unable to conceal her misery at the evening's turn of events — "such a battle, so close to the heart of Lune, would have destroyed us all as once it destroyed Gelmindel and the dwarf kingdom with it. This he must have known. This is why he ran — though Slag is right, he will bargain... if we give him the chance!"

"And what other chance is there?" Slag cried. "We're besieged! And were we to use the other doors, we'd leave this hall unguarded. Or, lady, can you put a closing spell on the door from this side to keep it safe while we go out another way?"

"No, it is too late... Whoever could do that now could also break the seal he's made, for this door is completely in his power and through means I do not understand. No... I had another course in mind."

She rose from her chair, thin and pale, tired and desperate, and something of the old craziness shone in her eyes again but mixed with a resolve to some immediate action.

"Lady," said Tholley, "will you not tell us what you have in mind?"

"I will not, for if he has the means to observe us as you say he has, then it's better to act first and speak last. Come, Lord Amlad," she said, addressing Slag for the first time by his proper name and title, "you alone have a right in this, a right gained by inheritance, labour, and loss. Bring a lantern and be my companion."

"Mother, what are you going to do?" Ristilian whispered, her voice trembling with unknown fears.

"Be silent, daughter," said Rymon gently, "stay with your husband and these others and help them guard the doors. Between you all you perhaps have power enough. Fear not. We guardians haven't dwelt in the wilderness all these ages just to fail in the end. Come, Slag!"

She strode towards the stairway which led to the upper levels, the dwarf hurrying close behind her. As they disappeared through the stone archway the last of the candles spluttered, flared and went out, leaving only the ten or eleven lanterns glowing softly from their wall-brackets.

"So ends — our wedding feast!" Ristilian cried and began sobbing uncontrollably. But Ilmarin was already kneeling by her side to comfort her.

In the upper corridor, high above the banqueting hall, the dwarf-king's lantern bobbed jerkily as he strove to keep up with the purposeful strides of his mistress. Only at the gallery's end did she pause at the round archway to wait for him.

"Stand well behind me," she commanded, "I shall need to step back quickly. Don't get under my feet!"

Facing back into the dark tunnel through which they had just come, she ran her hands out left and right from the arch's pointed top, round the wide sides and down to the floor. Then, swiftly and lightly she reversed the movement bringing her fingers together again at the apex above her head. There she stood for a long moment in complete silence — like a dancer turned to stone — until, with a sudden exhalation of breath, she stepped back. Even as she moved, the inlaid silver of the ancient inscription flared with a dazzling light, there was an explosion and all was dark again.

"Here, if needs be, we shall make our last stand," she said. "No creature, neither flesh nor phantom, can follow us through that door, nor can any of our own folk find us and try to interfere should things go against us. Any distraction could mean disaster, as could any help, however well meant. Only Osmarin could have assisted me; the others bring knowledge from the south which may not mix so easily with ours. Ristilian is too inexperienced, she would blunder."

"I have a little skill, lady," Slag whispered, as if they were of a certainty being overheard, "and this quarrel is mine now as much as yours. Do not deny me the duty of doing battle!"

"Quite so!" she said briskly, "I always thought the knowledge of your people might one day be united with mine. Come now!"

The myriad stars in the domed ceiling shone dully in response to Slag's one lantern, but in his eyes its light reflected with an angry gleam, for the cold rage of the dwarves had awoken in him, a rage that would fight to the death beyond all hope and reason for the chance of avenging what had been its own.

Rymon walked first to the right of the throne then hesitated.

"The other portal, too," she muttered. "Who knows what that devil has at his beck and call!"

She went to the door of the rooms given to Ilmarin and Ristilian and sealed it in the same manner. Then she returned to the west side of the chamber and peered closely at the wall.

"Give me the lantern," she said, "open the door, my hands are too big and clumsy for dwarves' work."

She took it, and Slag laid both his hands on the polished stone. He pressed gently, and after a while delicate writing appeared, shining from within the rock rather than from its surface, and it rippled and flowed like the veins of trapped quicksilver. "The Eye of Lune," it said.

"Make haste now!" Rymon snapped.

Slag pushed and the stone swung inwards to form a low doorway through which he disappeared. Rymon had to bend low to follow him.

"Do we leave it open, lady?" he asked over his shoulder.

"Ay, the danger's all before us now, none behind."

The tunnel curved round to the left, widening to form a tiny cavern, high enough for a dwarf to stand in — but Rymon was obliged to stoop. It opened outwards through a ragged mouth so overhung with rocks on the great face of the mountain that it was impossible to detect from below. But it gave a stealthy observer a good view of the plain and, by leaning out a little, he could also see at least part of the foot of the cliff, but still he would be concealed by shadows.

The moon, just approaching its full, was hidden from them, but by its light they saw a scene so strange that for a long time they watched uncomprehendingly. Tholley could have told them at once what they saw and would have warned them of their peril.

A company of people had assembled on the grassy space in front of the cottage around a large grey horse. But it was not the size of the horse that made Slag gape in wonder and made Rymon curse under her breath, for all the people who crowded together on the little pasture seemed to be clothed in fire. Their long garments waved and flickered with glowing lines of orange flame, and yet clearly they were not being burned. Their hair, too, which hung loose over their shoulders was all ablaze. There were nineteen or twenty of them, maybe, but impossible to count as they milled around swiftly in what could have been some kind of dance.

Slag leaned out over the ledge, squinting down at them in amazement. At last he pulled himself back and glanced uncertainly at Rymon.

"Well?" she whispered, "your eyes are better than mine."

"They are all women... and — and all the same!"

"One of them will be the leader. We must seek her out and destroy her first. The others will be but phantoms. We'll make the weapon together; you shall direct it, but I shall send it. What shall it be?"

"Spear!"

"Good! But we must hurry, they will not dance around for long, they'll be going into the mountain. Does any of them hold the silver mirror?"

Slag squinted down again. "No," he said.

"So much the better, they may not have seen us leave the hall. But it will make it harder to pick out the leader."

"But Lothur! What about Lothur?"

"One of the women. We must pick him out. Come now, the weapon!"

They knelt facing one another, each locking his gaze unflinchingly with the eyes of the other, and they thought of a spear, small, strong, light to handle, poisoned and wickedly barbed.

Suddenly Slag held it in his hands. At once he gave it to Rymon. She would not need to throw it. Already her strength had flowed into its shaft and she was having to keep a firm grip on it to prevent it leaping out into the night.

"Choose!" she commanded, "and point!"

He peered again at the swaying fire-dance.

"I cannot! They are all the same!"

"You must, I cannot hold it much longer. Choose!"

Slag pointed, more out of desperation than knowledge, and the spear whipped from Rymon's hand like an arrow from a bow. It struck one of the glowing figures between the shoulder blades, and with a shrill cry the whole company of dancers disappeared. The horse was also nowhere to be seen.

For a moment Rymon could not believe their luck. Then she laughed. "Well chosen, my lord!" she said and smiled at Slag triumphantly. But the staring out over the plain aghast. There, no more than two furlongs from the base of the mountain, were the women of fire, and amongst them, all silver in the moonlight, the grey horse. They no longer danced; they had begun walking, slowly and deliberately, towards the cliff. And as they came closer, Slag saw that some were pointing up at the mountain's face, and all of them were looking, searching for the place whence the spear had come.

Rymon cursed and pulled Slag back to conceal them both from sight. "Quick!" she said, "then it's no use attacking them with a weapon. We must fight them all!"

He glanced at her quizzically. It was hard to see her face for he had blown out the lantern and it was dark in the recess. There were only her eyes; they were seeking a way into his. He felt their sting and the piercing malice in them and he understood.

They thought of a company of dwarves, each like to Slag, but heavier and grimmer, with spiked maces and glinting axes, razor-edged. They thought of hags, like Rymon, but older, harder and bonier, utterly without compassion. Then they had them down the cliff, in front of the cottage and among the flame women, hewing and clubbing, gouging and strangling. And to each fiery woman there was a hag and a dwarf too, belabouring her. But the women were armed with long knives, one in each hand, light and deadly, and all fought in silence countering hatred with hatred, cruelty with cruelty. And where, up in the cave, king and mistress drove their army on with all their will, Slag felt the pain of every blade that pierced a dwarf, and Rymon the agony of every stricken hag; but they were resolute and made no sound, replacing each phantom warrior that fell, their eyes never wavering from the support of the other.

On and on they toiled, crouching in the Eye of Lune, their whole will bent solely to one bitter end: to destroy, and in the destroying to triumph. So absorbed were they, each in the mind of the other, that they were never aware of their enemy's strategem: for he, like them, also replaced his slain, so that the numbers on both sides remained constant. And just as he never found them, the cave having other protections around it than the mere shadows cast by sun and moon, so also they never found him, which was strange, for — standing clear to view in the doorway of the cottage — he took no pains to conceal his presence.

Hour after hour went by, and the futile nightmare became ever more a condition of mind with the invisible contestants, evenly balanced, none making any real progress towards gaining the upper hand. Then, just before dawn, the moon still hanging low in the western sky, all three became aware at once of their utter weariness and withdrew from the conflict.

For a fleeting moment ghostly shadows and glowing shapes reached out menacingly towards each other, then they were gone. The dreadful pantomime was over.

Rymon crawled to the edge of the cave and looked down into the colour-less light of the dawn. She must have fainted, she did not know for how long, and she hurried now to survey the scene. All was empty, the dancers and the horse had disappeared; but she scarcely dared hope that they had won. She was almost too weary and pain-wracked to care.

She felt a tap on the back of her hand. It was Slag. He was deathly pale, his eyes wide and bloodshot, and he seemed hardly able to support himself as he leaned forward on one hand. With the other he was pointing into the distance.

Rymon sighed heavily and screwed her eyes up with the effort of penetrating the gloom. But really it was easy enough to see. About a mile away, coming along the causeway which ran out like a pale ribbon over the great desolation, a group of figures was moving — glowing red figures, and among them, towering above their heads, a grey horse. They were all walking towards Lune.

Involuntarily, Rymon began to weep, softly at first, then in loud, convulsive sobs. Roughly, Slag pulled her back inside the cave.

"My lady, my lady!" he cried, greatly alarmed, "this will never do! We are not lost yet! Come, we must stop them before they reach the mountain. Only say, say what means shall we use!"

"Damn them! Damn them and damn him!" cried Rymon, "what means? We will drown them! Drown them in ice!"

Deep within the mountain, in the banqueting hall of the dwarves, Fal and his companions felt the chill that was being drawn down upon the Waste. From beyond the furthest north it came, from beyond the birth of the worlds, obedient to Rymon's will, drawn to the final discomfort and destruction of the fire witches.

They were not dancing now. They stood gathered about the silver stallion, smiling and laughing, for — behold — the hovel of Rymon had perished, or had been dissolved by the immensity of time which lay upon it, and the two pillars of the ancient gate stood out from the cliff clear and clean. And the horse stared at the portal and at the man who stood within it and whinneyed softly.

Alfeng stiffened and growled at the southern tunnel, his hackles rising like a mane, and Bereldan rolled into a tighter ball and whined, troubled in her deep sleep. But though snow and hail raged at the gate it never touched the horse or its fiery priestesses, who only laughed with a fierce ecstatic joy as their power grew within them.

Slag blinked, trying to penetrate the swirling whiteness and trying to wipe the ice from his eyebrows and beard with his freezing hands. He glanced at Rymon and it was on his tongue's tip to say that he saw no hope of victory this way. But his lips trembled and his voice failed him when he saw the face of his mistress. A bitter light shone from her eyes, more deadly than any frost or blizzard, and the pain of the ice witches of old smote him so cruelly that he recoiled against the wall of the cave. She moved towards him, her eyes wide with the horror of the cold, and appeared also to be about to speak; but only a terrible hiss came from her thin, stone-cold lips.

And at that moment the figure in the doorway below them felt his mastery come upon him and he nodded to the horse, and the fire women shouted in triumph and pointed at the mountain, and the one in the doorway laughed — a bubbling laugh, mocking and confident as at last, after many hours, he turned once more towards the darkness of Lune.

Then, too late, was Rymon aware of him and knew what he was — knew the power that was within him, creature of earth's fire, tormentor of the world's heart — the power of Gildor's ancient foe — and the phantom bane of Lune.

With a shriek she turned and scrambled back into the hall of stars, Slag stumbling blindly after her.

"Mistress, mistress!" he cried, "don't leave me!" But she did not hear him; she heard only, through the endless depths of rock, the tortured groaning of the deep. The fires would rise again, she knew, and they would all perish in them, yes, they would be licked away as ants from the galleries of the mountain. And the dragons would grow and feed on the vast swell of the burning stone which was already rocking the mountain on its foundations. Only the Lothur creature and the dragons would be left, she saw it all in one agonizing moment; yet as she unsealed the door and ran on through the dark tunnel towards the stairs she, too, laughed and through her cold, stiff lips she spoke.

"We have not been quite idle all these many years waiting for you! We have not guarded only by waiting, nay, we have yet some power to pit against you, demon of the evil heart!"

She was on the stairs now, running so swiftly through the dark that Slag was left behind, still weary and lame from the terrible hours in the cave. But Rymon felt the strength of her youth returning to enliven the wisdom and knowledge of her age, and foresight, too, came upon her, for even as she leapt down the last steps to the door of the hall she knew what she would see there and what she would do with it.

The guests were gathered at the near end of the table around the slender, upright figure of Ilmarin. Fal held his harp on his arm ready to play, and they were all facing the southern doorway. Ilmarin had raised his right hand which was shining with such brilliance that it was impossible to see whether there were any lanterns still burning. He was holding the gift which he had wrought over the forge-stone of the Delming, the gift of light which was his gift to Lune.

Rymon leapt at him, snatching the stone from his hand.

"This light is mine!" she cried, "mine and Lune's. You have no right to wield it!"

She stood holding the fiery jewel between her hands, and as the company watched, aghast, they saw the searing flame penetrate her and transform her, shining through her arms, her head and legs, until in seconds she became as a statue of alabaster, lit from within, and the streaming life of the blood in all her body shone and glowed as if she were made of flowing light.

Then Sulthind passed through the south door and stood before them, and he too was a figure of flame and shone with a terrible light.

"You come too late, creature of the south!" cried Rymon, and her voice rang like the clash of swords around the stone vaults high above them. Fal bowed his head in pain, such was the sharpness of the sound; but Slag knelt and wept, for his ears heard again the magic tongue of the Lady Varya, and when he looked through his tears he saw her, tall and lovely, the ageless queen, wearing the shining necklace the dwarves had made for her in the beginning of time.

But Sulthind saw only a foul hag surrounded by a frightened, broken rabble cowering at the hall's further end. He heard her words and could not understand them. He appeared to be about to speak but Rymon called in a loud voice, "Light meets light, flame meets flame, cold fire and hot fire, lord and dame!" And she hurled the stone with all her might in a shining arc across the room, crying a word which numbed the senses of all who heard it, and the fiery crystal struck Sulthind right in the heart.

There was a flash like a thousand lightnings and a noise so violent that it could not be heard but totally overwhelmed the mind, blotting out consciousness.

"I'm floating in the darkness, far, far away," thought something that was still Fal; "for an age and yet again an age floating in the unending dark. So it will ever be; so it has always been."

And knowledge of all else was wiped out in him and in all those who were with him.

TWENTY-SEVEN

The darkness ebbed and flowed silently through the dreams of those who returned, and even when at last they awoke it was long before they remembered Lune and what had happened there. For the cavern was to them as boundless and black as the land in which they had been wandering, it seemed, from eternity to eternity.

Slag was the first to realize that his head was resting on the hard floor of his own banqueting hall though even then he lay long striving to recollect all that had passed. Only when the final moments of the conflict were clear in his mind did he rise and busy himself with the lighting of lanterns and attempted to rouse the others.

Of the guests Fal was the last to return, for more than the others he had journeyed greatly in his dreams. And at last he had come to another cavern, which though distant indeed both in time and space was yet as familiar to him as anything in all his conscious memories.

Empty now was the place of his dream, silent with the weight of years beyond count, trapped air in a fossil ocean.

Then, in his dream, it was no longer empty, for in the middle, its branches heavy with a hundred thousand leaves, stood a tree, glistening with red gold. He cried out, torn between pain and joy, for this place he knew as he knew none other: the hall of Laurin — and of Andravel, and the centre of all their kingdom.

He reached out and touched the leaves, fearing that they would fade; but they were hard and firm between his fingers, and many hours passed as he stood and read the tales and wise sayings which were etched into the surface of the shining metal. For the script and the language were again known to him, though the words seemed tangled with riddle upon riddle.

But at last he wandered on and came to the cave of Skelgrist, his ancient adversary, where Bailor had stood without fear, and upright in its presence. Bare now was the ledge where the dragon had lain, for the slayer of King Andravel had never returned. Yet again he heard the dragon speak out its arrogance before Bailor, the tree-maker, who was neither dwarf nor elf, but for whom the dwarves would have died a thousand times.

"I will not listen," the voice thundered. "My mind is too full of thoughts far beyond your understanding."

Yes, the place of Skelgrist was now bare but Fal, feeling something in his hands, opened them and held them up before his face. And among his fingers shone the milky light of moonstones and on his palms the deep blue of the costliest sapphires, their light sparkling from a myriad facets like a sky full of stars.

———

He awoke in darkness and was at first unable to grasp the change and the loss.

"I have journeyed in distant lands," he said at last as he looked up at the worried faces of his friends.

"I know this world. You have called me back to it and I must acknowledge it; but I tell you truly, of all worlds it is by far the strangest." And then he frowned for, even as he spoke, the meaning of his words faded and the memory of his wanderings slipped from him.

As for the Mistress of Lune, she had perished, as she knew she would, uttering the most secret and terrible of the words which had been passed down to her — to save her friends and to keep her trust.

Slag said he would build a tomb both for her and for Osmarin who had also died a great and glorious death, and as long as the mountain stood, dwarves would read the story of their end, the story which now only he knew in full and which he would also engrave in the hall of stars. And he knelt in misery and beat his breast and said, "These walls will ever echo with the deeds of this summer's end, but one great shame and sorrow do they hold — that, while he lived, Osmarin stood all alone and was mocked by us, and by me, Amlad of the East, most of all."

Ristilian asked if he would build a monument for Aurvang, the Listener, for of him no trace had been found, and she felt sure that he, too, had died. But Slag said that it was not always the same with dwarves as with men and that one day, when he and his people were hardest at their labours, Aurvang would return. And he said he knew this for a certainty, though by what means he would not say.

Of Sulthind there remained nothing but the burnt floor where he had stood, and Tholley said this was the surest sign that their enemy had truly gone and was no longer a threat to the realm of Lune. But Slag would permit no-one to touch or clean the scorch mark on the flagstones or even to walk near it, nor did any desire to do so.

They found no trace of any building that had ever been on the cliff, not an outhouse, cottage, nor the shelter of the Bee Song, though this seemed to them the smallest of their losses, for the buildings and the magic boat could be replaced, but the Lord and Lady of the mountain they would always miss bitterly. Their food-stores, too, had disappeared, and those days would have been hard had it not been for the hunting of Frekk and Alfeng, for though the witch-snow that Rymon had brought had melted away, the sky was heavy and chill, and winter was not far off.

Ilmarin and Ristilian decided to stay and help Slag establish his kingdom, ruling in his place while he went to fetch his kinsfolk from the hills east of the Mirrorwend. But Fal and Feather wished to return to the south before the cold set in and make the journey impossible; even so, without the Bee Song they looked upon the distance between Lune and Gopley with some doubt, for there was little in the way of provisions to take with them. Then Frekk said he would come with them as far as the Starwell of Aurëlund and afterwards return to Lune to help feed those who remained there; and Tholley would lend them Bereldan, both to defend them and to carry them when they were weary. She requested only that the bear should make her winter sleep in one of Gulmer's barns and be sent back to her in the spring.

In the meanwhile they all helped Slag build a new house in front of the mountain — but well to the side of the gate in the cliff and not in front of it, and the hard work did much to revive their downcast spirits. Then they all made half a day's journey together so that they should make their farewells out on the causeway, between the mountain and the forest. The weather became sunny and mild, though it was by then far into the autumn, and faces which had not smiled for many weeks began to look glad again.

There was a pleasant breeze from the south-east that brought to Feather voices of her childhood, and she knew it had passed through the heights of the Forest of Hallin, where she was born. And Fal thought of the gardens of Vigg and Silfrintopp, for in that breeze they spoke to him again. And Frekk said it smelt of autumn and that they should be glad that the time of the gnats was now well past.

For many days Fal only listened and he contained the pain which was heavy within him; but at last he could bear it no more. It came unexpectedly when he and Feather were sitting together on the boulders where, only a year before, he had tended Rymon's goats.

"Even the Bee Song was a terrible mistake," he began, "and all that music of the Old Ones. It just led to more and more suffering — and now death."

"It wasn't your fault, you are not to blame," said Feather quietly.

"But it was my knowledge, my seeking — yes, my meddling that made it happen."

He wanted to shout but all he could manage was a hoarse whisper.

"Fal, things can't go right all the time, life just doesn't work like that... especially when you're trying to do something really big — like trying to change the world."

She caught his eye and, in spite of herself, laughed at him. For a long moment he was silent; then he sighed.

"Thinking I could change the world with a magic boat! What a pathetic and utter fool."

"The power can't possibly be in magic boats, in ancient paths, or in anything else... it can only be right here, within you."

Again he was silent, and she was not sure whether he disagreed or whether what she had said was too obvious to require comment. Yet it was the truth which too long he had been trying to avoid.

"But the shining of the path, Feather, and what happened on the Gop — that *is* the power."

"Perhaps it is, in a way. But the people who made the Gop, long ago, the people who laid the path, they must have controlled it from within themselves. Fal..." her voice dropped to a whisper. "Don't you see? It's not yours... You cannot control it."

He was looking at the ground, his face puckered with pain. She hesitated to go on, but she knew she must.

"You must seek that power as you would seek your dearest friend," — she laid her hand gently on his — "in your heart."

"Only you are my dearest friend," he said.

But Feather shook her head sadly and remained silent.

———

When it came to parting, Tholley said to Fal, "Your quest to fathom north and south has suffered something of a setback; for what happened when the Lady Rymon took the jewel and knitted it to her own power is still a mystery to all of us, and the little I understand of it is not what you are looking for. Yet I'll say one thing and hope it may be of some use to you: between a warrior's steadfast eye and the skill of his hand must live the fire of his heart!"

Fal stared at her stupidly, not understanding; Tholley laughed. "Look here," she said gently, "there's always this north and south in your mind, and the balance you talk about. But to get a balance you have to have something in between or the scales will just fall apart. The two weights by themselves are no good, you need the pivot."

"Some say the Starwell is the centre of the world," Frekk agreed nodding.

"And there was more in the Iron Mountains once than just iron and stone," Tholley added. "There was gold!" She took off her hat ready to wave to them. "I'd like to be in the Delming again before next summer, if you'd be kind enough to send the Lady Bereldan to help carry me there! Goodbye, and when you get to Gopley tell Gulmer I'll see him in the spring!"

Then Ilmarin, Ristilian, and Slag embraced them and assured them that they would all meet again before much time had passed, and they stood long upon the old path watching them as they walked towards the forest.

———

Once again Fal passed between the two moss-covered crags which were the gate of Aurëlund and entered the wild wood, and the pink of the heather and the gold of the autumn leaves had transformed all the forest about him. With him strode Frekk, clad in hunter's green, and between the two men Feather rode on Bereldan like a goddess of the spring passing silently by as the cycle of another year draws to its close.

Many creatures peered at them between the roots and branches of the thick forest, though even Frekk's skilled eyes were only occasionally aware of them. And when the beasts saw Feather's love for all their world they, too, thought the maiden herself, earth's lovely daughter, was among them. And the stillness deepened, as if all the golden wood looked upon her passing as a sign and a blessing.

That evening, when they had come again to the giant beeches, Fal found once again the place by the stream where he had sung to Feather and she had appeared before him.

"I saw you here robed in flowers," he said suddenly. "Were you looking in your mirror, did you know?"

She nodded and smiled as she slid from Bereldan's back. "Most likely I'd have known without the mirror, though the seeing would not have been so clear. As it is, I can recognize the place as well as you."

"The forest is very beautiful," said Fal shyly, "and this is a special place." Feather laughed and ran down through the ferns to wash in the fresh water, while Frekk unpacked some meat.

"I'm glad you like Aurëlund in the autumn," he said, "you'd like it in the winter, too, when the snow lies crisp and clean and icicles grow from the trees like crystals in the caves of the dwarves. There's even more magic around then than now — and better magic than in the stuffy air of dwarf-kingdoms, I can tell you!" He laughed for he was very glad to be back in his own country. "When we've eaten, Fal, you might be so kind as to sing for us — for us and for the trees! The forest likes your music."

"It didn't like it when I played at the Starwell," said Fal, wincing at the recollection. "It rejected me with all its force."

"With all its force?" There was genuine surprise in Frekk's voice. Then he smiled broadly. "You're very quick to jump to conclusions! And as for rejecting you — well, maybe it rejected what you were offering because it was expecting something else. I wouldn't be so sure that it rejected *you*."

"All the same I'd rather play here than there."

"I was asking you to play here — not there," said Frekk and began dividing up the meat.

When Fal tuned his harp he was again aware of the attentiveness with which Frekk watched him; yet now the hunter did not speak but only listened with closed eyes. Fal played slowly and thoughtfully for a long time until he was sure that the music was really in harmony with the forest around them, then he wove a simple melody into the bright sound of the strings.

> Where grass grew tall by woodland stream
> speak now no more of summer's dream;
> tree kings and queens with crowns of light,
> hold summer's gold against the night!

Great monarchs of the woods with me
sing of the autumn's clarity.

They were all silent for a while. Then Bereldan, who had been dozing and twitching after a meagre share of the meat, sighed, rose and trundled down to the brook to drink. She for one would not give up dreaming! Feather watched her for a while then said to Fal, "Are you going to take up your duties as master harper when we get to the Delming or will your search lead you away again, do you think?"

"I can't be a true master without the understanding I seek," said Fal shaking his head, "but we shall have to stay at the Forge now for the winter, especially with Ilmarin away. I was wondering whether we couldn't ask Frekk to invite the people of Lune to a wedding at the Delming when the spring comes!"

"Then there ought to be a double feast," said Feather, "Ristilian and Ilmarin must have another wedding banquet, shared with us and ending only in joy."

"It is well spoken," said Frekk solemnly, "the messenger hears and will obey. And since he can hardly be expected to miss such a princely occasion he also considers himself invited — both as guest and as chief provider of venison to the happy festivity!"

He rose and bowed, but Fal laughed and rolled over, making a grab at Frekk's ankles. "Have a care hunter!" he said, "there will be more than just a dozen mouths to feed at our wedding. We're not lonely folk like those of the north. Reckon with ten times the number and then double it just to be on the safe side."

"It is well, it is well! Permit me to bring a few of my kinsfolk from this land of Aurëlund and we shall provide all the meat you require for a double feast lasting three nights."

It was Fal's turn to look surprised. "That sounds like a marvellous bargain and very much to our advantage. But Frekk, where *are* your kinsfolk? We never come across any in the forest."

"No, we don't, though they come across us, I think. You see, I have something of a high standing among my people, and none would wish to disturb me in the company of guests unless they were bidden to do so. Yet if I called them they would soon be at hand."

"I'd gladly meet some of your kinsfolk," said Feather, "won't you call them?"

"To your wedding feast — gladly!" Frekk smiled mischievously, "but for the moment I must be off to hunt for tomorrow's fare. In the meantime you and Fal collect some wood so that we can spend the night in comfort — by a fire!"

———

The next afternoon they made their camp at the Starwell, and Fal knew that, as before, Frekk would leave him there to fend for himself, though Feather and Bereldan were now his companions and the hunter would not disappear into the vastness of the forest but would return, for the time being, to help their friends at Lune.

The clearing had become a different world. There were no flowers to be seen but, all around the grassy margin and under the trees, there was such a riot of toadstools as he had never imagined could exist together in one place: crimson, green, fawn and white, brown earth-stars and orange sulphur-tuft, flaky parasols, puff-balls, shaggy caps, and monstrous boleti in lurid reds and yellows. And all so vibrantly alive it was hard to accept that they were just growing where they stood. It would have been easier to believe that they had been caught marching out of the woods and were now awaiting their chance to invade the dancing-lawn from all sides!

As the three friends stood looking and listening a robin added its thoughtful comment to the scene like a shower of dew-drops and was answered by a rival from the far end of the glade; and where the sun was slanting through the trees, a thousand spiders' webs shimmered in every colour of the rainbow.

After a while Frekk said, "No-one has ever seen so many toadstools here. Is this Bee Song magic too?"

"My grandmother always used to call them 'the hidden ones'," said Feather. "I wonder what she'd have said to this!"

"In Aurëlund we call them 'fruits of darkness', but it's a strange name for the light shines upon them as much as on any other fruits of the wood-lands."

"Yet they're born out of the earth which is dark and also hidden," said Fal, "so perhaps both names are fitting."

"And there's much in their nature which is itself dark to all but the wise," said Feather, "though many make good eating. Is it all right to take some, Frekk? They'd make a wonderful stew with the venison!"

"It's all right!" laughed Frekk. "Mother Earth is glad to be appreciated! Do you know which are good and which are bad or shall I come round with you?"

"I know something, but little of their hidden uses. But if Fal gets the fire ready and you the meat, I'll gather some of the very tastiest."

Frekk nodded, and Fal was off collecting fallen branches even before she had finished speaking.

The hunter was impressed by her choice and said her skill would stand them in good stead on the rest of their journey for they would not need to go hungry.

After the meal, to the accompaniment of Bereldan cleaning her paws and grunting contentedly, Fal played again, though the music had a less flowing quality than before when they had sat near the brook, and was more in tune with the strangeness of the Starwell. Again he added words to the final part of the long improvisation, when his mood seemed at last to be fully at one with the glade.

> Where mosses green line root and bank
> and trees are standing rank on rank,
> dark earth sends forth a motley throng,
> red robins add their silvery song.
>> Toadstool and spider, seed and cone,
>> golden leaf and magic stone.

When he had finished, Frekk said, "It's not only your harp that carries the mark of the dragon, you know. Your music has it, Fal, and so have you yourself!"

"What do you mean?" said Fal, startled. "That song had nothing to do with dragons!"

Frekk's face puckered. "And what do dragons have to do with? They are guardians — guardians of the worlds your music sings of. You've forgotten, but maybe you should remember."

A drowsiness came upon them and none had the will to pursue the conversation further. Long before the light of evening had left the glade they were all asleep.

For a third time Fal saw the Starwell's dancers. Again the jewel-like flaming colours, again the sun welling up from the ground between them. But now the light was no longer empty; it shone as a garment round the figure that moved in the midst of it and who was the centre of that solemn dance.

"It is she! It is she!" The voices rang from far and wide as if all the multitude of stars had spoken, and the shining maiden raised her arms as if to bless the world. Yet even as she did so Fal saw the shadow like a chasm of darkness behind her. He looked hard, striving to penetrate the wonderful light, and stared with disbelief — for he had seen the shape of a dragon! It grew and grew, commanding his attention, capturing his vision, till all else around him faded.

He walked forward till the great beast loomed before him, heavy and ponderous, its horned head flat and menacing, viperlike, yet its eyes closed in deepest sleep. On an impulse he reached out to touch the massive body but even in the space between he met a force so terrible that he was roughly thrust back. To try again, he knew, would be mortally dangerous.

Only then was he aware that he was not alone. The maiden was standing by him and her warm light shone protectingly about him.

"The dragon is yours, then," Fal said.

She smiled, and a feeling of recognition, of age-old friendship awoke in him and he frowned, puzzled.

"He is the past," she said, "but you are the true dragon master! You have journeyed long to learn what the world needs of you; soon you must come into your own. Command the dragon! Bid him give you what he guards!"

"But he is the past, you say," Fal cried, "it is the world's needs now that I must learn, the needs of today! How can I ever command him without that knowledge? And if he is the past, then who — who are you?"

But already the vision was fading, and Fal woke to a damp chill dawn to find Frekk already departed and Bereldan licking his hands.

TWENTY-EIGHT

Mushrooms were indeed abundant that autumn, both in the forest and in the Iron Mountains. This stood them in good stead for it took them three whole days of searching among the valleys south of the Dodmoor before they were certain that they had found the ancient track again, the trodden paths having turned east and west across the moor. Wild plums were plentiful, too, and in one valley, still bright with green, well cropped grass, they found no fewer than twelve giant puff-balls, each as big as a loaf of bread and, when fried in a little deer-fat, as delicate in flavour as the tenderest of meats. Even Bereldan ate her fill that night!

And the next morning they found the glade of the wonderful music. All was silent there now. The birches which bristled out of the mound in the centre, white with the crusts of ancient lichens, had already dropped most of their leaves, carpeting the grass in bright yellow. Broad tresses of ivy hung down from the cliff and here and there holly bushes grew out of cracks in the rock. Of a doorway there was nothing to be seen.

Bereldan yawned and rolled up to sleep while Fal walked all round the tiny valley vaguely hoping to find something which would give them a clue. Feather stood long, looking at the mound which dominated the middle of the glade.

"The key lies there," she said at last. "There is a guardian in the rocks. The Bee Song took him by surprise, perhaps, but for wanderers like us he has always been ready. And yet he sleeps deeply — nearly as deep as the rock itself! You'll have to awaken him, Fal."

"I could try using the wisdom of Vigg and Silfrintopp to touch him. Their knowledge must be at least as old as any guardian of the earth!"

"Be careful. Awaken him if you can, but do not challenge him until you're certain what his powers are."

There was a snapping of twigs among the birches and a russet-brown squirrel leapt out onto the mossy boulders, chattering irritably. It bounded down the rocks, its bushy tail flowing after it, until it stood before the flat stone that Fal had selected for a seat. It regarded him with fixed, beady eyes.

"Has the guardian awoken already?" Fal laughed, "the music hasn't even begun!"

"He's more likely to want something to eat," said Feather, delving into her pack for a piece of very stale rye bread. "He's certainly not the guardian, but it's as well to make friends with any creatures that come to us here."

The squirrel began nibbling at the biscuit-like crust, and very quietly Fal began to sing:

> Where under sky dances fair wind or breeze,
> rustling in tree tops of valley and hill,
> come to the sleeper who lies here at ease,
> stir in the stone that is darkling and still.
>
> Rise, air of mountains, be drawn here to me,
> swirl around body, bring life back to limb,
> waft hair and loose tongue, put breath into lung,
> open stone eyes, waken mind dark and dim.

A wind was sighing in the birches, making them wave and bob at one another like excited children. The squirrel bounded back up the nearest swaying trunk and leapt away in alarm.

But the rhythm and key of Fal's singing had changed and the melody rose loud and clear above the soughing of the wind:

> Waken stone,
> waken rock,
> brush off moss,
> old limb unlock!
> Shake off tree,
> banish sleep
> stretch and laugh,
> dance and leap!

There was a stunning sound like splitting stone, so loud and high in pitch that his head reeled. Quickly he alerted his senses again but to his surprise, he could see no great difference in the scene before him. Only the wind had died, and the trees were still again, but he shook his head, refusing to let these mere appearances delude him. The silence had deepened into a presence and attentiveness, as if the forest were awaiting an event of enormous magnitude. He became aware of the pulse of his own heart, thumping in his ears.

Then he saw it. The glade around him was fading, growing thin and transparent, rippling like water. The world was disappearing!

He leapt to his feet, but it was too late. Towering above him like a colossal statue clad in vines and flowers stood the gigantic figure of a man. Cascades of blossoms formed a garment around him, they twined up his legs and arms, they grew out of his hair and shaggy beard. His eyes were closed, and his face, still full of sleep, was young and exuberantly beautiful.

Then as the giant's gentle eyes opened, his lips parted and he began to sing. At first no words could be distinguished in the liquid melody, yet the forest, now visible only as a shifting mist, responded at once. Trees grew and thickened, they changed shape, entangled their branches in one another's crowns, and burst into a rainbow world of colours and delicious fragrances!

Wherever Fal looked there where flowers; trunks and branches were all but disappearing under the canopy of petals. And each tree was different. What might have been an oak was transformed into gold as radiant as the sun, birches glistened silvery blue, others were shining oranges and reds. And through the richness of the giant's singing rose a chorus of bird song, a clamour of such exultation that Fal found himself wanting nothing but to dance off wildly among the trees, singing and laughing, to become a part of all the joy and loveliness. Now at last, at long, long last, he could be utterly and eternally happy!

"Don't move, you fool, or you're lost!" rasped a sharp, ugly voice close to his shoulder. He turned and saw, to his horror, that it was Feather. But she was growing goat's horns and a beard, and her eyes were tiny, blood-shot, and malignant.

"Be quiet!" he gasped, recoiling from the blasphemy of so mean a voice in this bursting of primeval spring-time. "Go away! You don't belong here, you don't understand. I've waited all my life for this. Go away!"

But already it was no longer a goat. It had shrunk to a sour-faced dwarf, in drab grey-blue, and it was scowling disdainfully.

"Never mind about that!" it snapped. "Play your harp, don't just stand there gaping! Sit down and play of sadness, of loss, of grief!"

Without knowing why, he obeyed. Yet his plaintive melody was merely taken up into the giant's singing and accepted, as if it had been created for no other task than to be a natural counterpart to the forest's awakening. Even so it gave Fal an undertaking of his own. He was not lost in the glory of the ancient song. It also made the giant aware of his presence.

The magic singing became livelier and more intoxicating as the guardian turned his gaze to where the harper sat. He commanded him to speed up his accompaniment, to break into a vigorous dance rhythm, while the childish eyes held Fal's attention as an infant grasps a plucked daisy in its fingers, careless and utterly possessive.

But now that the challenge was directed with purpose towards him, he instinctively defended himself. He played with doubled resolve a tragic dirge, a drawn out melody of heartbroken and irreparable grief, of friends betrayed and left alone without ever hope or possibility of consolation. Gradually the dreamy face of the ancient warden changed and his eyes became wakeful and keen. The lovely, ringing syllables of his song resolved into language that Fal could understand:

> Join the giving of the living
>   in the bud and leaf on stem,
> Join the swirling of unfurling
>   as the mountain blooms again,
> Where the forest-folk come leaping
>   shaking light from garments fair,
> Where the honey-dew drips weeping
>   from the blossoms in their hair.
> Join the petalling and pollening
>   where colours quicken space,
> Join the flowing and the glowing
>   in my lady mountain's face.

Then he saw the dancers, elves from the dawn of the world, who were all about him in rapid movement between the trees, scattering light in the shadows under the heavy crowns of the blossoming trees. But still he made his fingers find the notes of the terrible lament, and even as the dancers swept shimmering around him and the yearning to go with them grew to a piercing agony in his breast, he remembered the reason for his coming there and knew he could never command the giant as long as the singing continued.

How long he went on playing his dirge and striving against that ancient elemental will he could not tell, and when the end came he was not aware of it. He realized that he was sitting in the glade in the grey of evening, his fingers playing as if from habit. There were no blossoms, and though the giant still stood before him he was not robed in flowers but in lichens, grey mosses, and the dingy vines of old man's beard. An army of yellow toadstools had sprung up around his feet like squat, eyeless trolls, and a chill was spreading through the air. Night was falling.

The singing began again, though singing it could now hardly be called, for the voice was altogether flat, without resonance or tone. The eyes were closed, the countenance had lost the youthful freshness of its awakening and, through the mass of dark, tangled hair which now hid much of his face, the giant looked old and grim. The words of his song, if words they were in any tongue ever meaningful to man, were again quite unintelligible.

The glade darkened, shadows grew within ever deeper shadows, thickening to pools of a blackness which was no mere absence of light; it was misery and dread, a hollow loneliness, and horror beyond anything Fal had ever known.

"And I myself have called this upon me," he thought.

He sat, wretched yet still watchful, remembering his escape from Lune as a trivial adventure compared with this. Yet here there was nothing, only the gloom, the iron-grey dullness; the dread and despair were themselves the enemy, gathering to dissolve his being, his very self, into nothingness.

But he knew that this was not its ultimate purpose, it was only a preparation, a dark womb swelling to give birth to a higher power, a great being to be born of all that misery, that very hopelessness of which he had willed his fingers to play so steadfastly. He had won that contest, but the guardian had taken the victory from him — and was using it against him.

Very faintly at first the ground began to shake as if concealing an engine of unimaginable power. Yet its force was turned entirely inwards, giving nothing and taking all. From river and mountain, root and branch, from every creature, it drew and fed, bolstering its dreadful strength. Fal's blood faded from his cheeks, he felt his limbs drain and waken; but he could only sit uncertain, as if in disbelief, as the power in the trembling ground increased.

The giant himself had disappeared, for he had no place in this last deadly mystery, and his voice was lost in a far greater sound, a rush of noise so violent that the mind could not begin to grasp it.

Fal remembered the Starwell and the weakness he had felt there. But this time he was not free to withdraw from the contest, there was no standing up and walking off to return another day. There was no other, this was the final test, the ultimate blow of the hand of destiny, his last and most total failure. And he knew no remedy but could only sit lame and helpless almost longing for the terror to come and strike him down.

The boulders wavered, their substance collapsing into nothingness, as the gate between Fal and that diabolical vortex was flung wide open and the monster that had grown there leapt out from its depths, lashing out viciously like an angry serpent.

With a jerk it reared above him, and the shaking of the ground quickened to a mad racing of energy, faster and faster, till it was the only sensation of being of which he was still aware. There were no eyes, no jaws, only a darkness and a venomous will, and to that will he felt completely and hopelessly vulnerable. Then, with a deafening crack that all but broke his ears, two flames of lightning shot from its head and enveloped him in ice cold light. An eternity of chill and deadly pain filled all his mind, on and on, beyond all bearing. Then he was rocking, moaning, lost and bewildered, sitting on the stone again!

What had saved him from that first attack he did not know or care; he felt only the misery of his weak, swaying body. But the form of the dragon had faded, and he felt the throbbing of the ground heavy and deep as when it had first begun.

"Quick, Fal, our defences have been broken, they'll not save us a second time!"

He looked down and saw an elf of light, gaily clad in apple green.

"Quick, quick, before its strength is gathered again, play a dance, a merry dance! See, I'll help you, but it's you who must begin." The elf drew a silver pipe from its garment and looked at him with gleaming eyes, eagerly waiting.

The effort of lifting the harp from the ground, where it lay discarded in the moss, brought back some life into his arms and with a sigh he began to touch the strings. The first notes came almost of themselves, but the elf joined in at once, blowing delicately with a spritely rhythm as its pointed fingers flickered over the silver flute.

But now the hissing roar of sound, like the singing of the giant before it, resolved into words, slow and very solemn, as if the weight of all the world was being borne upon them:

> Rivers of dark
> flow into heart,
> draw from the root
> blossom and fruit
> sorrow and pain,
> profit and gain,
> in from earth's rim,
> dire and grim,
> oldest of old,
> 'ere tale was told.
> Nor heat nor light,
> darker than night,
> nor star nor moon,
> nor song nor tune
> was sure and true
> 'ere river grew,
> 'ere mountain lay.
> Darkness, hold sway
> again to gainsay
> where blood turns grey
> and into the heart
> is drawn in — the Dark!

In a flash Fal grasped the uniqueness of the moment: this was not the Starwell, where he had left in miserable rejection, nor was it Lune, where he had fled the two dragons. He was holding his ground! He was not giving in to this dark singer — for good or ill he was seeing it through! And he was offering it joy and merriment, the very best that he had.

There was no more draining of power, and though for a while the voice that came from the deathly shadow continued its ghastly prayer, Fal was beginning to take a real delight in playing with the elf and the infectious happiness of its music.

But the shadow did not fade again nor did it sink back into the ground.

He had not expected that it would. Instead it became more tangible, as if returning to the world the life it had stolen in a form that the world could accept: it was growing a body, a real body, animal-like yet lithe and slender! And even before it shrank to be a small black dragon no larger than a pig he could see that it was dancing: forwards and backwards to the rhythm of pipe and strings, its hooked claws scattering stones, earth, and leaves from the woodland floor, its golden topaz eyes fixed on the players. And although its neck arched proudly above its glistening chest, yet all the time it shrank, smaller and smaller, until at last all that was left was a lizard such as a boy might catch and hold wonderingly on his hand. Then it was off, scuttling over the ground and down between the rocks.

Fal stopped playing. A pallid light all about him showed that dawn had come. And in the cliff-face a five-sided door stood open, and he heard a gentle music coming from within the hill.

TWENTY-NINE

Fal had no idea how long he had been walking into the hillside, on and on. For utter weariness he must have slept on his feet, of that he was sure, and he felt only as if he were moving in a dream. His ordeal in the glade of the dragon was already remote and blurred in his memory, vague and improbable. Asleep perhaps... and he thought of the desolate land which had haunted his dreams at the Delming, the dreams which had first moved him to begin his search. Was this not that same blind fastness? Had he conquered in the glade merely to turn full circle and return to his beginning?

The tunnel had become quite dark; he could not remember whether he had seen any light shining from the entrance. He did not remember any light. He remembered the black crow which had ordered him to jump into the rocky pit. "Down, down!" it had cried, and he had obeyed it blindly — down into the labyrinth under the very crown of Lune. Blind, that might be it: he was blind to have obeyed the crow, now he had become blind! Instinctively he walked with arms outstretched, just as he had then, his hands touching both walls. Of course there was no music; if there ever had been any it must have stopped an age ago. Even his footsteps were muffled — perhaps he was deaf as well as blind. And it was becoming terribly cold. Panic began to clutch at him, needling his heart. He wanted to turn and run — but a hand gripped his arm from behind.

"It would be a pity to turn back now," said Feather, "it will not go on much longer!"

He did not know that she had entered the tunnel with him.

"You're right," he said, "it can't be far."

At last there was a light before them — he was not blind! The end was in sight, and the music had begun again, faintly but unmistakably.

A dwarf stood in the deep cavern and the light from his lantern was so dazzling that for a moment Fal could not see his face. And there was something wrong with the cavern, something Fal did not like. It was a strange place — yet strangely familiar; it appeared to have a mirror for its floor. His heart sank. Then he caught sight of the boat moored not far from where the dwarf stood and at once he knew it all: the cave of the two dragons, the cave with its perilous lake, and the boat — was his!

He gave a cry of bitter disappointment, yet as he did so the bearer of the light spoke.

"It's not what you think, master," he said, bowing gravely to them both. "and welcome to you, too, lady. It is an excellent meeting and one which brings me unearned honour." He bowed again and Fal noticed the golden circlet. Then he realized who it was.

"The wild king!" he gasped. "But I was only dreaming!"

The dwarf smiled knowingly and, nodding, cut him short. "Dwarves often have the privilege of walking in the dreams of men, Master Falimbravel. But come, you must continue your journey. If you would both do me the honour of stepping into the boat, it is my task to ferry you over the lake."

"It *is* my boat, isn't it?" said Fal.

"It is and it isn't, but not just because of dwarves' liking riddles!" His eyes sparkled. "It is certainly yours, though you won't be able to guide it here yet without me."

"But the waterfall!" said Fal with dismay.

"There are no waterfalls beyond *this* lake. The ordeals are never quite the same, you know. Do come now!"

For a long time they drifted in silence over the still water and the music came and went, now from this side, now from that, sometimes from all around them. The dwarf-king was using a pole to propel the boat, and Fal was wondering whether he should use his harp or the boat's familiar patterns to add to their speed. He glanced at Feather, but she, seeing that he was about to speak, shook her head and raised a finger to her lips.

The boat jolted. They had reached the further bank. He had not noticed that the light of the lantern had faded and that they had completed the crossing in bright sunshine. The edge of the lake was by a pleasant woodland and, where the trees gave way, the grass was full of the flowers of early summer. On this lawn ten musicians sat around a white stone table, each playing a different instrument, while into their wonderful music were woven the joyful calls of birds: cuckoo, lark, and nightingale, chaffinch and thrush.

Fal gave a quick glance over his shoulder. There was no cavern. Only the lake and the green forest rising ridge upon ridge into the surrounding hills. And all around, towering above the tree tops, were the distant snow laden peaks of vast mountains.

"Come, master; come, lady," said the dwarf-king, "you are to join the music. It is incomplete without you!"

Then they saw that at either side of the round table there was an empty place where, their guide assured them, they were requested to sit.

Playing his harp among the other musicians Fal was soon carried by such an ecstasy that he had little sense of time or duration and he did not notice, for what might have been hours, the variety of the instruments that were joined in making that heavenly sound — a lute, harps, and viols, a long trumpet and flutes, and, amid them all, a voice of such loveliness that he had to pause to listen to it. He saw then that it was Feather, singing from the seat opposite him, while around her were all the wind instruments, tunefully weaving together in clear and independent counterpoint. At his end were the strings, serving and supporting the endless melody of Feather's song; yet even then he did not recognize the company in which he found himself, for such was the importance of the music above any other thing that it was hard to concentrate on the players' individual features.

Only as he joined in again did he see who they were and was so startled that he nearly stopped playing. But the music seemed now to have grown in strength and import and it would not let him go.

To his left and right sat Tholley and Melauriën. Tholley, who was playing a large harp which stood heavily on the ground, gave no hint of being aware of Fal's presence, yet the strong bass which rang from beneath her fingers blended perfectly with Fal's faster line. Melauriën played a golden dulcimer, at the same time watching the musician opposite her and matching her notes carefully to his.

Beyond them on either side were Gulmer and Osmarin — the farmer, next to Melauriën, wielding a stumpy bow energetically on the strings of a bass viol, and Osmarin playing a lute with a prodigiously long finger board. He sat very upright, his gaze fixed on the distant mountains, his lips slightly pursed, while Gulmer was watching Tholley's harp and smiling broadly.

Ristilian, beyond her father, was absorbed in playing a wooden flute opposite Ilmarin whose bow ran rapidly over a smaller viol which he held upon his knees. Next to him was Rymon, drawing a pensive melody from a double-reeded instrument like an oboe in marked contrast to Frekk, seated between her and Feather, who was handling an enormous bassoon with dazzling virtuosity.

Individual as the style of every player was, all the parts supplemented one another and worked together in perfect harmony, each adding beauty to the whole, and the whole revealing ever new meanings within each separate line.

It was only at this point that Fal noticed the garments of the players. They were all wearing robes of a similar design, with a plain round neck and wide sleeves; but each gown was unique in colour. Feather was dressed in palest blue, Ilmarin in light purple; Ristilian's hair fell glistening, waist long, over a robe of silver, while Osmarin's garment was of cloth of gold. Tholley was in burnished copper, Frekk strong blue, and Rymon in sombre violet. The reds shone powerfully to Fal's left, Melauriën in bright vermillion and Gulmer in deep crimson. And to his astonishment he saw that he himself was clothed in rusty orange!

But the circle was not complete. Opposite Gulmer was Aren, dressed in pale green, blowing with great dignity into a slender golden trumpet, and next to him, in cutting emerald, playing a long row of ivory panpipes, was Sulthind! He alone of the musicians was watching Fal and his eyes glittered with mischievous recognition.

Then, as they played and sang, the sun set in scarlet splendour and stars began filling the darkening sky. All night long the planets wheeled above them and whether they were moving in harmony with the music or the musicians were inspired by the rhythms of the heavenly dance, he could not tell, but that all belonged to the one great symphony he was certain.

When the dawn came, swift and with a wealth of many colours, Feather's voice changed. Her singing became more measured, her melodies shorter and more precise, as if full of a joy so immense that for the moment it had to be contained. And Fal saw that there was now a child sitting on her lap who was watching him with large, thoughtful eyes. His golden hair seemed to be full of light, for the sun had indeed risen and was shining upon them all.

With a merry cry the child leapt upon the table, and Fal thought he was about to dance to the unceasing music. But he carried a bowl of crystal flashing with colours like the morning dew and full of cherries, bright burning red.

He first turned to Sulthind and, bowing to him, offered him the crimson fruit. The joy and mirth which came to Sulthind's face were so infectious that all the other musicians began to smile and laugh so that for a moment the whole group of wind players had to drop out of the music. When they joined in again, the panpipes added a tone so sweet that everyone had to exert themselves the more in order not to be out of place beside such an abundance of loveliness.

Then the boy turned to Rymon. Her stern face softened and a tear ran down her cheek as she tasted the heavenly food. And again the music changed and gathered strength.

So it went, backwards and forwards around the circle until at last it was Fal's turn. To him the child's face was very earnest, but as he fed him with the shining cherries Fal felt his heart glow with such a warmth and such a wildness that he was no longer aware of his immediate surroundings. He was carried out far beyond himself until, in unspeakable wonder, he found that the planets, sun, and moon were all around him and were part of him and he of them and he was circling in the heavens. Further and yet further out he grew until he lost himself in all the infinity of light and wisdom that the world contains.

———

There had been one last moment of glorious and boundless knowledge. He had clutched wildly at it, desperate to make it his own; but the stars had faded, the heavens had vanished as if they had never been. Now he had returned to a more familiar world, and it was hard and cold under his back. He had come once more to the glade, the mound of the terrible guardian, to the smell of broken toadstools and rotting autumn leaves.

"I was... all the universe," he murmured. Impatiently he thrust the crushing weight of longing aside. It was enough.

He fell to studying the cliff, the regularity of the fractures where the bare stone showed through, divided into massive blocks, layer upon layer, framed by the heavy green of the ivy. He knew there was no door now. The only light came from the grey of the sky, the only sound from the bear as she rummaged somewhere at the foot of the cliff. Spindlewood berries gleamed like flames out of the shadows and the red crest of a woodpecker flashed as the bird sped below the little tree. It was the very essence of perfection, all the poetry and song he had ever learned, and yet... and yet it was what he had always known, it had ever been so, that perfection, it was not new, no, not in any way.

He sighed, propping his head up in the palm of his hand. What had he learned then, where was the gain? There had been an ordeal... an ordeal and a vision... already a memory. Was that all?

He smiled. "I'm the biggest fool in all the world," he said aloud, "I've seen the stars and beyond the stars, and still I have to grumble." And yet he knew something vital was eluding him.

For a long time he lay there, thinking back, probing... the Delming, his nightmare dream of desolation, the windowless castle. Then the realization hit him like the blow of a hammer; but he could only whisper it to the fallen leaves. "Its me," he said, "me. That's what is missing, me. The world is alive with magic, and me the blank! I am the windowless castle. I *am* the desolation." He rolled over to face the other way. Feather was sitting there, waiting, looking down at him.

"It's time to go," she said, "winter's coming, and it will not be easy to find a way out of these hills."

For a moment he gaped, speechless. After the singing, the Child, the stars, this was so ordinary, so empty, he felt as if she had struck him.

"Perhaps you are a windowless castle, too," he muttered, "perhaps everyone is!" He stood up, staring at her, searching deeply into her eyes. "Everything is ordinary, that *is* the desolation. But I accept it, I take it onto myself, I will love the loss as much as the gain!"

She frowned for a moment, then smiled, as if his melancholy thoughts amused her. She leant forward to kiss him, but before their lips met her laughter faded. It had grown darker in the glade — as if a shadow had fallen upon them — but Fal could see she had become very pale. She was looking over his shoulder.

He turned. Towering over them was a mighty dragon — the sleeping dragon of his dream. Now its eyes were open, full of hidden light and mystery. He slowly reached out, and found there was no longer any resistance. For a moment he hesitated, then felt his hand numbing against the hard, ice cold skin. Almost at once it began to warm and throb beneath his touch. A power was flowing into him, a power he instinctively knew he could use and could control as his own. He remembered the maiden in his dream at the Starwell; she had called him a dragon master. She was not here now, but he no longer needed her protection; he could control the dragon by himself, draw the strength into his body. "I could change the world with this!" — the thoughts raced through his mind — "I could make the whole world blossom again, or I could lay it all waste, it's an unlimited power! No wonder Sulthind... "

He stepped back quickly and looked up at the dragon's face. It was gazing down at him with its dark eyes, watching, waiting. Then he remembered.

He gasped, his hands dropping limply to his side as his mind flooded with a thousand memories. And with a soft voice, resonant yet immeasurably gentle, the dragon spoke.

"Yes, Falimbravel, you have sought me these many lifetimes — but, you see, I have also sought you. Indeed, I have not often left your side."

Fal stared in wonder. Time ebbed away in great drifts. The silence was endless. "It was you who made me so restless," he said. "You were the tempter."

"Tempter? Yes, but also your advisor — betrayer and enemy, too, if you will, yet — in the end — your protector! Perverter of truth, yet guardian and giver of wisdom when the right time comes."

The silence throbbed around them, threatened to engulf them, then flowed away, defeated.

"I remember many things," said Fal slowly. "Yes, many, many things. The past is filling all my mind. But I do not see your wisdom, nor where you were."

"I was there when you were a mother nursing her dying child, I helped you when you were a soldier carrying his wounded friemd. When you begged, maimed, I sat with you by the wayside. You've been a farmer, too, and builder; king, queen, and peasant. Yes, we have struggled togetheu, you and I, through many lives of man. And it was not an easy fate. Yet in the end we have kept faith with one another!"

"Skelgrist!" Fal exclaimed. "But you have changed. You... you have become..."

"We have both changed and we both have grown — that was part of the bargain, though we did not know it then. Yes, we have changed... sometimes one way, sometimes another, today a sister, tomorrow a brother!" The dragon laughed, softly, rumbling like distant thunder. "You have defeated me and I'm the gainer, greater by far than Skelgrist of the Caverns could ever have been!"

"And I have become man," said Fal quietly.

"You have become man," Skelgrist agreed, "true man with man's true heart." It looked away for a moment as if deep in thought. It was Fal's turn to wait. After some minutes it slowly lowered its head till its chin rested on the ground in front of Fal's feet. It was purring like an enormous cat. "Are you satisfied, King Bailor of the Golden Tree?"

"You must not call me that," said Fal.

The dragon rumbled with amusement. "I won't," it said. "And soon you must give me a new name, too. That is also part of the bargain, did you not know?"

"What bargain?" said Fal, "I don't remember any bargain!"

The dragon's eyes opened wider. "It was not made with you, yet we are both part of it. The whole world is part of the bargain, did you not know?"

Then parts of Fal's vision of the stars began to return to him and he saw the earth in its place in the heavens, and he nodded.

"Yes, I suppose you could call it that. Though I don't know whether the giver of such bounty would think much of the expression." He remembered the boy with the bowl of cherries and he thought of Sulthind with his panpipes, laughing with surprise. "I'm not sure that 'bargain' is quite the right word for it."

"Forgive me," said Skelgrist rumbling again, "it's a dragonish way of looking at things. Perhaps you can find a better word. — And the maiden?"

The golden eyes glanced archly at Feather. She was standing at Fal's side smiling at them both.

Skelgrist laughed. "It is good! They say that a man cannot serve two masters. It's lucky that a dragon can."

THIRTY

Such is the story of Fal as he himself told it to the dwarves of the Forge, though much was added later after the first meetings between them and Amladorkaslagh, ruler of the Inner Kingdom of Lune, and both he and they have coloured it according to their understanding of things. I will take no issue with their interpretation, though many paths took turnings that they could not have guessed at, as you will see, and never have the dwarves come to know the true nature of it all. But the memories of Sulthind must also be allowed to speak, since their burden is great and must at last be shared.

We must speak at first of the time before out tale began, otherwise all that followed Fal's meeting with Skelgrist, the great dragon of Andravel, would not be understood in any way at all. Be patient, therefore, and listen while Sulthind tells his own tale.

———

My life began deep in the Forest of Hallin, where I was born of illustrious parentage, for my father was Kereoma, oracle and high priest of Hallin's hidden sanctuary. Of him and of my mother I remember little from those early years, and much now seems but an unlikely dream of paradise. More clearly can I see my childhood playmates, Fethilian and Timbelor, who were mine as I was theirs and as the forest belonged to all of us. But even in terms of human years that happiness was short lived, for Grindassil, to whom motherhood was as foreign as summer is to winter, fled for her crimes, taking me with her. Of that painful time only the merest fragments of memory remain, blurred shreds of hate which were gradually woven together into the pattern of my later childhood.

Southwards she journeyed, then westwards, having found a boatman who could be bribed into taking us across the lake to the Delming where she planned, as I suppose, to live, hoping to learn its secrets and to rule over it. But the discovery that the island in the lake was deserted and its buildings not yet decayed beyond repair, made her think again, for it had a source of power all of its own and the beguiling of many people at once in the Delming was, I fancy, beyond her.

So I was brought up on Grindassil's island, and though we became rich and acquired several servants, I was desperately lonely, for the servants were dour and unfriendly to me, as if specially appointed for their meanness, as perhaps indeed they were. For me the island was a waste and desert land, a place of no hope.

Things improved some years later when I became Grindassil's spy. She sent messages to the Forge, arranging that I should go there often as I needed to play with children of my own age, with Ilmarin and Fal, so that eventually I could learn their secrets. Sometimes they came to the island to visit us, but she discouraged their presence in the house, and mostly we played down by the shore in a world of massive rocks and caves. I was forbidden to take them through the house into the bowl of the hills beyond it, for in those hills quite close to us was the shallow stump of an old fire mountain, small but still active, brooding with ancient life. She had plans of using its power to feed her own. At first she only managed to produce a few fleeting illusions from the smoulder and foul smelling fumes, but it was a promising beginning and she did not want the mainlanders to know what she was doing there. So when my friends began climbing the trees in front of the house — they were very high and you could almost see down into the fire pits from their upper branches — she forbade me to bring them up to the house at all. She was sure they had already seen something to make them suspicious and her fears became so great that she even put out a rumour that she had died. I was forbidden any further contact with the Delming and life became more desperate and lonely than ever before. I was about twelve or thirteen at that time, the age when friendship begins to take on a new meaning. I made countless plans to run away, of course, but Grindassil was not having any of this and made sure I was watched night and day, year in and year out.

I began dreaming vividly of Fal and Ilmarin, and I began thinking a lot about my childhood friends in Halling again. Timbelor I had almost forgotten, for a while I could not even remember his name. But Fethilian grew and grew in my imagination, perhaps because Grindassil once told me that my father, Kereoma, had foreseen that Fethilian would one day be mine and I would be hers. So by the time I was sixteen she was my shining princess, a goddess of incredible beauty. Well, I did not of course know what had become of them, those little twins. They were no longer in Hallin, Grindassil said, but more than that perhaps even she did not know. I planned to flee to my father and ask him where to find them. But I wondered what the guardians of Hallin were and how they worked. I asked her but all she would say was that it was a secret of the trees and that nobody could enter Hallin. It was stupid to ask at all because although I did not tell her my reason for wanting to know, she guessed it was more than passing curiosity, and from then on her wretched servants were closer on my heels than ever before, while she spent more and more of her time down in the fire pits talking to her demons.

She even began forgetting my daily lesson. Oh yes, she made sure I learned a few things of her cursed sorcery and she went at it relentless and unsmiling, until I did, but little of it made much sense to me. Otherwise, I was left entirely to the mercies of her slaves.

They were a dire old crew, always following me around everywhere I went, or tried to go, attending to my needs, occasionally trying to strike up some sort of conversation. But I hardly ever spoke back to them, except to tell them to go and jump into the lake.

A strong and mutual dislike was nurtured with particular enthusiasm between myself and the two deaf-mutes which she had picked up somewhere on one of her secret visits to the mainland. One was grotesquely bow-legged, more than you would have thought possible, the other a hunchback called most inappropriately Grin, something I had certainly never seen him do, though we all have hidden talents. The name of the bow-legged one was Spad, a light-hearted blend between 'glad' and 'spat', perhaps, surely the more fitting name of the two. They were brothers. It was they who used to row me over to the town in earlier years. They still sometimes went by themselves if it was in the daytime, and they can hardly have done much to improve people's feelings about us. They would go round the market purchasing and even bargaining by sign language. Being mute they could not tell any secrets. Grindassil seemed to have them under direct mental control, so they were in every sense extra hands and feet for her. They seemed to adore her and hate me, and as I said their feelings for me were returned in kind.

The other servant was a bony creature I called the Spike, which was my interpretation of Speikunnar Derrad, though Spike the Rat would have served equally well. On the surface he was less grim than the brothers and would follow me around with a leering smile. I have never seen large birds of prey from close to but I imagine that vultures might look at their victims in a similar way, oozing anticipatory affection. Perhaps it is unfair that I talk of the Spike in this way for he was a very pathetic fellow and never actually did me any harm. My refusal to talk to him may well have contributed to the fact that I was always painfully clumsy in communication with words. I had a knack of upsetting the boat in any human relationship and the more I tried the more awkward I became.

Once visitors came, a gloomy couple from the far north, apparently seeking knowledge from Grindassil. She kept me away from their discussions, of course, but I picked up a little of it from something I overheard the woman saying to the man afterwards. It all went wrong, so much was clear to me, for the two of them stormed off leaving Grindassil spitting like a wild-cat. I think they would not agree to her terms in letting her join them in whatever they were doing up there in Lune. I wish now that I had tried to speak with them, for it turned out that these were the very people Fal was looking for a year or two later. Their names were Rymon and Osmarin.

What had actually happened between them and Grindassil I did not, as I say, know; but she behaved as if she had been threatened by them in some way or other, for after this time she spent more time in her fire pits than in the house, growing paler and wilder eyed every time I saw her.

If her aim was to gain control over the fogs and fumes which poured from the rocky fissures of her sanctuary, I was left in no doubt that she was succeeding, for a shadow world of enchantment — forests, moss-covered hovels, and turreted castles — would become visible behind the house. Then it would all waver and fade as you looked at it, but always it would return, tempting you to enter its net of illusion. And all the time her sulphurous fog spread and spread.

Then the eyes came, out there in the fog, terrible eyes, many of them, watching. And I kept more and more to the house, sometimes staying in my room for days on end. I entertained myself by working at some of the things I had learned from Grindassil's lessons — they had stopped completely by then — especially the exercises for what I called merging. You had to get right inside the substance of a stone, the sap of a tree, the mind of a beast. You have to float out of yourself and think of nothing else at all but where you are going, so to speak. In the early stages you cannot remember what happens after that, it is just like going to sleep; but you go on practising until you begin to dream inside the other creature. If you work hard enough you learn to wake up completely. I really enjoyed that; in fact it was the only thing I did still enjoy at that time. I used to practise a lot with Cronk, my pet crow, and it helped to take my mind off what Grindassil was doing — at first, at least. Until one of her fog people came up out of the pits, came looking for me across the island. It was summer, and in spite of the heavy mist I had ventured out for a walk — with the Spike trailing along behind, of course. I was on the cliff tops opposite the mainland when it found me.

For a moment I thought the fog had turned into some kind of magic mirror, for I was looking at myself, another Sulthind. Then it moved, and I nearly died of shock, of total, mindless terror. I must have sunk down to my knees for it stood there looking down at me, laughing and laughing as it watched my horror.

Then it became serious and threatening and stared for a long time without blinking, its damned eyes flashing like jewels.

"We don't need you any more," it said, then started laughing again.

"No, we won't ever need you now. But do not think of leaving. Always remember — this is your home. You will never want to leave it — never."

It stared right inside me, in and in and in. And I felt myself never wanting to leave. Home, I thought, yes; only this can ever be home.

But it did not work. I forced myself to remember other people, other places — Hallin, Kereoma, the waterfall, my friends at the Forge, Fethilian. I remembered Kereoma's oracle — that I would marry Fethilian.

Then I went wild. I turned and ran down the cliff path, skidding over the wet rocks, till I tripped and fell headlong onto the beach. After that I just rushed on and on, running and stumbling. I think I sat by the water and cried a lot. And when I had finished it had gone, and I knew I must get away from the island or perish.

The summer was bad enough, but the winter — the winter when the sun never shone — that was even worse. Grindassil's fog covered the whole island and it never moved, not for one day. I worked hard at trying to control her stinking vapours, but the best I ever managed was to tear a tiny hole in them like a window, so I could sometimes look out of the fog and see the town.

Two or three times, in the night, I crept down to the boat house, but there was always someone in there, waiting. Once, when it was only the Spike, I nearly got as far as attacking him, but he leered apologetically and assured me that help was much closer than I could imagine. He glanced over my shoulder and nodded knowingly. I panicked and ran back to the house — I have never been a very courageous person. Who knows what demons would have come to his call? — perhaps the other Sulthind again. And what else did she have lurking down in her fire pits? I preferred never to know.

In other ways I was getting stronger though, in spite of this deep seated leaning towards cowardice, for as regarded my ability to stay awake outside my own body and particularly as regarded being able to look at the world through Cronk's eyes, I had made considerable efforts. By the end of that desolate winter I could stay with him for hours at a time, often directing his flight far onto the mainland.

This in itself was a means of escape, though in the end it always meant returning to the island, where my body had been lying entranced and senseless. But it did make it possible to get the occasional glimpse of what Fal was up to over in the Delming and it made me unbearably aware of how lonely I had become, desperate beyond anything you can imagine. Evesdropping on Fal through Cronk's ears and eyes — this was how I found out about his plans to go north — only served to make everything all the more unbearable.

But we must go back a little to the end of the winter, to the day when Grindassil lost control of her fog. I was so overjoyed when the sun burst upon us that I seized Spad by the wrists and danced around the courtyard with him. When I saw her fury, though, I ran to my room and locked myself in. That was my mistake. If I had only gone down to the lake that night, or rather early next morning, before dawn, things might have turned out differently for us all.

At the time such blunders weighed heavily upon me. Again, it was my wretched cowardice which held me back in the face of a strong compulsion to go down to the shore of the lake. Instead, I locked myself in my room, and when, later in the day, I tried to leave, it was to find the door chained from the outside. She had locked me in — I was her prisoner.

Yes, Fal had come over to the island at dawn that day, but it was not me he saw. It was the other Sulthind, her jewel-eyed demon, that met him on the beach, enticing him to come up to the house. I thank the powers he did not. Both he and the dwarf maiden with him felt something was wrong and they would not come.

I do not know what devilry she had planned, but it was always her scheme by getting hold over a little to gain power over all. Yet it was the wrongness he felt over at the island that day which opened Fal's mind to seeing a disharmony, an incongruity in the world as a whole, and it was the beginning of his quest.

For me it was the beginning of an even worse imprisonment than before. I was never allowed anywhere without at least two of them guarding me, one on each side, and most of the time I was locked in my room. I thought of sending Cronk with a message to Fal but I knew that whatever I said he would look upon it now as a trap. He would never come.

Spring turned into summer and Fal left the Delming, journeying up the River Ironway. I am aware how irrational my feelings about this were, but I felt completely desolate after he had gone, abandoned, almost betrayed. I sent the crow to watch him but had to be careful not to arouse his suspicions. Cronk could not talk to explain himself and to be taken for a spy would have ruined my only link with my best friend. I was completely intrigued by the nature of his quest and I eventually sent Cronk up to Lune by a more direct route to see what awaited him there. In this way, through Cronk's eyes, I met Rymon and Osmarin again.

That was another blunder. If only I had been more patient and allowed Cronk to follow Fal all the way, I should have discovered Fethilian at Gopley Farm, and again many a later tangle could have been avoided.

Things changed as the autumn came on. Grindassil began to regain her control of the fog and her blank secretiveness gave way more and more to a look of triumph and uncontainable excitement. At first there was no explanation and no way that I could see of getting one. She rarely spoke to me now and I had not seen the Spike for several days; as for the two deaf mutes, they looked meaner the gladder their mistress became.

Then one day I heard a horse neighing in the courtyard. I could hardly believe my ears. We had never had a horse on the island, only a few sheep, chickens, and some skinny goats. I rushed to the window and saw the most unbelievable thing. A grey horse — it was a huge stallion — rearing on its hind legs as Grindassil whipped it again and again. She was laughing; yes, laughing. You will hardly understand how terrifying that was. She had never laughed before, never, not since I was a child. But now she was yelling with laughter as she flogged the horse. And the mutes, Spad and Grin, were watching, hugging one another with glee.

It was only when it was all over and the horse was standing there shivering and sweating, that I noticed its face. It had a familiar rat-like expression, a revoltingly unhorse-like quality. It looked around at her and leered. That was enough for me.

I rushed to the door and found thay had left it unchained. I had the sense to get myself under control and went out quietly.

Standing in the corridor was the other Sulthind. It looked very serious and spoke only in a whisper.

"Now at last the horse is finished and we can turn to more important affairs, my boy — more important to us all. At present I am you. Soon you will be me. Do you understand?"

I must have leapt back into my room and locked the door. I do not remember much of what happened next, only the horror and whirlwind of panic which has wiped out everything else. And yet one thing does remain, the realization and the despair it brought. I saw what anyone but a blind fool like me would have seen all along — that what I had prided myself on as being my especial strength, my talents at mind merging, was not my strength at all. It was a hideous weakness.

It made me helplessly vulnerable, I could find nothing in myself to keep it out, that demon in the white robe, only a bolted door was between me and it and I doubted that planks of wood were going to hold it at bay. 'Now that the horse is finished...' — that was what it had said. It was my turn.

I heard myself screaming, shouting out the names of Fal and Fethilian and knowing I had to stop, must stop, yes must or they will come, Grindassil and her demon, to merge minds, yes merge — as you are so excellent at doing, so excellent — you have prepared yourself so well for this, my boy. It was already beginning.

"I am not your boy," I yelled; then I knew I had to be quiet. Quiet and strong. Strong and controlled.

I stopped shouting and forced myself to think. There was very little time. I looked out of the window. The courtyard was empty now — apart from the horse — which meant she was on her way up to get me at this very moment, outside the door, with the Sulthind thing.

Ironically it was her latest creation that gave me my chance. I knew it was the Spike, of course — her devoted servant, her creeping worshipper. But now he was a horse, and he looked so grotesque and miserable down there that I could not help feeling sorry for him. My emotion was not particularly strong but it must have touched his mind for he looked straight up into my eyes.

"Help me," his thoughts whined. "In the name of all the powers, help me."

I knew this was my chance, the only one I had had for years, the only one I was ever going to get. I had to act.

I tried a quick mind merge with the Spike, just enough to suggest the idea of coming under the window. I must explain that our house was tall and narrow, almost like a tower, so jumping down from my room was not a thing to be easily undertaken. And I had no magical skills in anything like floating or flying, none whatsoever, to lighten the fall. It must have been a good thirty feet down.

What happened I can only recount as I experienced it, not by way of explanation, for I have none to offer; but my memories of that moment are quite clear. My mind pushed through the mist, on through the sky, upwards, in a desperate plea for help, and clung on to the stars. It was as if thousands of threads from my mind attached themselves to the delicate rays of twinkling light. You smile? It is beyond comprehension what a person can do in the moment of doom, that is my belief. I can only say what happened.

I floated down onto the Spike's back like a breath of air. As soon as I touched him, though, I regained my weight.

"Where, master, where shall we go?" his mind asked. "Not to the fire pits, please not to the fire pits."

"To the beach, faster than the wind."

As we raced off I tried to think what we would do. I had heard that horses could swim, though whether so far as to the mainland I had absolutely no idea.

I felt a stab of fury and hatred behind us and knew she was after us.

"Faster," I cried, "faster, faster!"

The Spike plunged straight into the lake without hesitating, as if all the demons of darkness were at his tail, as indeed they very likely were.

He swam strongly at first, but when we were a couple of minutes out from the shore he showed signs of distress and began twisting his head round. I could see the whites of his eyes as he was trying to peer past my knee.

"Just keep going, Spike," I said. "No need to look back."

I did, though. There she was, on the beach with the deaf mutes and the other Sulthind. They stood quite still, I think she was pointing at us. I guessed — correctly as luck would have it — that the demon would not be able to cross the water, and I had chosen a part of the shore well away from the boat house.

But the Spike kept whinneying and could not seem to get his head back straight again. I merged and asked him what was wrong.

"She's pulling me back, master, I can't help it. I will have to go. It is pain not to obey, ah pain — terrible, terrible."

He began squealing like a pig as I tried to fight Grindassil's command and keep his mind free. It was not going to work. He began curving back and I could see the froth just pouring out of his mouth.

I had never been a strong swimmer but I would certainly rather commit myself to the mercies of the water than be dragged back to what awaited me on the beach of that island. I threw myself off sideways and began thrashing around. My long robe clung to my legs and trying to pull it off I went under, my mind bellowing in despair. Then, in the midst of it all, a voice calling back from under the water, right into my head. It was powerful, calm — no words, just the question, what is wrong?

"Who are you," my mind shrieked, "who, where, what?"

Images flooded my brain, I saw myself as a boy after my first lessons in merging, trying to call a great beast from the depths of the lake. Then one day there came success, a soft tugging at the ankles in the water. Amusement was followed by disappointment.

"Did you not want to play, not want friendship?"

The child had not understood, was frightened, had never called again.

"But now you have called. Something is wrong?"

The voice spoke clearly, pushing my own frantic thoughts aside in one sweep. I let myself begin merging and at once felt the supple body, the delight in movement, the neck and tail long, floating, the huge eyes just above the surface.

"Come and help, then," I cried, "help, or I shall drown."

"Patience, little friend, the lake is large, but I am not too far away. Be patient."

Then silence. I had managed to pull the cursed robe up enough to begin treading water. The Spike was climbing out onto the beach, I could hear her laughing. They would all just stand there now enjoying the show, waiting for me to drown. I wondered how long the water creature would take. "Not too far," it had said. I thought if I was going to put my strength into treading water I might just as well swim — as far away from the audience the better. I tried to calm down, fixed my eyes on the Delming — I would otherwise swim round in circles, my left arm being stronger than my right — and began striking out.

It seemed to go on for hours and I got very cold. Several times I felt so tired I thought I would just have to give up and drown there and then, but always the gentle voice pushed at me: "Coming — patience."

Then it was there.

The water heaved and a massive neck thrust up between my legs, lifting me half out of the water. At the same time the head, shiny and dripping with water, swivelled round so that the dark eyes stared unblinking into mine.

"Safe now, little friend. Where?"

Yes, the face we had once seen watching us when we were boys.

"Where to, where?"

It occured to me that my appearance at the Delming was likely to be misunderstood; I had felt only hostile thoughts coming from there. The dwarves particularly, as I later realized, used to find my sort of humour offensive, and over the last year I had picked up an even stronger negativity which as yet I could not explain. Perhaps wait with going to the Forge.

"Where?"

My father, yes, I would go to Kereoma, he would help. I would go east beyond the river mouths, then travel overland up to Hallin. Too far to carry me? Amusement — no distance too far for her. Her? More amusement. The great eyes blinked seductively.

"Climb further up, little friend, or you will slip off when I begin to swim."

I wriggled obediently backwards onto the broad body. She was wider than a horse but softer and quite comfortable to sit on, except that my feet and ankles dragged in the water. Then she flattened her neck so that only her nostrils and the top of her head were still showing and we began to move. There was a lot of shouting going on behind us on the shore but I decided not to look. I was finished with the island and I most definitely never wanted to see Grindassil again. I concentrated all my thoughts on Hallin, the trees, Kereoma.

I had only the vaguest memories of what he looked like, not, I thought, because my time in the forest lay so far in the past; other people and places from my childhood I could remember quite distinctly, but for some other reason the face of Kereoma eluded me. I had the strange impression that he had only ever spoken to me from behind and that if I would turn round now I would see him. This had to be Grindassil's doing, trying to get me to look back at the island. Or was Kereoma really just behind me?

I decided to think of something else before I gave in and really turned round to see what that foul assortment of ghouls were up to. Change the subject; think of Cronk.

I had made him leave Fal and head straight for Lune. I had insinuated him into Rymon's household as the family pet and I tried to find out now what he was doing. But Grindassil was trying to probe into my mind and I needed more protection. Music forms a good shield, I have found, and I began going through a little ditty I had been writing. Music was not one of my talents, poetry was better, but by combining the two I could make a reasonable ballad.

So there I was, floating across the lake, feet completely numb with cold, my arms waving at the puffy clouds as if they were people listening to my song. By the powers, I was free at last, free and madly happy, for the first time in dreary years and years. Yes, it was a crazy enough scene to make a flock of chickens stand on their heads; but there were no chickens to see us, and no sorceress either, for we were soon out of sight of the island. That was just as well, for we must have been a very odd sight — the water monster with me on her back, and me bawling heart and lungs out into the summer sunshine. Surely the lake in all its history had never witnessed the like.

The song was crude and simple, especially as regards the tune, but it was my song, my very own, and I put all the joy of my soul into every word of it.

> Look a little longer at that swirl of mist,
>   at the dew or that ocean spray:

their light will surely shine and dance for you
 as long as shines the light of day.
And if you really look and heed them well
 and cast away your old despair,
you can move your mind right out on the wind
 just as only your mind can dare.

And then you'll soon be seeing that bright rainbow gate,
 ask the keeper there to let you through;
that land has all the colours of your wildest dreams
 that no-one can take from you.
And if you really look and heed them well
 and cast away your old despair,
you can move your mind right out on the wind
 just as only your mind can dare.

I must have sung it dozens of times, changing the words here and there a bit
until it sounded just right. I added a little chorus, by the way. It went:

Move out on the wind,
you can travel afar;
no need to pretend,
you just swing on a star.

The advantage of having a short chorus is that you can sing it again and
again. You can have lots of fun with it without getting too complicated.

But then the water monster began shaking so violently that I tipped over
and slid down her back and would have got another ducking if she had not
flipped her tail up really hard to prevent it. She stopped swimming and
lifted her head out of the water to see what was going on. Her face looked
different, all twisted up. I tried a quick mind merge: she was laughing,
that's what all the shaking had been about.

"Stop singing," she said. "It is giving me the most dreadful pains inside."

It was no use, we just could not stop laughing, neither of us. Somehow or
other I managed to scramble up her slippery back and stand up, balancing
there like a juggler, intoxicated with freedom, sunshine, and with the
enormous wonder, not to say insanity, of it all. My steed seemed to be
drawn into the madness as much as I was, for when, as I said, I stood up on
her back and began dancing up and down, singing even more wildly then
before, she gave a tremendous hoot, which must have echoed over the
whole lake, and jerked her back so that I shot up into the air like a stone
from a catapult. Then she rolled over on her back and caught me between
her flippers, turned me over and began spanking me.

It was too much. I nearly died laughing that day as she played ball with me in the sunshine far from any shore or meddlesome gaze. What an incredible way to begin my new life, I kept thinking, this I shall never forget. And so it has been. Yes, in my memories I ask a quite especial blessing for my water monster.

THIRTY-ONE

Fenli had always been an outcast. Even as a child she had been told how ugly she was so she had taken no care about her appearance and lived a life apart. And when she had become marriageable, the cruel mockery; that would have been enough to last her for ever. No, the agony certainly did not need renewing, even without the burning there had been no hope, for she was taller than other girls, and who fancies a mate that towers over him?

But the agony was renewed. There came that evening when she tripped over her own gangly legs and fell headlong into the fire. The red-hot ashes had the last and final word to say about her face, but the boiling stew pot came down as well and left her legs with long bubbly patches which healed bright red. And when it was all over even her own relatives shunned her ugliness as if she was bad luck in person.

So she fled, even to the very skirts of Hallin, and built a house up among the thickest branches she could find. She knew enough of hunting and gathering to still her bodily needs, and for company she had the trees. With them she spoke often but human kind she shunned, and after the first winter her people ceased looking for her. But among the trees she was a goddess that leaped and ran fleet of foot; and no guardians barred her way for the trees loved her voice, talking, singing, playing her pipes to them. Besides, she never sought to enter the forest's deeps. And since she kept far from any path that led in or out of Hallin, no-one ever trespassed upon her exile — though Fal may once have heard her — and no-one ever found her house, secure and hidden in the trees.

Until I came along, cutting northwards between the rivers, still fearing pursuit along the roads, avoiding villages and living miserably off the land. Berries and roots it was and nothing else, for it was too late in the year for birds' eggs and I had no idea how to hunt. So I was in a sorry state and more that a little fey from sheer hunger. When I saw her tall form rushing through the twilight, bow in hand, I must be forgiven for thinking that the guardians of Hallin were upon me. Her laughter when she saw me grovelling on my knees had no friendliness in it and she ordered me to be gone or feel her arrow through my throat. I took a chance and told her to do as she pleased as I should anyway die of starvation if she sent me packing. But even as I said it I knew the greater hunger was for companionship; and she knew it too, for I stayed with Fenli then, through the autumn and winter, and all the pent up love in both of us tangled, melted and mingled in a furnace of affection. She taught me to hunt and to fend for myself, but she also improved my singing and taught me some mastery of a simple three-stringed lute and a set of panpipes which she herself played with almost magic dexterity. It was an unbelievable time. She was in every way the opposite of Grindassil, who was beautiful but deadly cold; though seen from the left side Fenli had a grace which I have never found again.

She could have shown me the guardians, but I had lost interest in visiting Kereoma, perhaps secretly fearing disappointment or even rejection, while now I felt I had all. I still kept some contact with Cronk, and without him Fal would surely have perished in the black maze on top of Lune. But then Fal's whereabouts became a mystery to me; there was confusion and then utter silence. Eventually I ordered Cronk to fly southwards and find me in Fenli's tree house, for the weather up in the Waste, where I thought Fal must still be, was already becoming so severe that I feared for the crow's safety as well as Fal's. There seemed nothing else I could do to help him, at least until the grip of the snow and ice gave way.

The winter was vicious indeed, and happy as we both were in our home-spun blankets, the deathly freeze seemed to go on for ever. Hunting became difficult and Fenli would not use traps. At last we both became ill and started coughing day and night. She tended me as if I was a child, but while I gradually regained my strength, she coughed more and more until in the end she was wasting more blood than we could find in fresh venison.

When the thaw came she died.

There is no point in trying to put my feelings into words. Suffice it to say the fact that I had never before known physical tenderness until that marvellous winter was balanced by the leaden premonition that I would never know it again. The knowledge was as incontestable as a wall of granite.

I knew it was all up with me, I was finished, just as Fenli was finished. Two utterly starved souls had fed one another to the full; and now the feast was over. I did not complain. I made her a grave, or tomb rather, out of boulders, ferns and mosses. Then I went — northwards, I knew not where, with Cronk perched on my shoulder, as silent and miserable as I was myself. Of her possessions I took only her hunting bow, the musical instruments, one cooking pot, and a couple of blankets. The tree house I left tidy and secure, as I thought I might do worse than to return there one day; and I tidied the ground beneath the branches, too, so as not to make it plain to all and sundry that people had lived there. A tracker would have known at once, of course, but such folk were rare in those parts so close to the darkness of Hallin.

A nagging premonition told me that if I wanted to see Fal I would have to move northwards as fast as I could manage. But I had to eat. Sometimes I was able to shoot a rabbit and once a lame deer; in between I strummed the lute in the villages and farmsteads and sang a song or two. I prefer to think of it as entertaining rather than begging and it did a lot to improve my self-confidence. Once or twice I sang my rainbow song but more often some humorous ballads which I had made up to please Fenli. Her own songs I played only when I was quite alone.

Everyone was kind and friendly to the crazy young traveller, especially the children, who loved the funny ballads. Everyone that is except the grim old couple who run Lunt Farm, not very far to the south of the Gavelburg. They set the dogs on me and warned me to keep well clear of their land in the future. I lost Fenli's bow there, running away like a common thief, curse their sour old hides. I thought how well they would get on with Grindassil, and it turned out that the thought had more substance in it than I realized at the time. But more of that later.

After Lunt Farm I began sending Cronk out again to scout around and I even toyed with the idea of getting him to fly right up to Vond, the city of the many bridges, in case Fal had gone there. I decided against this for two reasons. First, a crow hanging round the streets of a town for any length of time might attract too much interest; it might even get caught or shot at, and I did not know what Vond had in the way of sorcerers. There were sure to be a number. Secondly, I still felt that Fal was closer than Vond and that our meeting was quite soon to happen. Cronk spotted him one morning travelling southwards towards the old castle ruins, as if he had just popped up out of nowhere. As it happened, he was still farther away than I thought and he did not reach the Gavelburg till the evening of the day following. I thought it would be a good place to camp and decided to try a little simple magic in the ruins to while away the time, trying to adapt my mind merging talent to reading the memories of the past, so to speak. The result was nearly disastrous and put me terribly to shame; but you will have read Fal's account of all that and how Ilmarin turned up in the middle of it all, taking us both very much by surprise. That was all grim enough in itself, the whole business with the phantoms of the burg, I mean, but it was nothing compared with the nightmare which followed our little party round the camp fire. My stupid behaviour in the ruins had attracted more to it than the attention of the spooks, I'm sorry to say, and destroyed all that I had hoped of my reunion with Fal.

We had had a wonderful evening together, chatting and singing. In the end it had grown late, and Ilmarin and Fal had both rolled up by the embers and gone to sleep. I was too excited to follow them yet and had begun making the fire up for the night as it was beginning to get frosty. Part of me was happy again, everything was working out so well; and I was such a fool, an unbelievable idiot. Did I really think she was going to let me get away from her and be a free adventurer, as Fal had become, master of my own destiny? I had kept no watch, taken no precautions since I had found Fenli. A new life had begun and I had done nothing at all to safeguard it. Well, that night put an end to my merry chatting in a matter of minutes.

I can see it so clearly even now, the cold stars sparkling in the black sky, the flare of the firewood, then the voice calling from the shadow of the woods. All I could make out was a tall figure, apparently clothed in white. You will scarcely credit my stupidity, but the fact is that I thought it was Fenli come back from the dead to speak with me. To think it was a woman at all let alone one who had been so close to me! Pathetic creature that I was, I walked straight off, away from the safety of my friends and the fire, following the beckoning of a shadowy white hand to a heavenly rendez-vous.

Of course it was the other Sulthind, it had caught up with me at last, and this time it was better prepared for my reaction. It kept me totally para-lyzed, I felt literally turned to stone; I tried wildly to shout for help but I could not even breathe let alone shout. There was nothing I could do; and it just stared with its glowing jewel eyes, just stared. It did not even bother to say, "Hello, Sulthind." It began pushing thoughts straight into my mind, trying to worm its way right down into my feelings. Accusations. The sufferings I had caused Grindassil hunting for me in the snow, the heart-breaking loss of her child; the ice of the river cracking as they rode over, she and the Spike, she nearly perishing in the freezing water. Accusations of ingratitude, ingratitude that must be punished to set the balance right. Grim laughter. Then pictures of her rescue by the kind people at Lunt Farm. So she had been there, actually already been there when I had tried to approach the place. You merciful powers! But she was well now, very well again, very strong; and I must go to her at once, now, this very moment.

I found myself fingering Fenli's panpipes in the pocket of my robe, my left hand must have been on them — just by chance, as the saying goes; and the feel of them under my fingers was putting grit into the foul creature's dough — its spell, I mean. I let out a terrific yell which was answered at once by someone round the fire, I think it was Ilmarin, and then all hell was let loose. I punched out at the spook and that seemed to set it off shape shifting. It developed a golden bull's head, became a serpent of flames, scattered into an army of rat-sized ants all glowing a sickly yellow, scuttling around me. I kicked out at them like mad, and it became a ghastly thing all made of icicles, frosty needles, and pain.

I ran. Very cowardly, I know, but I am not ashamed, I was just not up to that sort of thing. I found myself racing off through the forest in the dark, stumbling and screaming like a lunatic. There was a most terrible hulla-balloo behind me, a lot of shouting and flashing lights; I suppose Fal and Ilmarin were fighting it. I know I should have helped them but there was nothing I could do, really nothing. Terror had completely won the day, I just had to keep going — until, as I suppose, I hit my head on a low branch and knocked myself out cold. That must have been my salvation, for my guess is that I blanked out for the other me, for the spook too, I mean, and so it could not find me. Be that as it may, it was suddenly light in the forest and I was alone — alone with a headache like a dagger in the back of my head.

I have never felt such a terrible pain. I must have sat there for hours, totally blank and miserable; but in the end I somehow managed to pull myself together and find my way back to our fire. It was a filthy mess, ashes scattered everywhere, the lute was burned to a virtual cinder. There was nothing else — except Cronk's charred remains some way from the fire towards where the phantom had appeared. It was seeing his pathetic little body that did it, made up my mind once and for all, to start a new life and leave every element of the past, even the better sides, completely alone. I turned straight round and ran off, not southwards to follow Ilmarin and Fal, for they had said they would go back to the Delming; I had had enough of it all, and anyway Grindassil, I knew, was somewhere in that direction.

No, I went the other way, I would get rid of her once and for all, begin again, even take a new name. I would go to Vond.

———

I have often enough reproached myself for deserting my friends the very same night that I found them, abandoning them in the face of a danger which only I fully understood. This cowardice seemed part of a shameful pattern as far as my character was concerned and it often weighed heavily on me. In all truth, though, I must say that at the time it did not occur to me that Grindassil and her devil would give Fal and Ilmarin a second glance. It was myself she was after, as far as I knew, and I was convinced I could not even begin to stand up to her. Fear and only fear flooded my mind, escape was the one straw worth clutching at; and the more I thought of Vond and the blessed anonymity I might find there, the more it seemed like paradise on earth.

And in some ways it really was, for I became happy there again — for a while. But I must not paint too fair a picture of it, for Vond is a shabby town, whatever else is said of it, uncared for and dirty, though it has a quaintness in spite of that. Its many bridges would be handsome enough if it were not for the stinking tidal waters that seem to linger permanently under them instead of flowing away as decent water should. The whole town is built of grey stone, famous bridges and all, like an everlasting twilight, and it would be a dull looking place but for the decorative style of the pointed roofing which adorns the houses. No two gables are quite alike, and their slender spikes, twists, and arches give the eye pleasure enough to make up for some of the rest.

But there was more to Vond than grey stone and pretty roofs. I soon became quite attached to the ramshackle old port and derived immense satisfaction from walking the busy streets day by day without being recognized. That is the greatest attraction about city life for me, it is like being a living paradox; for while walking in a surging crowd you are not known. You are seen and acknowledged but not judged. No-one shuns you because of who you are or whose you are. So while being one of many you can be fully yourself, strange though it may seem, and that I found a marvellous relief.

I opened up a little business, first on a cheap market stall then in a private house just off a main street — for fortune telling. I called myself Gribbar Tornadis, a rather typical sort of name for Vond, and soon did rather well. My shop sign styled me as palmist and personal advisor, but though I did have some knowledge of the lines on a hand it was mostly mind reading, making sense of what people silently told me; and then giving advice. Sometimes there were young couples asking whether it was propitious for them to marry, or rich men wanting to know how to get yet richer. There were family problems, people in despair, in love, in debt, seekers of revenge and seekers of refuge. My reputation spread rapidly, which was most agreeable as far as earning a living went, but it also had an unbelievable effect on my self-confidence, and as spring wore on into summer I began to feel quite happy again. In the evenings I usually went to a little drinking house at the corner of Northbridge Street and became part of a rather rowdy but not unintelligent company. One of them in particular, Jundar Glim, whose grandparents had come to Vond over forty years before, had quite an influence on me. Often, late at night, when the others had gone home, we would go up onto the walkway above the inner courtyard of the tavern so we could look out over the roofs of the town. He knew the names of all the stars, not just of the constellations, I mean, but the names of every single star. And he knew their stories, their history, the sagas of their peoples. He was a wonderful friend and I soon opened my heart to him and told him of Fenli, as she lived in my memories, and of Fal, Ilmarin, and even of Fethilian, though she was but a tiny child when I last saw her. Jundar did not comment or sympathize, he only listened and puffed thoughtfully at his great hooked pipe; listened and shared. He was the very best kind of companion.

It was late one evening or, to be more precise, well into the night, when I realized how much I was changing. We had been walking home together, as we often did, and were standing on the Silversmiths' Bridge. It was another of our favourite star gazing posts, for unlike Vond's other bridges it was quite uncluttered by houses or shops and gave us a good view of the night sky. It had been cloudy for more than a fortnight, I remember, so we stood longer than usual on the narrow hump of Silversmiths' watching out for shooting stars. We had stopped chatting for some time and were just staring up at the sparkle above us. I felt a sudden blow, or tug rather, as if the whole sky had jerked me out of my body, and I was floating above the bridge, hanging onto the stars again, but this time I was really high up in the air. The bridge looked quite tiny down there and I could see the whole city, that's how high up I was; yet I could see my body standing next to

Jundar who was apparently staring up at me and pointing. The next moment I plunged right back down into my body, like a gannet diving into water, and found myself looking up at the stars. Jundar was still pointing and had his mouth wide open.

"Did you see that!" he asked. "Keep looking over there, towards the Lion, there might be another one."

There wasn't and I wondered what he had seen; but thinking about it all the next morning, it came to me that the ability to go so far from my own body was a new strength, one that I had been acquiring unwittingly in Vond merely through the daily practice of my profession. By helping others, you might say, I had actually been helping myself.

One good thing I may well have learned from Grindassil was the instinct never to let things go to sleep but always to move on, to look for the next foothold in the cliff — while you still have the strength to climb. It was quite a problem, for the last thing I wanted was to become conspicuous to the local sorcerers or, worse still, to Grindassil herself. But I knew I had found a vital pathway and I had to know where it led. The chances were, I thought, that I did not need Cronk any more, and the possibilities in that thought made me very excited. On the other hand, to go off shooting around in the sky seemed possibly quite dangerous. So I worked out a compromise. I would reach out much further than I had been doing, without the crow, that is, but I would stay rooted in my own body, hidden — you might say — by the harmless mask of Gribbar Tornadis, the fortune teller.

I began by trying to meet people I knew, clients, friends from the tavern, and so on, wherever they were in Vond. This turned out to be easier than I had expected. I could locate anyone straight away just by imagining their faces clearly and suppressing every other thought. I could listen to them or even, for short spells, look out through their eyes, though this required a great deal more energy than it had with Cronk's predictable mind. The moment it began to bother them, though, I would withdraw, for it is quite against my nature to control other people.

Jundar was easy as I knew him so well, and I soon explained to him what was going on so that we could turn it into a sort of hide and seek game in the little markets and back streets of the town. But I never told him about floating up under the stars. I felt strangely shy about that part of it and decided to find out first exactly what it could lead to.

In the meantime I worked out a few other things — how to get more control and power into the Gribbar Tornadis part of me. We would walk through the markets together at the busiest time of the day, Jundar acting as a bodyguard to see that I was not jostled or pesterd, while I opened myself as wide as I could to the staggering medley of thoughts and emotions in the noisy throngs around us. I say 'noisy', although the moment I concentrated on people's minds, the whole street dimmed and became outwardly quite silent. Day by day as we practised this I could focus on a larger number of patterns of thought and surges of feeling. Occasionally the sheer diversity of it all would become just too wild and I would be forced to break loose and jump back into my eyes and ears, so to speak. But all the time new areas of my own mind were shaken out of their lethargy and brought to life. It was an exciting time.

At first Jundar acted merely as my protector, but after a while we tried switching roles at least once on every excursion; and though he never proceeded beyond the most elementary experience of mind merging there is no doubt that Jundar was becoming my pupil — yet never my disciple, for first and foremost he was my friend.

Our companionship was remarkably effortless; I think because we had a similar sense of humour and could laugh in an understanding way at some of the weird characters we tangled with: a shifty pair of beggars, a most odd woman who was convinced she had a pebble rattling around in her head, a musician who was thinking more about the women passing by than the notes he was playing. Sometimes there would be thoughts that were extremely unpleasant to share, but these were the most strengthening, for they had to be fought and held firmly in check — an inferno of revenge, an abyss of loss, a filthy quagmire of despair. These were emotions I met with often enough during the times when my clients came to me; but then I had to deal with only one at a time, and sitting in my room, in my own chair, things were a bit easier. Out there in the busy street it was rather like wrestling against some sort of giant centipede — with legs of unexpectedly varying length.

Activity in the by-ways of Vond is at its height in the early evening, especially during the hour before sunset, not first thing in the morning as you would find in market towns. You may have heard of city streets packed with people all trying to go in different directions. If you cannot imagine what such a throng is like go and visit Vond and sample the teeming life of that curious old port. I found it more and more to my liking as I came to cope with such large numbers of people.

When we tired of our sport we would go and eat with our friends at the little tavern I mentioned earlier. Incidentally, it had a rather odd name: The Knipering Drake. No-one seemed to know quite what it meant, even the landlord had no idea. The inn sign, which, he said, was a copy of the ancient one that had once hung there, showed some sort of dancing dragon, or so I reckoned it was, with its tail held in folds over its back. It made me determined to find out one day where the notion might have come from that dragons danced and whether 'knipering' was some particular step or posture in those dances.

But I am wandering from my tale. What I want to convey to you is the unique nature of those carefree months in Vond, for they did not, alas, outlive the summer. It is even more important to show you how I developed the powers which were later so vital to me. Through this daily practice my mind became increasingly versatile until I could see more through another person's eyes than they could themselves. Distance ceased to have any bearing on the matter; all I needed was to know someone well enough, no matter where they were, to be able to form a clear picture of them in my own imagination. So it came about that I saw that first voyage of the Bee Song as it flew over the shining path between the Forge and Gopley Farm — but only as a helpless spectator. I say helpless, because the dangers they were running into looked overwhelming. Oh yes, I saw the elves and I saw all the beauty. I saw the dark castle and its foul history, too; how the lords of the Silver Highway, as they had called it, had wielded dreadful powers, and how they had used them to destroy the lands of the north — until strife among themselves had led to their own destruction. I saw Fal awakening those deadly powers, especially as he took the Bee Song over the Gop itself. I tried using my own mental energy to protect them but knew I could do nothing to sweeten the poison which was gathering like a fester of puss under the ancient stone; for the rock which marked the convergence of the paths was, I saw, the key to it all — the key and the doorway to all the power and to all the disaster which Fal was setting out to mend. And now that very power was awakening against them.

Ironically it was Grindassil who saved them, not I. Against her intention, I need hardly say, for the storm she sent at them was meant to wreck their craft and perhaps finish them, too. But they met the tempest just before they crossed back over the stone. Had they done so it would have been their end for sure. As it was, they were close enough to the cursed thing to unleash its power but just too far away to receive the punch. Grindassil's storm got in the way instead.

Any attempt at direct contact with Fal and his companions met with violent rejection. I knew by now of course that it was Fethilian they had with them, but she was convinced that I was responsible for the theft of her mirror, which my father had once given her, as well as for the storms. Her mind was completely closed. I knew I would have to find a way of approaching them, probably by making the journey to Lune myself; but this set me something of a dilemma for I had no desire to leave my friends at Vond. Perhaps Jundar and I should set out together and he could make the first contact for me. That seemed a likely solution. But then there was Kereoma's oracle. I reasoned that if it had to be fulfilled then the powers would see to it and Fethilian would eventually turn up at Vond. Again and again I was on the point of discussing the matter with Jundar but always became oddly tongue tied and in the end I never got as far as mentioning it. Our time ran out.

I cannot judge what our pleasures or sorrows may mean in the totality of greater patterns, in the lives of those who for a time are our companions; but after Vond I had for a while the crushing certainty that to be my friend was to attract disaster and that the hatred of the dwarves of the Forge might have been founded on something more than hollow prejudice.

For as it had been with Fenli, now it was with Jundar.

His cry for help came during one of my afternoon sessions as an advisor of destinies. From a dock-side trader I had purchased a cheap crystal ball which I pretended to stare at while I was actually scrutinizing the mind of the man before me, in this case no less a dignitary than the mayor of Vond himself. I was of course eager to make a brilliant success of this new client and was giving every bit of my attention to him. Fortunately the consultation was nearly at an end and I had said pretty well all that was going to be necessary. The ball turned bright red and seemed to pour blood out all over the table. For a moment I was too startled to move. it was obvious that the mayor did not see it; he had been going on and on about his latest mistress, convinced she was not being honest with him, and things of that sort. First there was the blood gushing out of the crystal then the most terrible scream went off in my head. The room went black. Then the scream again. It was Jundar. I leaped up in panic, made a garbled apology to my client and shot out into the street. I headed straight for Jundar's lodgings, everyone trying to get in my way as they always seem to when you are in a hurry. I thanked the powers that at least I was not wearing my long robe. It had been a warm summer and Jundar had persuaded me to buy a light tunic and trouser outfit in one of the markets. I ran like a hare, dodging in and out, even leaping right over a loaded wheel barrow which seemed to appear out of nowhere.

But his rooms were empty. I knew he had to be nearby and I knew he was dying. There was just enough life in his mind to guide me and then enough to show me what had happened when I at last found him, though he was already past speech. It was on a side walk under a bridge — I can smell the reek of that putrid river even to this day. He smiled. We touched hands and I saw how it had been. Thieves, seamen from far away, strange voices. Then he was gone, fading out of his body like the mist in the warm morning sun. Yes, that is how I saw it.

And then a shadow fell on us. A couple of the sheriff's men with their bright yellow arm bands, looking down at me with a peculiar grin.

"Not often we're quite as lucky as this," one of them said.

I scanned their minds, saw they had no interest in whether I was innocent or guilty, they were not accusing me. There was only desire, burning greed, to win commendation from their superiors, anything as long as I swung.

I threw the whole strength of my mind at them, just punched out with all I'd got. One of them reeled backwards, straight into the stinking water; the other, the one who had spoken, just crumbled up where he stood. And I was off running again as if all the wolves of darkness were at my heels.

At my lodgings the mayor had gone, leaving his fee on the table.

I packed in seconds, clothes, money, panpipes, and I was on my way out of town before the sheriff's rabble had time to get themselves organized. It was obvious which way I would go — follow the Mirrorwend upstream, westwards, into the Waste. I would go to Lune.

THIRTY-TWO

In the two weeks or so that followed I was more glad I risked the time to linger in Farley, the last village of any size to the west of Vond, to buy as much dried meat and biscuit as I could carry. Being late summer, almost autumn, there was no shortage of ripe brambles by the wayside, and the water of the river soon became clean enough to drink. But the journey was strenuous and longer than I had reckoned with, leading in the end to a vastness of barren land, as lacking in any form of vegetation as it was in human inhabitants.

The details of that journey, my third headlong flight from danger in just one year, are of little enough interest, except for the extraordinary dream I had while resting in the shade of some wild apple trees down by the river. I had only stopped for a bite to eat but was so tired from the endless walking that I must have dozed off in the warm afternoon sunshine. It stands out clearly in my memory because on the whole my dreams used to be rather depressing. In another way too it was quite unusual because there were no people in the dream at all.

I found myself surrounded by an enormous swarm of bees. They were not angry or threatening in any way, just very noisy, and my whole body seemed to vibrate in tune with the throbbing roar that the countless thousands of wings was producing. That noise was golden splendour, magnificence and majesty, terror and comfort, all in one. And it carried me away, straight into the most superb sunset I have ever seen. I was spread out, floating around in the light for what seemed hours and hours. And then the sun really did set. The sky became dark. I remember a moment of fear as it occurred to me that bees never fly at night, and I had never been so far from my body before. But out of the darkness the bees began to shine like a host of fireflies and then gradually became quite still against the black sky. They had become the stars of a radiant universe.

A simple dream, but it was the last thing of beauty that happened to me before the events at Lune changed my life for ever.

In spite of the bees I did not walk to Lune in a happy frame of mind. Jundar's death still lay like lead in my heart, of course, and I was expecting a painful and perhaps even impossible struggle when I met up with my friends. I reckoned that to restore those friendships was likely to be harder than anything I had ever attempted and I stewed and stirred around with my thoughts endlessly as I tramped across the last miles of the Waste, wondering how best to approach them. It did not occur to me to anticipate any other than just that one problem; all dangers, I was certain, had been left far behind. Yet as I covered those last miles Grindassil was there before me, and even while I was stumbling over the rocky screes at the base of Lune, the fateful night had already fallen, the wedding had begun, and Grindassil was sending her phantom in to interrupt the feast.

I was so befogged by my own problems that it never occurred to me to ask myself what might be going on inside the caverns of Lune; I only saw my own dilemma. As I realized later, this considerably increased the power of the Sulthind phantom. It had been bloatering itself on my weakness in a way that I could not have even imagined at that time. Yes, I was remarkably blind. But do not misunderstand me; I do not suggest that to be naive is to be free from blame. The crucial fact of that moment, though, was that I had veiled myself in darkness, closed my mind completely off, for I wanted my arrival to be a surprise. That was how the disaster came about.

My approach to the entrance of Lune was so careless that the powers must surely have favoured me with their protection otherwise my story would have ended there and then.

I clambered round the last cliffs to the east of the cottage and saw the grey horse — standing there in the moonlight right in front of the door. Its attention was tightly held as if listening, concentrating on what was going on within, so it did not notice the stupid clatter of stones which I made, stumbling with shock as I dived for cover. Nor did the woman see me who was standing beside it, half hidden by its towering bulk.

I felt as if I was falling to pieces with terror; but if some saner part of my mind just managed to register the fact that neither the Spike nor Grindassil knew I was there, any relief which that knowledge gave me was soon outweighed by the extraordinary nightmare that followed.

I was wedged down between some rocks just under the cliff face and, I thought, in deep shadow; but even so I expected to be discovered any moment. Fortunately Grindassil kept herself busy putting all her energy into increasing her own nightmare, as you might say. I can only describe parts of it to you as the magical pressures around me were so overpowering that I must have fainted several times. It was like being struck by lightning over and over again. Anyway, the next thing I remember seeing was the Sulthind phantom come bursting out of the cottage as if the mountain had spat it out. But there was something wrong with it, it was all top heavy, all the wrong shape. There was a black thing writhing round its neck. At first I thought it was a monstrous lizard, then I realized it was a dwarf and that it and the Sulthind creature were actually fighting. The dwarf seemed to be exploding with fury but suddenly drew its violence inwards and appeared to be trying to burrow right into the phantom. The two of them, the light and the dark, began dissolving into one seething mass. The horse had reared and backed off leaving Grindassil, speechless with rage, in front of the contestants. It looked for a moment as if she could not make head or tail of what was going on, literally I mean, and all the while the black fury and the pale horror were entangling one another more and more, shredding each other into strips. There was a humming and eery crackling noise as the whole thing began spinning, faster and faster, like a whirlwind of black and white. Then it was flashing with brilliant colours, so bright I had to shade my eyes.

You might think from my description that this was all rather fascinating; in fact it was a horror, an obscenity beyond what I am fully able to recall.

Then above all the whizzing and crackling there was laughter. It was Grindassil. She had sorted the problem out and knew what to do about it, and the knowledge was amusing her immensely. She took a silver mirror out of her gown and held it under her chin, tilting it as if she was reflecting herself onto the spinning colours. There was a deafening explosion and I must have lost consciousness for some time, for when I looked again the scene had changed completely. The phantom had gone and she was surrounded by flaming replicas of herself, there must have been a score of them at least, all dancing around her and shrieking madly. By the powers, I have never experienced such a terror as then, I was sure my end had come.

But they were not looking for me. Their only concern was to adore their creator, to share her triumph, her power and her joy.

They did not have long to share it, though, for armed dwarves seemed to be popping up out of the ground everywhere and began attacking the women. I think some of them looked like old hags — the women, I mean, not the dwarves — but I cannot be sure now. And I must have kept fainting, for the power of the most violent evil was all about me like a suffocating cloud of smoke.

I have no idea how long I had been lying there but I very slowly became aware that it had become unbelievably cold, colder than I ever thought was possible. As my head cleared, I discovered that my lips were frozen together and I could hardly feel my legs. I knew if I stayed there I would freeze to death.

I could not hear anyone out there now and I knew I had to act fast or die. I managed with difficulty to scramble out of my hiding place and somehow blundered my way towards the cottage. I knew I had to get inside, hostility or no, it was the only chance I had left. Somehow I would get them to understand. Except that the cottage was not there; it must have vanished while I had lain senseless in the snow. Instead there was a pillared archway, like the entrance to a castle.

Then I caught sight of the women again. They were further away then they had been before, grouped around the horse, watching me, laughing. The Spike must have recognized me, too, for he gave me a friendly whinny as if he would have liked to have helped me, but I did not stay there long enough to give him the chance. I was into the doorway and running up through the tunnel like a madman, tripping and stumbling. Once I fell heavily and may have broken my right arm, for it hurt terribly, but my panic drove me on. I had to reach my friends in the hall, I had to make a stand with them against the unspeakable evil that stood at their gates.

There was some sort of magic barrier at the end of the tunnel but I threw my whole mind against it and shattered it, right in front of the long table where they all sat frozen with terror. They stared at me as if I was a ghost and I found myself shouting at them about uniting our strength, theirs and mine, with the power of Lune, with the Earth's fire, against the menace which threatened to destroy us all. They did not seem to understand or even hear, and I began yelling at them that there was no time. Ilmarin had grabbed a shining thing off the table and stood holding it as if to keep it away from me, and all the time I could feel Grindassil and her damned dancers flowing up the tunnel behind me.

I began weeping and screaming, when the most unimaginable thing happened. The further end of the chamber disappeared or rather opened out so that the hall turned into a gigantic chasm going on and on for miles into the distance. It was all lit by flames, flickering and reflecting as if the whole landscape was made of mirrors; and in the middle of it all stood the most unbelievable creature. She was some sort of giantess or troll, so immense and gross that she was almost as wide as she was tall. She wore what looked like an iron crown on her head. Her lips were huge and gaping and lined with teeth like splinters of rock, and a roaring noise came out of her mouth like an avalanche. It was so loud it was making the whole mountain shake. There may have been words mixed up in it but I could not understand them.

Then a couple of dragons appeared, massive and grotesque, one on either side of her, but even they looked tiny compared with her vast bulk. Somehow she had got hold of the thing of light that Ilmarin had been holding. I heard myself laughing hysterically, I tried to stop but I just could not get control of myself. Then she threw it at me and the mountain exploded in a blaze of flame and noise. For a moment I thought the whole place really had burst from the roots up but then I realized it must have been some sort of illusion, for I found myself floating right up above the mountain, looking down on the black labyrinth and the rocks and all the snow, just as I had once seen it through Cronk's eyes.

I must have stayed like that for a long while, for I remember seeing the stars rise and set many times. I saw the sun and the moon and the planets rolling round and round the sky, and I saw the ice melting and colours gradually return into the world.

Then I went back down into the mountain.

They were all sitting around in the gloom and the cloak of misery they wrapped around themselves was very unpleasant. I tried to talk to them but it was obvious they could neither hear nor see me. I tried to communicate directly with their minds but it was quite impossible, though I could hear all of them and read their thoughts with the greatest of ease. I looked everywhere for my body and was at first very puzzled that I could not find it. Then I understood.

I wanted to begin screaming again but somehow kept control this time, and I even managed to force myself into a state of great calmness. There was a number of things I had to find out and I knew I would not achieve anything by getting into a panic; enough harm had been done that way already. I wanted to know exactly what had happened in the hall of Lune when the troll queen had appeared and I needed to know where Grindassil was with her horse and her gang of fire dancers.

The answers to the first question were not at all easy to come by, for it meant listening in to the minds of the survivors, and it soon became obvious that they each experienced that frightful scene in completely different ways. None of them had seen the giantess with her dragons, for instance, and they all seemed to think that Rymon had thrown the weapon at me. The other common ground was that they all believed the Sulthind phantom and myself were one, or rather that the phantom was me. So their hostility towards me had increased even beyond what it had been after the storms at Gopley. The phantom must somehow have killed Rymon's husband, Osmarin, and of course they all thought I had done it.

I felt extremely wretched. Everything had gone wrong, except perhaps that Grindassil had gone off and had failed to conquer Lune. I decided I had better find out where she was and what she was up to, for it was hard to imagine that she would really accept defeat, especially since success had so nearly been in her grasp. I had run away from danger too often, and no good had come of it. Now it was time to do the other thing and look danger right in the face.

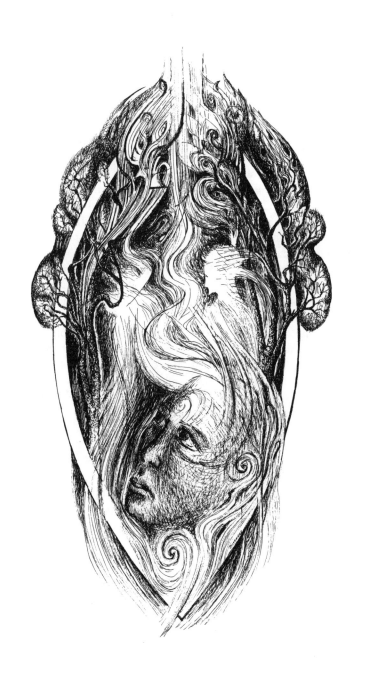

THIRTY-THREE

My guess that Grindassil would go south on the path that led by Lunt Farm turned out to be right, and she was nearly level with Fenli's tree house when I found her. She was riding along half bent forwards, either sunk in her own thoughts or perhaps exhausted. Her flame-coloured gown was in tatters and the horse looked in a sorry state. A cautious probe of her memories told me that she had lost more than just her phantoms when the troll queen had — well, killed me, I suppose is the correct expression; for Grindassil had been leading her women in through the outer tunnel and had very nearly reached the entrance to the banqueting hall. Another moment and her body would have been destroyed with mine, trapping us in the same world together.

I was following her down the trail musing upon this alarming thought and thanking the powers that things had turned out otherwise, when she reigned the horse in, turned round and looked in my direction.

I was already so used to being invisible that it had not occurred to me that she would be aware of my presence. I had not a moment's doubt, however, that she was looking straight at me. She dragged the Spike round, rather brutally, and sat there waiting. You may think that fainting with fright is a purely physical phenomenon, but I can assure you from experience that the body is in no way needed for the mind to lose consciousness. At that moment I had the utmost difficulty keeping a grip on myself.

"How very touching," she smiled. "Such an unexpected display of filial devotion — trailing along like a faithful hound. Would my darling son like to be his mother's little dog?"

She must have seen my terror for she sat there sniggering insanely while the Spike snorted and twitched as if she was burning the skin off his back. I saw more than that, though. Scared as I was, I could see that she had precious little power left; she needed people, she needed the earth, her fire pits or the caverns of Lune. Without them she would fade. She had to return to the island now to renew her strength — she had no power to coerce me.

She saw that I knew. But she still tried to get the upper hand through skill and through scorn; and besides, she needed to hurt and frighten me.

"You are damned now, Sulthind," she spoke quietly. "Your body is gone but you are bound to the earth for all eternity. Your only hope is in serving me — your friends cannot help you, they can't even see you, nobody can. You are damned." She looked serious and pleading. "I am your mother,

Sulthind. Why can't we work together?"

I felt weak and faint, but I knew I had to hold on or be lost indeed.

"Why?" I said. "Why should I side with you?"

"I have just told you. Anyway, you have no choice, no choice at all."

And then the smile came back. She had not been able to keep up her show for more than a moment, and that moment had not been long enough.

"What do you offer besides slavery?" I asked.

"You know what I offer, Sulthind, I offer power — beyond anything you have ever imagined. I am learning to waken the ancient magic, the magic of the earth. But you are right, I am not strong now — and in that you are to blame. But for your blundering I should be Mistress of Lune and from there mistress of all the world. You can be glad that I forgive you. Come home with me, Sulthind, you must be mine again."

"Your latest phantom, another dagger in your hand? What would you do with me if I did come with you?"

"I am your mother, Sulthind, don't you understand? You are mine, we belong together — come home."

I felt myself going, drifting under her spell. It was her smile that saved me. She could not get rid of it a second time and its very falseness undid all the weaving of her spells.

"If you want another slave you'll have to go and fish him out of your cess pits at home," I said. "My path does not lie with yours and never shall."

She started laughing again. It was meant to be disconcerting and to cut and hurt, but there was not a trace of love in me for her, not the tiniest fibre, so she could find nothing to cut. She saw that she was beaten.

"There is one other thing you might as well know then," she said. "It is not only your father who has the gift of foresight, I too am a prophetess. And I tell you this, Sulthind, faithless child, we shall meet again — but once only. And at that meeting you will see where your destiny lies. For I speak now truly that wherever you turn you will find only cliffs and dead ends. You have no path Sulthind. Any chance of that was destroyed at Lune. You are a ghost, a trivial phantom, invisible to all the world except me. Whatever you were or might have been, that ended at Lune. Now I am your only hope. Through me you will be born again."

I quickly scanned her mind to see whether she was lying and found to my considerable disquiet that she spoke indeed with the gift of a seeress; but the precise import of what she said seemed vague and hidden even from her. One thing was quite clear: I would never go along with her whatever her words meant.

"I see you speak the truth," I said calmly. She smiled. "But I will not follow you, not now nor ever."

She looked puzzled for a moment as if genuinely surprised.

"I offer you a share, you fool," she hissed. "I am your only hope."

"I will not come," I said.

She shrugged with a careless gesture, but as she turned the Spike round to ride on I glimpsed the hate and anger in her eyes. I tried to read what was in her mind but she was shielded now and I had no idea what she was thinking. I felt an almost overpowering impulse to run after her, but it only lasted for a moment. One way or the other I did not want any of her power; but strangely my feelings were in a turmoil and I stood there a long time before I could muster enough will-power to go on my way.

I did then what was long overdue — I went to see my father, the oracle of the Forest of Hallin; for I reasoned that if Grindassil could see me then surely Kereoma would be able to see me as well.

But even now I was uncertain. If his talents were similar to hers, what surety did I have that he was not just as dangerous as my mother? After all, there must have been a close friendship between them at one time; and if he was a true seer why had he not seen Grindassil for what she surely was, a witch of the worst imaginable kind?

Yet whatever the danger, I knew I had to see him, even if she was right and all my ways did lead to dead ends. So be it, I was dead anyhow as far as the world was concerned.

If I thought the meeting with Grindassil had left me untouched I was soon to think otherwise, for I fell into a terrible depression of self-pity and misery as I dragged my feet across the grasslands towards the forest. Yes, I say dragged my feet, for I clung to all I had been like a dock root clings to clay, and though walking and other familiar movements were something of a make-believe I used them desperately as a crutch to self-confidence if not to sanity. I also needed to lie down and sleep sometimes, though now just a third of the night was ample to refresh me.

It was in the night when I came again to the eves of Hallin and saw the trees there as my bodily senses had never seen them. In the glitter and flow of starlight they shone in the most delicate rainbow tints, casting a shifting light about them which moved and pulsed rhythmically almost as if they were dancing. It was an awesome sight and I stood for many hours watching it quite unable to gather the resolve to go on, to penetrate that magic sea of colour. The stars whispered and sang, the trees turned and danced, and I was weak with a new kind of terror, born of a vulnerability which could find no straw to clutch at. Do not ask me what I feared. I do not know. My mind had passed beyond knowing in that night, beyond logic and rationality. I was an empty place through which the beasts of the forest passed, puzzled yet challenging, staring at my terror with accusing eyes — owls, a stag, a pair of badgers, and many smaller folk, glaring, scorning my lack of courage, passing contemptuously on their way.

It must have been after hours of this torment and madness, close to dawn, when the man came. He too stood staring for a while but his gaze was friendly and soothing.

"Be still," he said.

A silence seemed to fill all the world at his command, and the trees stopped dancing. A stag stood next to him and the man rested his hand on its neck. Nothing moved. They stared but I was not frightened any more.

"You must come with me," he said.

He made a gesture which was half beckoning and half like opening an invisible door. He began walking off into the forest, and I followed him, leaving the stag by the pathway, its head lowered now, gazing after us.

We walked for hours, it must have been half way through the morning when we came to the waterfall, the one I remembered from years before.

"Wash your hands in the stream," the man said. I wanted to tell him I did not have any hands but I saw he already understood.

"Wash them all the same," he said. And he smiled.

I still hesitated, it seemed such a stupid idea. I realized my rationality must have been coming back to me. Who was this smiling man who told me to do the impossible? I tried to look into his mind.

"Wash your hands first," he said. "Everything else afterwards."

I pushed my ghost hands into the spray of the waterfall, cautiously, though the whole thing seemed so ridiculous. First the spray turned into a rainbow, then the waterfall, blazing, wild. And the colours poured into me like a flood, a rushing landslide of energy.

I thought I had exploded, a human volcano destroying itself all in one moment. And yet I was still there, a raging pillar of fire, its flames consuming themselves even as they grew.

The mind is very strange. I expected to hear myself screaming and imagined I heard my own voice, but it was the silence which in the end made me realize that it was all over and that I had been standing there for quite a long time.

The man was still smiling. "You need never be afraid again," he said.

I looked at him wonderingly, the bearded face, the mixture of old and young, strong yet perhaps not so very much older than myself. His thoughts were unshielded now.

"You cannot possibly be my father," I said.

He laughed. "I am the only Kereoma in Hallin. But there is a better place to talk, my son. Come into the house."

He turned and walked on, away from the water. A tide of peacefulness had overcome me, a happiness mixed with utter exhaustion. I just stood there watching him go along the path.

He paused and looked back.

"Come up to the house, Sulthind. You will like it there."

I do not remember much about the forest dwelling from my childhood, mostly the thick carpets and the tiny shuttered windows; perhaps because its one room was so enormous that it was beyond a small child's comprehension, though I do have a faint recollection of the rows of wooden pillars. I think because we were not allowed to play among them. And there are some lingering images in my memory of the many wooden steps which lead up to the doors, for the house, or hall rather, is built on stilts well above the forest floor.

I followed him in — Kereoma, my father, it was extremely difficult to reconcile my expectations with this young and athletic person who bounded easily into the house taking the steps three at a time. Yet the mood of peace which had entered into me smothered bewilderment even as it grew; I did not really care who he was, this bearded man with the kindly eyes.

I found myself sitting on a couch. He had gone to a cupboard and was taking out a loaf on an ancient breadboard with a knife heavy enough to fell an ox.

"I don't eat," I said.

"That's fine, the waterfall will give you all you need." He laughed. "But I do eat and I'm half starving. Any idea how long you were standing by the water?"

He threw me a quizzical look. I did not answer.

"Well, it's close to sundown now and it was before midday when we reached the falls, and anyway I haven't eaten since yesterday. It was in the middle of the night when I rescued you from the Guardians."

"The Guardians? The trees?"

He smiled but did not answer at first as his mouth was full of bread and butter. Then he nodded.

"They were kinder to you than most. Those who don't run away are likely to go mad. Some don't even survive. Hallin is a place of power."

"I know," I said ruefully. Then after a pause, "Do you live here alone?"

He nodded, his mouth was full again. "Ever since Grindassil left I have been alone — the Hermit of Hallin. Sometimes there are visitors, legitimate ones, who come for the oracle. You know about that?"

I did not answer. I was thinking about Grindassil. She was wrong then, she had lied. She was not the only one who could see me.

"She's your wife," I said.

He looked puzzled as if he had not quite heard what I said.

"Grindassil — she must have been your wife."

The smile had completely faded. There was no doubt now that he did not understand me.

"Grindassil — my wife? I don't quite know what you mean."

He spoke slowly, peered at me from beneath a heavy frown.

"But if she is my mother she must have been your wife."

He leaped to his feet so suddenly I thought he was going to attack me. Then he began to laugh, incredulously, uproariously. I was totally at a loss. But he got control of himself and stood looking down at me for a while stroking his beard. At last the smallest trace of the amused twinkle returned to his eyes.

"Grindassil!" he said. "Grindassil is my sister. Your mother died when you were very small. Grindassil killed her."

The room reeled. I thought he had toppled over, everything was going the wrong shape, then I felt him holding my hands. I seemed to be lying on my back on the floor or I may have been floating just above it. This time I really did hear myself screaming; but he held me calmly, quite still, waiting.

"You need never be afraid again," he said. "Never forget that."

At last I quietened down, but we did not speak for a long time. Instead, thoughts flowed between us, images, memories, that gathered and quickened until I was seeing the past as if it were the present although it must have all happened so long ago. I saw her now, my mother, my real mother, terribly young and innocent, I saw their love for one another, hers and Kereoma's. Then Grindassil, insisting on coming to live with her brother in Hallin, the jealousy, the closed mind, the pool of dark secrets. And the other family, Gulmer and the old lady, her daughter and the little twins, the friendship of the two mothers, their strange disappearance. I saw Grindassil's pretended outrage and sorrow, and I saw her trying to take the children as her own; then Gulmer's family fleeing, Grindassil's odd smile, and Kereoma's first suspicions, still unable to believe.

"Why could you not see her truly, father, you the oracle, greater than Grindassil?"

"Oracle, yes, my son, but not much of a seer and certainly no sorcerer. She could keep her mind well shielded — at first."

"You didn't follow us when she fled, stealing me from you to train me as her slave?" Question upon question raced through my mind, I was battling against a flood of anger and resentment.

"My powers had become entirely bound to Hallin, Sulthind. She did well in choosing the island for her little realm, and she was well protected there. I could only wait until such a strength as I had managed to give you came to fruition, until you found your own way back to me."

"But now it is too late — I am dead."

He let go of my hand. I became aware that I was no longer floating over the floor but sitting upright on the couch.

"You don't look very dead to me," he said. There was a silence between us for a while. Did he not understand?

"But to everyone else I am dead. I have no body that anyone can see, so I'm as lonely and hopeless as I was on the island, I'm — I'm a ghost."

"No you're not, Sulthind, you're nothing like a ghost. Have you forgotten the Gavelburg. Yes, I've seen your past this last hour just as you've seen mine. Listen, all of us are led to the fulfillment of our destinies and each one is different. You will find yours. You have made some impressive strides on your own path these last months whatever you may think. Look how you resisted her on the road the other day. Do you think you could have won that battle if you were a ghost?"

I could not listen to what he said, I was sinking into self-pity.

"But what of Fethilian, of your oracle? Or did Grindassil lie about that as well?"

Kereoma looked surprised. "So she told you about that?" He thought for a moment. "No, she did not lie. At least, exactly what did she tell you?"

"That we would be married one day."

He pursed his lips. "That is what my oracle said, yes, that is true. But 'married' can have many meanings, and oracles do not speak the language of the everyday world. And again, my son, remember I am not a seer. I do not always understand my visions; they are like dreams, strong and with the compulsion of truth about them but in symbols which are often hard to understand."

"So I might not be one day married to Fethilian?"

"You will be for sure, Sulthind, though just what that means we shall have to see."

I thought of another explanation. "If your oracles are not in everyday language, father, could it be that the name is wrong? I lived with Fenli when I escaped from the island and our love for one another was — well, limitless. The names are similar — a little."

He shook his head slowly. He had seen Fenli in my memories.

"It is not a matter of names or of words that sound like this or that. Your destiny lies with Gulmer's daughter, who lived here with us in Hallin when you and she were children; do not doubt it."

"But if she cannot even see me?"

"She will see you when the time comes and she will see the truth of who you are; and she will see the misunderstandings that have been. She will know it all in one moment and you will be her friend. And then you will have to be very brave, very brave indeed. The choice will be yours and yours alone."

"What choice, father, why will I have to be brave?"

"I speak as I must, Sulthind, but I cannot see what that danger will be; though I suspect Grindassil will be part of it."

"She said that I would be born again through her. What a monstrous idea!"

"She spoke truly, though believe me, she did not understand what she spoke, for in this one respect her gifts are just like mine. She told you this as an oracle, without understanding. You will see what she meant when you find her again, of that have no doubt."

He paused for a moment, frowning.

"And there is someone else, or something, that will also be reborn; something neither she nor you have yet met. But I do not understand all this, any more than you. It's a puzzle, yes, it truly is a puzzle."

There was a silence. I could think of nothing else to say. In the end he went over to the hearth and began making the fire up. He shivered as if it was cold. I had no such sensations, at least not in connection with the seasons of nature. Emotions from other people, moods of places, they were the weather to which I now responded.

He pottered about getting a meal ready. I just sat there thinking about it all, reviewing my new memories, the young mother with the baby boy, the murderess with her sickening pretence of grief. It seemed to be only yesterday.

When I at last looked up, my father had already finished his meal. There were candles burning. It looked as if he was going to bed.

"What do you do at night?" he asked.

"Sleep, part of the time — then walk around, look at the stars; think."

"Do not go beyond the waterfall. Not yet. Tomorrow we will talk again."

There were no stars that night. The clouds hung thick and low and it rained without ceasing. I stood till dawn by the waterfall letting the spray and the drizzle pour through me. It was refreshing and healing, like a sparkling music, but words cannot capture its quality. When the sun rose the sky cleared. A robin sang then by the falls and for a moment I thought I could remain standing there for ever. But I knew that was not to be. I went back to the house and was strangely relieved to find him up and about preparing breakfast.

"The people will come soon," he said. "don't be alarmed — and don't try to speak to them."

"What people, father?"

"The wardens who look after me. Once a week some of them come up with supplies and see if there is anything I need. And if there are supplicants to visit the oracle, they will come, too."

There were no supplicants, and the four people who appeared, three women and a man, with supplies and clean linen in wide carry-baskets, did not stay long. They were cheerful but showed great respect for Kereoma, chatting only in whispers as they changed his bedding and did things around the house. Kereoma thanked them and asked them to tell the assembly that all was well. There was a quality of ritual about all this, but I did wonder whether everything was really always well and what would happen if it was not. But another thought also occurred to me.

"Father, I heard Fethilian talking about the mirror you gave her as a child. Grindassil stole it from the farm at Gopley. What can she do with it?"

He looked surprised. "Very little, I should have thought. It belonged to my grandparents who were both craftsmen and sorcerers, of a good kind. I doubt the mirror will do much for Grindassil."

"What is it meant to do?"

"It is meant to look afar and to project thoughts, helpful thoughts, to the people it sees."

"I think I saw Grindassil use it for something else before the gates of Lune."

I told him of the battle and the creation of the fiery dancers. Kereoma smiled. "Was there a noise when she did that? Did you see the mirror again?"

I tried to remember. The crash had been deafening, enough to have brought the mountain down. She certainly was not holding the mirror afterwards, but she may have put it back in her gown. Kereoma shook his head and smiled.

"She will not have put it back in her gown, Sulthind; it can only be used once for such purposes. It will have destroyed itself. That is a pity; but I am glad she doesn't have it any more, it is not for the likes of her." He smiled grimly. "She must have been desperate to have done that."

I stayed for many days and many nights in the forest of Hallin until at last Kereoma said I was ready to go, for he assured me that although I had been strong in resolve when I had met Grindassil on the road, the encounter had drained my strength more than I knew. I asked him if he had any idea where she was at that moment.

"There is no way that I can ever have direct knowledge of Grindassil, my son, I have thrust her out utterly. And I say this to you, that even when you feel stronger than you do now, for who knows what powers and friends you will find on your travels, do not try to see her with your mind, neither from close by nor even from any distance, for now she will be waiting for this very thing, and then your destiny would fulfill itself before time. You must find another way — and be patient."

"But if she's waiting for this last encounter she may seek me, and if I may never try to look in her direction, how can I know when she is near?"

Kereoma thought a while in silence. At last he spoke slowly and with hesitation. "I do not know, my oracles are mostly riddles even to myself. Yet it seems to me that she will not seek you — she knows you are destined to seek her."

"How can I seek her and avoid her at the same time? And not use my mental powers to know when she is near? Your advice seems impossible to follow, it makes no sense."

He smiled and sighed. "My oracles usually do not make sense, I'm sorry to say. There is always a chance, though, that at the right moment you will have to follow her wherever she goes yet keep always well away."

"Until the right moment."

"That's it"

"And if I have to keep out of her sight how can I ever know when that moment comes? It seems totally ridiculous!"

"You will know. I cannot help you more than that."

"But I don't want to follow her, I want to keep as far from her as possible."

"I know, but then you would stay as you are for ever and ever. In the end you would become a ghost indeed, a tired shadow whose friends have long since died."

"My friends have already died — Fenli and Jundar."

"And Fethilian? You must go now, Sulthind, go and find Grindassil but keep away from her. Just make sure you know where she's gone and what she's up to — to begin with."

"And you have no idea where she is!"

"She was riding southwards when you last saw her."

"Back to the island."

"Or to the Delming."

"The Delming? What would she want at the Forge?"

"I don't know. You had better go and find out."

We walked past the waterfall together, back to the place where he had found me on the forest's edge. There were no rainbow colours now. The forest had become wintry and drab, as grey as the heavy clouds which seemed to be trying to keep all the light out of the world. The only bright thing was Kereoma's smile.

"Keep walking," he said. "If you fly, she'll see you."

I felt extremely miserable and very reluctant to go. "I hope we meet again, father," I said.

"We shall, we shall," he smiled, "just make sure you do all the right things. Don't lose your nerve."

"I have already," I said. I think I might have managed a glum sort of smile. "I've lost them all, every one."

He laughed. "That won't make it easier, I'm afraid. Just remember — keep your feet on the ground."

I turned round many times as I walked back towards the road. He was always standing there waving, a tiny figure all in brown amidst the black of the bare trees.

THIRTY-FOUR

The gloom did not lift all the way down to the Delming. Towards the end it was beginning to grow worse, and when I finally approached the North gate of the town it was worst of all. Although it was early evening, you would have thought it was the middle of the night the way the town was all closed up and silent. There just has to be a watchman, I thought, and I stood around for a long time peering up at the walls until I found him, huddled in a shady recess instead of walking up and down as they usually did. The fellow obviously wanted to stay out of view. I tried a cautious mind merge with him and found panic, terror at having to remain alone up there, alone, exposed to... her. I began to feel exposed myself and glanced around hastily but there was no sign of anyone else, not a single soul. I tried probing him again to find out what had happened, but there was only confusion and self concern which just about smothered everything.

I had no difficulty getting through the closed gate — though on the whole I had been trying to maintain every detail of my old habits, it seemed the only way to keep sane. There are times when you have to set yourself a few rules in order to hold things together, but now it looked as if I might have to be breaking them rather often, at least as far as walking through closed doors was concerned.

The main street which leads down to the Dwarves' Gate was empty, or at least appeared to be so at first. Then a woman stepped out of a doorway, glanced nervously around, and hurried across the road into another door-way. This sort of thing happened several times, sometimes two or three people would be out at once, but they never stopped to speak to each other. And always this glancing around, especially up towards the North Gate. They could not see me standing there, of course, but I wondered if I stood there long enough whether I would find any exceptions and how I would react if there were; think of the dwarves, for instance. They would set off a most dreadful pandemonium if they spotted me of all people walking towards their precious Forge. I smiled at the thought but knew I had better do something to find out what had been going on. My guess was that she was not in the town at the moment and that they were all terribly fright-ened she might return. Even so I kept a careful look out.

The first dwarf popped out just as I reached the walls which guarded the Courts from the north. It happened so suddenly that I had no time to get out of the way. He went right through me and out the other side, grunting to himself like an old hedgehog. So they could not see me, either, I realized with no inconsiderable relief. To have had the whole community of the dwarves on my heels like a pack of hare-hounds would have been unpleasantly inconvenient. Another little fellow appeared out of one of the houses, more cautiously this time, peeping up and down the street before scuttling through the doorway which led into the dwarves' part of the Forge. I was particularly glad this one was not able to see me, for I recognized him as Theck, a rather nagging creature who had always been very quick to take offence in the days when I used to visit Fal and Ilmarin. I decided to follow him, not into the dwarves' quarters, though I had always been curious to know what it was like in there, but through the long almost tunnel-like gateway which led into the Forge itself. I went slowly as I felt there might well be someone of ability in that innermost sanctuary of the Delming guarding it.

There was.

Even as I stepped through the inner door, before I had any chance at all to look around, I was frozen solid, turned to ice or iron, I could not even move my eyes to see what held me in such an unbelievable grip. I tried to remember what Kereoma had said about not ever needing to be afraid again, and why he had said it, but it was no use, no use at all — I was totally overcome with maddest terror, there was nothing else in me, it had the power of a hundred storms, of all the winds, darkness, lightning, all brought together into the grip of one gigantic talon just about to crush the being out of me. My mind gave way, I was sure it was the end of me, the absolute end. But it was not the will of that terrible force to destroy — not yet — it wanted me for something. And I just wanted to scream, and scream and scream, but even that was impossible.

Then it spoke.

At first I could not understand what it said, it was nothing but a noise which ripped and tore at my very roots; and the fact that I could make no sense of what it said added even more to the pain and terror; while it — and I — were coldest steel.

In the end it must have quietened down a little; I think its first explosion of rage had come to an end — and its words began to make some vague sense. It seemed to be asking something, repeating a question, endlessly, the same words. I suppose it realized that I would never understand if it kept me paralysed to such a degree, and its grip relaxed, just a little.

"Where is she?" it said. "Where is she?"

I could not speak. It released me a little more and I managed to turn my head and look at it.

It was a dragon. For a moment I thought that it must be one of her phantoms and that this was the cause of the town's distress. But it did not feel like one of her creations — it was too direct, too real, and a slave to no-one.

"Where is she?"

I made a heroic effort to speak and managed to say something about the unusual pets they kept at the Forge nowadays. The icy grip tightened again.

"Play no games with me, Lothur of the Island; I have seen you in the mind of Fal and in the memories of the dwarves. You are in a poor position to engage in any form of amusing conversation. Just tell me where she is."

"You don't understand," I managed to make myself say, "there are two Sulthinds, two. The other one is her slave. I have nothing to do with her. Nothing at all — any more than you have."

The golden eyes blazed with fury and I'm sure my end would have come there and then, but at that very moment Fal came in. He looked pale and worried, at the end of his tether, I thought — but the dragon's grip prevented my attempting any mental contact with him.

"Who are you talking to, Skelgrist," he said. "I'm sure I heard voices." It was obvious that he could not see me.

"I thought there was an intruder," the dragon answered, "I must have been dreaming."

"Do dragons talk in their sleep?" Fal forced a brief smile. "And anyway you're supposed to be guarding the Forge."

So it was called Skelgrist; and it was not going to tell Fal that I was here. That seemed ominous to me. It meant that it wanted to finish me off in its own way, without interference. I was horribly afraid but kept trying to think of Kereoma and kindle at least a trace of courage within me. It did not seem to work; I felt utterly abandoned. Then Kereoma spoke — "You have only your cowardice to fear; there is no need to be afraid."

The dragon must have heard it too, for it jerked its head up, listening. "There *is* an intruder here," it said. "I am sure of it. I heard a voice."

"A woman?" Fal asked, "Grindassil?"

"It was a man, the voice of a man."

"Strange" said Fal. "But I do not think it is Sulthind, he has no power to come here, and anyway he would not dare."

The dragon's talons tightened round me. It became so cold I began to lose consciousness.

"Forget Sulthind," it said. "I am certain he can never trouble us; quite certain." It chuckled with a sort of grating rumble, like boulders rolling over each other.

"Tholley said he could never again trouble the realm of Lune. But what about the Delming?"

"Why suddenly this concern about Sulthind? It is Grindassil we have to worry about now — Grindassil and Feather. Lothur can never harm us."

The ice in my mind splintered into a thousand colours, whirling in a dazzling vortex of pain. What by all the powers did he mean, Grindassil and Feather?

But I heard Fal speaking again. "It is strange, Skelgrist, but the last thing she said before she went was, 'We must go to Hallin; perhaps it wasn't Sulthind's fault after all.' I was going to ask her what she meant, but then... it happened."

I made a desperate effort to see what was in Fal's mind, but Skelgrist squeezed me almost at once. I just caught a glimpse of that final scene, Fethilian and Fal walking alone in the hills outside the walls, then Grindassil, all in black now, the grey horse, her scorn and laughter, Fal's terrible anguish. So that was it. She had taken Fethilian. But for what purpose? And why were these two here, why not trying to get her back?

I read the answer, from Skelgrist now. The island was deserted, they had searched everywhere; they did not know what to do.

"Go and rest, Fal," the dragon rumbled, "leave me alone for a while; I am at the gates of an answer to this riddle."

Fal was about to object then shrugged and went to the door. He turned and frowned at Skelgrist, obviously puzzled, needing to know more about the dragon's thoughts. Instead he said, "Do you often sleep, Skelgrist?"

"I never really need to; I only bother to doze when things get really dull."

Fal forced another smile. "Let me know if you think of something."

He closed the doors behind him. I was alone with death again.

"Alone with your *second* death," said the dragon.

I jumped at this unexpected chance. "If you can read minds then you can see that I'm telling the truth."

He let go of me suddenly and withdrew his claws, folding them under his chin with a swift movement. Then he kept still for a long time, his head resting on his glittering paws, the golden eyes watching me unblinking. His mind was completely shielded. I made no attempt to move but opened my memories to him.

"Your mind is vague to me, Lothur, cloudy, like a dirty puddle. No, I cannot read your thoughts, only Fal's and — partly — Feather's,when she is here. You could easily hide half your mind behind what you are trying to make me think. And I don't need entertaining."

"There must be some way to show you."

"If I wanted to be shown... No, do not try to move; I'm thinking about you."

Now the first terror had subsided I was beginning to find all this extremely exasperating.

"Perhaps you are right," he said, "there are two of you, two Sulthinds: the one you are showing me and the one you are hiding. Where is she?"

"I don't know where she is," I screamed at him, "and I'm not hiding anything from you."

"Losing your composure would be dangerous, Lothur. I believe you are sensible enough to see that I have no way of testing your claims. But I do have ways of — forcing you a little."

I could see this was going to lead us nowhere. I decided to try a different approach.

"Listen, Skelgrist," I said, "you call yourself my second death. You are wrong; only Grindassil can be my second death. You are looking for her, I am trying to avoid her."

He snorted with contempt. "Your mother — your death? Try a more amusing riddle, I'm usually quite good at them."

The claws slid forward a little, ever so slightly, but it was a warning. Yet it was true what he said, dragons do like riddles, I had to take the chance.

"I have to avoid her," I tried again, "because she is my doom; but because she is my doom I cannot avoid her."

"Go on," he said.

Then I made a stupid mistake, trying to move too fast. "If you would only let me speak to Fal's mind, I could explain all this to him in a moment."

He leaped to his feet with a growl and hung over me menacingly. "If ever you try to do that I shall destroy you utterly," he whispered. "Never let that thought cross your mind, never ever again."

But his threats admitted a future at least; if he was going to finish me now the warning would be meaningless. I was winning, and the claws were keeping away.

"You have understood, Lothur of the Island? And remember — I never need to sleep."

"Yes," I said, "I have understood. Incidentally, I do need to sleep sometimes, in case you wondered." I felt I was getting too confident and beginning to wander from the point. I decided to come straight out with it. "If you come with me I shall lead you to her, I cannot avoid my doom."

It was an oracle and I could see he felt the truth of it. He lay down again and went back to the unblinking stare. What was it Kereoma had said about not losing my nerve? I knew that to crack now would be fatal.

"Where would you take us?" he said.

I had to think fast. I made a quick decision. "First we must go to the stone on the Gop, for it is the crossing of many paths. One of them has to be the right way."

"It is a place of many dangers," he mused. "But you are right; there are doorways at the Stone. Most of them are best avoided."

I said nothing, it was better to let him think.

"How do I know you will not betray us?" he murmured after another long silence.

"I expect she could find you herself if she wanted to, and staying in here is not likely to find her."

"Unless she comes to bargain."

"She can come to bargain on the road much easier than here."

He thought again for a while. "It is nonsense and truth all knotted up together," he said, "but you are right: there is no better way."

He was still staring. I feared I had won him over too easily. There would be more to it than this, I thought, wishing again that his mind was less perfectly shielded. I wanted to know who he was and how he came to be in the Delming's very centre, a dragon lurking at the heart of the Forge. I did not enjoy riddles as much as Skelgrist appeared to, and this particular riddle was quite beyond me.

After another period of respectful silence I decided to ask. I tried to think of subtle and circumspect ways of approaching the question but I was tiring rapidly and I could not think of one.

"Who are you?" I asked.

He still stared.

"You cannot force me to find my doom; doom cannot be forced."

"You will find it anyway," he grumbled. "You just said so."

"I didn't, but I say again: you can hold me captive if you will but you cannot force me to lead you; only my doom can guide us, I cannot."

"So?"

"So I demand to know the nature of..." I was about to say 'my companion' but was quick enough to see the tactlessness in the phrase. I changed it to "Fal's companion."

Another bout of this cursed staring, but I contained my impatience this time. At last the answer came. He cleared his throat with a rasping cough and spoke very quietly.

"You said there were two Sulthinds. I do not know if this is true, but I know that it could be." A long silence; then: "I am Fal's other self; his lower self, some might say, but it is too soon to judge such matters; though not too soon to say that the day will come when that will all be changed. Yes; but in this shape I have been bound to him — not since the beginning of time — but since his fate began to take shape. And because his destiny is bound with Feather's I belong to her also."

I nearly shouted that he must be mine, too, if he was Fethilian's, but fortunately I managed to keep a grip on myself. And I had the feeling the dragon had not quite finished. It was my turn to watch and wait.

"I am the burden he has borne," he said, "and we have fought to many a bitter end. I am the Guardian of his Doom."

This was beyond me at the time, but the word 'guardian' was clear enough. I decided to leave it at that and change the subject.

"Do you agree to set out then?" I asked.

"Fal is weak from nights of sleeplessness and now he slumbers deeply. We will go tomorrow. And we will do as you say."

―――

It was a strange company that processed through the main street the next morning, Fal — tired and miserable — riding on the dragon's back — and myself an unseen companion walking next to them. Melauriën came to the dwarves' gate to wish them well — I cannot say "us", for Skelgrist refused to tell anyone that I was with them. A few townsfolk turned out to watch them go, others peeped from their windows. I thought many of them were as apprehensive of the dragon as of a conflict with Grindassil, but I could not probe their thoughts without risking retribution from Skelgrist, for one of the conditions of our strained fellowship was that I did not use my unusual mental abilities in any way without his agreement. Another was that I stayed close to him at all times, though he assured me that his own mental powers could devastate me almost as much at a distance as when he used his claws — they only served to put the effect beyond any possible dispute, as he charmingly explained.

None of us had the slightest idea whether we were heading in the right direction, and I had already secretly admitted to myself that the plan I had suggested was very much a child of desperation. It would have been more sensible, as I told Skelgrist in the course of the morning, if I had sought Fethilian mentally, but the dragon would not hear of any mind merging except with himself, and then only to a slight degree; just enough to be able to converse without attracting Fal's attention. I begged him, not for the last time, to let me explain myself to Fal, but he would not hear of it, and warned me that I had better keep to one suggestion at a time. I wondered whether it would ever be possible to win Skelgrist's confidence, and this worried me unceasingly, for in a confrontation with Grindassil it could be fatal to be confused as to the matter of allegiances.

For the moment Fal seemed to think that Skelgrist was guiding him and I wondered what would happen when we came to the Gop and none of us had the faintest idea what to do. In the meantime Fal was in the blackest of moods and sat hunched on the dragon's back completely blind to the world around him. He ate almost nothing but slept fitfully that night under a clump of old pines, Skelgrist and I keeping watch from both sides.

I asked the dragon if he ever ate, but he assured me that he was almost as much a spirit being as I was, that he needed only to drink in order to maintain his physical form. This was the nearest we came to conversation on that first day, but I did think that even that modest exchange was quite a positive sign.

During the night another possibility occurred to me. Skelgrist had warned me against the use of any mental merging, presumably because he feared I would betray them. I wondered if he would object to my probing the trees and animals that we passed. I could justify this on the grounds that their perceptions, though of a different nature from ours, might form a trail of memories which could be of at least corrective value in our search. I needed another Cronk, of course, but failing that my new inspiration gave me the hope that by the time we reached the Gop I would have improved my position considerably.

I began with the pines under which we were camping. I probed into them very cautiously and received images of stars and clouds, sunshine and rain. Skelgrist asked what I was doing and I told him that it was my nature to be aware of my surroundings. He showed mild interest but no alarm and expressed no objection. I had difficulty suppressing my elation and had to concentrate for a while on remembering Fenli and her tree house to cover my emotions. Then I tried again. I found some mice and a young owl, and the world under the pines burst into a flood of different dimensions as I touched their minds and demanded to see as they saw. Skelgrist showed little interest and again my biggest problem was to conceal the rush of hope which would have certainly given away the whole thing. I knew I would have to proceed slowly, step by step; one hasty move and my only chance would vanish for ever.

The next day I concentrated on cows. From the point of view of finding a trail this proved to be of no use at all, they seemed always to be far more conscious of each other than of anything else, but that did not matter — I had to practise. I knew that by the time we reached the Gop my plan could and must succeed. Even now we were as likely to be going in the wrong direction and losing precious time. I tried not to think too much about what Fethilian might be going through. I supposed, like Fal and Skelgrist, that Grindassil would use her as a hostage, to bargain with; but several more unpleasant possibilities occured to my mind and I felt the sooner we found out the truth the better. If only Skelgrist would allow me to contact her directly, but he would entertain no discussion on this point and warned me to keep to animals. I had every intention of doing so.

The third day, after we crossed the Runeway, I switched to horses. Still Skelgrist raised no objections, though I feared my plan would become obvious to him at any moment. There were two of them grazing up on the hillside and they proved to be most co-operative and observant creatures. I kept up my contact with them long after they were lost to view, and still Skelgrist suspected nothing. I hardly dared believe my luck, but kept probing them playfully as if merely to relieve the tedium of the journey until we were only a half a mile or so from the Gop. The massive green pyramid would block our path further on and I knew the great stone was up there behind its collar of trees, marking the interchange of hidden paths, of terrible ancient energies. And still I thought of horses, and of grazing, and galloping, sparring, mating, and of watching.

It was almost evening as Skelgrist plodded slowly up the hill, Fal still an inert heap of misery on his back. We came over the brow and there it was, black, threatening. I noticed Fal was huddled over his harp now, and the unpleasant thought struck me that he might try to use it on the Stone as a last resort.

"Skelgrist," I said, "remember the stone is very perilous. Do not awaken it."

He stood there growling at the cursed thing while Fal seemed lost in another world; and I still tried to think of horses.

Then he took a step closer — and I thought of the Spike. I concentrated on his nature as a horse, while Skelgrist bowed before the Stone as if he was going to charge it and challenge its evil nature in head-on combat. And I imagined the Spike, more and more clearly, the grey horse, the cowed subservience. I waited till Skelgrist was completely taken up by his study of the Stone — then I moved right into Spike's mind.

I was immediately dragged into a vortex of the most sickening emotions — fear and despair, humiliation, cruel laughter, crushing bondage with the knowledge that there would never be release. I was struggling wildly to avoid being caught and drowned in this world of terror, and I went on struggling until I was quite certain I could remain free.

Then I forced my will on his. It was pathetically easy, he was already so broken.

Where is Fethilian? I asked, and I made him show me. I saw Grindassil, all in black, and Fethilian tied with leather thongs, and the whip, the merciless whip, and flames — blue flames. Why, why? Then I saw — it was to break Fethilian too, to make another slave, another devilish transformation. But it did not work, Fethilian could not be broken — not yet. And I felt Grindassil's lust, revelling in the pain she caused, I heard her laughter.

But where, where are you?

This was more difficult, and for a long moment I thought he would be unable to tell me, there was for him no 'where', only 'here' and 'now'. But I had to know and know quickly, before Skelgrist stopped what I was doing. I pushed hard on the Spike's mind, taking the risk that he might crumble completely and become unconscious; I tried to hold back some of my power and hoped I could still press something useful out of him. Show me where, show me, show! Confused images, weary travelling, often by night, but westwards, clearly westwards, past Old Running, then further, further to the west. Rocky chasms, gorges, the thunder of a waterfall, the horse stumbling with weariness and always the whip. Where now? Mountains, steep paths, always westwards. The cavern, the cavern and the throne; a tree in a cavern, and power, terrible power. And blue flames, always the blue flames.

There was a flash of light and a flattening release of energy. Fal was on his back in the grass, and Skelgrist, towering high on his hind legs, appeared to be enveloped in a swirl of dazzling green which was pouring out of the Gop. He began staggering backwards, the light flowing after him like a liquid, burning, punishing, stinging. Without thinking I leapt into the dragon and thrust against the pain. The brilliance faded. The only green was from the grass, and the stone was black.

I sprang clear before he had time to recover, and was half way down the hillside fearing a terrible reaction. But none came. I looked back and could see Fal lying there motionless but apparently still clutching his harp. He looked as if he might be dead. At first there was no sign of Skelgrist, so I went up again to see what had happened. He was stretched out behind the stone, his head pointing away from me, so I had to creep around him, trying to keep my mind totally withdrawn. I came face to face with the golden eyes, waiting, watching. They showed no sign of recognition or emotion, just the cold stare, unblinking.

This time I'd had enough of it. "You're all right, then," I said, "but what about Fal?"

"He has only fainted, he will recover."

The dragon raised his head a little and rested his chin on his paws. He still stared.

"You rescued me, little wizard, saved my life when you could have escaped. I wonder why."

I gasped with frustration. But he went on.

"You did something else too, while I was struggling with the Stone. Something else. What was it?"

I did not answer. I was trying to make up my mind whether he was really grateful for my intervention and had taken it as a sign of friendship or whether he had already decided that I must have other motives which served my own ends; in which case my disobedience would still be punishable on the same terms as before. He stared. And Fal lay there unconscious. Surely he needed help, but in this state of idiotic deadlock it was going to be difficult to help anyone; my dice had already been cast. I decided to throw all my money into the hat, too, there might never be another chance.

"Listen, Skelgrist, I told you already that my intentions..."

"Don't try to tickle the dragon behind the ears, little wizard, just tell me what you did, that's all."

I sighed. "Very well; yes, I disobeyed you while you were — occupied, but only slightly. I did not try to contact Fethilian with mental search."

His eyes opened wider. "How sensible of you. And stop telling me what you did not do and begin telling me what precisely you did do, before I get upset."

So I went right into it. "She has a horse, Grindassil has a horse, called the Spike."

"Your mother has a horse, yes?"

"She is not my mother, Skelgrist, but if you want to hear what I have to say, will you be quiet and let me finish! This horse is part of her devilry, it was once a man, a servant of hers, now she has enslaved him completely and..."

"And turned him into a horse! Fascinating. Go on."

"The horse hates her and has already helped me once before, last year, when I escaped from her island. I managed to look into his mind to find out what was going on."

"And... what *is* going on?"

"She is trying to break Fethilian so that she can enslave her, too."

"Turn her into a horse?"

"I don't think so, something different. I did not have time to see. The energy from the Stone hit you, and I came back."

"I understand. And where are they?"

"To the west. I saw mountains, narrow gorges, an agony of weariness, it must have been a terrible journey."

"How is she trying to break Fethilian."

"She is starving her, whipping her, many times a day, in the middle of the night, her resistance is cracking."

The dragon growled. "They are still in these mountains?"

"I saw a cavern, a hall, with an ancient throne... and a tree in the cavern, glistening with a peculiar blue sheen."

Skelgrist raised his head with a jerk and let out a serpent-like hiss.

"Do you know of such a hall?" I asked.

"I know of such a hall. Yes, indeed, Sulthind, I know of such a hall; once it was mine. It is like the Gop, a place of power. She must not rule from there, she must not, it would be the bane of us all."

He stood up and shivered, stretching his neck and claws, snarling with fury. But I had noticed that he had called me Sulthind instead of Lothur, and I knew I was winning.

"Where is this hall, then?" I asked.

"It is in the west, as you say. Alas that I am not a flying dragon, for we have need of haste."

He scooped Fal up in his paws and, holding him in his scaly arms like a baby, began waddling off down the hill with him, not towards Gopley but away to the left, westwards, straight into the setting sun.

THIRTY-FIVE

The next morning Fal was again riding on the dragon's back and once more I begged Skelgrist to let me speak with him. I tried elaborating on the value of being fully united should an unexpected encounter with Grindassil be thrust upon us. He was friendlier about it this time at least, but argued that there were still some things concerning me that he did not understand and needed to know. I offered once more to open my mind completely to him, but even as I did so a difficulty occurred to me which might well cause a serious setback in our delicate relationship. I need not have worried. Skelgrist had no intention of entering my mind unreservedly and admitted that he still feared some sort of trap, especially as since my rescue on the Gop he rated my mental powers much higher than before.

"You want to defeat Grindassil," he mused, "this I can now believe, and you want me as your ally to help you defeat her. But what then? What if you plan to snatch her power from her to your own ends? Tell me, Sulthind, what do you purpose when all is done? What are your own ends?"

I explained to him yet again that I was every bit as desperate to rescue Fethilian as he was and that I had no further thoughts or plans. But I was treading the most dangerous ground, for if I let him know that we had spent our early childhood together, Fethilian and I, and that my father's oracle foresaw an even closer future, surely Skelgrist would react with terrible jealousy, for he regarded the bonds between Fal, Fethilian, and himself as indissoluble and, I guessed, not in any way to be extended to include me. Even as I pondered this dilemma my fears were confirmed.

"There is something else in your mind, little wizard, something I cannot see, only as a shadow behind whatever else you tell me — something I do not like. What can be hidden there? What is lurking in that shadow?"

It was too much to risk, too much by far, especially as Kereoma's prophecy was dark to me, too, its meaning concealed in total paradox.

"Whatever it is that worries you, Skelgrist, one thing is certain: I am not interested in power, neither over the whole world nor over any single individual in it. The future is as cloudy to me as it is to you, but I know we must help Fethilian and we must check Grindassil, or in the end we shall all be slaves."

He grunted, still not satisfied, and I felt we would get no further with it for the moment. Fal, at least, became less dejected that afternoon and even began to sing a little, though to a terribly melancholy tune, but I still

thought that was a good sign. Then by the fourth day we came up to the
fords which led over to Old Running. Skelgrist decided to spend the night
on the north bank where a new village had sprung up. I was glad of this, for
Old Running was a deserted and partly ruined town, a relic of a more
prosperous past, and since my ordeal at the Gavelburg I was wary of ruins.

As in the other villages we passed, the dragon and its pale rider were a
great attraction, and it was difficult to get rid of the gaping crowds. But at
least hospitality was always forthcoming, this time lavishly so, for everyone seemed to fancy winning the favour of a friendly dragon. Skelgrist
asked to be granted the freedom of the local well or spring, which he often
did, he said, particularly if it came from deep down below the rocks, and
on some occasions he would drink quite astonishing quantities.

I asked him that evening about his own origins and whether he had ever
been a baby dragon and if so, how long ago. He found these questions
rather amusing and it was some time before he would answer.

"Dragons were once formless powers, the thoughts of the world. That
was a time of boundless energies, of unbelievable abundance. And you
might say we were knots in those energies, places where the power flowed
and turned about itself, gathering its strength."

"Dragons were places? Like the Gop?"

He snorted with contempt.

"Places in the flow, not in the landscape. Like storm-clouds, or winds,
whirlpools below a waterfall. But not in the wind or the water: in the tides
of power when the world was young."

"You remember that, Skelgrist?"

"Like a dream."

Fal was asleep, breathing heavily. I thought perhaps Skelgrist had begun
dozing too.

"Whirlpools don't have heads or tails," I whispered, experimentally.
"Or eyes."

He chuckled. "Everything changes. There came a time when there were
lizards in the world, huge, like dragons, but mere beasts that grazed and
mated and bred — like cows today. Yes, mere beasts. And yet they were
majestic, Sulthind, majestic and wonderful."

"Don't tell me the whirlpools grew jealous?"

"We desired form."

He was silent for a while, and I felt he was remembering.

"We needed form so we could grow, even as the world was growing. We
needed it and we took it; and we became the guardians, the guardians of
the earth's life, in streams and wells, chasms, mountains.

"It was a time of peace and harmony, of worlds turning within worlds.
And in every world, in every layer, we were the guardians.

"Then the humans came and the harmony was broken. The power
whirled once more and formed new knots — in them. Many of us found

this new power very interesting, irresistable, I suppose you would say. We needed that power, too. We entered their hearts and the world changed even more. So did we. Yes, so did we."

He chuckled again. "But I have never been a baby."

He seemed to find the picture of himself as a tiny youngling increasingly funny and kept cackling and grunting to himself for hours, making any further conversation impossible. In the end I must have fallen asleep.

After that there was the unending journey, or so it seemed at the time. We came to the flatlands of the west, dry and bare, and apparently uninhabited. At least, for the first few days they were dry, then the ground began to get swampy, and Skelgrist fell into a mood of dejection which almost matched Fal's. He would not drink the water, for it was brown and stagnant, and it seemed to me that he was weakening. Of mountains there was still no sign, but the clouds were low and dark, and it must have been bitterly cold, for Fal sat huddled up in his blankets, coughing and moaning, and Skelgrist became less and less talkative.

Then, one night, the blizzard came. I suggested making a hollow in the snow and resting, but he would not hear of it, and stumbled on in the pitch dark, claiming that he knew just how far the mountains were and there was no time to rest. In that I thought he was probably right, but the snow was gathering into drifts and I could see how his strength was being drained by it. If only I dared go on ahead. But, as he had said, I did indeed look to stand side by side with him against Grindassil and I dreaded facing her alone, especially if the cavern I had seen through the Spike's eyes was a place of power and she was already in possession of it. I began secretly to wonder whether we would not anyway be too late, for the days had turned into weeks and who knew whether Fethilian could hold out till we reached her? I had to fight hard not to fall into the same depression that seemed to be wasting my companions.

All the next day the blizzard raged, and again I begged Skelgrist to rest but he would not even answer, plodding on slowly as if entranced, his jaw set grimly, the fiery eyes glazed and unseeing. In the end he just had to follow my advice and dug a cave in one of the drifts. Fal slept fitfully between the dragon's paws, but even in his sleep the coughing went on.

"Skelgrist," I said, "Fal is sickening. We cannot go on like this. He at least will die, even if you do not."

For a long time he did not answer; I could see his golden eyes staring into the blackness as if looking far away. I tried to be patient but soon I could not stand it any more.

"I could go on alone, I may have to go on alone — unless you can think of something. But for now we must get to a proper shelter."

"Therefore we must go on." He was silent again for a while.

"The mountains are not far now; that is why the snow has come upon us." I thought he had finished, but he added: "Look again."

I did not understand him; there was no image behind the thought that I could catch.

"Look through the horse again. Tell me what you see."

It was the middle of the night. I did not think the Spike was likely to be awake.

"It does not matter. If he sleeps, you can try again later."

Strangely, after having gone to such lengths to develop this method of spying against Skelgrist's wishes, I was now reluctant to try it out a second time. Perhaps I dreaded to find out that the worst had befallen Fethilian and that at least that side of our quest was now beyond all hope. No doubt that was part of it. But there was something else, elusive, mocking yet drawing me. I tried to justify this vaguest of premonitions to Skelgrist, but, not surprisingly, he could see no sense in it, except, as I said, bearing in mind that the Spike is Grindassil's slave and not a friend or servant of mine as Cronk was.

"That was so when you did it before, up on the Gop," he argued irritably.

"But what can we learn that could change our plans? What is the point?"

"Until we've learnt it, how can we say? And as to plans, that's just it, we don't have any. We have to learn more. Try."

I entered the Spike's mind very slowly, still feeling oddly ill at ease about the whole thing. At first there was nothing — blankness, numbness; I was sure he must be asleep. The thought occurred to me that even if he was, it might just be possible to read his memories, perhaps in a more controlled way than when he was awake. This was a new idea to me, and the appeal of its logic drew me on.

I found confusion, and terror, but so stiffened with despair that clearer thoughts were slow and weak. I did not believe he was sleeping — no, it was something quite different, something uncomfortably alien. I withdrew and told Skelgrist what I had seen, if seeing is the word for it. He showed remarkably little interest and even less sympathy for my doubts.

"Try again," he said. "Go further in."

I went back slowly until I had reached the same point as before and then pushed until I could begin to feel the whole body. I tried to find the hooves... and found hands... human hands and feet... and the body sitting... on some sort of chair. No, he was not asleep, but his eyes were closed; and there were straps, binding him to the cold stone... a chair of rock!

"Open your eyes," she said "now!"

He snapped them open... and I was looking straight into her face. Energy flowed from her, poured in a swift torrent, engulfing the mind as a winter flood sweeps up a single autumn leaf and carries it away. There was no possible resistance. His bonds snapped like threads and his body reeled out of the chair. Her eyes had grown enormous, they filled the whole room.

I struggled frantically to get out. I knew that if I didn't, whatever was happening to the Spike would happen to me, too. He certainly wasn't a horse any more but he would not be human for much longer either, I was sure. Strangely perhaps, I knew with the one part of my mind which I could keep calm — that she could not see me, that it was only the Spike she was watching. And I could hear her laughter, shrieking with joy. I fought against her with all my might but it was no good, it was wrong to concentrate on her at all, but there was nothing else, just her and her damnable flood of power. The Spike seemed to be threshing all over the floor and had lost any vestige of shape or identity. I went wild, it was like trying to swim up a waterfall, drowning, screaming under water.

Then it was gone; I was in the darkness and the snow once again. And Skelgrist was watching me. I knew he had pulled me out, without him I would have been lost.

For a long time neither of us spoke; there seemed to be nothing worth saying. It was his turn to break the silence, anyway.

"Did she see you?" he asked.

"I don't think so, almost certainly she didn't, but I can't be really sure."

"What was she doing?"

I said I had no idea. I was too shaken to think anything at all.

"She was changing him again," said Skelgrist, "using the powers of that place to cause a much deeper transformation. You were right then. You had better not try that doorway again."

"Change him into what?"

"I wonder," he said, and was silent again.

The dawn had come, light filtered down into our little cavern. Skelgrist pushed a tunnel out through the snow but quickly drew his head back in and sealed the entrance.

"The storm is still raging," he muttered aloud, "the very sky is against us."

Fal was awake now, too.

"I can use the harp," he said, "I have music which can change the weather."

I told Skelgrist that if the blizzard was Grindassil's doing, attacking it magically was the surest way to announce our presence.

"We will die anyway," he spoke into my mind, "Fal and I, if this goes on much longer. And you alone — we have just seen you are not nearly strong enough. Let him try."

Fal began to play the most extraordinary music I had ever heard. I had to withdraw my mind from it as in my shocked state I couldn't bear the sound. And it went on for hours, or so it seemed; just the music, there was no singing with it, only the harp.

In the end it seemed to stop quite suddenly.

"I must eat now," Fal said.

He unpacked one of the bundles he had with him and got out some black sausage, bread, and goat's cheese. He ate silently for a while, picking at a little of this and a little of that; but it was the best meal I had seen him manage since we had left the Delming, and it was clear that his weird music was good for the player whatever its effect might be on the weather — or on me!

"Skelgrist, do go out again and see what's going on," he said at last, his mouth still full with the last bite. He was unplugging a flask of wine to wash it down.

The dragon returned through the ice-tunnel he had made like a dark shadow, spreading gloom.

"The snow is falling less wildly now, and the wind has dropped, but falling it is. If your music has worked it has not worked enough. We shall still perish if we go on in this."

Fal was silent for a while, as if testing his own thoughts for their truthfulness before he spoke.

"Skelgrist," he said, "the music has worked; yes. I'm certain of it. But it's not just the weather we're fighting; there's something else, something behind it. It's Sulthind's mother doing this to us, and that means she already knows we're here."

"Whatever 'here' is. Unless the snow stops, I cannot find our way. We are lost, Fal; and I dare not go on while the snow falls."

"But if I try again with the music it will mean pushing really hard against her. If she came to us now, while we are as weak as this..."

Skelgrist pondered for a long time, and I took the opportunity of interrupting, speaking directly into his mind.

"Listen, Skelgrist, her strength comes from deep within the Earth, she has no power in the frozen air. I saw that at Lune, the cold defeated her, she needs the heat of these old fire mountains. And I believe she'll wait for us at the place where her strength is greatest. But we must stop the snow, we must."

I nearly added "before Fal dies", but felt it wise to suppress the thought, though the danger of our predicament was surely obvious to both of them.

"Get rid of her enemy, the cold? But you are right, at the moment it is our enemy more than hers." He pondered again for a moment; then he spoke aloud to Fal. "If she knows we are here already, it would perhaps be foolish to appear weak... as weak as we are!" He snorted. "No, Fal, you must stop the snow. It will worry her and she is likely then to withdraw into the hub of her new kingdom and wait for us. She will be better prepared, but it will at least give us time — and maybe a chance to regain our strength... perhaps."

He looked at Fal with sad eyes and I could see he had little confidence in what he said.

Fal played once more, pausing again and again as he was forced to yield to spasms of coughing. But each time he began it was with a new vigour and determination. At last he stopped and looked up.

"Try now," he said. "Look again"

He rested his head in the crook of his elbow while Skelgrist slithered down the tunnel. Again the overpowering urge to speak to Fal, to try to comfort him, give him strength even, if that were possible. But I knew that now, at any rate, Skelgrist was right, it would be too bewildering, too complex for Fal to come to terms with me.

The dragon returned triumphantly.

"It is clear," he shouted, "crystal clear, we can see the mountains! Come outside and look!" I think he nearly added "both of you", but I did not need to be persuaded. I was through the tunnel before Fal and found myself under a blue sky, in brilliant sunshine. The snow still lay crisp and undisturbed, but — glory of glories — the whole western horizon was jagged with peaks, peaks of the most amazing mountains you can imagine, tall and spiky, as if they were created only yesterday, and flushed with pink as if caught in an eternal sunset.

"They are still distant." said Skelgrist, "two or three days at least, but now we know where we are and we can take the shortest way."

"You mean you know exactly where she is — in all that?" said Fal doubtfully. "And how are you so sure she's here at all?"

"Dragons have exceedingly long memories, and — yes — I know exactly where the Hall of Laurin is. You will remember later, maybe. It is buried deep among the greater summits, a rounder mountain, quite different from any you see, and of a darker stone. Only the top is flushed with the colours of dawn, from the rose garden, as they say."

We made good headway that afternoon and Skelgrist refused to rest, even at night. But then we ran into another spate of trouble. The stars clouded over and a warm wind sprang up from behind us. Fal slept on the dragon's back and Skelgrist did not seem to heed the change, but the thaw came swiftly, and before dawn he was wading deep in slush.

Here and there were rivulets of clean water that he could drink from, but that was the only good thing about it. It seemed more and more likely that below the ice there was a vast swamp which if the worst came to the worst might last right up to the foothills of the mountains before us.

Skelgrist stumbled and wrestled with the mud, often sinking up to his belly in the icy ooze, sometimes finding firm ground for a few paces before flopping down again. I wondered how long he was going to last, for it seemed to me that each struggle to free himself from the swamp's clutches took a little longer than the last.

But by evening the ground was firm again, and Skelgrist said we would be in the foothills before morning. He told Fal that there was an almost direct way between the peaks to Laurin's mountain on the road that led over a narrow but deep ravine. There was a bridge of stone, he said. I asked

him how long ago it was since he had been that way, but he said it was of
no consequence, for the bridge was as indestructible as the mountains
themselves. I hoped he was right, but said nothing. To choose any of the
longer ways would mean going through at least one of the old fortresses
which guarded the little towns and villages, frequent among the hills,
where Grindassil might have obtained dangerous allies. I wanted to ask
him how he was so sure that there were no new settlements since his last
visit, but he seemed to be battling with his last strength and I thought it was
better to hold my peace. Instead I asked, "How far is it from the bridge to
Laurin's Hall, Skelgrist? Shall we see the mountain from there?"

"You'll see it before the bridge, and beyond the bridge there's only one
more valley; and after that you will be at the gates."

"What sort of gates?" — I remembered the modest entrance to Lune.

"It's not like Lune at all," he said testily, "not at all. But be silent now,
you will see."

The journey up through the green valleys of the foothills took nearly
three days. We passed a hamlet of shepherds on the opposite side of the
valley early in the evening of the first day and they all turned out to wave at
us, or rather at Fal and the dragon, but they were the last living creatures
we saw. Even the lush forest which clad the lowest slopes of the mountains
was empty and silent, and though it was still winter, as I kept reminding
myself, the total lack of any bird call by day or owl by night made me feel
uneasy. I was desperate to seek with my mind among the trees for the
reason for this, but I agreed with Skelgrist that whatever was behind it all,
we did not want to risk tangling with it.

"The whole land is watching," he said, "that at any rate even I can see;
watching and waiting."

"It's waiting, Skelgrist, but waiting for what? For three mighty heroes to
come and crush the monster in its lair? You're completely exhausted, Fal's
ill, and I have about as much power as a fly in a puddle of water. I keep
telling you I'm not a wizard or a sorcerer or anything else. There's nothing
we can do, absolutely nothing."

"And it's too late to turn back! Poor Sulthind! If the heroes run away the
monster will follow them. Yes, she's waiting, waiting and watching. Do
you think you'll make us stronger by prattling on about it like a nagging
old woman?"

That was all I could get out of him. He seemed to be getting angry, and I
did not think that would help us either. But I knew we were walking to our
doom, both of us. That was a total certainty I now carried within me.
About Fal I could feel nothing beyond concern, tinged perhaps with
disappointment. He just sat staring, unseeing, as if his mind was already in
a different world altogether.

The forest came to an end that night and we went on over clean rock,
which I could see was more to Skelgrist's liking, for he began walking

briskly even though the going was steeper than before. The weather had cleared again, too, and the stars were thick above us in a moonless sky. But there were no narrow gorges, no tumbling waterfalls. Where was the path I had seen through the Spike's tormented eyes?

"She did not come this way," Skelgrist rumbled. "I know these hills better than she ever did. We should be even wearier if we'd have followed in her footsteps. At the bridge the ways will meet."

By dawn we had crossed the pass, or rather we had reached its summit, for the land did not plunge down on the other side as I had expected but stayed almost level in a great rocky cleft between the peaks.

"This valley is on the top of the world," Skelgrist said aloud. "You cannot remember, Fal, but it was once a busy place, a habitation of dwarves. It is strangely silent now."

Ominously silent, I thought; as bleak and empty as our own fate. And it struck me then that none of us had spoken of Fethilian for quite a few days. Was it that we had all secretly given her up for lost or were we too occupied with our own hopeless plight, drawn on to a hollow doom without even the will-power to call a halt let alone turn back? I began remembering her as a child and wondered, I think for the first time, what experiences she may have had later in her childhood at Gopley. I felt a strong surge of affection for her and of rage at my own eternal impotence.

"Sulthind?"

The voice rang clearly out of the crisp mountain air, even echoing for a moment on the side of the valley nearest to us, and I glanced around, bewildered.

"Don't get nervous, little wizard," rumbled Skelgrist's mind at me. "She won't come at us here. She'll wait till we get to her mountain."

So he had not heard it. I had to work hard to conceal my agitation.

"You are Sulthind, the child in the forest?"

I wanted to reply but experienced an overwhelming reluctance to do so in front of the dragon, and to have reached out with my mind so close to the very source of our peril might have opened up a channel to Grindassil. Instead I tried to keep calm and quietly turned my thoughts to Fethilian's presence, silently inviting her to look into my memories, to share all I had lived through, all that I was. There came, I thought, a rather puzzled response, a silence countering my silence. Then understanding, warmth, surprise and relief. But almost at once the presence withdrew, and we were alone again. A residue of pain and suffering seemed to hang in the valley for a while like a mist; then that too faded.

Skelgrist was watching me strangely. I realized I had stopped walking. We had come almost to the end of the valley, for the sky opened out in front of us — another twenty paces and we would get a view of whatever lay before us. There was a low ridge yet to climb, dark against the crimson disk of the setting sun, then we should see.

"How do you like this place?"

I was not sure whether the dragon had spoken to me or to Fal, for he had expressed the question vocally. But he was looking at me still, and Fal, as I then noticed, was sound asleep, upright on Skelgrist's back but his head slumped forward, mouth sagging, in deep slumber.

How did I like this place? It was a world of grandeur such as I had never imagined could exist. Each peak stood splendid and arrogant, undefeatable. The thought occurred to me that if I had to submit to a doom of eternal bodilessness and slavery, this would not be such a bad place to suffer it — surrounded by such queenly splendour. At the thought of 'queenly splendour' I frowned.

"Skelgrist," I said, "I think we are in danger — in very great danger. She is attacking us."

He had lain down on his belly, his head resting on his paws, golden eyes staring.

"Not until we cross the ridge, until we see the mountain. We are hidden still up here."

His eyes glazed over.

"I am very tired," he mumbled. "I will sleep now for a while."

"Sleep, Skelgrist? No!"

It was too late, his eyes were closed. I was alone, alone and naked on the threshold of Queen Grindassil's eternal realm.

THIRTY-SIX

The sun had gone and the first stars were glittering from the east along the valley behind us. I was at a total loss to know what to do. For some reason I was not actually afraid, just numb and empty, terribly empty.

There was a flicker of movement on the ruckle of boulders leading up to the ridge, the outline of a human figure. This is it, I thought, the second meeting, it has come as I knew it would; but I will not flee, nor will I become her thrall without a fight; this is my moment.

I picked my way over the stones. But it was not Grindassil; it was Fethilian, dressed in tatters like a beggar girl, long faced and frowning.

We stood and stared at each other, quite a long time, I suppose. She glanced at the sleeping dragon and Fal, spreadeagled over his back, hanging on as if they were flying over the clouds in a world of their own. Then she looked at me again. I opened my mind to her again so that she could see.

"You are like me," she said sadly, "I did not know."

I did not understand her for a moment, then I realized that she was transparent, too, I could see the rocks behind her.

"You are dead, Fethilian!" I gasped. "We are too late."

"I'm not dead, Sulthind. My body has suffered more than I could bear and — yes — it is near to death, very near. I don't have the strength to hold on to it any more. I think perhaps I am dreaming. Will you help me?"

I glanced desperately at Skelgrist. If only they would wake up. But there was no sign of that. It did not occur to me to try to wake them.

"Perhaps I'm dreaming, too," I said. I did not have the remotest idea what to do.

"Come with me, help me put strength back into my body. Perhaps together we can find a way."

I hesitated. I really did not know. Abandon Skelgrist and Fal, leave them up here, helpless and vulnerable?

"Please, Sulthind. I shall die soon if you do not help."

Her eyes grew larger and shone as if she was weeping, but there were no tears.

Still I hesitated. It seemed such a hopeless thing to do. She took another step towards me and stretched out a hand. I took it and we walked over the ridge together, like children, hand in hand.

At first I thought the world had disappeared. It was a bowl of emptiness, miles across, a black pit slung between a dozen jagged peaks and the glitter of distant glaciers. And in the blackness floated the lump that was Laurin's mountain, hunched and muscular like the head of ancient bull.

An irrational terror flooded through me, I was struggling not to scream, not to be drawn down into the bottomless dark, the sucking mist, that world of endless nothing.

"My body is in there," Fethilain said.

Blue lights began to flicker over the rounded hill, lights that were of the darkness, rich and deep as sapphires; and the stars blazed out in the black sky. I thought my mind had gone.

"It's the power she's calling up out of the mountains," she whispered. "She will destroy the rose-garden — look."

On the rounded summit among the sapphire flames there were flickers of red, but faint and unsteady.

"She cannot do it yet. This is only a beginning. She has been too busy trying to break me, and trying to change her horse into a creature of power."

I was overcome with the whole spectacle, the pit and the blue fire on the mountain, and I did not think to ask whether she had succeeded. But I was soon to find out.

"Look," she said, "we cannot enter the gates. They are closed. If we touched them she would see us; but there is a side door we can use."

We came to a narrow chasm, a jagged fissure not more than twenty paces wide, but very deep, the chattering stream-way in its depths lost in blackness.

"Did you fly across?" I asked.

"No, flying would attract her attention at once. But there was a bridge here, long ago. I can recall it for our use, out feet need only the mind's support, Sulthind, and with our thoughts we can call the bridge back. Watch."

She let go of me for a moment and stretched both her hands out over the abyss. At once the bridge shone out, faintly at first, but in a myriad dancing colours as soft and delicate as a moon halo.

"Will she not see?"

"There are no windows on this side; only the gates, and they are closed. Look."

"I can't see with the shine of the bridge in between."

"Then come over." She took my hand again and a marvellous warmth flowed into me. But I was seized with reluctance to step onto the bridge.

"It's perfectly safe," she said.

I did not doubt it — for us. But what about Skelgrist and Fal, if they awoke and tried to follow? The dragon had been wrong about the bridge; we were cutting ourselves off.

"There are steps down the cliff," she said, "further down the stream. It's a longer way round, but Skelgrist will remember. Come now, Sulthind, there is not much time."

The bridge vanished the moment we had crossed it and the night became silent again as the babble of the stream faded from our hearing. Then I could see the gates. They were immense. At first I had taken their outlines to be a natural part of the rocks, but now it was clear that two lofty doors, many times the height of a man, slender and pointed at the top, were set in the mountainside. Beneath them hundreds of steps were carved into the stone, vanishing in the endless dark below.

"We cannot go that way," she said again. "Come."

She led me down to the right towards the edge of the black mist.

"It's not really black, only dark. Do not fear it. Only hurry now."

She began skipping lightly from stone to stone, and the memories of our childhood awakened so urgently within me that I expected any moment to hear her merry laughter. But her mood was desperate.

"If your body dies, can we not escape together?" I suggested.

"You can, perhaps; but through my body she will hold me."

"Then how did you manage to get out now?"

"She was busy with her wretched Speikunnar, all her strength is going into that."

I was just going to ask more about what had been happening to the Spike, but the mountain answered the question before I could begin to form it.

There was a deafening boom, that echoed like thunder all around the peaks, as the two great doors, high above us, were thrown open. A blue light, pale but as steady as moonlight, poured out across the valley making the rocks glisten like a thousand pearls. Then with a rush it came.

Huge, yet elegant and slender, shining with fire, blue and gold, a dragon leaped from the mountain like the upthrust of a gleaming sword. As its wings flashed open its roar of challenge was a scream of pain, harsh and searing, and it sped up and over the ridge, into the upper valley from which we had just come. There was a bellow as Skelgrist awoke, then a splintering and crashing of rocks as the battle began. I thought of Skelgrist, numb and exhausted, and I knew he would not stand a chance.

"We are too late," cried Fethilian, "she has finished with him, now she will turn to me. Run!"

She seemed to throw all caution to the winds, leaping over the boulders in long arcs that no body of flesh and bone could ever have accomplished. In a minute we were through the darkness and racing up the side of the mountain like tongues of fire.

There was a tiny postern left open, and we sped through a passageway abandoning all semblance of human movement, but flying like the wind itself. Hall after hall we crossed with never a door closed against us and never a sign of habitation until we came to the throne room — the hall of the Golden Tree.

In the centre, facing the doors, was Andravel's chair of stone, the throne of the dwarf kings, flanked on either side by bowls of sapphire flame. Behind, in the shadow, the Tree, the silent witness of ancient wisdom. And on the throne, slumped and lifeless, was the body of Fethilian. Of Grindassil there was no sign, nor was there any feeling that she was nearby.

"Yet the doors are closed again," said Fethilian. "She must have been here."

She pulled me over to the throne and looked down at the tortured wreck of her body.

"It is not dead, but I do not have the strength to bring it to consciousness any more. Watch."

She faded into it and left me standing there alone. Nothing happened for a moment, then the body on the throne gave a trembling sigh and stirred a little. Fethilian appeared next to me. She looked pained and haggard.

"You see, there is nothing I can do. I must get my body out of the throne, Sulthind, it is the hinge and lever of her power. Help me."

"But how?"

"I don't know, but we must hurry. She will return. I will go in again and you will put your hands on mine. No, cross them, like this, so that your right is on my body's right. Try to flow all your warmth into me."

I was doubtful, and the ominous emptiness of the hall was weighing on me. The Tree felt like a silent watcher, disapproving, contemptuous even of our plight. But Fethilian had gone, her body was twisted round so that I had to kneel to get my hands into the position she suggested. I tried very hard, pouring love through my hands, into her. But it was no good. She did not even sigh this time. I thought she was very near to death.

Then she was standing next to me again. She was actually weeping now, with diamonds of light running down her cheeks, flashing blue from the magic flames.

She stared at me in helpless horror.

"There is perhaps one other way."

Her eyes were growing larger and larger. I thought desperation was going to break her. I had no idea what to do, I only knew I was failing again, as always, and that time was running out.

"Come in with me, Sulthind, perhaps together we have the power."

I stared for a moment, frozen with astonishment.

"Please try."

We went in together. It was to experience pain, terrible pain, drowning, fighting the dark, endless dark, suffocating weight of arms, head, shoulders.

"Together, Sulthind, together."

I joined with her. We became like one person, an ecstasy of affection, flooding warmth, a vortex of love.

"Sulthind, try."

The weight of hands, moving, the softness of a woman's body; sitting up now, eyes open, sitting on the throne — looking at Grindassil. She was laughing.

"So this is your latest piece of drôlerie! Oil and vinegar in the one bottle! How novel! And how careless of you, Sulthind! As careless and as useless as ever you were. But I did warn you. Now you can both sit there and wait. Wait for your joint rebirth!"

She laughed wildly. She was obviously quite mad, but I was not frightened of her, even though we could not move on her damned throne. Fethilian and I huddled in to one another, warming, strengthening each other, wondering what she was going to do.

She pointed at the floor around the throne and a circle of blue flame sprang up, cold and cruel as ice, enclosing her and us within it. I tried experimentally to get out of Fethilian's body, but there seemed to be nothing to grip on. It was like trying to pull yourself out of a pond by clutching at the air. Fethilian hugged me closer within her, loving me, comforting me.

"You cannot get out, you fool!" whispered Grindassil. "Do you not realize where you are?" She smiled. "You will never get out, never. And this flame," she pointed to the ring of fire about her feet," contains all the agony of the world, all the pain there has ever been or can ever be. Look at it well, Sulthind, soon I shall bring it in to you. It will be yours."

A shudder of fear swept through me, but Fethilian mingled warmly with me, caressing my terror, soothing me.

"The two of us together," she said, "we will bear it. She cannot deal with us both at once; do not fear her."

"Have you already... ?" I began.

"Yes, of course. Alone, it is terrible. Together we have the strength."

I was doubtful and would have panicked, but Fethilian kept me totally enclosed within her. Grindassil appeared to be dissatisfied with the size of her ring of fire and was struggling to move the two stands with the bowls of blue flame further way from the throne. The fire on the stone floor flowed out with them and I wondered if they governed its position.

"How very vexing," she said. "We had just moved them in after Speik-unnar's wonderful transformation. But we shall need plenty of room for this. It was to have been a queen of ice who could rule here in my stead. But the two of you together would make a most attractive ice-dragon. Have you brought any extra warm clothing with you, Sulthind?"

She began laughing insanely again, on and on, while we just sat there watching her and waiting. And in spite of all her warmth and reassurances, I could feel Fethilian's doubts getting the better of her. Her breathing quickened, and as I merged with its rhythm I realized how long it had been since breathing had been part of my experience of living.

THIRTY-SEVEN

Grindassil stopped rather unexpectedly in the middle of her orgy of laughter and frowned, as if another irritating thought had just occurred to her. She swung round and walked out of the ring of flame, her black gown swishing like sand about her feet. I noticed that she wore nothing on them, her ankles appearing bare at every step. She held up her arms to the great doors and, without touching them, swung them open, silently this time, into the blackness of the night. A wind seemed to be blowing and Fethilian and I could hear it sucking around the doors. It rose suddenly and one of the doors must have been caught in it, for we heard it hit the wall with a clang. Grindassil shouted something and stepped outside. The stars seemed to blaze up around her head with anger and the wind howled, plucking at her long hair so that it lifted and flowed as if water had risen over her head. She raised her arms defiantly to the sky, but the wind shrieked even louder. She staggered, and I hoped for a moment she would be plucked away. Instead, the stars vanished in the blackness and there was a stunning crack as a bolt of lightning struck the ground just in front of her. Our eyes pulsed with light for several seconds, and when we could see again it was to find that she had come back in the hall, with the doors closed behind her.

"Speikunnar has bungled, the cursed fool!" she hissed, and her eyes glowed with fury. She came and stood right in front of us, her eyes locking with ours. I was sure she was going to do something there and then, but whatever was going on outside continued to distract her.

There seemed to be bells ringing, faint but insistent, somewhere on the mountainside. But in Fethilian's mind I saw the image of a harp. Her heart raced, I was whirled around in her emotions. Joy! Fal at least then had survived the dragon's attack, though we both doubted that he could do anything now by himself.

But the bell-like tones continued, forming a little melody now, growing slightly louder at each repetition until the doors themselves began to resound, first quietly, then louder and louder until they were booming like gigantic gongs. I wanted to put our hands over our ears, but the throne held us completely frozen.

It was hard even to blink. Grindassil stood within the ring of blue fire with her back to us; she seemed to be preparing herself for something. Then it happened. The doors flew open and the wind burst in. For a moment I thought the flames would go out, they flared wildly then dwindled. But they formed a thin line, a thread of unbearable brilliance, in what I guessed was a perfect circle.

Still she did nothing, while the wind tore at her slender black gown. Fethilian's hair was torn over our eyes, and for a moment I could not see at all.

Then it was gone, the wind was quite still, and Fal stood in the doorway, the waning crescent moon resting, as it appeared, just on his head. He walked in slowly, looking around for a while as if he was trying to remember something; then he walked straight across to Grindassil. The flames had leapt up again and he stopped in front of them. He looked at Fethilian, sitting upright on the ancient throne. We managed to force a slight smile, I think, but it was beyond our power to speak.

Obviously Grindassil was reckoning to do all the talking.

"Come no closer, harper-boy," she said. "One touch of the flames and they will consume you. Only I can control them. Watch!"

For a second all the flames vanished, leaving us in utter darkness; then they were back. Fal had not moved.

She sniggered.

"The harpists of old were renowned for their courtesy," she sneered. "Please do tell us why you are here."

Fal pursed his lips and stared at her for a while. Was he playing for time or was he, as I feared, at a total loss to know what to do? I tried to make mental contact with him but she had completely sealed us in. We tried again to smile, but I feared it might come out as a leer. He looked deathly pale and I reckoned he had used up his last strength in storming the gates. If I was right, it was only a matter of time indeed — before she had him at her mercy. She obviously had the same thought.

"Your friend, Fethilian, is in need of a little healing," she said, "that is why she is sitting on the throne of power; I can cure her there. If you wish, you can help me — your music, perhaps. But you seem to be in no small need of healing yourself — Falimbravel. Or should I say 'Bailor'?"

She laughed as Fal's eyes widened in amazement. But still he said nothing; he just stared at her. I feared his weakness would overcome him and he would faint. Grindassil was eager to follow up her advantage.

"She doesn't know about all this, does she, Fal? Feather thinks you have come here because of her. Shall we tell her the real reason?" She laughed. "She does not need you. She has all she can ever want. I shall make her a queen of unimaginable powers and she will not want to share; she will rule by herself. Yes, I shall leave her alone. I have other things to do, many other things. Very soon she will have all she needs."

She paused. I could not see her face but I could feel her smiling at him. "You cannot prevent it. But I will allow you to watch while the transformation takes place. You will never have seen anything so wonderful, Fal, so splendid, not even in the Forge." She leaned forward and spoke quietly to him, almost conspiratorially. "There are forces of change here, unbelievable energies, such as nowhere else in the whole wide world."

She spoke so softly I could hardly hear her.

"I have mastered them. Look!"

She raised her hands slowly to her head so that her finger tips rested just above her ears. A circlet of silver light appeared round her hair, spinning, I thought, at tremendous speed.

Fal did nothing. She laughed again, still holding her fingers to her head.

"Watch, Falimbravel, watch!"

His harp clattered to the ground and his arms fell to his side.

He watched her, spellbound.

"Closer now, watch closer!"

A crown of icy white light, brilliant and painful to look at, extended slowly upwards from her head, narrow and vertical, brighter and brighter, while the air was filled with an unbearably high buzzing noise, tearing at the ears and brain, destroying thought, ripping and shredding like a thousand razors at consciousness itself. And as the sound grew the ice-crown became taller — taller and taller.

"Look how it grows, Fal; look, look!" she shrieked.

The noise stopped. The crown must have reached the roof. It looked as if it could not make up its mind whether to remain as this searing cold light or to turn into real ice or crystal, for it kept wavering and flickering. Then it steadied: it was hard light, that is how I must describe it — crystal-hard light, and colder than any ice the world has ever known. And its brilliance was beyond all bearing.

Fal was lucky; he was able to shield his eyes but we could not move.

"No, Fal, no; you must look," she commanded him.

His arm slowly dropped again, numb and helpless.

"Watch how Feather becomes a great queen, watch. And how fitting, how wonderfully fitting that you of all people should be my guest to see it! You who once gave up the kingship, begging that another should rule here in your place. Can you think of a more masterly touch of destiny, that you should live to see this crowning — of the Queen of Laurin's Halls!"

She began turning towards us, and made as to lift the crown from her head. But there was a movement in the doorway, an immense shadow seemed to have entered there. The crown flickered and trembled, blazed for a moment, then vanished. A voice boomed out of the darkness.

"There is another, then, that should be here since Bailor has been called upon. You spoke of courtesy, great lady. Small courtesy to leave me in such a sorry state to perish on the mountainside!"

We were still blinded by the agonizing light of the ice-crown and at first the blue fire on the floor seemed too weak to illumine the chamber.

The shadow had moved closer, next to Fal. Then I saw. It was Skelgrist, torn and lame, but dark and menacing as I had never seen him before.

Grindassil's shoulders had stiffened with rage but as she studied the dragon she held out her hands towards him in mocking invitation.

"Forgive me, poor, noble Skelgrist," she laughed, "for thinking you had perished with my dragon in the watery ravine. How foolish of me to forget that running water is but grist to your skill, or whatever the saying is. Have you to come to replace my beloved Speikunnar?"

"Your lover, your husband, you mean?" growled Skelgrist. "I come to fight, lady, to fight light with darkness, pain with sorrow."

"You will meet your end," she said softly.

"I shall meet my end," he agreed, "at last, yes, at last, I shall meet my end. Here at the beginning my path runs out."

"The serpent bites its own tail?" she whispered. "No, Skelgrist you never had a path. And the pain of all the world stands between us."

With a snarl he leapt at her and the blue fire rushed in a fountain of light to meet him, clothing him in swirling brilliance. He rose up on his hind legs, pawing the air wildly, jaws agape in a soundless scream, a pillar of living flame. Then he fell on her.

For a moment she appeared to withstand the shock, but the fire spread to her and on, up, building a new crown of light.

She screamed, again and again, but still she did not move. Their arms reached out, hers and the dragon's, as if trying to embrace each other. For a moment they stood upright together, united by fire, upright until the dragon fell, a tumble of broken limbs, yet massive, within his robe of flames.

But Grindassil remained standing even as she burned, her screams no longer audible against the ear-splitting hum of the new ice-crown, dripping liquid blue light down into her flames.

Then it was all gone.

It was very dark, there was no more burning, and we found that we were standing — we — I — in front of the throne. I could just make out a shape where Fal lay senseless on the floor. I hurried over to him.

"Fal," I said, "Fal. It is Feather. Wake up."

I cannot say how long it was that I knelt there caressing him, waiting, the stars moved across the doorway, ages passed, the constellations turned and seemed to change their shape. But at last I noticed that it was becoming light. Sunlight flooded into the hall, and the dawn songs of many birds echoed around us. The air was heavy with the scent of roses.

Fal sat up and for a moment frowned.

"Feather!" he said. "You are safe!"

But his attention had already been caught by something else and his eyes looked past me, widening in amazement.

I turned; and I saw what he saw.

There, on the charred skin of the ancient dragon, stood a young woman, childishly innocent and breathtakingly beautiful. Her hair flowed down over her white gown and around a girdle of the darkest blue. Stars sparkled on it like the stars of heaven. Then, as we watched, the girdle changed. It paled and flowed with the colours of dawn, turquoise and pink, the palest yellow, lilac and gold. She laughed merrily and stepped out of the dragon's skin. For a moment she hesitated and she looked stern while her robe became a rich and royal blue, the girdle plain, of clearest silver.

I realized then that she was looking at me — as if uncertain what she should do. Did I know what had to happen to restore the balance of all that had been done, that Fal could never be mine?

I knew. I had known it since Skelgrist had first appeared — it already seemed years ago — in the glade of the mushrooms, after the contest. I nodded my assent.

She smiled and the gentler colours returned.

"The Spirit of the Dawn," murmured Fal, entranced.

She laughed and shook her head.

"You must call me Skella," she said. "I am the queen of the rose garden." She seized his hands. "And you, Fal — you are the king!"

"You the queen — I a king? How may this be?"

He was completely enraptured and held onto her delicate hands as firmly as she held his.

"I through fire — you through endurance," she smiled, and I saw she wore a wreath of wild red roses in her hair.

I left them talking, discovering each other, and went out onto the hillside to meet the spring-time sun, which had burst so suddenly upon us.

———

All this was many years ago, so many, many years, and much has happened both in joy and sorrow in between.

Fal and his dragon maiden stayed in the west and tended Laurin's rose garden once again. The dark mist has never returned and where once it hung a town has now grown up at the foot of Laurin's Hill. Already it has become a second Delming and will one day bring light and hope to the lost lands beyond the mountains.

As for myself, I have been Mistress of the Forge now this many a year, since Melauriën passed from us, and Sulthind and I have been as one, even as the witch-woman intended, but to our bliss, not sorrow. Yet he has never been my prisoner. He is free to come and go as he pleases, though it seems a long time since he did so, for we are old and take great comfort in one another.

Even around Lune the lands are full of life and magic again, as Fal had known they would be, and there Ilmarin has tamed its dragons and music sounds once more on the terraces of fair Gelmindel. One day I shall visit them again, one day, Ilmarin — and his Lady Ristilian.

May the grace and blessings of all the Great Ones be upon you who read this. Dance, my people, dance with the trees, the wind, the sun and the moon. May joy be with you.

> O glory of the wonder-wood,
>   fair leaf and blossom bright,
> your dance brings back the meadows' green
>   at ending of the night.

STARWELL

1. Times will come, times will go, _ the pat-terns run, the _ pat - terns flow, where rocks crum-ble, moun - tains grow. _

The tunes are long, the dance is slow,
the patterns drawn by heels and toe
are never done while star worlds glow.

What blossomed once its fruits still show;
the pattern weaver seeks to know
where to reap, where seed to sow.

SONG OF THE WASTE

The grey eyes of the stone-lands sing of more than whis-per-ing dreams;

si-lent seeds in win - ter ___ know best what sum-mer means. _ Be-

-gin-ning, once, and cen - tre, the migh - ty land _ of Lune, where

bare rock reigns and ___ si - lence: cry - stal

moun-tains of the _ moon. ___

Listen, and learn the story
  of how the land shall wake again!
The stone has not forgotten
  who shall end its ancient pain.

The Tree once more shall blossom
  and the golden light shall run,
bursting up the pathway
  like the fires of the sun.

THE MAGIC BEE-SONG

Accompaniment: a quiet, rapid picking pattern till bar 17.

In the mountains there are serpent paths
    still hidden from your sight;
Yet even the fierce giant kings
    know dawn will end the night.
The spirit of the rising sun
    who is your oldest friend
Will come again to touch your eyes
    and make the long night end.

Forthcoming books by the same author:

ORVELLIN

Orvellin waits, he is the watcher of Vond. He has seen all that happens there, has watched for more years than he can count. He has watched for so long that he has forgotten why he came to Vond and why he must never leave it. Then a ship sails in from Anneke-Del, and Orvellin knows that he *must* remember.

Orvellin is a companion volume to *Fal, the Dragon Harper,* and will be published by Hawthorn Press in 1993. Please write to us with an advance order (to be invoiced on publication).

SONGS

FROM LORD OF THE RINGS AND FAL

Peter Patterson is a musician and composer as well as a storyteller. He has composed hauntingly beautiful tunes and group arrangements for different instruments for a number of Tolkien poems. These have been played by groups such as *Dragblod* and other choirs and orchestras. We plan to publish, either separately or together, the songs for *Fal* and for the *Lord of the Rings.*

Please contact us if you would like to place an advance order to help with publication.

Other books from Hawthorn Press:

FESTIVALS, FAMILY AND FOOD
Diana Carey and Judy Large

This is a resource book for exploring the festivals — those feast days scattered round the year which children love to celebrate. It was written in response to questions from Children and parents such as "What can we do for Christmas and Easter?" "What games can we play?" "What can we make?"

Packed full of things to do, food to make, songs to sing and games to play, this is an invaluable resource book designed to help you and your family celebrate the various festival days round the year. The Observer.

200 × 225mm; 216pp; limp bound; fully illustrated; ISBN 0 950 706 23 X

THE CHILDREN'S YEAR
Stephanie Cooper, Christine Fynes-Clinton and Marÿe Rowling

Crafts and clothes for children and parents to make.

You needn't be an experienced craftsperson to create beautiful things. This charmingly illustrated book encourages children and adults to try all sorts of different handwork, with different projects relating to the seasons. Over 100 potential treasures are described, decorations and even children's clothes.

267 × 216mm; 220pp; sewn limp bound; illustrated; ISBN 1 869 890 00 0

Forthcoming books from Hawthorn Press:

FESTIVALS TOGETHER
Sue Fitzjohn, Minda Weston and Judy Large

This is a resource guide for celebration, and for observing special days according to traditions based on many cultures. It brings together the experience, sharing and activities of individuals from a multi-faith community — Buddhist, Christian, Hindu, Jewish, Muslim and Sikh. It draws on backgrounds as diverse as north and west Africa, The Caribbean, China, India, Ireland, Japan, New England, The Philippines and more. Its unifying thread is our need for meaning, for continuity and for joy.

ALL YEAR ROUND — CELEBRATING FESTIVALS
Ann Druitt, Christine Fynes-Clinton and Marÿe Rowling

Brimming with seasonal stories, activities, crafts, poems and recipes, this book offers a guide to celebrating festivals, with ideas and things to make throughout the seasons.

If you have difficulties ordering from a bookshop
you can order direct from Hawthorn Press
1 Lansdown Lane, Lansdown, Stroud, Glos. United Kingdom GL5 1BJ

Telephone 0453 757040   Fax 0453 757040